TWILIGHT IMPERIUM

From the glittering halls of Mecatol Rex, the powerful Lazax Empire rules supreme across the galaxy, enforcing an ancient doctrine of strength and peace.

But their once-mighty rule is failing.

In the shadows, the Great Civilizations plot against the crumbling regime they are bound to, determined to break the chains of their authoritarian masters, claim their independence, and destroy anyone who opposes them.

But their freedom comes at a heavy price. Once the spark of war is ignited, it will consume everything in its path until nothing remains.

The galaxy will burn.

And the empire must fall.

TWILIGHT IMPERIUM™

The Twilight Wars

EMPIRE BURNING

Robbie MacNiven

First published by Aconyte Books in 2024

ISBN 978 1 83908 303 7

Ebook ISBN 978 1 83908 304 4

Cover art by Tobias Roetsch

Galactic map by Ryan Hong

Printed in the United States of America and elsewhere.

9 8 7 6 5 4 3 2 1

ACONYTE BOOKS

An imprint of Asmodee North America

Mercury House, Shipstones Business Centre

North Gate, Nottingham NG7 7FN, UK

aconytebooks.com

Dedicated to Gwendolyn Nix, who helped bring this book to life. More novels should be dedicated to their editors!

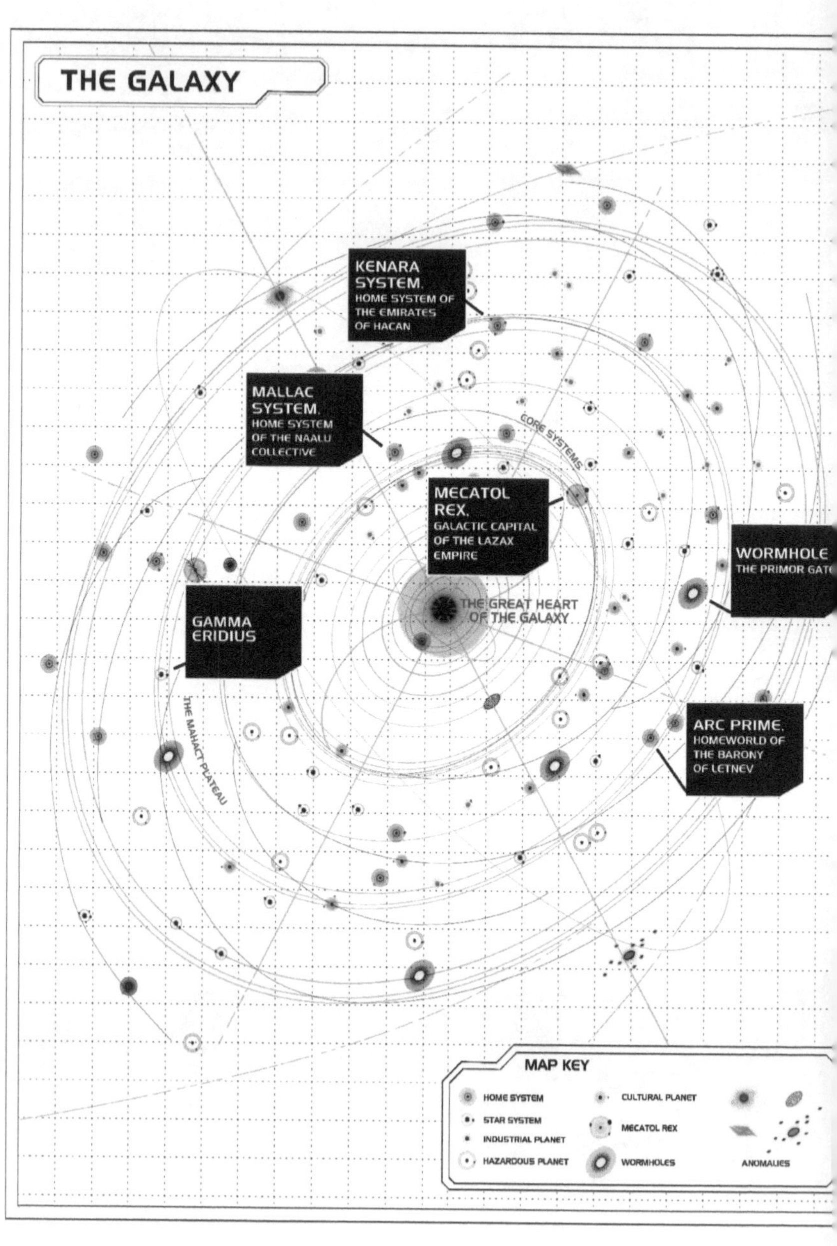

THE GALAXY

KENARA SYSTEM.
HOME SYSTEM OF THE EMIRATES OF HACAN

MALLAC SYSTEM.
HOME SYSTEM OF THE NAALU COLLECTIVE

CORE SYSTEMS

MECATOL REX.
GALACTIC CAPITAL OF THE LAZAX EMPIRE

WORMHOLE
THE PRIMOR GATE

THE GREAT HEART OF THE GALAXY

GAMMA ERIDIUS

THE MAHACT PLATEAU

ARC PRIME.
HOMEWORLD OF THE BARONY OF LETNEV

MAP KEY
HOME SYSTEM
STAR SYSTEM
INDUSTRIAL PLANET
HAZARDOUS PLANET
CULTURAL PLANET
MECATOL REX
WORMHOLES
ANOMALIES

PART ONE

CHAPTER ONE

Alshaz Orbital Station,
the Kenara System, Home of the Hacan

"None of this would be a problem if you just let me kill him," Drusha said.

He'd spoken loud enough for the rival delegation to hear, but they were all too experienced at this kind of game to glance over at them.

"There's enough killing in the galaxy without resorting to violence against fellow Hacan," Akenzi responded, just as loudly, then added with a stage whisper, "Besides, do you think I can afford to hire someone without any links to our clan?"

Drusha's mane bristled with amusement, and he looked over at Hamlar's gaggle of sycophants for any hint of a reaction. Still there was none – the five Hacan, robed in the green and gold zenfar robes of the Dazeshi clan, continued to converse among themselves in low tones while acting as though Akenzi and his brother, Drusha, didn't exist.

"They're good," Akenzi said, flashing his fangs. "In a boring kind of way."

"Truly, though, not enough trade disputes are resolved with honor duels anymore," Drusha said. "What has become of the ancient traditions of our people?"

"I think they call it 'civility,'" Akenzi said. "We need to display a bit of that, if our people are to become the masters of the galaxy."

Drusha just growled, glaring across the antechamber at Hamlar.

Akenzi was being facetious, and with good cause. His levity was a front, a disguise that he hoped would conceal his nervousness. Years of planning and speculation, of negotiations, bargains and concessions, had led to this – a meeting with representatives of the Hacan Council to resolve the legitimacy of his proposed venture to the Boreas Gap, in the face of opposition from Magnate Hamlar and his clan, the Dazeshi. Akenzi was convinced his entire future, perhaps his very life, would be decided in the next few hours.

What if you fail? That was what his father, Zamaq, had asked him that morning, over a pot of freshly brewed channa, before he had taken the shuttle from his clan's dust-sled up into orbit.

It was the most pointed of questions. What if all his efforts had been in vain? What if he had miscalculated, and the council ruled in favor of Hamlar?

Zamaq was a planner. During his younger days he had amassed a fortune trading gerr root products along the Fornax Axis. He had monopolized trade with multiple embattled factions and ensured that his merchant vessels had been able to pass unharmed through half a dozen war zones. The galaxy might be in the throes of the greatest, most devastating conflict since the fall of the Mahact, but that didn't mean a Hacan couldn't turn a profit.

Zamaq's every action was carefully considered, and he had a plan for every outcome. He had built the fortunes of his clan on the solid foundations of prudent investment. But that had never been Akenzi's way. He believed in high risk and high reward. The galaxy was on fire, and if he didn't take what he wanted, someone else would.

He knew the answer to his father's question. If he failed to secure rights to the Boreas Gap, he faced ruination, ostracization, disgrace. Everything would unravel. Bargains with his affiliates would break down, trust among his contacts would collapse, and his debts would become uncontrollable. It was all unthinkable.

He had told his father he did not play to lose, and that he would return to his clan's sled later that day with a trade and settlement charter for the Gap. Zamaq had sighed, finished his channa, and bidden his youngest son goodbye.

"They are late," Drusha grumbled, picking at the hem of his zenfar – blue edged with silver, the colors of Clan Muktat.

"Deliberately so, no doubt," Akenzi said, trying to sound unfazed. "The Council likes to make its authority clear. They might make us wait an entire day-cycle if it pleases them, but any lateness from us would see our case summarily dismissed. This is what we call 'an asymmetric bargain.'"

Drusha had spent over a decade as a section leader with the ordri of the Emirate of Tumak, an honored service that had come to an abrupt end after a particularly lethal encounter with a Sardakk N'orr Tekklar Elite. It had cost him his right arm. Akenzi considered it a good trade – the N'orr had, apparently, lost his head – but Drusha had never seen it that way, not since the cybernetic limbs he had been offered as replacements had failed to take, and he had been discharged from the ordri's service. Now, he acted as Akenzi's chief of security.

"Lateness isn't the way with the ordrim, deliberate or not," Drusha said dispassionately. "When a time is given for a briefing, that is when the briefing will happen."

"And therein lies the difference between soldiers and traders," Akenzi said.

"I wish I was still a soldier."

Akenzi sensed genuine pain in his brother's voice. Among Zamaq's four offspring, Drusha alone had chosen not to enter the family business. He had always favored more direct forms of aggression than the types usually enacted over the bargaining table – as soon as he was of age, he had joined the Hacan's armed forces.

A little over a century earlier it might have been seen as disgraceful for the firstborn of a well-respected and successful magnate like Zamaq to become an ordri warrior. That was certainly no longer the case. Since the overthrow of the Lazax and the collapse of their empire, war had been the galaxy's only uniting constant. And while every merchant worth his aurei stacks knew that war could offer ample opportunity for profit, the Hacan had still learned swiftly about the importance of strong military capabilities, of forces beyond the simple mercenaries and hirelings magnates had relied upon in ages past. The likes of Drusha were part of a new hierarchy within Hacan society, necessitated by the understanding that might carried a value all its own. Now, the voice of the warrior held as much weight as that of the merchant. Well, almost.

"Give it time, my brother, and I'm confident you will find there are many similarities between war and commerce," Akenzi told Drusha.

The door to the antechamber slid silently open as he spoke, admitting a mechafamiliar. It was an automated construct built of chrome plates, its main body and head node circular, levitating thanks to discreet antigrav plates. It floated with a light thrumming noise through the chamber until it was between the two delegations. Then, with a ping, its head node began to project a three hundred-and-sixty-degree viz display.

It showed an old Hacan, his gold fur faded to brown and flecked with silver, dressed in a red and gold zenfar and sporting a data-monocle fixed over one eye. Akenzi recognized him as Kalzid, the senior council member who had been assigned his dispute case.

"The panel will see you now, eminent magnates," the elderly Hacan declared, voice pulsing from the comms band circling the mechafamiliar's middle. "Please proceed through to the hearing room."

The transmission cut off, and the familiar began to hover back the way it had come. Akenzi went after it immediately, determined to get there ahead of Hamlar. Drusha followed, casting a withering glare back at the Dazeshi Hacan, along with a low growl that left them in no doubt that they should not get too close on the tails of their rivals.

Akenzi kept pace with the mechafamiliar. Such expensive automated units were relatively rare nowadays. They were Hylar inventions and had typically been constructed and maintained with the expertise of the Jol-Nar. As a child, Akenzi remembered his grandfather owning one, and Zamaq claimed they had been commonplace, fulfilling tasks from household care to administration. That had been many decades prior, and now mechafamiliars were either poor, unreliable knockoffs, or they were kept only by those who could afford either the services of rogue Hylar engineers or had a direct alliance with the universities. Akenzi knew either possibility could be the case when it came to the Hacan Council.

The familiar led them along a corridor and through a second set of doors, into Alshaz orbital station's main hearing room. The lighting was low, the way the Hacan favored it. The far wall was dominated by an observation port, allowing a spectacular view out over Hercant. Kenara, the tri-system's star, was setting beyond the planet's horizon, leaving the upper rim of Akenzi's homeworld gleaming with the harsh yellow brilliance of its deserts. The outlook was interrupted only by the bulk of other stations and the winking streams of lights that marked the vast amount of orbital traffic passing through the planet's upper atmosphere. Since the near annihilation of the galactic capital on Mecatol, no other place in the known cosmos besides the wormholes received as much stellar traffic as the home system of the Hacan.

In front of the observation port was an elegant, curved desk topped by a series of active data panels, projecting the evidence and reports already submitted by Akenzi and Hamlar for the three figures seated behind it – Kalzid and his two subordinate councilors. The chamber's furnishings reflected the wealth and good taste of the council – there were holo-busts of senior members, including Kalzid himself and the current Quieron, Amalia, alongside a curated array of antiques, from an ancient Hercant amphora to a first generation Lazax data recorder circlet, all displayed in alcoves along the walls. The bare decking plates that constituted the floor in much of the orbital station had been covered by a grand Arretze sandsilk rug, red and embroidered with the Council's elaborate crest in gold.

Had Akenzi been dealing with anyone else, he likely would have spent time inspecting the artifacts on display, making a show of his cultured leanings while hunting for any information that might be useful in forthcoming dealings. But this was the Hacan Council. They would not take kindly to such obvious forms of gamesmanship, and Akenzi intended to be on his best behavior. At least until things got serious.

"Venerable Councilors, you do me a great honor this day-cycle," he said, already beginning to address Kalzid and his underlings while Hamlar entered behind him. "Hopefully we can find a resolution to a matter that I know has detained us all for too long."

The trio of councilors looked unimpressed, and Kalzid ruffled his silvery mane in apparent annoyance.

"Less of the 'venerable,' if you please, Magnate Akenzi," he said. "You can honor me with brevity."

Akenzi did his best not to read anything into the brusque response. Kalzid was infamously short-tempered, and Akenzi had no wish to bait him. Maintaining a warm, confident exterior was important. He inclined his head respectfully and held his tongue.

Hamlar joined Akenzi before the trio of councilors, leaving his flunkies at the back of the room where Drusha was likewise prowling – Akenzi could only hope his older brother remained the master of his aggressive tendencies.

"Kalzid, it is good to see you again, old friend," Hamlar said. Akenzi suppressed the urge to scoff. Old friend? How trite. He knew full well that Hamlar and Kalzid had served briefly as part of the same trading consortium operating out of Verix nearly two decades earlier, but Akenzi had done his due diligence on all of the Council members assigned to his case – there was no indication of close collaboration with Hamlar or Clan Dazeshi in the past. If there had been, Akenzi would have already pre-prepared a conflict-of-interest complaint form.

Kalzid merely grunted at Hamlar and cleared his throat with a gravelly cough.

"This is Councilor Kalzid, at hearing session two-one-seven-three, relating to Magnate Akenzi Muktat's request for trade and settlement rights to the Boreas Gap, and Hamlar Dazeshi's registered dispute with said request. We are now in session."

Akenzi noted the mechafamiliar had taken up position off to the side of the desk, a winking red light on its head node indicating that it was taking a viz recording of the proceedings.

"Our purpose here today is to hear the verbal petitions from both interested parties, ahead of the Council making a final decision," Kalzid went on. "I call upon the Muktat to make their statement. I will add only that we would be indebted to Magnate Akenzi if he bears in mind my earlier comment about brevity."

"Of course, Councilor," Akenzi said smartly, taking a step forward so he was not only closer to the trio behind the desk, but blocking the mechafamiliar's line of sight to Hamlar, momentarily obscuring him on the recording.

"Given you are all Hacan of wisdom and experience, I will not burden you with platitudes," Akenzi began. "You will all be aware that I lodged a request for exclusive trade and settlement rights to the Boreas Gap a little over a year ago. Specifically, I am seeking formal recognition for a number of enterprises already receiving my sponsorship regarding the Gap.

"There are three habitable planets in the subsector that constitutes the Gap – Exilon, Boreas Majoris, and Boreas Minoris. All three once held protected status under the Lazax, but since the empire's dissolution, I believe it is not inaccurate to say their jurisdiction no longer holds sway."

He paused, hoping to garner an early agreement, but the councilors merely watched him until he continued.

"None of the planets mentioned are currently inhabited by high-level sentients. There is some evidence of a primitive avian civilization on Boreas Minoris. All three worlds are possessed of a number of valuable natural resources, including senkium ore and grade B taban gas. I believe the council already have the list I have provided via reliable, independent prospectors relating to such assets. I hope they would agree, a hub in the

Gap capable not only of facilitating taxed, above-board trade, but also of extraction and collection, would almost certainly prove to be a profitable enterprise. I hope it is the Council's view that I am worthy to lead said enterprise. My associates and I need only the Council's formal approval to begin business."

"And just what associates are those?" Hamlar said abruptly.

"There will be time for you to interrogate the applicant once you have delivered your opening statement, Magnate Hamlar," Kalzid said.

Akenzi narrowly suppressed a satisfied swish of his tail, hidden though it was beneath his zenfar.

"Correct me if I'm wrong – and I'm sure you will – but are you saying there are already Hacan of Clan Muktat operating within the Gap?" Kalzid said to Akenzi, adjusting his data-monocle.

"No, noble Councilor," Akenzi responded, silently cursing himself at having given the wrong impression before. "No Hacan vessel – at least, none from Clan Muktat – have entered the Gap, or are even present in the subsector! My earlier reference was to my efforts in contacting private prospectors and amassing the necessary backing for the venture. A chartered fleet, robust supply chains, security – the groundwork has been laid for every eventuality. I am happy to elaborate further on any of those elements."

"In due course," Kalzid said. "But first I will call upon Magnate Hamlar to make his statement. Also, would you please step back, Akenzi? You're interrupting the recording."

Akenzi hitched his zenfar and did so, hoping he appeared magnanimous. Hamlar began to speak.

"My thanks for upholding my right of contestation, eminent councilors. I could not help but notice that throughout Magnate Akenzi's statement of interest, he failed to make any reference to the most obvious reason for the establishment of an outpost in the Boreas Gap. It is what we might call the Tuuran in the room. I am, of course, referring to the planet of Gamma Eridius."

The urge to respond to the accusation – true though it was – nearly proved too much for Akenzi, but he managed to maintain his silence. He watched the three councilors carefully, hunting for any hint that would point toward whether they were receptive to his rival's arguments or not.

The zenfars, the traditional garb of the Hacan, made that difficult. Unlike many other species, Hacan facial expressions were a poor indicator of attitude. Social cues were transmitted by the position of the ears, the movement of the tail and, in male Hacan, the bristling of the mane. Drawn up over the head and with its skirts hanging over the tail, the robes concealed all such instinctive responses, and with good reason. The last thing a clever trader wished was for his body to betray his thoughts in the midst of negotiations. The zenfar had helped solve that problem for millennia, and it was currently helping to guard the attitudes of Akenzi's judges as they listened to Hamlar.

"For the record, Gamma Eridius is a class A habitable world, rich in tyrentine and with possible osmium deposits that lies just on the far side of the Boreas Gap, within the active travel distance of the Alpha Wormhole. Its resources render it potentially more valuable than any of the three planets mentioned within the Gap itself. No major power has claimed it since the collapse of Lazax authority."

"I submit to the Council that Magnate Akenzi's ultimate aim is not merely to establish a presence in the Boreas Gap, but to use said presence as a staging post for the strip-mining and exploitation of the near priceless resources of Gamma Eridius. This in itself is a worthwhile venture, and I applaud the Muktat magnate for his great efforts in making such an operation feasible, but I deplore his attempts to claim exclusivity rights. A prize as lucrative as Gamma Eridius cannot possibly become the private fiefdom of one single clan. It should be open to the healthy competition of at least one trade consortium. Gamma Eridius is a feast that all Hacan should be capable of sharing in, if they are able to provide enough funding and venture capital to warrant a space at the table."

"If I might offer a reply, noble councilors," Akenzi broke in, unable to hold back, but Kalzid raised a wizened hand.

"You may not, Magnate Akenzi. You have had your say."

Akenzi heard a soft growl from behind him, and prayed to every desert spirit he could remember the name of that his brother wasn't about to assault Hamlar or one of his flunkies.

He inclined his head respectfully to Kalzid, not looking at Hamlar, though he heard the triumphal swish of his rival's tail brushing over the Arretze rug.

As Akenzi had feared, Hamlar had cut straight to the heart of his scheme. A Muktat presence in the Boreas Gap would indeed make mining operations on nearby Gamma Eridius feasible. Once, the Lazax Empire had controlled the planet directly, though the discovery of tyrentine – a substance highly valued for its use in biosynthetic meld products, particularly in the fields of medicine and cybernetics – had come late and efforts to extract it had still been in their infancy when the rebellion against the empire's rule had broken out. Akenzi had read enough about it and had spoken with enough explorers and prospectors over the past decade, to become convinced that the planet was a viable growing concern. The rumors of osmium ore deposits only enhanced its appeal. Open up trade through the Gap, start extraction, and Akenzi would have the potential to elevate Clan Muktat into the uppermost echelons of the Hacan's trade hierarchy.

The Dazeshi, of course, wished to stop all that. Rumor had it Hamlar himself had been considering Gamma Eridius as a possible venture for years but had unwisely sought rights to exploit the planet directly, rather than occupying the nearby Gap first. His efforts had become caught up in competing interests and the Council's bureaucracy. At least one report Akenzi had spent a great deal of time and effort tracking down claimed Hamlar was already conducting unofficial, illegal operations on Gamma Eridius, hence why Akenzi had stressed that no members of his own clan were even in the subsector – if the Council refused him permission to occupy the Gap, his next plan was to try to expose Hamlar's illicit dealings, and lodge an appeal.

He supposed he could have told his father that he did have a plan if his current efforts failed after all. He doubted Zamaq would approve. Like Drusha, he placed too much stock in old ideals of honor. Akenzi was sure his father had been far less scrupulous in his younger years, back when he had actually been earning his fortune.

"Thank you both for your statements," Kalzid said. "You are dismissed while I confer with my colleagues. We will make a final review of your verbal reports and the evidence you previously supplied. You will be called back in in due course."

"How was that then?" Drusha murmured as they passed back along the corridor. "Did it go as you expected?"

"Broadly," Akenzi said, deciding he'd rather not go into the finer points of the meeting's difficulties. "But the outcome remains impossible to predict. It's a waiting game."

"And I suppose it really is too late to kill that Dazeshi sand-sucker?"

"A little, yes. I'd say you could petition the Council to allow it, but it would probably be at least a year-cycle before they even managed to schedule the preliminary hearing."

The two rival parties reoccupied the antechamber. Time dragged. Akenzi tried to busy himself by inspecting one of the artifacts decorating the antechamber – what looked like a huge, desiccated Tuuran tusk, partially sheathed in gold. The text of the holo display being beamed in front of the relic stated it was the remains of the ancestor species that had eventually evolved into the Tuuran, and claimed it was the oldest example of its kind on – or now above – Hercant.

As Akenzi looked at it, the tusk rattled against the brackets holding it. At the same time, the lights, already dim, dropped almost to nothing before automatically restoring.

Akenzi's ears twitched with momentary confusion.

"Did you see that?" he asked his brother.

"Shields," Drusha replied with the same kind of certainty Akenzi reserved for matters of commerce. "The station's shields activated."

Akenzi did not question his brother's knowledge. But why would the shields of a Council hub need to activate with such suddenness that it caused the entire system to experience a momentary power drain?

He looked at Hamlar and found the older Hacan already gazing at him.

Neither said anything, and Akenzi realized they were probably thinking the same thing. Was this some kind of trick? Some distraction, or deliberate manipulation? An effort to force the Council to adjourn before reaching a decision?

Just then, the mechafamiliar returned.

"Councilor Kalzid will see you again," the automaton buzzed in its artificial voice. That confirmed to Akenzi that something untoward was afoot. As much as the waiting had pained him, he had been expecting the councilor's deliberations to last much longer. Was the case really so clear-cut? Or was something else happening?

They retraced their steps back to the hearing room and found Kalzid and his fellow councilors still seated, waiting for them.

"We have reached a unanimous verdict," Kalzid said brusquely. "And one that I'm sure you will both respect."

Akenzi steeled himself. This was happening too fast. Something was wrong. He found his eyes drawn to the observation port behind the stately trio. There were lights there, more than the usual flow of orbital traffic. New constellations had been born, and more were visibly departing neighboring platforms as vessels left their docks or diverted their headings.

"It is the Council's belief that there is indeed merit in the proposed venture to the Boreas Gap," Kalzid said, recapturing Akenzi's attention. "The preliminary work shows a tolerably high likelihood of profitable margins. However, the Council is also mindful of the dispute raised by Magnate Hamlar."

That wasn't what Akenzi wanted to hear. He opened his mouth to interrupt, only to find himself staring through the port once more as a ship passed dangerously close to the station, its engines blazing.

Akenzi didn't consider himself especially conversant in military matters, but he knew enough to recognize the broad stern and sleek midsection of a war zebek, an ordri cruiser. It was practically burning its engines out trying to get somewhere, gliding with urgency across the port's field of view. As Akenzi watched, the space around it shimmered. Like Alshaz orbital station, it had triggered its shields.

"Noble Councilor," Akenzi said, interrupting Kalzid in the politest way he could conceive. "A thousand apologies but… I think there might be a situation developing that requires our attention."

The old Hacan flashed his yellow fangs in displeasure, then followed Akenzi's gaze. All three councilors turned to look at the cruiser as it swept purposefully past the observation port, heading away from Hercant.

"I'm sure it's nothing," Hamlar said.

"That very much does not look like nothing," Akenzi said as a second ordri vessel heaved into view, a bulky carrier this time.

"Its launch ports are open," Drusha growled from the back of the room. "It's about to deploy its interceptors."

"Whatever is happening, the Council's will has already been decided," Hamlar said testily. "Please, Councilor, continue!"

Kalzid looked from the carrier ship to Hamlar, seemingly frozen with uncertainty. Just then, the savant that made up part of the desk's data display began to ping urgently.

Kalzid tapped at the display in front of him to transmit the call to the earpiece he wore, then sat staring into space as he silently listened to what was being said. He looked at Akenzi and Halmar.

"Magnates, forgive the impropriety," he said. "But it would appear we are under attack."

CHAPTER TWO

Alshaz Orbital Station,
the Kenara System, Home of the Hacan

"What did you offer him?" Akenzi snarled. "Aurei? Shares? Who else is involved?"

Hamlar responded to each accusation with stony silence, but one of his subordinates wasn't so restrained.

"How dare you make such claims?" the younger Hacan barked. "We will report this! You will be disciplined for contempt!"

"We'll also be disciplined for ripping your scrawny little arms off and shoving them down your throat, you Tuuran-fathering welp," Drusha growled. The Dazeshi subordinate's zenfar had slipped back off his head, and his ears visibly went flat at the scarred former ordri warrior's tone.

Akenzi and Drusha had been thrown in amongst Hamlar's group as they all hurried toward Alshaz station's bridge. Akenzi's efforts at diplomatic detachment had broken down, and he had confronted his rival on the way.

"You already knew the verdict," he pressed. "That was why you were trying to rush it through before it was interrupted! So, what did you offer Kalzid?"

Hamlar remained silent. Akenzi knew he was desperate. Everything pointed to the fact he had been outplayed, but the game wasn't finished yet.

The fact that the Hacan home system was apparently under attack felt like a secondary problem. Kalzid had said that a war fleet – race unspecified – had just arrived in-system, and that everyone currently on board Alshaz was being asked to gather at the station's bridge. He had refused Hamlar's demands that the Council's verdict on the matter of the dispute be formally delivered before the session adjourned.

"I know you have a presence on Gamma Eridius already," Akenzi hissed at Hamlar as they carried on along the final corridor toward the bridge. "But I'm still willing to negotiate, despite your underhanded tactics. Retract your complaint log and we can talk about a split venture in the Gap. I have shares I'm still looking to sell."

They arrived at the flight of stairs leading to the bridge's blast doors. Hamlar halted abruptly and faced Akenzi, his Dazeshi underlings surrounding the two rival magnates. Akenzi suddenly realized how tall Hamlar was, finding himself close enough to see the sheen of the akaba resin he used to weave the fur above his eyes into sharp points, and smell the expensive jupa oils and incense he used on his pelt and mane.

"You seem to be laboring under misapprehensions, Akenzi Muktat," the older Hacan said, glaring down at him imperiously. "And things might go more easily if I dispel them. You and that family of drip-farmers that you call your clan are wholly unworthy of claiming a prize like Gamma Eridius. I will warn you once, and never again – abandon your claim, and walk away. It might not leave you with any pride, but at least you'll still have your petty fortune intact, not to mention your life."

Drusha snarled and took a step toward Hamlar. The Dazeshi didn't flinch, and Akenzi instinctively put a hand on his brother's broad chest, pushing him back.

Hamlar did not wait for Akenzi to compose himself. He strode up the stairs and onto the bridge, leaving his rival boiling with anger.

"He insults us all," Drusha said furiously. "This is worthy of a clan feud! Let me go after him!"

"No," Akenzi managed to say. "He wants that. He's clever. I've underestimated him before, and I won't again."

"You speak too highly of him," Drusha growled. "He is an arrogant fool! He should be taught a lesson."

"I plan on teaching him many," Akenzi said. "But not yet. Come on."

He moved his paw from his brother's chest to his shoulder, patted it, and headed up the stairs.

Alshaz orbital station was not a military instillation, and its bridge hub was small and undistinguished, a circular space with a clear, reinforced plasticon ceiling that showed the constellations beyond, along with the lanes of disrupted space traffic. Visiting claimants, applicants and Council staff were not expected to visit such an area, and the fact that seemingly all those currently acting as guests on the station had been gathered there implied something very untoward was happening.

Akenzi assumed it was an overreaction to some minor incursion. It had been a month since he had returned to the Kenara system from his latest business trip, and in that time everywhere from the dust-sleds to the orbital exchanges had been rife with stories of the war's latest progress. Apparently, the Sol Federation had won a desperate naval battle off Malpar IX, and the Ardanil had been forced to surrender to the Letnev after their homeworld had been annexed by the Barony. Most of all, talk was circling of a future Sardakk N'orr offensive, one that was going to finally break the long, bloody impasse that had developed between the insectoid species and the Hylar of the Jol-Nar Universities.

Akenzi would believe it when he saw it. The whole galaxy had been locked in conflict since long before he was born, and in all that time the Kenara system itself had never been invaded. The Hacan were negotiators by both profession and inclination, and while the other great civilizations had torn one another apart they had navigated the worst of the storms and expanded their monopolies, no longer fettered by the limiting edicts of the old empire.

Sometimes, the other civilizations tried to challenge that. Hacan fleets, territories and trading posts had been attacked. Always, however, the threat of a cessation of commerce had been enough to ensure such aggression did not spread. The Hacan had made themselves almost indispensable to each of the great civilizations by acting as the go-betweens for all manner of vital supplies, and even the most aggressive Federation admiral or Sardakk Swarm Leader knew depredations against the Hacan would soon begin to have negative consequences. Akenzi suspected a particularly powerful delegation fleet had just arrived and startled some picket drones, or another gaggle of pirates had lingered for too long, hoping to get lucky with a wayward merchant lugger decelerating in past the system's edge.

He realized almost as soon as he entered the bridge that his assumptions were wrong. The center of the space was dominated by a viz projection screen that was beaming a three-dimensional representation of the Kenara system into the air above it. The interlopers were obvious – a thick wedge of red triangles spearing in from the upper-right quadrant, moving in-system. If each one represented an enemy vessel, Akenzi knew he was looking at an invasion fleet, and they were headed not only into the heart of the Kenara system, but toward Hercant.

Most of the Hacan crowding the bridge were councilors or their staff, but the different-colored zenfars of a variety of different clans were scattered among the red and gold. Hamlar was off to the right, so Akenzi moved left. He was still simmering with anger at what the other magnate had said. This wasn't the place to cause a scene. Hamlar would want that.

"That won't be enough," one Hacan councilor said loudly to the station master, who stood on a platform next to the raised viz plate. "They're Letnev! We can't expect them to show restraint!"

That at least answered Akenzi's first question – the fact that the incursion force was from the Barony of Letnev certainly wasn't reassuring. Akenzi had few dealings with them, and for good reasons. They were cold, militaristic and aggressive. Their main imports from the Hacan were the fuel and fodder necessary for the factories on their ice-ball of a homeworld – Arc Prime – to continue to churn out their vast array of war machines and void ships. And now, ironically, it seemed a good portion of those ships were being directed toward the Hacan.

"Where is Sword Fleet?" another Hacan shouted. "We're supposed to–"

A burst of light cut the speaker short. Akenzi bared his fangs in annoyance, half blinded. He feared for a moment that the station had been struck by some sort of projectile, but there was no noise or notion to accompany the brilliance.

"What was that?" one of the assembly exclaimed. As their sight returned, every eye fixed back on the viz projector. The station master, after a pained pause, answered.

"I think… I think they just hit Kalmar orbital station."

Low growls of dismay ran through the bridge as Akenzi spotted what the station master had already seen – the marker representing another of the orbital platforms above Hercant, dangerously close to the one they were on, had turned red. He stared at it, hardly daring to believe the horror it represented – a whole orbital station gone, along with hundreds of lives.

"This is an act of war," a Hacan councilor exclaimed.

"And we're on the front line," another added. "We need to evacuate!"

"Have they hailed any of the homeworlds?" another Hacan asked. "Or the stations?"

"You all know as much as I do," the station master said. "Please, give me a moment!"

Akenzi saw him gesture toward the communications bank that circled half of the bridge's wall. A voice came in over the speakers around the viz display, chopped up by static. The pair of Hacan comms operators working at the bank adjusted dials and levels, and the voice came back, accompanied by a shimmering in the viz display. Gone was the three-dimensional star chart, replaced by a glowing green representation of a face Akenzi recognized, though he had never seen her in person – it was Quieron Amalia Farik herself.

The elected ruler of the United Emirates looked out over the frightened gathering, her leonine features framed by a fine zenfar and surmounted by a gilt data circlet.

She was young, not a great deal older than Akenzi, but she was the daughter of Musfar Farik, and that ensured respect. The Farik clan was considered by most to be the most powerful of all the Emirates, grown mighty off the Sarween trade, and by Musfar's clever brokering and politicking. Many had anticipated that with his death the Farik would slip from their heady pedestal, but Amalia had done enough to secure the votes required for her own election to Quieron and had since stabilized the clan's position at the pinnacle of Hacan society.

"Alshaz station, forgive my interruption," she said, her voice clear now over the speakers. "As you are doubtless already aware, an emergency situation is developing. A war fleet belonging to the Barony of Letnev has entered the Kenara system and has launched an unprovoked attack on Kalmar orbital station. I am going to have to ask, however, that you do not attempt to evacuate."

Everyone stared in silence as Amalia continued.

"We have received a transmission from the Barony fleet. They demand that a senior representative attend them immediately, that all platforms remain anchor-locked, and require that our warships deactivate their shields and muzzle their guns. Their intention, I have no doubt, is to hold us to ransom."

One councilor finally found his voice.

"Outrageous," he cried. "This is a violation of every treaty we hold with them!"

"It is," Amalia agreed. "I believe the Letnev have grown desperate. The war has turned against them since their defeat at Jost, and the annexation of the Ardanil is not enough to placate the Baron's lust for expansion. In their need for aurei and resources, they see us as an easy target. I intend to disabuse them of that belief, but we must buy time. Sword Fleet is mobilizing.

"The system pickets and those vessels scrambled from the docks above Hercant are not enough to hold the Letnev at bay. The main system defense fleet is currently launching from Arretze, on the far side of the planet from the Letnev, to shield their preparations from them. It will take time to conduct a gravitational assist around Arretze and reach the point of incursion. By then, with the firepower the Letnev have at their disposal, they could have leveled half of the orbital assets above Hercant."

"Including us," Councilor Kalzid said from amongst the crowd. "Alshaz is the next station in their path. We should already be evacuating!"

"That is why I am transmitting to you directly," Amalia said. "I am asking for you to remain in place. If a mass desertion of Hercant's orbit takes place, the Letnev will become suspicious. It may cause them to open fire again, and your evacuation will likely not be complete before they do so."

"So we are to be hostages?" a Hacan in the robes of Clan Afesa demanded, her tone strained. "We are just to sit here under the Letnev guns?"

"For the time being, yes," Amalia said. "But there is more that some of you can do. I have already mentioned that the Letnev demand representatives. They will expect us to send a delegation to their flagship to try to negotiate. If they have come here to extort us, they will need to make their demands. Receiving them and making a show of talking may slow them enough to maneuver Sword Fleet into position."

The bridge met the Quieron's words with silence, each Hacan following the line of reasoning to its natural conclusion.

"Negotiating in bad faith, to stall the Letnev ahead of a reprisal," a voice said eventually. It was Hamlar. "It would be suicide for whoever boards their flagship."

"It would be highly dangerous, yes," Amalia admitted. "Senior members of the Council have already volunteered to go, but I fear there is a possibility the Letnev may simply use them as hostages."

"Only a fool would try to entreat with the Letnev while we prepare to attack them," Hamlar went on. "Even if the delay is successful, they will find themselves on board the Barony flagship and potentially in the midst of a naval engagement. With the greatest of respect, my Quieron, once the Letnev realize the duplicity involved, it is a death sentence."

"Perhaps," Amalia replied. "But lives have already been lost. If we are not seen to comply with their initial demands soon, they will summarily destroy another orbital station, and Alshaz is now their closest target. This may be the only option that will save most of your lives."

"I'll do it," Akenzi said. Every face turned toward him, but he kept looking up at Amalia's transmission, seeing her gaze fall upon him.

It had been a struggle to utter the words, but as soon as he spoke, he knew he was making the right decision. He had made a career turning problems into opportunities. This would be no different.

"Speak and be known, son of Kenara," Amalia commanded.

"Magnate Akenzi, of Clan Muktat, oh wise Quieron," he said, throwing in a deep bow for good measure.

"You are the son of Zamaq Muktat, of Hercant," Amalia said. "Your clan has prospered under the direction of your sire."

"It has, my gracious Quieron, and in no small part thanks to your beneficent rule," Akenzi said, not caring if he sounded like he was groveling. He had never had an opportunity to speak to the Quieron, and there seemed to be a good chance he never would again.

"You understand what I am asking you to do, Akenzi Muktat?" she said.

"I believe so," he responded. "I am to meet with the commanders of this incursion while acting as a representative of the Council and feign negotiations while Sword Fleet mobilizes."

"Precisely," Amalia replied. "Speed is vital. They are attempting to use aggression to mask the weakness of their position. We must keep them busy until our own hand is ready to be played."

"Yes, wise Quieron," Akenzi said. "I am prepared to act, for the safety not only of those on this station, but for the survival of all Hacan. I can only hope prosperity will remember my efforts."

"This is foolishness," Drusha said as the transport compartment of the shuttle thrummed around them.

"I told you, you could have stayed on the station," Akenzi replied, once more adjusting the red Council robes he'd been given before they left Alshaz.

"I didn't say I disapproved," Drusha said with a humorous glint in his eye. "It reminds me of when we were young. Do you remember the time we crashed that auto-controlled toy sled into the council dome right when Father was about to seal a deal with Clan Igben?"

"You ran in after it, and I stayed back and denied all knowledge of what had happened," Akenzi said, tail swishing with amusement at the memory.

"And when Father made me clear wet sand out of the moisture vents as punishment, you shared the work without him knowing. You didn't have to. I'd have been mucking those clean for days by myself."

"I couldn't let you take all the blame," Akenzi said. "Or at least, I couldn't let you take all the *punishment*. We're clan. Family."

"And Father still sealed the deal with the Igben."

"He's everything I aspire to be," Akenzi said, meaning it.

Would their father be doing this? Certainly, it was hard to imagine him approving of it now, though in his prime, who knew? It was unbelievably impulsive and risky. Drusha's word – foolishness – had been overly kind.

But a good trader knew when to seize the moment, knew when to take the long odds. Or was that a good gambler?

Akenzi had always considered the two activities to be closely related.

"On final approach," clicked the voice of the shuttle's pilot over the compartment's intercom. Akenzi undid his restraints and stood up, Drusha mirroring him.

He had been impulsive, even by his standards, and now he was committed – with great risk came great reward, and right now he needed something to work with if he was to sway the anticipated judgement of the Council. It was a huge gamble, but what was the alternative? Meekly accept the Council blocking his venture to Gamma Eridius? The fates had handed him this opportunity.

He wondered briefly whether he should have ordered Drusha to stay behind and spared him almost certain death. He consoled himself with the knowledge that his brother would undoubtedly have ignored such an order.

"Remember what we discussed," he said to Drusha, trying to focus on anything other than the fear welling up inside him. "I'm a senior member of the Council and you're my bodyguard. I have been authorized to negotiate on behalf of Quieron Amalia and the entirety of the United Emirates."

"Won't they think you're a little young to be a senior councilor?"

"They're Letnev. I doubt they can accurately tell age differences in our kind," Akenzi said, hoping his scorn was not misplaced. "Just let me do all the talking. You can pretend to be mute, if you'd like. Maybe the N'orr pulled out your tongue after they cut off your arm?"

Drusha growled at the blithe humor but said nothing more. A shudder ran through the frame of the shuttle, and Akenzi knew they were beginning to dock.

They had watched their approach toward the Letnev formation earlier, on the viz monitor located above the door leading to the cabin blister. It had shown the incursion fleet, a formidable cloud of dreadnoughts, cruisers and carriers in battle array, shields active and guns run out. Drusha had identified them as they had drawn nearer, reeling off a catalogue of sizes, classes and armaments the way Akenzi might have been able to list the salient points of a trilateral investment treaty.

"That's a *Viscount*-class carrier," he said, indicating the behemoth at the heart of the Letnev formation. "It'll be their flagship, though I'm not sure which one it is specifically. I never served against the Letnev."

"Well, whatever you do, don't let them provoke you," Akenzi had urged him. "Just stay ready. When they realize what we're doing they'll probably try to kill us immediately."

"So, it'll be an entire capital ship full of one of the most militant warrior cultures in the galaxy, versus the two of us? I like those odds."

As they had drawn nearer, the viz display had started to distort, and now, as they docked, it was nothing but a fuzz of static, presumably scrambled by interdiction tech on board the carrier. They'd be exiting the shuttle blind.

The transport shuddered once more, and a light above the primary exit hatch switched from red to amber. Akenzi took his position in front of the hatch, again adjusting his borrowed robes. They smelled of another Hacan, and he didn't like the unfamiliar scent. Drusha took his usual post, slightly back and off to his right.

"He did know, by the way," the veteran Hacan said abruptly as they endured the wait, feeling the final tremors running through the deck underfoot.

"What?" Akenzi asked, confused.

"Father. He did know you helped me with the moisture vents on the sled. He told me, years later."

"He's clever," said Akenzi, amused by the memory. "Or wise."

"What's the difference?"

"If you're clever, it becomes wisdom when you get old."

Akenzi again wondered whether their father would approve of this venture. Certainly, he doubted many of those on board Alshaz station considered him clever. He had caught Hamlar's eye as they had left the bridge, and sensed amusement in his posture. He suspected the Dazeshi thought he was making a deadly mistake, one that suited Hamlar perfectly. Let him continue in that assumption. By the time he accepted that he had been outmaneuvered, it would be too late.

"Docking procedures completed," came the pilot's voice over the intercom. "I'm about to disengage the hatch. Stand by."

CHAPTER THREE

Grand Carrier Mordaunt, Flagship of the Barony of Letnev's First Grand Fleet

The hatch opened, and Akenzi and Drusha passed through the venting hydraulic steam and down the ramp beyond. Akenzi immediately felt a bitter chill.

They were in one of the carrier's docking bays, a wide hangar of cold steel and strip lighting. The Hacan shuttle had settled into a landing berth, flanked by ranks of jagged Letnev space-fighters, their wings cinched up and cockpits bowed forward against the decking plates like predatory avians at rest.

There was a Letnev delegation waiting for them at the bottom of the ramp. Warriors mostly, presumably the fleet's marines, encased in black lacquered ferroplate and carrying vicious-looking energy carbines. In front of them was a figure in an immaculate uniform – white breeches and a maroon jacket trimmed with silver lace and epaulets and emblazoned with silver and gold badges that Akenzi took to be either medals or signifiers of rank. He was tall, for a Letnev, with a high-boned, haughty face, a grayish complexion and white hair that he wore bound up around his crown.

Akenzi drew his strange smelling zenfar tighter around him

and descended with what he hoped was stately grace. In that moment all fear and doubt evaporated, the way it did whenever negotiations began.

"Surrender any weapons you have in your possession, immediately," the uniformed Letnev demanded, speaking in univoca, the old, universal tongue of the empire. It was the sort of crude, brusque opening Akenzi had been anticipating.

"I am a Councilor of the United Emirates, and I come unarmed," he replied. "Our people are not natural warriors, such as yourselves. My companion here is my bodyguard, but he bears only a plasma pistol."

"Hand it over," the Letnev demanded.

"Do you expect that the two of us will storm your bridge and take control of your flagship with just a single sidearm?" Akenzi asked. "I have come here to negotiate in good faith. I expect basic courtesies in return."

"Check them," the Letnev snapped. Several of his soldiers stepped up, leveling their weapons, while another produced some sort of scanning wand and ran it up and down the pair of Hacan. Akenzi hoped Drusha would submit without a fuss. As far as stalling for time went, every little bit helped, but he didn't fancy being gunned down while they were still in the docking bay – he had few doubts the Letnev would do just that if they suspected any duplicity of the firearms/explosives variety.

The scanner beeped and winked red when it passed over Akenzi's chest.

"What's that?" the Letnev running the scan demanded.

"My savant," Akenzi replied.

"Take it out."

Akenzi complied, removing his savant and proffering it. As far as communications devices went, it was an expensive piece. It was edged in Tamari gold, its glassy screen made from crystal mined on Pelerath, renowned for both the quality of its display and its connectivity.

"It doesn't look like a savant to me," the Letnev declared.

"I suspect we have quite different tastes when it comes to such things."

"Confiscate it," the Letnev commanding the welcoming party ordered. Akenzi snatched his hand back, the device still in his grip, privately amazed his voice sounded so calm even with a plethora of charged energy carbines being shoved in his face.

"How do you expect me to communicate with my superiors without this? I'm happy for you to scan it individually. I'll even show you it in use. But you will not take it. Besides, it's a clan heirloom. Such things have great importance in my culture."

In truth, Akenzi had acquired it a year earlier, a sweetener in a deal over jebba spices with Clan Garash. That wasn't important right now – what was important was flagging the device as potentially dangerous without actually losing possession of it.

The savant was subjected to another scan, and the Letnev commander made him activate it and demonstrate its capabilities by contacting the shuttle still sitting at their backs. Eventually, he ordered Akenzi to put it away.

"My name is Sub-Captain Celan Waizakil II of the Grand Carrier *Mordaunt*," the uniformed Letnev said. "How should you be addressed?"

"I am Wushar Farik of the Great Clan Farik," Akenzi lied, knowing how the Letnev put stock in ranks and titles. "Second Head of the Council of the United Emirates of Hacan. You may address me as Councilor Wushar."

Waizakil's expression gave a rough idea of just what he wanted to call Akenzi, but he gestured instead for the Hacan to follow him, his marines falling in on either side.

"The First Admiral, Count Tarquilian Zorias, will address you on the bridge," he said.

"Does the count have the authorization required to negotiate?" Akenzi asked, maintaining a stiff, formal persona.

"He does," Waizakil said, as though the answer was obvious.

They were transported to the flagship's bridge via a rail pod, a spherical compartment that was able to carry passengers throughout the great vessel without them having to traverse a host of corridors and lifter shafts. Akenzi had never seen the like before, though they seemed like an ingenious way of moving around the interior of such a huge vessel.

The bridge was as he had expected – a grand, warlike space full of military bustle. It was box-shaped, with tiered platforms rising like a ziggurat at its center, each level occupied by the machinery and command stations necessary to oversee the vessel's running and coordinate the actions of the wider fleet. At the pinnacle sat a command throne, an unnecessarily large seat that appeared to have been carved from some sort of black bedrock that Akenzi assumed had a relevance to the Letnev. Around the throne was an array of banners, black and purple, white and green heraldic emblems that he guessed were the flags of the fleet and its senior officers. Trust the Letnev to take the concept of "flagship" literally.

Akenzi wondered whether its bitter cold – a far cry from the temperatures used in most chambers on a Hacan ship – was a deliberate attempt at compromising his ability to negotiate, but he suspected such subtle tactics were beyond a blunt gathering of Letnev warriors.

The walls that surrounded the ziggurat were banded by strips showing the space beyond the hull, covered with all manner of trajectories, tactical markers and viz projections. Akenzi wasn't sure if they were true observation ports, or screens showing what the carrier's devices were picking up in the space beyond. Kenara filled the one to their left, the brilliant white star of Akenzi's home system covered in a screed of crimson and amber target locks – it seemed like every platform and merchant vessel in the tri-system was currently being held in the Letnev's sights.

Access from the base of the ziggurat to its peak was provided by an autostair, a two-way rotating mobile system that Sub-Captain Waizakil motioned Akenzi and Drusha onto. They rose up between the Letnev bridge crew and their stations, keeping their gaze fixed on what awaited them.

Akenzi assumed that the Letnev sitting in the black throne was the fleet admiral, Count Zorias. He had always found military panoply childish, and this particular Letnev was even more ridiculously attired than his subordinates. His scarlet coat practically dripped with silver and gold braid and gleaming medals, while his long hair had been pulled back into a tail, with the corners in front of his ears curled into a trio of ringlets.

He rose from his throne as Akenzi and Drusha reached the end of the autostair. He was not the only one at the bridge's pinnacle. Two other Letnev stood on either side, both less extravagantly garbed. One was uniformed similarly to Waizakil, while the dress of the second was demure – an off-white overcoat with the Baronial sigil on its left breast. The garb put Akenzi in mind of some sort of medical practitioner, though the Letnev's face did not – it was brutally scarred and more wizened-looking than the others. Ironically, given he was the only Letnev on the bridge not wearing overtly military clothing, he struck Akenzi as the most dangerous.

Waizakil and a section of his marines had followed Akenzi and Drusha up the autostair and remained surrounding them at the top. The sub-captain spoke up.

"Introducing Decorated First Admiral Count Tarquilian Zorias, Count of the Ice Fields of Treas, victor of Garaman Prime, Conqueror of the Trennaian Nebula and commander of the First Grand Fleet, by the will of his most glorious and honored Baron Zornn."

Akenzi looked at Zorias as he was introduced and was thankful that the Letnev was presumably unaware that the swaying of his tail under his zenfar indicated his amusement. He offered the shallowest of bows and introduced his alias.

"I'm Wushar Farik."

A painful silence followed, and Akenzi realized the whole bridge had gone still and was looking at them. Good. A few less eyes on the displays, hunting for any possible signs of an armed Hacan response to the incursion.

"Your name means nothing to me," Zorias said in a voice that was almost comically high-pitched to Akenzi's ears. "Who am I treating with? I must know that you have the authority to negotiate!"

"I am the son of Quieron Amalia Farik," Akenzi lied. "She rules all the United Emirates. I am an honored senior Councilor and come bearing the full authority of every loyal and honest Hacan who calls the Kenara system home. A home you have, on this cycle, seen fit to invade."

Had it not been for the seriousness of the situation, a part of Akenzi realized he would have probably been enjoying this more.

Zorias waved a hand, and the uniformed figure to his side hastily pressed a part of the control panel built into the throne's arm. There was a thrumming noise, and the air around the three Letnev and the two Hacan distorted, shimmering as though amid an intense heat haze. Akenzi recognized a void glove in action, presumably built into the decking plates beneath them.

It would mask what was being said and largely shield those within from the eyesight of the rest of the bridge. It afforded a degree of privacy befitting high-level negotiations. That would make phase two of the plan a little easier.

"I bear a list of demands, drawn up by Baron Zornn herself," Zorias began to say, but Akenzi cut him off.

"I would be indebted if you would introduce your companions," he said, still stalling. "I, too, would know just who I am negotiating with. This is my bodyguard, Drusha."

Zorias's face contorted – Akenzi was adept at reading the facial expressions of other species, and while Letnev were more reserved than the likes of humans, they weren't too dissimilar. The admiral was annoyed.

"This is my aide, Lieutenant Ogthorn," he said, gesturing dismissively at the lesser-uniformed officer to his right before indicating the scarred Letnev on his left. "And this is Gondar."

"And who is Gondar?" Akenzi asked, looking at the third Letnev, the one who Zorias had failed to name a role or title for.

"Gondar will be observing negotiations and asking questions he thinks relevant," Zorias said.

"I did not ask what he would be doing, I asked who he was," Akenzi said, maintaining eye contact with Gondar. The Letnev's expression was icy, but he summoned up a tight smile. It left the Hacan feeling vaguely disturbed.

"That information is not relevant to these negotiations," Zorias began to say, but to Akenzi's surprise Gondar cut him off.

"I am here at the personal dispensation of Baron Zornn," he answered. "Consider me an… interested observer."

Akenzi gave a little bow of acceptance. "Very well. You were saying something about a list of demands, Count?"

"Yes, the list," Zorias said, snapping his fingers at Lieutenant Ogthorn. Another depression of the throne's control panel, and it beamed a holo text projection before the two Hacan, a long series of univoca bullet points.

"In summary, the Barony of Letnev requires tribute," Zorias said. "Terridium, Grade B taban gas, exotrite. You will take note of the quantities. All of this is to be delivered to my fleet within the next two day-cycles. Every tri-hour segment that passes without at least one partial delivery to my transport haulers will result in the destruction of one of your ships or orbital stations. Is that clear?"

"It is clear," Akenzi said slowly. "It is clear that you have, and are intending to continue to commit, acts of war against the United Emirates."

"This is not war. This is negotiation."

"Not the kind of negotiation we Hacan will accept. Negotiating with a kijit to the throat is not negotiation, it is robbery."

"A kijit?"

"A knife."

Zorias scoffed. "In my opinion, you people are thieves and cowards. You avoid the worst of this war and play one side off against the other, all the while thinking only about turning a profit. Well, that ends now. The Barony of Letnev will not stand by any longer and allow you to extort the rest of the galaxy."

"Those are outrageous accusations, Count Zorias," Akenzi said, privately more than happy to get caught up in base insults as long as he could draw them out. "The galaxy's present state is in no small part thanks to the warmongering of your Barony. Only the Letnev could see a civilization that pursues peace and decide that it deserves to be attacked and brutalized. Do you think any other great power would adhere to your demands, especially after the entirely unprovoked aggression you have shown? You have already killed hundreds!"

"And I will kill thousands if you do not report these demands to your Quieron and see that they are met with alacrity!"

Akenzi paused, his apparent shock only partially feigned. He had expected something like this, but the brutality and the arrogance of the Letnev, laid bare, was monstrous.

"The amounts you are demanding are unfeasible," he said. "The tri-system is not a military depot or a mining hub. Do you really expect us to possess this quantity of terridium, for example?"

"You feign poverty, yet your wealth is known the galaxy over," Zorias said. "You will provide as close to the required amounts as possible, and any shortcoming will be submitted in the aurei. That is something you cannot claim you do not possess."

"Pure extortion," Akenzi said, affecting a bitter tone.

"You can pay with more lives, if you wish," Zorias said, then snapped at Ogthorn, "Have the *Indomitable* charge prow lances and prepare to fire on the closest Hacan merchant vessel."

He looked back at Akenzi, speaking over him.

"Be under no illusions, Hacan. I have full authorization from Baron Zornn to turn your three little balls of sand into glass."

"And you will have none of what you came for," Akenzi said, deciding it was best not to outright tell the admiral he was a sand-sucking idiot. "If we could dispense with the aggression, we might discuss the practicalities of any potential… agreement."

It was Zorias's turn to hesitate, and Akenzi carried on.

"I am sure my people can provide you with resources and aurei. But we need to know how and where to deliver them, and the timeframe involved. We need coordinates, carrier tags, shipping clearance lanes. We cannot simply make what you wish appear in the holds of your ships."

Talk of genuine logistics went some way toward cutting through the haze of aggression that appeared to be clouding Zorias's mind. He said nothing at first, until Ogthorn asked him a question.

"Shall I order the *Indomitable* to open fire, sir?"

"Tell Captain Cheva to keep the lances primed," Zorias said without looking at the subaltern. "But do nothing more without my command."

Grudgingly, the admiral allowed himself to be drawn into something akin to a normal conversation. Akenzi dug into every factor and problem he could conceive of, from the safe transferal of potentially volatile Grade B taban gas to the amount of haulage that would be required to shift the amount of terridium the Letnev were demanding.

"Ships will need to come from Arretze and Kamdorn as well," he said, seeing an opportunity to mask the approach of at least part of Sword Fleet. "We do not have all of this on Hercant alone. In fact, as I was departing to conduct these talks, there were already transports being dispatched. It would be helpful to us all if you didn't open fire on them."

More precious time was wasted as Akenzi tried to extract tangible promises that the Letnev wouldn't simply demand more once their first requirements had been met. They both knew the reason there would be no further extortion was because the Hacan would be better prepared next time, but neither could admit that. Instead, Zorias made airy references to a possible treaty between the two civilizations.

Throughout it all, he did what he always did during negotiations and tried to think from the perspective of his opposite number. The ferocity of Zorias's negotiating was not born out of natural Letnev militarism, he was sure. The admiral was entirely aware of the precarious nature of his position. He was essentially performing a heist on a grand scale and knew that speed and aggression were his best weapons. Akenzi was working to undermine that, but he hoped he was doing it with enough subtlety to avoid detection. He was thankful the Letnev had sent a military figure to head the negotiations, rather than someone who actually knew what they were doing.

Zorias's patience started eroding. He refused to make any concessions about the time it would take to assemble so much exotrite and demanded that all aurei payments be delivered as hard currency. He ordered that Akenzi immediately transmit his list in full to the Council.

Akenzi took out his savant and pretended to beam the holo readout Zorias had provided to the shuttle that had brought them to the carrier, claiming it would be relayed from there to Hercant's orbit. He even feigned slow connectivity, sensing Zorias getting closer and closer to snapping.

He wished he could check in with Drusha, no matter how briefly, but didn't want to risk drawing attention to him or derailing the work they had done so far – he had hoped they could communicate in their own tongue, but Akenzi hadn't dared try that yet either. He very much doubted Zorias or Ogthorn knew the Hacan language, let alone the Muktat clan dialect, but he couldn't be sure there wasn't technology that would automatically translate whatever they said for them. He also had doubts about the third Letnev.

Gondar seemed like the wild card. He had said nothing since his vague comments at the beginning, had simply observed the exchange in silence. There was a sinister air to him, watchful and calculating. Had Akenzi not been so busy outmaneuvering Zorias, he was sure he'd be trying to figure out what Gondar's true purpose was.

The fact that he was about to become integral to the next part of the plan wasn't reassuring, but even Zorias would become suspicious if Akenzi suddenly decided to swap places with where Drusha was standing, on his right.

"What time can we expect the first transports?" Zorias was saying. "Need I remind you that failure to meet our timetable will result in more collateral damage?"

"What you call collateral damage, I call the mass murder of my people," Akenzi said with genuine anger.

"Do not test me, Hacan. This has taken long enough already. The first tri-hour is almost over, and nothing has been delivered bar assurances. Do not think I am oblivious to the wiles of your kind."

It was a struggle not to tell Zorias he was very oblivious to the wiles of his kind, but Akenzi bit his tongue.

He wished he had a way of knowing how well the preparation of Sword Fleet was progressing. Zorias's threats to destroy a Hacan vessel meant there was only so much more stalling Akenzi could do. He didn't want to be responsible for hundreds more deaths, even indirectly.

"I think you are growing desperate, admiral," he said, deciding he was almost out of time. "In fact, I think your entire Barony is desperate."

"What do you mean?" Zorias snapped.

"I mean there is no way the Barony of Letnev would countenance an invasion like this unless your war efforts had become dangerously strained elsewhere. It is clear that you lack resources and have resolved to try to acquire them by force from what you think will be an easy target."

It felt good to be shrugging off the cautious respect Akenzi had been feigning, good to watch the outrage mount, and a slow realization dawn as he went on.

"You were fools to come here. Fools to believe my people are weak, or easily exploited. Do you think we have not been threatened before? That we have not faced extortion and aggression? Did you really expect us to meekly surrender to you while you murder our kin? You do not know us Hacan at all, admiral. And now you will pay for that mistake."

"How dare you–" Lieutenant Ogthorn began to shout, recovering before his admiral, but Akenzi ignored him, still speaking to Zorias.

"Order your fleet to muzzle its guns and deactivate its shields."

"Why in the name of the glorious ancestors would I do that?" Zorias demanded.

"Because if you do not, I will kill everybody on this bridge."

CHAPTER FOUR

Grand Carrier Mordaunt, Flagship of the Barony of Letnev's First Grand Fleet

Lieutenant Ogthorn reacted with commendable speed. He deactivated the void glove shielding the Hacan and the Letnev high command from the rest of the bridge, and in an instant Akenzi and Drusha found themselves surrounded by leveled carbines.

But Drusha had been as fast as the Letnev subaltern. He snatched Gondar by the throat, yanking the mysterious figure against his broad frame and baring his fangs.

"Nobody move," Akenzi shouted, heart hammering, tail stiff, one hand raised. In it he still held his savant. Its screen glowed red, and it began to emit a high-pitched beeping tone, making several of the nearest Letnev flinch.

"One more twitch and it detonates," Akenzi went on, baring his own fangs for good measure as he looked at Waizakil and his marines. "It'll destroy this bridge and kill everyone on it. So lower your weapons!"

Hesitation. Akenzi looked fiercely at Zorias, who was frozen in shock.

"Do it!" Akenzi shouted, his voice ringing through the bridge, otherwise silent but for the insistent, dangerous beeping of the savant.

"Lower arms," Zorias said, finally finding his voice. Ogthorn looked as though he was about to complain but thought better of it.

The marines slowly lowered their carbines.

Akenzi glanced at Drusha and his hostage. The Letnev had probably thought a one-armed Hacan was little threat, and they were now discovering just how wrong they were. Drusha had his arm locked around Gondar's shoulder and chest. His claws were out, and his fangs bared against the Letnev's collar, his eyes gleaming with predatory intent. Gondar was perfectly still, his expression icy but unafraid.

"If you shoot my bodyguard, his death-grip will still tear out this one's throat," Akenzi said. "And if my vital signs cease, the device in my hand is programmed to detonate. So, I would once again recommend that everyone remain very still, and that you give orders for your fleet to power down!"

"How do we know that device is really an explosive?" Ogthorn blurted out.

"Do you want to test it?" Akenzi snapped, privately terrified that he would try to do just that.

"Why was it not scanned?" the lieutenant dared continue.

"It was," Waizakil said.

"And it didn't come back as dangerous? Then it isn't an explosive!"

"It did… I computed it as an error," Waizakil admitted.

"You idiot," Zorias barked at the subordinate, finding his voice. "You've singlehandedly endangered this entire venture! You will be standing trial when we return to Arc Prime!"

"If you return," Akenzi pointed out. "That is up to you now.

Do as I say, and nobody will be hurt. You'll be able to leave the tri-system in peace, which is more than any of you deserve."

Akenzi didn't actually know if they would be allowed to leave in peace, but it was the kind of offer he hoped would keep him and his brother alive.

Of course, the device in his hand wasn't an explosive. It really was just his savant. He had simply activated one of its light effects and turned on the alarm that usually woke him in the morning.

The thing that gave it a veneer of believability was the fact that Drusha had fired his plasma pistol next to it before they had taken the shuttle from Alshaz. The weapon discharge and its blast residue had covered it, rendering it "hot" to most devices set to scan for military-grade or dangerous particles. It had shown up as a weapon for the Letnev earlier, even when it quite clearly wasn't, but that was now enough to create doubt.

"This is outrageous," Zorias said. "You think you can hold my entire fleet to ransom?"

"Did you think you could hold all three of the homeworlds of the United Emirates to ransom, admiral?"

"You may think yourself noble for sacrificing yourself like this, but all you have done is guaranteed the annihilation of your people. Even if I am slain, my fleet will react with all the force that such aggression calls for."

"You think this is our last card?" Akenzi asked, and Zorias frowned. Wondering if the Letnev weren't familiar with the concept of card games, he tried again. "This is not the only option remaining to us. Since the beginning, we have been preparing to eject your fleet from our system. We needed only time to gather our strength, time that you have now given us."

"Impossible," Zorias said, sounding aghast.

"Anything but, admiral. Check your displays."

"Scanning station, I want an immediate report on all hostile ships within the engagement zone," Zorias barked.

A few more precious, tense minutes ticked by as the flagship's crew collated the necessary data. Akenzi wondered what they would find. Perhaps Sword Fleet was still hours from being able to deploy? If so, how long would the savant's threat hold the Letnev at bay? It would only take one to find their courage and take a shot or lash out and attempt to bring one of the Hacan down, and his effort would be revealed for the flimsy, foolish gambit it was.

"Scan report collated, admiral," one of the junior officers called, and the observation port showing Hercant and its orbital traffic blinked and enhanced, covered with new tags scrolling with information.

"Multiple Hacan vessels moving on a contact heading. All military-grade. Classes translate into six cruisers and three capital ships, one possible carrier. We aren't sure if it's also military, or a merchant vessel. Their shields are active, and they will be entering effective weapons range in just under ten minutes at their current rate."

"Your cargo is here," Akenzi said, unable to suppress a vicious sense of relief. "And that cargo is death."

"How?" Zorias shouted furiously at the scan officer. "How have they been allowed to assemble and approach?"

"They used the merchant lanes and the planetary orbit as cover while–"

"Shut up! Communications, message all vessels! Target-lock shift to oncoming hostiles. Fire on my command!"

"You forget yourself admiral," Akenzi snapped, thumbing the audio on his savant so the beeping of its alarm grew louder. "If one of those orders is transmitted, you all die! Lower your shields, and we can still find a peaceful resolution!"

"Kill him," Lieutenant Ogthorn said. "Even if it means death for all of us, it will free the rest of our captains to act. The First Fleet cannot be held to ransom like this!"

"We are ready for you now," Akenzi responded just as stridently, looking Zorias in the eye. "Your death will be in vain, and your fleet will be decimated."

Zorias hesitated, and in that moment Akenzi recognized that for all the medals and decorations and military bombast, beneath all his arrogance and anger, First Admiral, Count Zorias was a coward.

"Can you really afford to lose your fleet, admiral?" Akenzi pressed, trying to give him a way out that didn't expose his lack of courage in front of his underlings. "Can the Barony afford such losses, at a time when it desperately needs every warship? Today has been a bad day for your people and mine. Let's not make it an even worse day for yours."

"Just how do you think this ends, Hacan?" Zorias hissed.

"I'm glad you asked," Akenzi said. "After you've deactivated your shields and I've heard from my Quieron over your comms array, myself, Drusha and Gondar are going to board the shuttle we arrived on. You might imagine that once we're off your bridge you'll be able to seize us without worrying about any collateral damage, but rest assured I will be in touch with those Hacan warships the entire time. At the slightest suggestion that I have been harmed or impeded, they will open fire. That goes for my shuttle while it is space bound, too. Once I am safely back among my kindred, then you will be allowed to depart. You have my word on that."

"The word of a Hacan," Zorias said bitterly. "And one who has been lying to me since I set eyes on him!"

"Destroying your fleet wouldn't make sense, from a business perspective," Akenzi said, trying to stay rational. "It would mean a full-scale war. You won't want to add another front to the conflicts you're already fighting in, and my people have no interest in direct conflict. You have a low esteem of us Hacan, so you will accept surely that survival and profit are our priorities."

As he spoke, he cast a warning look at Ogthorn, who currently seemed the most likely to go for his sidearm. If he did, there was nothing Akenzi could do. Negotiations would be at an end.

But, like Zorias, the subaltern kept his weapon holstered.

"Order to the fleet," the admiral said eventually, after further hesitation. "All ships… lower shields and muzzle weapons batteries."

"But, admiral–" Ogthorn began to exclaim, but Zorias turned on him.

"Be silent, lieutenant, or you'll be joining Waizakil on charges! The rest of you, follow your damn orders! Send transmission! And hail the oncoming fleet!"

Akenzi found himself wondering what he would do if Sword Fleet refused to communicate or, with the Letnev's shields lowering, if they decided to simply open fire. Those were all factors well outside his control, and he had to hope Quieron Amalia had explained the situation to her commanders.

As it was, it was Amalia herself who answered the transmission request, patched through via Sword Fleet's flagship, *Pride of the Golden Sands*.

"I see you have found sense, First Admiral Count Zorias," the noble Hacan declared, her head and shoulders transmitting via a holo display that formed part of the Letnev's throne. "And I am also pleased to note that my ambassadors are still alive, though seemingly only thanks to their own initiative. I suggest you stop pointing weapons at them."

"And I suggest they remove themselves from my ship," Zorias snapped.

"I'm sure they'll be happy to oblige. I must also inform you that the commanders of Sword Fleet wish to see you destroyed. What you have done here today is an outrage. Still, I would not be known as a warmonger, like your baron. My only demand is that you leave this system immediately, and never return without invitation. There will, of course, be severe economic sanctions, once I have discussed further steps with the Council. But you should be thankful that you can depart here alive."

"You have not heard the last of this, you foul animal," Zorias said, seemingly in a desperate last-ditch attempt at saving face. "You have made an enemy of the Barony of Letnev this day!"

"That only makes us the latest on a long list of foes you are embroiled against. Now, I suggest you release my ambassadors and take your leave."

The transmission cut out. Akenzi watched Zorias closely, saw the slump in his shoulders, the sudden weariness that indicated defeat.

"Sub-Captain Celan Waizakil II," the Letnev commander said, sounding drained. "Your marines will escort these beasts from my bridge and back to their shuttle. Lieutenant Ogthorn, you will accompany them. Afterward, confine Waizakil to the brig."

"Let's go," Akenzi said to Drusha in their clan dialect as the marines formed around them. "And not too close," he added to the Letnev, flashing the savant still in his palm.

Drusha growled deeply and yanked Gondar to the autostair.

They made it to the docking bay, and Akenzi experienced another moment of raw relief when he found that the transport was still in place and seemingly untouched.

"Just keep going," he told Drusha as they approached the lowered ramp. He was privately amazed Ogthorn hadn't simply ordered them gunned down as soon as they were off the bridge.

He suspected it was a good thing that Gondar was their hostage after all – whoever he was, it appeared nobody on the carrier wanted to take a risk with his life.

They passed up the ramp, Drusha hefting his Letnev prisoner into the shuttle ahead of Akenzi, who paused in the hatch and gave the savant one final wave.

"Remember, any aggression against this shuttle will see not only this carrier destroyed, but your entire fleet with it."

He stepped fully inside the transport and looked at Gondar and Drusha, the former still in the fearsome grasp of the latter. Akenzi thought for a moment, then activated the intercom and ordered the pilot to delay takeoff, then spoke to his brother, again using the Hacan tongue.

"Let him go."

He sensed Drusha's surprise. "You mean, out of the shuttle? While we're still docked?"

"Yes. He isn't the hostage now. Their entire fleet is. I don't think holding him will make a difference."

"He's helped get us this far."

"And I would rather avoid further diplomatic incident," Akenzi pointed out. "We take him with us, his return will need to be negotiated. It could be used as a cause for provocation by the Barony. And I don't want to be the one whose name is tied to that, not after the good work we've done today."

"Wise," Gondar said. Akenzi stopped and stared at him.

It seemed his misgiving about speaking in the Hacan language earlier had been well-founded. The Letnev had clearly understood what had passed between him and his brother.

"It isn't real, is it?" the Letnev went on in Akenzi's language, his pronunciation crude but passable. "The bomb."

Akenzi hesitated, glancing down at the savant in his hand, then imitated a Letnev mannerizing and shook his head. It was difficult not to want to show these brutes just how thoroughly they had been outplayed.

"I suspected so." Gondar nodded.

"If you thought it was fake, why didn't you stop me?"

"The device may not have been real, but your companion's fangs very much are."

"True," Akenzi said. "It is good you didn't underestimate our physiology, even if you underestimated our skills at negotiating."

"Not a mistake I will make again," Gondar said, and Akenzi believed it.

Drusha released him. The Letnev looked between them, as though searching for one last sign of duplicity, or perhaps committing them to memory. Then, he silently departed.

Akenzi immediately rushed to the intercom and transmitted to the shuttle pilot.

"Get us out of here."

"You don't seem concerned," Drusha said as the transporter returned to Alshaz orbital station.

"Should I be?"

"If I was that admiral, I would have us both annihilated as soon as we were off the ship."

"But you're not that admiral, thankfully."

Drusha grunted. "We are both still warriors."

"That Letnev was no warrior," Akenzi said dismissively. "I looked into his eyes. When he realized he had no power over us, there was nothing to him but fear. Not like the one I let go. He seemed more like a warrior than any of them."

"No," Drusha said.

"No?" Akenzi repeated in surprise.

"Not a warrior, that one. A killer."

"There's a difference?"

"Not always. But sometimes. I do not think you should have released him. He is dangerous."

"We've taken on an entire Letnev war fleet, just the two of us, and won," Akenzi said with a satisfied rumble, deep in his chest. "I think we can handle ourselves."

In truth, part of Akenzi did expect to be obliterated by a Letnev bombardment during the transferal back to Alshaz, so it was with concealed relief that he stepped on board the station, knowing that its shields were up.

He and Drusha were greeted by roaring cheers. The bridge was still packed, and the Hacan hailed the Muktat duo like returning heroes. Akenzi refused to search for Hamlar in the crowd, but instead accepted the acclamation with a sweeping bow.

It was only afterward that he noticed the nearest Hacan were wearing orange garments, fringed with gold.

Clan Farik had come to Alshaz. Akenzi found himself standing before his Quieron, flanked by her courtiers and aides. He bowed again, properly this time, trying to overcome his surprise.

"Noble Quieron, I did not expect to see you here," he admitted, though he supposed he shouldn't have been surprised. Amalia was an astute leader, and this was the sort of crisis she would want to be seen in the midst of, controlling.

Amalia accepted his bow with a graceful spread of her arms, a Quieron's greeting.

"Welcome back, honored magnate. I speak for all here when I say I am relieved to see you safely returned. You have saved thousands of lives, and thousands more livelihoods."

"I am sure any other Hacan would have done the same," Akenzi said, hoping Hamlar was within earshot.

"Regardless, your selfless courage deserves its just reward. Name it, Magnate Akenzi, and I will see it given to you."

He knew he had to be careful with what he said next. He couldn't be seen to deliberately undermine the Council – especially since several senior members were present, including Kalzid – but he also knew that it was now or never. His biggest motivation for confronting the Letnev hadn't been selfless courage.

"I am honored that I could be of assistance to my fellow Hacan," he said. "But in truth, there is one matter in which you might be of great assistance to me, glorious Quieron."

"Speak it," Amalia said, Akenzi suspecting she enjoyed acting as the benevolent ruler, dispensing gifts before her subjects.

"I have been attempting to build a business venture to an area of space known as the Boreas Gap – you may well have heard of it. Progress has been positive, and profit seems likely, but there have been… unexpected difficulties with acquiring trade and settlement rights. If it is not too presumptuous, might I ask you to review my case and render a final judgment?"

Amalia watched him closely, and he briefly feared she was about to refuse him, maybe even chastise him for overstepping and questioning the efforts of the Council, even indirectly. A Quieron's powers were not as absolute as the likes of the Baron of Letnev, and all clans knew the balance of authority was a delicate one.

Then Amalia spoke, and welcome relief flooded through Akenzi.

"I will ensure that your venture is not in vain, Magnate Akenzi. Sarawa, you will see to this?"

The Quieron gestured at one of her orange-clad Farik courtiers, who bowed and glanced at Akenzi with glittering eyes.

"Of course, my Quieron," she said.

Akenzi unleashed a flurry of grateful platitudes, trying not to overdo it. He told himself that nothing was settled yet, that until he had a transcript of the trade and settlement rights in his hand, it wasn't yet real.

But in the moment, he knew a ferocious sense of triumph greater than any he had felt before. He looked across the gathering and found Hamlar, still present.

The green and gold zenfar might have guarded the Dazeshi magnate's other tells, but it couldn't disguise the bared fangs, a level of unabashed aggression that almost triggered a mirror response in Akenzi.

He had won, this time, but Hamlar was leaving him a message – there were plenty of games still to be played.

CHAPTER FIVE

Touchdown Zone Gamma, Galier

Galier was worse than Mortalia had imagined it.

She smelled it first, over the chemical reek of the shuttle's suborbital fuel engines. It was the stink of raw sewage and stale bodies, cooking in the heat.

The Winnaran stepped out into the glare, pausing to get her bearings. The transporter had alighted on a landing platform that appeared to be little more than a circle of packed dirt, scarred with the marks of plasma thrusters. A ramshackle shanty town surrounded it, a warren of scrap buildings and makeshift prefabs, rising like a jungle mountain toward a cluster of spires that seemed to shimmer and warp in the midday heat.

Touchdown Zone Gamma. That was all this place was known as, a landing point for medium-sized orbital traffic that dropped right in amidst the sprawl of the refugee camps that had accrued around the planet's original habitation centers.

Mortalia had known it would be a desperate, dire place, but she still wasn't prepared for it.

She had seen the planet from orbit, as Conveyor *SC7* had approached Galier's exosphere. Most of the transport ship's holds were without ports, but the one hired by the Hope Corps – the group Mortalia had attached herself to – had the luxury of a small viz screen showing the space outside. As *SC7* banked on its way through the clear zone to the lock-in coordinates for atmospheric entry, Mortalia and the Corps had gotten a view of Galier and the graveyard of Federation and Barony warships entombing it.

The world itself was ostensibly a human colony, yet the Sol Federation hadn't administered to it for over a decade.

The wars had come to the planet, specifically a series of vast naval engagements between the Federation and the Barony of Letnev, fought across the space of five years. After what was now known as the Fourth Battle of Galier the Federation had been victorious, but at a brutal price. In an effort to shorten its defensive perimeters, it had abandoned the very planet it had spent so much blood and material defending. It had left behind the human colonial population, and the devastation of its conflicts.

Thousands of hulks choked Galier's orbit. Some were wholly intact, dark and foreboding tombs framed by the backdrop of the great blue-and-green planet. Others were gutted or partially wrecked, their innards spooled out in glittering clouds of slowly drifting debris. Many were now unrecognizable, shattered and charred corpses damned to eternally hang above the world they had died to claim.

The volume of the wreckage made it difficult to enter Galier's orbit. It took military-grade shields to withstand collision with even small pieces of battle refuse. Access was only possible by following a series of marker buoys navigators had charted through the worst of the remains over the past few years. That was one of the paths *SC7* followed.

Galier had been almost locked up by the ferocity of the fighting it had witnessed, and the warring factions no longer wished to spend capital to hold it. The planet's surface was still habitable, with areas of temperate climate and good soil, but besides that it lacked the resources required to feed the destructive machinery of the great civilizations.

That had turned it into a haven for the many souls in the sector fleeing the violence of the fighting, or the persecution that inevitably sprang up around it. Conveyors like *SC7* – ugly old lugger ships owned by unscrupulous or desperate captains from all manner of species – accepted their last aurei or valuable possessions in exchange for passage to a world that, it was said, would not be troubled by the great and terrible armies and fleets still carving up the old Lazax Empire. Of course, what the refugees found, if they survived the brutal conditions of the conveyor holds, was an existence every bit as miserable and desperate as their former lives.

"Someone has to do something," Amma had said as they had watched *SC7* navigate the orbital wreckage. "And even a little is better than nothing."

That might as well have been the Hope Corps' unofficial motto. Amma was a Winnaran, like Mortalia. There were a few others among the Corps, as well as a few humans, a pair of Hylar and a single Letnev, whom Mortalia kept well away from. His name was Dragomar and, from what she had overheard, he was a disillusioned ex-Reaper pilot who had chosen to abandon the Barony after one combat action too many. A deserter like him was the last sort of person Mortalia wanted to interact with. She had been careful to avoid conversations with him since she had boarded the conveyor at Hadron's Point.

Someone had to do something, apparently, and the Hope Corps were those someones, a pan-galactic aid organization founded to bring assistance to planets devastated by the ongoing wars.

Mortalia wasn't a member of the Corps. As far as she was concerned, their efforts were akin to trying to put out a furnace fire with a cup of water. Commendable though it was, compared to the devastation being wreaked the length and breadth of the galaxy, it was utterly futile.

She had broached as much, carefully, to Amma not long after she had met her. It had been a while since she had interacted with a fellow Winnaran and, as it often did, the attitude displayed left her privately scornful. Amma admitted there were uncounted billions currently in need who they would not be able to reach or help, but she hoped that doing the good she was capable of was still better than nothing.

Mortalia felt as though the Corps was little more than a confederation of naive young individuals from semi-privileged backgrounds trying to make themselves feel good while their superiors creamed the top off charitable donations, but she kept all that to herself. For a modest fee this Hope Corps expedition to Galier had given her a berth in the tolerably clean hold section they had rented out on board Conveyor *SC7*, apparently satisfied by her claim that she was a journalist trying to bring the horrors of war to the attention of the great civilizations. The idea had sounded even more hopeless and preposterous than the Hope Corps' stated aims, but it had worked so far.

Such deception was a necessary part of her true quest, and a sad reality faced by Winnarans the galaxy over. A century ago, such measures would not have been necessary. Winnarans had been amongst the greatest benefactors of the Lazax Imperium, working as aides and administrators as part of the empire's galaxy-spanning bureaucracy. Mortalia's own grandparents had been senior clerks in the Office of Chancellery, the financial hub of the galaxy. They had owned their own apartment, on Mecatol Rex itself, the capital world of the empire. They had been looking forward to an early retirement, but the Sol Federation's war fleet had opened fire, and the empire had begun its final fall toward crashing, burning annihilation.

Mortalia could believe such things only because she had seen the picture stills her mother had managed to keep with her through the hard years of her own upbringing, during the evacuations, the long-haul voyages and the periods of imprisonment and extradition as the fabric of the empire was ripped apart around them.

She knew her kind would never know the peace and security they had once enjoyed ever again. And she was going to make the ones responsible for that pay.

"I hope we meet again," Amma had said as they had left the shuttle ramp. Mortalia had smiled and agreed.

Now, she intended to get away from the shuttle and its aid cargo as quickly as possible. She had seen the Hope Corps at work before and knew soon this part of the refugee camps would be completely overwhelmed with desperate people, striving to get at the food and necessities the Corps had descended from on high with.

The largest of the slums that had sprung into existence across Galier – known only as the Sprawl – spread out before her, festering in the heat. It was high summer, or so the atmospheric and climatological log on her savant told her. A bad time of the year for those with little water and less food and shelter, or those species who didn't deal well with such conditions. The latter would include the one she had come all this way to meet. Just another reason to hurry.

She drew up her glare-hood and headed into the Sprawl.

She found trouble fast, as was so often the way. She swapped a few ration bars for information from the first locals she encountered, a stinking family of Saar hurrying toward Touchdown Zone Gamma, their thick pelts matted and greasy. Mortalia had answered their anxious questions about the cargo of the newly arrived shuttle, and they had pointed her toward the Dreghouse, one of the largest forums outside the pre-existing city at the heart of the Sprawl.

She hurried through the twisting dirt alleys, keeping her glare-cape cinched tight around her. It was a drab garment, one she had chosen not just because it would help combat Galier's heat and light, but also because it wouldn't draw attention. She was out in the unknown here, and in truth it was only her iron sense of determination that was keeping her going, so far from any source of comfort or familiarity, down amongst the galaxy's most desperate and impoverished.

In one alleyway she paused briefly to check her projector. It was a square device, small enough to sit in her palm. When activated it beamed a discreet holo projection of her parents into the air above it. For all intents and purposes, it was one of her few personal items. In reality, it contained a beacon, allowing it to act as a rudimentary, concealed comms device, not dissimilar to a crude savant.

Mortalia found the projection of her parents pitched at a slightly blue hue, meaning there were no new transmissions, and that her companions were within nearby scan range. That was good news. She assumed they had made it planetside with the Hope Corps cargo.

She carried on deeper into the Sprawl, discovering that she had taken a wrong turn past a thrumming makeshift energy hub. The narrow lane she found herself in, packed with junk and refuse and stinking like an open sewer, was partially cut off by a trio of figures. Two of them were Saar but they didn't look like a family hurrying to reach an aid transport. Their focus was on a third individual, a human, male, grubby, looking emaciated and scrawny next to the two big brutes.

"The last time was your last chance," one of the Saar was growling at the cornered human in crude univoca. "You're all out of luck. We're taking you to Nezdra. You, and your family."

Mortalia had heard that name before. She had done what research she could on Galier and had gleaned more from Amma. There was no universally recognized planetary authority – the human colonists still considered themselves its rulers, but had realized they could do nothing to stop the influx of refugees, and generally focused on keeping the worst of the masses out of the original settlements, now called the Core Cities. Out in places like the Sprawl, control was exerted by a volatile mix of semi-legitimate collectives and communes, violent gangs and everything in between.

Unfortunately, Nezdra appeared to fall under the "gang" umbrella. He was a human but consorted freely with all species in his ongoing quest to prey on the destitute.

Mortalia began to turn around yet realized she was too late. The human being interrogated looked at her, and the two thugs followed his gaze.

"You," one barked. "Stop!"

Mortalia knew she had two options, neither of which involved trying to outrun the Saar on their home turf. One was to stop and talk. The other was to stop and hope the things following her would intercede on her behalf.

She glanced at the surrounding rooftops for them but could see no sign that they were with her just now – she would simply have to trust in what her projector had shown her. She had been almost entirely unaware of them on board Conveyor *SC7* as well, though she knew they had made a lair for themselves in the ship's stuttering air recyc vents. Sometimes she got a sense of when they were close, as though after so many years in their half-felt company, she knew on a subconscious level when they were nearby.

She didn't have that sense now. That only left the first option.

The Saar were on her, dragging their human captive alongside them. They loomed over Mortalia.

"Don't get a lot of Winnarans around these parts," one of them grunted. "And that's a clean, fresh-looking shroud you've got there."

"New arrival from that shuttle, perhaps," the other hypothesized with a bestial leer. "Want to tell us what cargo you're carrying?"

"It isn't my cargo," Mortalia said, wondering if she could talk her way out of this. "It's the Hope Corps'. I was just hitching a ride."

"Maybe you should come and tell Nezdra about that," one of the Saar said. "He always likes meeting new arrivals."

The other one reached out and snatched her wrist, watching her closely for her reaction.

"You should let go," she told him.

"Why?" he demanded with a grin, his fangs a rancid yellow.

"Because if you don't, it will end badly for you."

The Saar laughed. Mortalia felt a stab of annoyance, potent enough to overcome her concern. She let the brute keep ahold of one arm but reached under her glare-cape with her other and pulled out a small metal plate.

"Do you know what this is?" she demanded, holding it up before the pair. They studied it, and she saw realization dawn on the face of the one still gripping the human.

"What's a Winnaran doing with one of those?" he demanded.

"That doesn't matter," Mortalia replied. "What matters is your friend here lets me go."

"What is it?" the nonplussed Saar asked his companion. He explained just what the small plate and its embossed seal meant.

"How do you know it isn't fake?" he asked. "Why would they trust a Winnaran with that kind of authority?"

"You still don't seem to be grasping the situation," Mortalia said, letting her anger show through. "Let me make it easier for your little brains to comprehend. Let me go or die!"

"Nobody talks to us that way," the Saar who hadn't understood her full identity snarled, making their human captive whimper. "Little offworlder with a trinket like that, you think you can just come here and order us about?"

He yanked her arm. It was the last thing he ever did. The other Saar was telling him to let her go when the first one went suddenly stiff and turned to look at the object that had materialized in his shoulder.

It was a slender barb, about the length of one of Mortalia's fingers and slightly thinner, seemingly made from a pale, plasticon-like material. A look of confusion passed over the Saar's face, and he made no reaction when Mortalia ripped her wrist free from his grip. Then, a dull, vacant look entered his eyes, and he collapsed backward onto the refuse-littered dirt.

So, the projector beacon hadn't been lying. They had been following her after all.

The second Saar was already running, abandoning his human captive, but it was too late. He managed a few yards before he was hit as well and went down as the synapse venom in the dart locked out his muscles and then rapidly shut down his organs.

Mortalia faced the human. The man was shaking and sniveling, too afraid to even move.

She looked up at the rooftops and, though she caught nothing but the barest hint of movement, raised her hand and clenched her fist.

Not this one.

No more darts fell. Mortalia looked at the human.

"You should go," she said.

The man didn't seem capable of speech, but he managed a nod. Mortalia brushed past him, stepping over the Saar bodies.

She had hoped this wouldn't happen, at least not so quickly after arriving planetside. It cut down all the timeframes she had been working with.

She slipped the small plate back into her glare-cape and began to hurry.

CHAPTER SIX

THE SPRAWL, GALIER

Not all the wreckage from the four great naval battles that had beset Galier had remained in orbit.

Debris had rained down on the planet's surface, scarring and pockmarking it. While much of it had since been scavenged for scrap, some ships were still well enough intact to serve a function for Galier's teeming new inhabitants.

That was how the Dreghouse had come into being. It was one of the foremost marketplaces in the Sprawl, and a Federation cruiser played host to it all. The ship's aft section was still largely in one piece, and the Sprawl had sprung up over, around and within it, like a woodland fungus working its way across and into a great, fallen log.

The huge furrow ploughed up by the cruiser's impact had become part of the marketplace. The sides of the long trench were crammed with stalls and seller shacks, forming a parade toward where the cruiser's rear fuselage loomed, towering over the surrounding scrap city.

Mortalia hurried along the furrow, paying no heed to the hawkers and vendors, trying also not to linger over the miserable poverty of the place.

Here the divisions of the great powers had been laid bare as hollow and meaningless. All species intermingled and suffered together, all endured hardship, all strove to survive, and none cared for the politicking of barons and councils and kings, or the sector-spanning campaigns of great generals. This was the reality for billions the galaxy over, ignored by the great and the good.

Mortalia knew there was no time to ponder such matters. Introspection on the state of the galaxy could wait until she had achieved what she had first set out to do almost a decade earlier. She was on a quest, one that had defined her life, and one that she hoped would soon be complete. So, she ignored the begging of the rag-clad urchins, stepped over a human who was sprawled, seemingly inebriated, in the middle of the furrow pathway, and waved aside the sellers trying to push broken old savants, lucky charms or steaming, foul-looking local delicacies into her hands.

In the shadow of the fallen cruiser's fuselage, the true marketplace began. The engines themselves had long ago been stripped out, leaving gaping, blackened holes in the ship's rear. Mortalia entered the cavernous space, hearing the echoes of the hubbub within.

The cruiser's innards had been gutted, and now its bridge and hangars formed a hall of rusting metal plates and disused pipes and ducts. Part of the ceiling had fallen in, allowing the light of Galier's star to lance down onto the scene below.

Unlike the rickety stalls or spread blankets of the hawkers infesting the landing furrow, the structures that had been built within the old ship were semi-permanent. A mass of shacks and scrap-hovels had grown and spread inside the vessel, creating a painfully narrow maze of passages and alleyways through what had once been vast hangar bays and weapons platforms.

The whole place, partially encased within the broken and decaying hull, was alive with activity. Most of the shops had open fronts to display their wares, and buyers and sellers intermingled freely, packing the spaces between the ramshackle buildings. The air was busy with a hundred different languages and thick with the smells of zestbread and roasting tusker, grease and sweat-musk.

Mortalia moved with purpose, keeping her head down, not making it obvious that she was searching for somewhere without knowing exactly where she was going.

Most importantly, she knew the kind of people to avoid – the vicious-looking Shikrai with the molting plumage lounging with a tankard of equally vicious-looking swill outside a brew shop, the trio of Letnev, armed to the teeth, strolling across the old mesh decking plates like they owned the whole place, the heavyset Saar and his mean-looking companions, decorated with gold jewelry, making their way out of a stew shack as others scrambled to get out of their way, clearly aware of their high standing in the web of gangs and cartels that ran the Dreghouse. Mortalia made sure she didn't catch any of their eyes, and hoped rumors hadn't started to spread yet of two Saar goons who'd turned up dead in an alleyway near Touchdown Zone Gamma.

Rumors always traveled too fast in places like these.

There was a slope to the ship's interior. Mortalia descended it, heading toward the far end of the hulk's interior. That was where the data she had acquired – at great danger and cost – claimed the place she sought was to be found, in amongst what was known as the market's prow. There the poorest traders congregated, the buildings little better than the shacks packing the furrow outside.

Mortalia doubled back in an effort to check she wasn't being followed but found no sign of a tail among the teeming crowds. Nor could she see her companions, though she trusted they were there. Sometimes, if they were especially close, they would signal to her by tapping on a nearby surface – two beats, a pause, then three, *tap-tap… tap-tap-tap* – but the hubbub around her was too much for that.

She located the shop she was looking for. Makar's Emporium, crammed beneath a sagging bulkhead in one of the final side-corridors of the marketplace. Its narrow frontage displayed a series of computation consoles, an array of savants and an old-pattern autofamiliar whose head node tracked Mortalia as she approached. The blinking neon sign above the doorway proclaimed that this was the finest Hylar-run mechanical shop on Galier.

Mortalia had her doubts about that, but she wasn't here for Hylar tech savvy. After a furtive glance over her shoulder, she pressed the door's entrance pad and stepped inside, deactivating and pulling back her glare-hood as she went.

Makar at least seemed to have a technological grasp on air conditioning – the atmospheric recyc unit clattering noisily on the ceiling was the first thing Mortalia noticed, along with the welcome cool it generated. She found herself in a cramped place packed with shelves bearing all sorts of machine clutter, from autofamiliar parts to holo units and viz players. Most of it appeared to be covered by a layer of dust. Even the illuminator bars overhead were stuttering and filmed in grimy yellow.

Mortalia passed between the stacks, trying to gauge if anyone else besides its patron was in the shop, but it didn't seem like it. Business looked bad, and that suited her perfectly.

"Good middle-day, stranger," said a voice in clipped, precise univoca as Mortalia rounded another jumbled set of shelves. Before her was a shop counter, and behind it was the Hylar who had addressed her. He was one of the Jol subspecies, tall, his gray scales patchy and flaking with age. Like all his kind, he was an amphibian, and wore an old-looking, patched enviro-suit to survive on Galier – his head was encased by a glassy containment sphere, the orb filled with slightly murky-looking liquid.

"Are you Makar?" Mortalia asked.

"That I am, my lady," the Hylar said with the slightest of bows and a small smile. "And how can I be of assistance to you this fine, bright day?"

Hylar didn't smile often, but Makar was clearly used to at least trying to adopt some of the mannerisms of his customers. Mortalia approached the desk.

"I have something to show you," she told him. He chuckled, voice given a slight synthetic buzz by the vocalizer that made up part of his containment sphere's gorget.

"I doubt there is anything you could show me that I would find interesting, Winnaran."

"Are you certain?"

As Mortalia spoke, she drew out the plate and placed it carefully on the counter.

The Hylar looked down at it, and his aura of professional friendliness disintegrated. He locked eyes with Mortalia, his expression now more befitting of a Hylar – cold and guarded.

"I think you should leave."

"Not until I have what I came for."

"And just what is that?"

"Information."

"Of course. But what kind of information?"

"It relates to an incident not long after the start of the war. One that you witnessed."

"I don't know what you're talking about," Makar said.

It had taken years to track him down. Even with all the considerable assistance her backers could provide, there had been innumerable dead ends and false leads. Months had been wasted as she had endured the cramped, infested holds of interstellar luggers and the dangers and discomforts of all manner of stack-city underbellies, bleak outposts and old battlegrounds.

He wasn't the only lead, of course. There had been others she had tracked down over the course of her quest, but they had all led either here or had only been able to give her rumors and suggestions. She needed corroboration. She needed an eyewitness.

"Your parents were the station masters at Pell's Point," Mortalia told the Hylar. "Some time after the Federation opened fire at Mecatol Rex, they logged a Lazax ship that refueled at the Point."

"Hundreds of ships refueled there," Makar snapped. "A whole Letnev war fleet came through at one point!"

"But this wasn't a military vessel, or a diplomatic courier. It was a private civilian cruiser, a Lazax one, registered to an Imperial politician. And it was heading out-system, beyond the sector."

"How do you expect me to know that? You said yourself, my parents were the station masters, not me."

"But you were present. You were young, but not so young you don't remember. Woken by your parents being roused by an incoming alert signal, late one night-cycle. The war was still fresh, and rumors were circulating constantly. There had been a complete cessation of shipping. But then this lone vessel, tagged to a Lazax politico. Running, it seemed. What could it mean? Would there be others pursuing it? Could you find out from them just what had happened back on the capital world?"

"There were three," Makar said eventually, his expression as cold as any Hylar Mortalia had seen.

"What?"

"It wasn't one ship. Three. All Lazax."

"What about the rest of it?" Mortalia demanded, focusing on the number involved later, forcing herself not to become sidetracked by the mere mention of the existence of the Lazax. "I'm right, aren't I?"

"They refused to open comms with us. Their aurei was good though."

"And while they transferred it, you were able to tap into their systems, weren't you? Access their nav-markers. Work out where they were going."

"You think we'd be capable of that?"

"You're Hylar. Always one step ahead of the rest of us when it comes to technology. Pell's Point isn't a big fuel hub. There are only so many locations they could be going if they were heading outbound. But which one? What did you find in those ship systems?"

"Why would we want to know where they were going? It was just three more ships."

"It wasn't though, was it? You'd heard the rumors. A senior Lazax politician, a member of the imperial council even, fleeing Mecatol prior to the Federation attack, and still on the run as everything descended into chaos. Some say he was in league with the humans that bombarded the capital world, others that he knew what was coming and wanted out. There are a string of reports tracing his progress to Pell's Point. Your station was the last in the line, at least back then. But where did he go after?"

"Why should I tell you?" Makar said.

"How's business?" Mortalia asked.

"Don't mock me, Winnaran," Makar hissed, his gills flaring and causing bubbles to form in the murky fluid of his containment sphere. "How does business look to you?"

Mortalia reached into her cape again – slowly, so as not to startle the Hylar, and withdrew a small, glassy black bar. She placed it down next to the plate with a singular, pronounced clack, and slid it across the counter to Makar.

"From where I'm standing, pretty good," she said.

She could sense the Hylar's mistrust as he stared down at the untraceable aurei stack.

"It's good," Mortalia told him. "Fully loaded. Run it if you want."

Makar did just that, sliding the aurei stack through a currency block reader on the counter while the Winnaran pocketed the plate that identified her.

"There's more where that came from," she told him. "But only if you tell me where those three ships were going. Where did you triangulate them to?"

Makar told her. She spent some time digesting the information, then informed him an associate would deliver the second aurei stack within the same cycle.

"Don't bother," he said, to her surprise. "Just go. You're trouble, and I've no doubt your 'associate' will be as well. I'm going to use what you've already paid me to buy passage out of here. You won't find me again."

"As you wish," Mortalia said.

Before she could add anything more, she heard a knock at the door. She realized Makar must have sealed it remotely at some point after she had entered.

Makar moved, but not to unlock the door. Instead, he swept out from behind his counter, heading for a door in the back of the shop and beginning to input a code into its control panel.

Mortalia realized what was happening and threw herself to one side just as the door blew. A shape barreled through the smoke, a shape that included a raised beam pistol.

She dove behind a row of shelves bearing a clutter of tech junk, hearing the pistol's whine followed by the *snap-snap-snap* of discharges.

Still struggling to get through the back door, Makar was hit by the flurry of searing lasers. The door hissed open, but too late for the Hylar, who dropped out of sight behind the counter.

Mortalia had no idea if the sudden invasion was because of the Saar that had been killed earlier, or whether she'd simply been unlucky enough to be caught in the midst of a gangland hit. She didn't suppose it would make much difference, as far as her not becoming a target was concerned. She had the information she needed. That was all that mattered.

To stay meant death. She scrambled on all fours toward the counter. The figure who had swept through the door half saw her through the clutter on the shelves and opened fire again, but the machinery on display took the worst of the fusillade, old junk cascading down around her as it was blasted off the shelves.

She managed to get behind the counter and kept going toward the open back door. Makar was convulsing on the floor in front of it. He hadn't been hit directly by the pistol, but his containment sphere had been shattered, its precious liquid spilling out and leaving the gray-scaled amphibian choking to death on Galier's hot, stinking air. Mortalia knew there was nothing she could do for him – a few seconds more and her fate would be just as thoroughly sealed as his.

She scrambled over him and out onto the rusting decking plates that constituted the alleyway outside, pursued by more beam pistol shots that burned holes in the wall of the shack opposite.

Panting, she got to her feet and ran, stumbling over refuse clogging the narrow space. She didn't know where her companions were. She could only hope they were still nearby and had caught the sounds of weapon discharges.

Left – that would take her to a main thoroughfare. At best the presence of witnesses might put the attackers off, at worst it would slow them down. She almost tripped over more wreckage, and raced past another opening to her right, then quickly decided to double back – more shapes loomed in the end of the alleyway, the narrow walls funneling the telltale whine of another energy weapon rapidly charging up.

Wrong choice. The sharp right-hand turn led her to a dead end, a refuse-filled space between the last of the shacks and a section of bulkhead now almost lost behind a mound of stinking, decaying junk. Mortalia swore viciously and turned at bay.

All she could do was pull out the plate and hope against all hope that it would give them pause.

Her pursuers advanced along the alley toward her, weapons leveled, and she got a proper look at them for the first time – one Letnev and one Shikrai, the off-white plumage of the latter daubed with pink gang markings, the former with similar tattoos marking the left side of his pallid face. The Shikrai had a needle bow and the Letnev a beam pistol. The third member of the hit team, a Saar, was hanging back at the entrance to the dead end, presumably acting as lookout.

"If you do this, there'll be consequences," Mortalia called to them, trying to sound confident. There was only one way of surviving this. "Turn around and go back, and I'll make sure my friends don't hear about this."

"Nobody's going to hear about this, besides Boss Nezdra," the Shikrai chirruped scornfully. He was at the front, half a dozen paces away now with the Letnev keeping an angle on her over his shoulder.

"Take her," the Letnev said.

The Shikrai loosed his bow.

There was a cracking, zipping sound, and a clatter. Mortalia had reflexively closed her eyes, expecting the needle arrow to drill its way through her body and leave her sprawled against the slope of rubbish behind her.

Instead, she opened her eyes to find the Shikrai staring at the shorn launch beam of his weapon, and the arrow that had clattered to the decking plates instead of launching into Mortalia's chest. Something had sliced the bow a split second before the Shikrai had loosed its projectile, rendering it abruptly useless.

That something now darted past the gawping Shikrai and slashed at the Letnev. The ganger barked with pain as his hamstring was sliced, and he went down on one knee. He squeezed his trigger as he went, and Mortalia flung herself aside as red bolts of brilliance spat indiscriminately past, punching into the rubbish and slashing burn marks into the walls.

The wicked, curved knife Mortalia's companion carried caught the Letnev's throat as he went down, free hand directing the pistol's spasmodic discharge into the deck. By this point the Shikrai had recovered enough to reach for his own dagger but had only drawn it halfway before another of the lethal figures had dropped down from the rooftops, directly onto the Shikrai's back. He let out a shrieking squawk that quickly became a blood-curdling cry as a short, telescopic razor-spear – extended – was punched through his plumage and down between his shoulder and collar bones, running him through vertically.

Both the gangers dropped. Their killers were already on the move again, and Mortalia kept herself pressed to the wall as the Saar at the far end of the passage opened fire.

The brute only got off a few shots before the last of the Winnaran's trio of companions struck, a venom dart consigning him to the same fate as the two who had tried to accost her earlier that day.

A sudden, terrible quiet descended on the alleyway. Two of Mortalia's rescuers immediately scaled the walls back onto the rooftops, but the third approached with a hunched, darting run that made her take a step back, almost falling against the junk heap. They had been in contact for years, on and off, but a part of her still feared them.

"Hylar is dead," the creature told her.

"I know," she replied.

"You have what you need?"

"Yes. I think so. I know where we are going next."

"We go now then, quick. Gun sounds will draw attention."

That was true. She nodded her thanks, and hurried toward the end of the alleyway, stepping over the bodies of those who had been sent to kill her.

Makar had given her what she needed, after all these years. Confirmation.

"Where?" her companion called after her, still standing at the dead end. She looked back at him.

"The Boreas Gap."

CHAPTER SEVEN

Interstellar wreckage, the Exiles' Path

"Did you hear that?" Lekaan asked.

Vexar looked at her sharply and held his breath, listening. He found he could detect nothing, bar the beating of his own heart and the soft humming of his sealed suit. He shook his head, the motion clumsy in the void protection gear. Lekaan remained silent, so Vexar spoke out loud.

"What did it sound like?"

"Like… knocking. Or footsteps?"

"This place is old. Hundreds of years old, and most of it preserved by the cold. There'll be plenty of things that can knock."

"You're really not making me feel any better, Vex."

"Plenty of innocent things, I mean! We ran the scans five times. There's nothing living on here with us. There's an atmosphere in here, but it's not breathable. We're alone."

"Yeah. That's what makes it worse."

Vexar sighed, trying to be patient. He could understand why she was struggling. This was a literal tomb, after all, cast adrift in the depths of space. They had found seven bodies so far, all mummified by the interstellar cold. They didn't appear to have been part of the station's old crew but looked more like vagrants who had been using the place while it was still semi-inhabitable and receiving passing traffic, maybe even before it had been cut adrift from its stellar anchor. At some point, however, the last ship had come by, and there had been no more. They'd starved or run out of oxygen.

It was sobering, imagining being stranded here. Vexar found himself continuously checking and rechecking the connection marker on his suit dome's heads-up display, the one that showed he was still in contact with their own sprint ship, the *Grand Dominion*. It was anchored portside of the largest, most intact part of the space station's wreckage. While it had been battered by debris over the decades, most of the station was still traversable, though its artificial grav generator had long ago failed, its heat pumps had burned out and its oxygen tanks had depleted. That was why the pair of Winnarans who had boarded were relying on void suits they had brought with them from *Grand Dominion*'s inventory.

"I can take you back to the shuttle if you'd like, and I can go on alone," Vexar said, not wanting to drag Lekaan after him when her nerves were so obviously fraying. Privately he realized he should have brought someone like Mond or Kazi, both of whom Vexar considered the toughest members of the group. But Lekaan, quite apart from being his partner, was also easily the best tech expert among them, and he doubted he would be able to do much in the way of deciphering whatever could be salvaged from the station's data banks without her. It was a relief, then, when she did her best to shake her head in the bulky suit.

"No, it's all right. We've come this far."

And that, Vexar supposed, summed them all up. This had been years in the making. Most of them had dedicated their whole lives to getting this far. They had sworn the Resurrectionist Compact. They were Winnarans, servants of the one true empire, inheritors of it alongside the Lazax. They had lost everything. They couldn't give up now.

Like all his fellow Resurrectionists, Vexar was far too young to remember the empire itself, at least from before the war. He had vague memories of a Lazax his grandparents had worked for as part of the imperial tithing operation on Hondar. She had sought shelter with his parents on Winnu during the collapse, believing that, of all the peoples in the galaxy, the empire's loyal administrators would protect her. Like many other Lazax, she had been mistaken, and both she and Vexar's parents had eventually been hunted down and killed by the Letnev.

Vexar had been too young to fully appreciate the horror of those days. While Mecatol Rex had fallen in a matter of hours, the death of the empire had been slow and painful, stretching out for over half a century. When the Lazax his parents had sheltered had been killed, some had claimed she was the last of her kind, the last of that noble people who had once overthrown the Mahact and created an imperium of peace and enlightenment in their stead.

Vexar didn't believe she was the last. He didn't believe his parents had died in vain. He had joined the Resurrectionists because they believed in that same principle, that there were still Lazax living, surviving, somewhere in the galaxy. As Winnarans loyal to the old empire, Vexar and his companions had sworn to find and serve them, in the hope that one day, against all odds, the shattered imperium could be pieced back together again, and stability could be restored to the galaxy.

It was a duty Vexar had pursued all his adult life. And it had led him and his band of companions out here, into the depths of space, to a waystation, wrecked and forgotten except in a few fragmentary tales. Stories that linked it to the true last Lazax.

"There's no one else here," Vexar reiterated, hoping to convince himself as much as Lekaan.

"It's probably just Clunky anyway," she agreed, glancing back at the silent mechafamiliar. Vexar knew her well enough to be able to tell she didn't believe her own words either, but she seemed determined enough to go on. That was why Vexar loved her.

They continued, moving along the dark, bare metal corridor, slow and awkward in their suits, the stab beams of their flashlights the only illumination. There was a slight upward tilt to the deck, forcing them to ascend. Vexar was almost tempted to kill the antigravetic clamps that were keeping them securely anchored to the decking plates, but he didn't want to be caught floating should anything sudden occur.

Lekaan went ahead, seemingly intent on proving herself after her moment of doubt. She reached the corridor's end first. It was a solid hatch bulkhead, shut.

"This should be it," she said, pausing to check the flickering green holo scan being projected from her suit's vambrace. The *Grand Dominion* had done multiple, thorough sweeps of the wreckage from different angles and across different spectrums. Vexar was glad the Resurrectionists had spent so much on a ship with such powerful systems. They had been able to pick the nearest point of ingress on the old station and make their way with relatively little difficulty to this point – the entrance to the bridge.

Lekaan tried the access panels next to the entrance hatch – long dead – then attempted to use the manual opening lever. It refused to budge.

"It's sealed," she told Vexar.

"Stand back," he advised and called up Clunky.

The mechafamiliar was crude, at least compared to the types of automated intelligence Vexar had heard the Lazax once possessed. Such machinery was becoming rarer, just another indication of the slow and brutal degradation the galaxy was experiencing without the peace and unity of the empire.

Whatever the limitations of Clunky's boxy design and mode of locomotion – whirring treads rather than the sleek suspension of antigrav units – the machine was suited to this particular operation. Its chassis had been rigged up with a high-concentration beam projector, a device usually employed in asteroid mining that the Resurrectionists had purchased from the market on Shenchetch Minoris for this very purpose. They'd also fitted Clunky's underside with a few of the gravetic clamps and stabilizers from the boots of spare void suits, ensuring the station's lack of gravity wasn't an issue.

Vexar called the familiar up along the sloping corridor and pinned its attention to where Lekaan wanted the beam to hit using the pointer beacon he had strapped to his cuff.

"That should shear through the primary pin bolt," Lekaan said.

Vexar didn't question how she could be certain. He had long ago accepted she knew much more about these sorts of things than he did.

There was a high-pitched whine as Clunky triggered the hi-con beam emitter. A continuous line of orange energy no thicker than an ink inscriber speared the hatch. Vexar watched as metal blistered and deformed, starting to give way.

It seemed to take an age. Vexar checked his oxygen levels – still above sixty percent – and the reassuring presence of the *Grand Dominion*. He tried a quick comms blip, but it was chopped with static, cut up by the surrounding wreckage.

There was a thud, ringing through the deck underfoot, and the hatch shuddered and groaned. It was followed immediately by more ringing sounds on the deck, except this time they came from behind, rather than the hatch – one-two-three, in rapid succession, each louder than the last.

To Vexar it sounded like someone was using the noise of the hatch locks breaking to try to run up the tunnel toward them.

He turned with some difficulty, heart suddenly racing, and pointed his flashlight back down the corridor. The narrow beam of harsh white light picked out nothing but old pipes and decking plates.

He noticed Lekaan looking at him.

"You heard it that time, didn't you?" she said, accusingly.

"Let's just get in there," he said, glancing the way they had come one more time before turning back toward the now-open hatch. "The sooner we can get back to the shuttle, the sooner we can be on our way."

With leaden steps, they entered the bridge.

The space was partially illuminated by starlight. A plasticon dome, thankfully intact, formed much of the ceiling and part of the walls, and would once have allowed the staff manning the bridge to look out over the station's four refueling spurs. All but one of those were now broken off, leaving the bridge and the body of the station below it like a lonely, drifting watchtower.

The mesh decking underfoot groaned as Vexar stepped on it. His breath caught, but the floor held, and he carried on.

The bridge's center was a circle of control nodes and data banks. There were words emblazoned above the computator consoles, text stamped in univoca, picked out by the roving of the Winnaran pair's flashlights and the glimmer of the stars. Lekaan read it out.

"Pell's Point."

"That's the station name," Vexar said. "It was a refueling hub on the routes to the Outer Banks and the Exiles' Path.

But when the war started most of the outer settlements and colonies were abandoned by both the empire and the great powers. Work dried up and the station was abandoned and cut adrift."

"And this is where they came through?" Lekaan asked. She didn't need to specify who she meant. Figures of near myth, a story repeated by Winnarans still loyal to the old ideals of the empire. The last of the Lazax.

"That's what we're here to find out," Vexar said.

Clunky trundled in after them, and Vexar stooped over the back of the chassis and unclamped the power block. Used to fuel the hi-con beam emitter, it would now hopefully serve to stoke old systems back to life.

Lekaan spent a few moments surveying the bridge's primary computator, then directed Vexar on where to plug the block in. There was a brief period of suspense as nothing happened. Lekaan tried several switches on the various control panels. Vexar was considering advising her to give it a smack – only half-jokingly – when there was a sudden electrical crackle, and a whine.

Light blazed, first across the viz screens and input boards in front of them, and then from the bars overhead. The two Winnarans blinked and squinted uncomfortably. The illumination flickered but held. Vexar matched Lekaan's grin.

"Hylar-made, probably," he told her. "Nothing matches their technology, even after half a century of disuse."

"Shame they were so swift to betray the empire," Lekaan pointed out. Vexar couldn't argue with that.

He stood beside his partner as she leaned over one of the input boards and began to stab at the keys, forced to go slow by her thick, clumsy gauntlets. Vexar tried not to fret, his nerves mounting. So much rested on this. The group's funds were almost dry. They had the fuel and supplies for one more voyage, one more stab into the unknown, chasing a dream. After that, even the last remaining diehards would have to accept that they had failed.

Lekaan worked her way through the system access on the primary viz screen. It was partially broken, fuzzed with static, but enough was discernible for Vexar to see that she was coming up against a digi-security barrier. She pulled a data stick from a pouch in her suit and inserted it into one of the computator ports, then resumed her inputting.

"That should get us close," she said. "They didn't bother with anything but basic shield protocols before they left, because they'd wiped the system."

"But does that not mean we won't be able to retrieve any data from it?" Vexar asked.

"How long have you known me, darling?" Lekaan smirked. "I've got enough here for a full system renewal. It'll just take a while to analyze."

She pulled out and inserted another data stick, lips pursed, the light of the screen reflecting from the glassy dome of her suit's head. Vexar knew when to let her work, trying not to fret. He looked up past the glare of the screens at the hatch they had entered through, still lying open. Thanks to the light within the bridge, it had been reduced to a semicircle of utter blackness, a yawning maw with only the void beyond it. Vexar stared into it, then suppressed an involuntary shudder and looked back at the screens.

The work went quicker than he had hoped. Lekaan was able to restore much of the aged system and begin transferring it remotely to *Grand Dominion*.

"It will take too long to do a deep dive from here," she pointed out. "We can analyze it once we're off this hulk."

"As long as you have everything you think we'll need," Vexar said, wanting to spend as little time on board the abandoned station as her.

"I think so."

Finally, Lekaan retrieved her sticks, and they began the slow egress. Vexar kept trying to force the memory of the station's strange sounds from his mind, knowing he couldn't freeze up now.

After what felt like an age, they made it into the shuttle and back on board the *Grand Dominion*. The rest of the Resurrectionists – about three dozen Winnarans in all – gathered anxiously on the bridge as they waited for Lekaan to run the analysis, while Vexar ordered their helmsman, Dronno, to put as much distance between them and the remains of Pell's Point as possible.

As they moved on a new heading, Lekaan let out an exclamation and gestured toward the bridge's holo display. It blinked with a screed of data, parts of which she rapidly highlighted, fingers dancing across the input board.

"The stories were true. Here. And here. The station master recorded not one, but three ships, time-logged within the window we calculated. They couldn't match the hull tags, but they've triangulated possible out-system routes. The same ones you were trying to work out, Vex."

Vexar's eyes scanned the findings, his excitement replacing the dark trepidation that had settled over him at Pell's Point. He looked at Lekaan, unable to suppress a grin. She nodded at him.

"It's what we thought. The Boreas Gap. And beyond it, Gamma Eridius."

CHAPTER EIGHT

GAMMA ERIDIUS, THE BOREAS GAP

Something darted through the murky depths, a flash of yellow and blue in the gray brine.

Harial Tol had been tracking it for the past few minutes. There had been a whole shoal of them, but they had broken apart, perhaps to hunt, or to avoid being hunted. Tol's own potent aquatic senses had detected no threat, so she had followed one through the waters, hoping the vibrations being caused by her savant – sealed in a plasticon pocket to her arm – wouldn't disturb it.

The fish flitted through the capillaries of a bank of underwater rock, seemingly searching for something. Tol swam up onto the rock's top and crouched there, waiting for it to reemerge once more before diving down with a lithe thrust and a kick of her webbed toes. Her spindly, soft-boned hands closed around it like a cage as it darted back out, encasing it without harming it.

She raised the fish and looked into its eyes, wondering, as she often had before, if it possessed any comprehension that, billions of years ago, they might once have been kin, or at least possessed the same evolutionary markers that had led to the independent development of life on her homeworld of Nar, and here, on distant Gamma Eridius.

Of course, the idea was foolish. She turned her gentle grip back and forth, admiring the markings on her catch's scales, glittering and iridescent in the light diffracting through the waves above. Her own scales were not wholly different, orange and blue stripes and a crested head-fin, though age had removed their luster and was increasingly causing them to scab and flake.

She wondered what this fish was called, whether it had a name at all. It reminded her of lightbursts. There were great shoals of them back on Nar, shimmering clouds of color that streaked the clear, shallow depths of the planet's warm oceans. Or at least there had been when she had last visited. She hadn't been to Nar for almost a century now.

Her savant was still buzzing. Her gills shivered with unrest. He was always calling on her. She was tired, and while Gamma Eridius' seas were a far cry from the crystalline waters of home – they were cold and deep and gray, more like Nar's neighboring planet, Jol – they still allowed her to escape, to leave behind the responsibilities she'd been burdened with for so long now.

She released the lightburst and watched it dart away, into the gloom. She remembered as a child being told that the memory spans of many smaller amphibians were minute compared to that of a Hylar and wondered if in a few moments more it would even truly be able to recall this encounter.

Sometimes she wished she could so readily forget.

She set out, back toward the shallows.

Tol had left her enviro-suit on the rocks by the shingle. As she put it on – not bothering to dry her scales beforehand – she had to bite back a groan. Her body ached whenever she was outside of the water's embrace, and only submerged could she be free of the burden of her increasing years.

She was a Nar Hylar, spawned in the aquatic city of Nuun-Dascha, and so was more capable of terrestrial adaptation than her Jol cousins. She could breathe for short periods of time out of the water, needing only the semi-regular moisture bursts of the enviro-suit to remain sufficiently hydrated. Still, though, life was always more manageable beneath the waves, and now more than ever.

She finished sealing the suit and flared the crest along her head, allowing the water from it to cascade down over her features. The savant had ceased its buzzing, she noticed. She doubted that was good news.

Behind her the ocean stretched, a churning expanse of slate-gray that eventually met the equally brooding sky at some distant point. Before her was the coastline of Pangaria, the largest temperate continent on Gamma Eridius. The narrow shingle gave way to a rising, forested ridgeline, the coniferous trees tall and jagged. Gamma Eridius was a rugged place, a planet that gave the impression that it was still experiencing the vigor of youth. A far cry, then, from the leader of those who had chosen to settle it.

Tol was about to trudge inland when movement caught her eye. She looked up, into the dark, leaden clouds, and witnessed a black speck inscribing a slow arc through Gamma Eridius's heavens. It was much too far up to identify, but she suspected it was the reason her savant had been buzzing so insistently.

Settling her suit, she hurried toward the woodland track.

Ibna Vel Syd was waiting for her in the roots of the needle-bough.

Tol ducked into the hollow space that lay beneath the gigantic tree the settlers had taken to calling the Eridius Arc.

The tree stood at the center of the ridgeline's crest, a king surrounded by the spear-like tips of the thousands of guards that made up its forest. Tol had carbon dated it not long after the establishment of the settlement around it, and discovered it was over twenty-five thousand years old. It had stood here, proud beneath its gray skies on the edge of existence, while the accursed Mahact Gene Sorcerers had dominated the galaxy, while the Lazax had risen up to defy and defeat them, while they had in turn reigned across their great empire and now, while that empire burned. Tol wondered how long it might yet endure.

The roots of the Eridius Arc plunged deep into the rocky soil of the ridge, but at their center was a hollow, large enough to act as a chamber. That was where Ibna Vel Syd had made his home, part throne room, part lair, at least to Tol's mind. She had helped rig the space with something approaching modern comforts, including an energy generator and heat valves buried in the soil, providing electricity and temperature control. They partially powered the machinery that filled much of the hollow, most of it transported from the enclave's space cruisers. Much of it played a vital part in keeping Ibna alive.

"Where have you been?" he asked as Tol entered. His voice was low and dry – it reminded Tol of a Jol Hylar who had been out of the water for too long.

"I didn't know I needed to regularly report my location to you," Tol said coldly, approaching where he was reclining in his charge cradle, set in amongst the thicket of ancient roots that made up the far wall.

"You are of vital importance," Ibna responded. "Not just to me, but to all of us here. Your safety is paramount."

Tol wanted to tell him that she didn't care whether her safety was paramount or not. She was tired, and still Ibna drove her on, demanded more of her than anyone else in the enclave. Sometimes she thought she hated him.

She also could not deny that he was a visionary, and surely the last hope of his entire species. Tol had met him decades before they had fled to the edges of existence together, when she had been working as a freelance doctor naively trying to end the suffering of the galaxy singlehandedly. Ibna had been in his pomp then, a member of the Lazax imperial council, one of the empire's foremost administrators. Even then, though, there had been a weariness to him. He had been closely involved with events immediately preceding the start of the war, especially the infamous blockade of the Quann wormhole. Ibna had failed to stop the impending apocalypse but had at least foretold it. After the Lazax emperor had failed to heed his warnings, he had gathered those who would believe him and fled the imperial capital on Mecatol Rex.

The decision had proven wise. Seeing the weakness of the Lazax, the Sol Federation had descended on Mecatol and leveled its once-great cities and palaces from orbit.

In the ten decades since then, the rest of the galaxy thought it had hunted the Lazax to extinction. They were wrong. Gamma Eridius was now acting as the cradle of the last spark of an empire.

"Your absence would not be an issue if you would permit me to monitor you," Ibna continued.

Tol suppressed a pang of anger. They had discussed this before, many times. Against her better judgement, she had agreed to implant much of the enclave with the locator tags and monitoring chips that enabled Ibna to know the whereabouts and vital signs of his people at a glance, but she would not submit to the same. She was not Lazax, and while she accepted Ibna's role as the enclave's leader, she would not surrender that degree of autonomy for anyone.

"If my nonconformance is so much of a problem, I'm sure you could find another Hylar doctor," Tol said, failing to contain her frustrations, knowing she was being facetious. Along with another Hylar medic named Rondu and a bio-scientist called Zeth – the former Nar-born and the latter from Jol – she was responsible not only for the health of the enclave, but also for the modifications that had kept Ibna going well beyond a natural span of years.

Those modifications were evident on Ibna as he ignored Tol's sharp comment. Much of the Lazax she had once known before the fall of the empire was gone, replaced by gleaming chromatic metal or dull synthetic flesh. Almost half of Ibna's cranium was cybernetic, as were three of his four upper limbs.

The simple, rustic robes he wore hid even more. Over the past century Tol had performed over a dozen major invasive surgeries on the former Lazax councilor. One of his lungs was entirely synthetic, his hearts – which had failed on three occasions – had an accentuator that was practically driving them at this point, and a good deal of bone in his left side had been replaced by fiberplast. There were also three major pieces of hardware in his skull, heavily modulating his cranial functions. Those were just the major internal modifications. By last count, Ibna's life was being prolonged by fifty-two separate pieces of medical technology. Rondu and Zeth sometimes quipped that he was held together with tyrentine, the naturally occurring mineral that could be refined into the synthetic plast necessary to mesh the mechanical with the organic. Of course, they never said such things within earshot of any of the Lazax.

At first, Tol had viewed the extension of Ibna's life as a challenge. Every ounce of biomedical science at the disposal of the Hylar had gone into trying to maintain the proud, aging, bitter leader of the Lazax. They had used up much of the medical stocks they had originally brought with them from Mecatol Rex, and had bought, bargained and stolen more over the decades, particularly from a Jol-Nar research laboratory they had been forced to raid at one point. Most precious of all was the tyrentine itself – that was much of the reason they had ended up here on Gamma Eridius. The planet was rich in the mineral. The ridgeline where their settlement had been sited was partially composed of it, to such an extent that only rudimentary digging had thus far been necessary to supply enough for Ibna's purposes.

Providing enhancements to the other Lazax that made up the expedition had been considered by Ibna though thus far only a few minor operations had been attempted, most prominently the implantation of the monitoring chips into the enclave's youngest members. The facilities on Gamma Eridius had simply not been sufficient to make large-scale cy-inlaying feasible.

At first, such modifications had seemed like the small concessions necessary to keep hope alive. Eventually, though, it had become Tol's reason for being. Her every effort was now spent attempting to stave off the inevitable encroachments of age, disease and decay on Ibna. He was more than just the leader of the enclave, he was its figurehead, their guiding beacon in the darkness that had swallowed up the galaxy. He had, in his own way, become the last emperor of the Lazax, and Tol had come too far with him over the decades to be able to give up on him, or the families that still cleaved to him as their only hope of salvation. Now, the carefree days of her youth, studying medicine at the University of Biomedical and Genetic Advancement on Jol and imagining making the galaxy into a better place, felt like they belonged to a different person, in a different lifetime. They may as well have been.

"Another ship arrived in-system," Ibna said, dredging her up from her bitter thoughts. "Another commercial skiff. There are drones in the sky. The scanners can detect them. They're combing the area. It isn't safe for you, or for any of us out there."

"That's been happening for years," Tol pointed out.

"And for years, we've ridden our luck … with what luck we've had on this forsaken journey."

Tol sighed. This old hurt again. "No one could have predicted the catastrophic failure of the mass-drive on the *Syd*."

"A failure that forced us to hide in the shadows as we leapt from planet to planet, terrified of everyone and everything–"

"What you must remember is we found the materials to manufacture replacement parts. Surviving *is* the journey. We've done that."

Ibna took a deep breath as if to steady himself. "My worry now is the frequency of contact with outsiders is only increasing."

Tol could not deny that was true. Gamma Eridius had not been the place they had set out for so long ago. The failure of the mass-drive was only one problem on a list of steadily growing issues. Gathering enough materials to fix it had taken years, sourcing the abilities to manufacture them even more so. Other life-saving materials had ran out, including tyrentine. One journey after another had followed, from one false haven to another, searching for sanctuary, for shelter from the storm of war that was ripping the great civilizations apart. They had kept going for decades, from one increasingly distant and fallow corner of known space to another, from abandoned stations to asteroid belts and ice-locked rocks far from the heat of any star.

Eventually they had found Gamma Eridius, following a fraught trip through the Alpha Wormhole. Ibna had always resisted stating it would become their permanent home, the base of a new Lazax Empire-in-exile, but they had now spent longer here than they had anywhere else.

They had lost many on the way, most to age and sickness. Some had simply given up and abandoned the rest, content to meet their fate. Others, specifically Head Researcher Mordai, had become fascinated with Tol's knowledge and how it could extend life. Besides Ibna, there were only a handful of other Lazax still living who remembered the flight from Mecatol Rex, and many of them had been children at the time. Marchu Mal Serrus, Ibna's old friend and confidant, was the only Lazax of a similar age – without the benefits of cy-augmentation, Tol was convinced only her determination not to abandon Ibna was keeping her alive.

"You want to go again," Tol said, deciding to cut to the quick. "Is that the real reason you were pinging my savant? You wanted to drag me here to tell me to pack up, get ready to do it all again? And again, and again?"

"We have to be ready," Ibna croaked in his dry, dead voice. "As always. Contingencies prepared. That's the only reason we've survived this long."

Tol wanted to scream at him, to tell him that stolen medicine and cybernetic implantation were the only reasons he had survived this long, but she knew it would do no good. They had endured this debate, shared it back and forth between themselves, many times in recent years. She knew how it ended.

"What about the tyrentine?" she asked instead. "Without it, further operations will be next to impossible."

"We have stocked enough for the time being," he replied. "Besides, if I must risk my own health in order to ensure the safety of the rest of the enclave, then so be it."

Tol bowed her head, accepting that he would not be moved.

"Do you want me to tell the others?" she asked quietly. "I can swim down to the ships tonight if you'd like?"

"No, not yet," Ibna declared, and unplugged himself from his cradle. He reached with his one remaining organic hand for the polished staff of white moontree wood that rested against one of the roots. Tol realized he was trying to get up and moved instinctively to help him.

"Rest this hand on my shoulder," she said, guiding him, trying not to wince as the heavy metallic grasp of one of the cy-limbs clamped against her slender frame. With a crack of old bones and a whirr of new enhancements, Ibna slowly found his feet.

"I wanted to share my thoughts with you first," he told her, wheezing slightly. "Hopefully I'm wrong. Hopefully another relocation proves unnecessary. But I wanted to warn you ahead of time."

"Because you knew I'd be unhappy, and you wanted time to convince me."

"Because I value you more than anyone else in the enclave. Now, walk with me under the pine boughs, and let us talk of happier times, and try to remember why it is we strive so hard to keep enduring."

PART TWO

CHAPTER NINE

JUNKER SHIP, THE KLAST SYSTEM

Makar had traveled a long way before meeting his ungracious end on Galier.

The Boreas Gap was, according to the star charts Mortalia had been given, half a galaxy away from that scrap-locked world. In more peaceful times traversing such a distance by the quickest route – through the Alpha Wormhole – and on a swift craft might have taken between a month and six weeks. But these were not peaceful times. Traditional travel lanes had been cut and bisected by warring factions. Once-busy trade and transport hubs were under the control of one or another of the great civilizations or closed entirely. Once-free systems had become no-go zones or heavily fortified bulwarks where civilian shipping ran under the threat of bristling star forts and the guns of garrison armadas. Beyond them, pirates and renegades harried shipping.

Thanks to all this, it took Mortalia almost three months just to reach the subsector adjacent to the Gap.

She had ridden her luck at times, avoiding Federation inspection teams at Leros III and making an expensive last minute ship change at Quirst to avoid Hacan-enforced tariffs.

Her luck ran out at Klast.

Reaching the system had been one of her goals, and she had hoped that getting that far would give her a straight run at the Gap. Klast was on the Outer Banks, its worlds uninhabitable gas giants or freezing ice balls. The only habitable zone was Port Rathen, a space hub that, even in the days of the empire, had operated as a barely legal freeport. Since the collapse of the Imperium it had, by all reports, become a lair for pirates and a den of larceny.

Mortalia anticipated little difficulty in bribing or intimidating her passage from there to the Gap. That plan evaporated when the nameless junker ship she'd hitched a ride on after Quirst finally arrived in-system.

She was slumming it in one of the junker's main holds, so didn't know exactly what was happening until it was too late.

The hold itself resembled a slum cast into space. By the smell of it, during the junker's more reputable days it had transported some form of cattle, but now it was crammed with flesh cargo of a different kind. Like the Sprawl on Galier, it was filled with destitute refugees, cast adrift on the tides of war, and among them lurked less honest and savory characters, individuals who would be perfectly at home once they reached the scum-dens and lawless bars of Port Rathen.

Mortalia had considered doing what she had done on SC7 and bartering for a better berth, but such a thing hardly existed on a rust hulk like the junker, and besides, her funds weren't limitless. She wanted to make sure she still had a healthy sheaf of cred-bars when she reached Gamma Eridius. So, she had found herself a slender strip of decking plate and rusting wall near one of the hold's refuse-littered corners and kept to herself, subsisting on the nutripaste and brackish swill that the ship's crew deigned to dole out as rations to their passengers.

It was a grim existence, but Mortalia didn't care. Her quest was almost at an end. She could feel it.

She knew something was wrong when the hull around her stopped vibrating with the throb of active engines. They should have been making their final approach toward Port Rathen, but instead they were idling, practically adrift.

Nervous rumors began to swirl through the crowded hold. The captain had misjudged the voyage, and they were becalmed, without fuel. Pirates were holding them to ransom. The captain was going to demand further payments from the passengers before completing the final leg of the journey.

Mortalia didn't engage with anyone around her. She surreptitiously looked for any sign of her companions but, as was so often the case, couldn't find them. She had caught their signal, tapped through the venting systems near her – *tap-tap…* *tap-tap-tap* – but besides that there had been no contact. Their mastery of stealth never ceased to amaze her. Still, not knowing exactly where they were was rarely reassuring.

She felt the urge to check her projector but suppressed it. She didn't want to draw any attention to herself, no matter how well disguised the beacon was.

The unrest among the crowded passengers grew. There was no sign of any crew members. People left to see what was happening in the neighboring holds or tried to take the elevator platform up to the ship's decking spine, but they found it unresponsive, dead.

The lights overhead flickered, and the hull shook, not the reassuring thrum of the engines but something that sounded more like a hard impact.

It was followed by a clattering sound – the elevator was operating again. Mortalia expected the appearance of crewmates, deckhands, or even the captain herself. Instead, she heard screams coming from the corridor lying between the elevator and the holds.

She scrambled to her feet and looked toward the entrance

and realized that every plan she had carefully laid was about to be undone.

A creature had appeared in the entranceway to the hold. It was insectoid, but standing on two legs, its other two sets of limbs cradling a tarsus glaive. Its hide was chitinous, off-green, and strapped with webbing pouches, while its head was broad and flat. Two sets of black eye clusters surveyed the hold with glittering, unknowable intelligence.

It was a Sardakk N'orr warrior, a swarm-trooper, and there were many more of its brood kin behind it. They chirred dangerously as they stalked into the hold, and the screaming spread as people scrambled back, desperate to avoid the sweep of their strange, deadly-looking weaponry.

Mortalia had little experience with N'orr. They were unlike many of the other great civilizations, singular in purpose, united behind the beliefs of their people. Individualistic N'orr or breakaway broods were not unheard of, but they were rare. Mortalia had little idea how to even converse with one if they didn't speak univoca, let alone bargain with them.

There was a stampede to get away from the N'orr as they moved around the hold. The crude blanket dwellings or plankboard shelters that had been erected to give some illusion of privacy and separation between different groups of passengers were trampled, and Mortalia was thrust back against the wall. She controlled her breathing, fought down the panic, making sure she kept her arms raised so she couldn't become pinned and helpless in the crush.

"Desist," one of the invaders barked, the words delivered in a univoca machine buzz by an ambassador translator kit worn around its elongated neck. "Comply and you will not be harmed!"

Mortalia's heart sank. It became apparent what the N'orr wanted. They were herding the passengers through a channel in their ranks and out of the hold.

The N'orr deepest into the space began to snatch at refugees with their extra limbs and haul them out. There was more screaming and crying. Mortalia was shepherded with them, afraid someone would try to draw a weapon. If they did, it would be a massacre.

She reached down for her projector, thankful the eyes of the rest of the hold were on the N'orr, and triggered it, twisting one of its dials and depressing a button in its side twice.

Do not engage. Wait.

Whether or not her companions would obey the instructions, she didn't know. Right now, she couldn't worry about them. They had saved her many times before, but they weren't going to bring down a whole brood of N'orr boarding warriors.

Mortalia allowed herself to be carried along with the flow. She avoided looking at any of the boarders, keeping her gaze lowered, knowing anonymity was the safest option for the time being. N'orr wouldn't care about the plate she carried in her pocket. In fact, it was likely to actively endanger her if they found it.

Just where had they come from? Were they raiders, pirates, a breakaway brood? Or was this a Sardakk incursion? She noted the markings stamped or branded into the chitin plates on the shoulders of their upper arms, but she didn't know what they meant.

They were herded out of the hold and began to take the elevator platform, group by group. Above them, the junker's decking spine was packed with more N'orr, and there was still no sign of the crew. The refugees were being channeled to the starboard docking bays. That, Mortalia decided, might be a good thing. The N'orr appeared to have complete control and could have easily slaughtered them all in the holds if they wished, or even simply destroyed the junker from afar.

Others were considering the situation less calmly. One particularly brave or foolish Saar was angrily shouting at the nearest boarders, demanding to know where they were being taken. The N'orr simply stared back at him with their glassy, unblinking black eyes, silent, uncaring. Other refugees hustled the Saar along.

There were N'orr shuttles waiting for them. The group was further subdivided and urged along now by tugs and chittering exclamations. One Saar stumbled and almost knocked over several people around him, nearly creating another panic. Mortalia drew her glare-cape tight as she left the junker's decking and stepped onto the N'orr transport.

The shuttle's transport bay was ribbed metal, with a clear, crystalline substance for its roof and upper walls. The sides were fitted with strange devices that Mortalia took to be the cradle clamps that would secure any N'orr being transported. They remained unused, the physiology of the new passengers failing to match the safety devices of their captors. Instead, they stood, herded into the long, narrow space, worried features underlit by the light strips that ran along the outer edges of the decking plates.

As the main hatch sealed shut, Mortalia realized that there was no conceivable way her companions could have followed her. For the first time in years, she was truly alone.

The shuttle shuddered with takeoff. Mortalia almost lost her balance but was steadied by a tall Xookchen woman next to her. She nodded her thanks but resisted the urge to say anything. Now wasn't the time to be making friends.

There was a stomach-churning lurch as the grav systems kicked in, taking over from the junker as they left its orbit. Mortalia realized the substance plating the roof and upper walls was clear enough to allow passengers to be able to see the space beyond. And that was when she understood exactly how desperate their new circumstances were.

Port Rathen was a freeport no longer. The station itself was visible off the port bow, a great mountain of duranium and terridium with a bristling halo of docking struts and habitation platforms, winking with the lights of a thousand illumination runners.

The size of the armada that had assembled around it was even more impressive. Mortalia was not familiar with the exact classes of military vessels, but she knew Sardakk N'orr ships when she saw them, and there were dozens arrayed around Port Rathen. It was an invasion force, and Mortalia doubted a pirate backwater like Port Rathen was its final objective.

The Sardakk N'orr were preparing for a grand offensive.

And the nameless junker had accidentally delivered them all right into the middle of it. Mortalia wondered how long it had been since the N'orr had seized the system. Port Rathen made sense – once pacified, it could act as a fuel and supply depot, and its isolation meant none of the great civilizations would detect the N'orr buildup until it was unleashed. She had heard rumors during her travels that the Sardakk were preparing for an offensive, but no indication that anyone knew just where or when it would fall. Now, she had unwittingly found the area where they were building their strength.

The course of the shuttle shifted, and the fearsome display began to envelop them as they passed between the N'orr vessels. It seemed as though they weren't headed for any one ship, but for Port Rathen itself. That made sense, she supposed. The station's inhabitants were presumably being corralled there, forbidden from leaving and allowing news of the N'orr arrival to spread. Ships would be dock-locked, and ports and berths sealed. Mortalia imagined the N'orr had been capturing and bringing in traffic arriving in the system since the beginning of their occupation.

The station loomed, its great central bulk like a jagged moon, and one strut in particular grew more clearly defined against the mass of space-bound metal as the shuttle made for it. It was a docking berth, and it embraced the transport as it slotted with a shudder into its atmospheric seal.

The refugees were ordered from the shuttle and on board Port Rathen by more chittering N'orr warriors. Mortalia was again swept along, out into the docking bay. Other refugees from earlier flights were packing the area. There was a swell of pushing and shoving, and shouting broke out next to her as a Saar barked something in its clan dialect and lashed out at the knot of humans beside him.

A fight erupted. People screamed and shouted as they tried to push away from its epicenter, creating a wave of grubby, desperate bodies.

Mortalia fought to stay on her feet. She heard a rising susurration, like rain from a sudden downpour hissing in the eaves of the moontree grove her parents had sometimes taken her to during her childhood holidays. She realized it was coming from the N'orr.

They were communicating in their dialect, seemingly unsettled by the disorder in front of them. Their strange weapons came up and started to hum.

"Stop," Mortalia shouted, throwing herself against the tide and managing to force her way to the Saar, who had a squirming human in a chokehold. "You're making them angry! You're going to get us all killed!"

The Saar wasn't listening or didn't understand. He half turned and snarled at Mortalia, driving her away with a swipe of his furry forearm.

The blow caught her awkwardly and she fell, sprawling across the deck. The small plate that had eased her way across the galaxy slipped from her pocket.

She scrabbled desperately at it, managing to snatch it up and hide it again, still on her hands and knees.

That was when the beam pistol sounded, a vicious zipping noise accompanied by a flare of light, right above her.

Mortalia screwed her eyes shut, anticipating that the N'orr were about to indiscriminately return fire and massacre the entire docking bay.

Instead, she found herself looking at a pair of scuffed, thick-soled boots between her and the N'orr. She looked up, heart racing, and found a tall, broad human woman standing over her. She was dressed in what looked like an old set of white Federation fleet officers' pants and a short leather jacket, her long, dark hair tied into a thick braid that hung draped over one shoulder. Her face was buff and humorless, puckered by a scar under her left eye. A smoking blast pistol was gripped in one gloved hand, muzzle pointed at the bay ceiling.

"Welcome to Port Rathen," the woman declared in a loud voice to the crowd, before locking eyes with Mortalia.

"Get up," she ordered.

Mortalia obeyed. The Saar had let go of the human, and both parties had disentangled themselves. The N'orr hissing had died back to a low rustle, but their weapons remained primed.

"Despite what you might have heard, troublemakers aren't welcome here," the human went on, again speaking to the crowd. "You're going to be brought into the port proper, processed, and given what space and food we can spare. There isn't much. We're oversubscribed as it is."

A few of the braver people near Mortalia began to ask

questions, but the human waved her pistol, and they became silent again quickly.

"This isn't a question-and-answer session! Get moving. And whatever you do, don't antagonize these insectoid bastards. We've had enough trouble with them already and I promise you, they won't think twice about slicing you up and eating you!"

The crowd began to shift toward the open blast doors at the end of the bay, and the N'orr finally lowered their weapons. Mortalia tried to lose herself in the masses again, knowing she had made a mistake in trying to break up the fight. As she went, she heard the human speak to her again.

"Not you, sweetheart."

Before she could protest, she was grabbed by the wrists by several other individuals, a Letnev and a simian-like Hondril, both clad in scraps of armor and bristling with sidearms and blades – they clearly weren't part of the refugee intake.

"What're you doing?" Mortalia demanded.

"I told you, we don't like troublemakers here," the human said.

"I was just trying to stop us all from getting killed," Mortalia exclaimed.

"We'll see about that," the woman said, snapping her fingers at Mortalia's captors. They led her away from the rest of the crowd, past more N'orr, toward a set of side hatches.

Mortalia decided against struggling, for now. She was afraid, knowing there was no way her companions could have made it off the junker on board the N'orr shuttles. She was on her own, in unfamiliar territory, with only her wits to preserve her.

The human directed her through one of the hatches. A dingy room lay beyond, seemingly a storage space stacked high with crates and vac-sealed containers.

"Wait outside," the human ordered her two underlings. They obeyed, withdrawing and clamping the hatch shut behind them.

She raised her beam pistol once more and pointed it squarely at Mortalia's head.

"Don't move," she ordered. Her voice was calm, and the pistol's aim was unwavering. Mortalia was certain she knew how to use it.

"What are you doing?" Mortalia asked slowly, suppressing the instinctive urge to flinch away from the leveled weapon.

"Show me the plate," the human said. "The one in your breast pocket."

"What plate?"

The human fired. Mortalia flinched and felt the heat of the energy beam passing by her face. Her left eye was momentarily blinded by the flare of crimson light, and she heard a thud and a hiss as it burned a hole in one of the crates behind her.

"I'm not playing," the human declared. "I saw you drop it. Clumsy of you. Now show it to me."

"Why?" Mortalia snapped, trying desperately to get a gauge on the stranger.

"I want to see if it's real or not. And then I want you to tell me how you got it."

Mortalia pursed her lips, knowing she was out of options. Even if her companions had made it off the junker somehow, they weren't getting in here to aid her.

"Slowly," the human urged as Mortalia reached inside her cape. Maintaining eye contact, she gradually drew out the plate and held it up.

"It looks very real," the human conceded after a brief inspection, keeping her distance.

"That's because it is."

"I suppose we'll find that out for sure soon enough. They're coming."

"Who?"

"The Letnev. We got word out to them, before the N'orr blockade was complete. The last courier ship to leave the system."

"Well then… since I've shown you mine, how about you show me yours?"

"What makes you think I've got one?"

"If you didn't, or if you thought I'd stolen this one, I think I'd already be dead."

The human smiled coldly.

"In that, we are in agreement. What's your contract code?"

Mortalia hesitated again, not wanting to surrender more information to the stranger, but she was very much at her mercy.

"Two-five-eight-six-seven-two."

"Only three digits out from my own then. We must have joined at the same time."

To Mortalia's silent relief, the human finally lowered the pistol and reached into her hip pocket. Sure enough, she had one of the plates as well, the crest identical to hers, though the information stamped beneath differed.

"My name is Samy," the human said. "Or at least that's the one I use around here."

"I'm Mortalia."

"Sounds a bit grim."

"It's a bit of a grim galaxy."

"Don't find many Winnarans like you," Samy went on. "Hence my caution."

"You won't believe how many times I've heard that," Mortalia replied bitterly. "Does anyone else on the station know you sent a message to the Barony?"

"Oh, they know, though they don't know exactly who I am. I work for Kanbos as an enforcer, and he trusts my word."

"Kanbos?"

"He runs Rathen now. It used to be a league of different captains, but times have been hard, and there were too many disputes. Kanbos was elected in an emergency vote when the N'orr showed up. He's a good sort, as pirate lords go."

"How long have the N'orr been here?" Mortalia asked. "Do we know what they're planning?"

"Almost three month-cycles, and no, we don't. They've been building their strength here all this time. Constant reinforcements. In truth, I'm worried the Barony might not come. They probably don't want this fight. Now come on, you've asked enough. I brought you in here to ask you the questions, not the other way round."

"And are you satisfied with my answers?" Mortalia dared ask. Samy looked at her, eyes cold and hard, but she smiled.

"For now. Come on. Let's go and meet the boss."

"If it's all the same to you, I'd rather not. I don't want a high profile here. My objectives don't involve Port Rathen. I was only intending to use this place as a stopping off point."

"That may be, but I'd like to keep you where I can see you. This is my turf, and I still haven't decided if you're trouble or not."

"Do you think our sponsors will approve of you keeping me here?"

Samy laughed. "Oh, trust me, you're free to go as soon as you're able to. As soon as the N'orr have gone. But until then, your best chance of survival is sticking by me, and I'm going to see the boss. So, you're coming, too."

CHAPTER TEN

Port Rathen, the Klast System

Samy introduced Mortalia to Captain Kanbos.

She led her to Port Rathen's control hub, the space at the pinnacle of the great station's sprawl. The highest point of the duranium mountain, it was a reinforced plasticon dome that looked down across the plunging slopes and docking struts and out over the Sardakk N'orr fleet that hung in space around it.

The hub itself was befitting a pirate lord. Most of the machinery and operational systems looked old and currently deactivated, but it possessed an almost primeval grandeur, with poles and wracks bearing skeletal trophies, a dizzying assortment of weaponry and the banners of what Mortalia took to be the freebooter captains who called the station home. There didn't appear to be any of the Sardakk N'orr present.

The hub's center was a wide pit ringed with seating, where the pirates had presumably held court. Now its edges were unoccupied, though the center was full of a rough assembly. The gathering included half a dozen different species, and all were armed to the teeth and sporting an outrageous display of scars, missing limbs and cybernetic replacements. They were talking loudly among themselves as Samy led Mortalia inside.

In the midst of them was what could only be described as a throne. It looked like an old command chair from a warship, possibly Sol Federation, though it had been heavily modified with a higher, more imposing backrest and holsters for a set of expensive-looking solid-round Saar-stopper pistols. Atop the throne, the master of Port Rathen presided over his vagabond kingdom.

Kanbos himself was a Rokha, a black-furred felid whose garb alternated between practical and lavish. He wore maroon jodhpurs and what looked like a tough, scaled zergon hide coat, knee-length and reinforced with a ferroplate demi-cuirass. The coat's shoulders were heavy with silver epaulets, like a Federation or Barony naval officer, and a sword of similar design rested against his throne's side. The black fur of his mane was glossy and braided with dozens of small gold ringlets, while on his head rested a broad-brimmed black hat bright with lush feathers.

Mortalia glanced at him before assessing the figures around him. There was a Hacan, a tall and lean specimen with a tatty mane and small, round data lenses resting atop his muzzle, which he adjusted to get a better look at Mortalia. He was not wearing the robes of one of the great trade emirates, but dressed similarly to the rest of Kanbos's cortège, with a hide jacket and a glare-cape hanging off one shoulder, and a beam pistol strapped to his hip. His presence, seemingly subordinate to Kanbos, was a surprise. Rokha were distant relatives of the Hacan, and it was a stereotype that Hacan considered themselves the superior of the two species of felids. Still, out here was a long way from the power bases of the United Emirates. Any Hacan operating in a place like this was unlikely to be an adherent to traditional values and beliefs. The same went for the figure standing on the opposite side of the throne – a Jol Hylar, clad in a leathery enviro-suit and a full containment sphere. He, too, was likely a long way from the oversight of the Universities of Jol-Nar. The important thing, as far as Mortalia was concerned, was that there appeared to be no Winnarans or Letnev among Kanbos' inner circle. That at least made things less complicated.

The Rokha was having a sharp-sounding conversation with the Hylar but cut off as he saw the new arrivals.

"There you are, Samy," Kanbos exclaimed, his voice rich and deep. "Where have you been?"

"Making sure the new arrivals are settling in," Samy answered, halting before the throne and stepping aside for Mortalia. "I thought I'd bring this one to see you. Her name's Mortalia. She broke up a fight in one of the docking bays, probably saved everyone there from being mowed down by our new insect overlords."

"It would've been better if they had," Kanbos growled. "We can't take any more. Even if they don't force any new arrivals on us, water and oxygen will be gone in another month. Yush here was just telling me."

He gestured at the Hylar, who hadn't so much as glanced at Mortalia.

"Even with rationing, conditions will rapidly deteriorate," he said, voice buzzing from the vocalization grille of the water-filled containment sphere encasing his pale, amphibian head. "I have recommended that we cease supply to certain decks, beginning with those housing the new arrivals."

"I won't," Kanbos said, cutting off any potential argument from Samy. "Yet. I don't want a mutiny on my hands, not when I'm trying to organize one of my own. So, how'd you end up here?"

The question was directed at Mortalia, and she found herself under the gaze of the entire hub. She stood tall and cleared her throat.

"I'm seeking my fortune," she said.

There was hissing and laughter from the piratical assembly.

"Then you won't fit in here," Kanbos said with a wry tone. "Not anymore. Fortunes be damned! We're all just looking to survive!"

"I didn't know the N'orr had claimed the system," Mortalia admitted. "Why are they here?"

"You think they'd tell me?"

"Well, they haven't killed you. So maybe?"

Kanbos grunted and brushed at one epaulet before replying.

"They haven't killed us *yet*, but if they keep us in these conditions for much longer, wiping us out would be preferable to letting us run out of oxygen. Not even you would last long, Yush."

The Hylar showed no amusement at what seemed to be a quip. Kanbos carried on addressing Mortalia.

"They let us live, but they control everything. The docking bays and launch chutes, the shields and weapons systems, the power supply, the comms, even the air recyc. They've made us prisoners on board our own station. Any sign of trouble, and they've said they'll blow us to pieces. We aren't at liberty to leave, and every time a new, unwitting cargo like yourselves arrives in-system you're taken and crammed in here with the rest of us. They don't want any word getting out that they're here."

"Thankfully, they didn't stop the last courier leaving the system when they arrived," Samy said quietly.

Kanbos nodded but said nothing more, and Mortalia assumed he didn't want to speak of his scheme in front of a new arrival.

"You've shown initiative, but you're another mouth to feed, another set of lungs breathing my air," the Rokha said, his tone becoming brusquer. "So, for now, you're going back among the new arrivals. We'll have to wait and find out whether you're going to be of some use to me."

He waved a hand, and seemingly that was the end of Mortalia's audience. She glanced at Samy, who shrugged – there was nothing more she could do for the time being.

Two of Kanbos's thugs closed in but didn't lay hands on her. They led her from the hub and back down, to the lower decks.

It was a waiting game, Mortalia realized. A wait to see just what form of death reached them first.

Mortalia spent several uneasy cycles crammed into one of the station's habitation blocks, sharing an apartment designed for maybe a dozen people with over double that number. She did her best to avoid attracting attention and tried not to worry about the fact that she had put her fate wholly in Samy's hands. Was she working with anyone else directly? Did she have companions, like Mortalia's? And if she wasn't who she said she was… well, Mortalia supposed she would already be dead if that was the case. It didn't help her with her own plans, however. She knew she would have to be patient, and work her way through it, the way she had always done in the past.

During the third hour-cycle, Samy came and found her.

"Kanbos has decided it's time," she said as she led Mortalia back along crowded corridors and up along juddering elevator plates to the hub. "And I convinced him to include you. I hope I'm doing the right thing."

"You really think you can take them all on?" Mortalia asked, lowering her voice as they passed a brood of N'orr guarding one of the upper deck junctions.

"Can we kill the ones on this station?" Samy said, rephrasing the question. "Yes, absolutely. Kanbos and his crews are a vicious rabble, and this is their turf. Can we fight the fleet surrounding us? Almost definitely not, but at this rate we suffocate or starve anyway. Pretty sure we'd all rather go out with a bang."

"How long have you been here?" Mortalia asked, noting how completely at home Samy seemed on board the station, and how familiar she was with Kanbos and his senior crew.

"Long enough," Samy said evasively. "They need eyes everywhere."

Mortalia knew better than to press. She wouldn't have wanted to answer similar questions about herself.

They reached the hub. Kanbos wasn't there to receive her, but the place was busy with activity.

As with the first time she had visited, there didn't appear to be any N'orr present. Either they had foolishly decided the hub, with much of its power and its connectivity with the rest of the station cut off, was not important enough to station troops in, or Kanbos had managed to negotiate for it to remain the sole realm under his jurisdiction. Either way, it was allowing the station's inhabitants to organize their mutiny seemingly without being detected.

Samy led Mortalia to a table erected along one of the disabled control banks that once would have regulated Port Rathen's energy systems, before the N'orr had taken direct control at the power source, buried in the station's bowels. It was spread with a dizzying array of weaponry: beam pistols great and small, shot pistols and rifles, needle launchers, vicious-looking daggers, particle grenades and even ferroplate swords. It was a fearsome display, and Mortalia simply stared at it.

"Take your pick," Samy said, raising one beam pistol before

her and slapping an energy pack home. It was only then that she noticed Mortalia's hesitation.

"I've never met one of our kind who wasn't… familiar with these sorts of tools," the human said. Mortalia shrugged her slender shoulders.

"We aren't all killers. That's not what's required of us."

Samy watched her closely, saying nothing. Mortalia fought back the urge to admit to the existence of her companions. Sharing that sort of information would do no one any good, and besides, they weren't with her anymore. They might even be dead. She was on her own.

"This one," Samy said, indicating one of the weapons on the table. "Solid shot, but packs a punch, enough to crack N'orr chitin. Easy to use."

She lifted the snub-nosed sidearm and showed Mortalia the chamber for the rounds, the safety, and how to cock it.

"I'm meant to take this back to the habitation blocks?" the Winnaran asked.

"Unless you plan on punching the N'orr to death when it all kicks off," Samy said. "Something like this, you can keep concealed. The N'orr aren't doing checks on anyone. They think if they control the port's systems, they control the port itself, and they know their fleet surrounds us. Just don't go waving that around beforehand. We can't trust everyone on the lower decks, especially among the new arrivals."

"Wouldn't that include me?"

"Well, prove your doubters wrong, Winnaran. Keep all this under wraps and wait for the word."

"We don't know exactly when it's going to start?"

"Oh, you'll know."

CHAPTER ELEVEN

Port Rathen, the Klast System

Samy was right.

Another two day-cycles passed. Mortalia stayed in the crowded, squalid hab block, enduring the bitter nutripaste and the lack of privacy and cleanliness. She kept the pistol hidden, and she waited, and she tried not to worry about what she'd gotten herself into.

It wasn't for herself that she feared. It was the thought that, now that she was so close, she might ultimately fail at the task she had spent her life working toward.

During the beginning of the station's evening shutdown, one of the unkempt human youths from the family that comprised around half of their block's inhabitants came scrambling into what had once served as the kitchen area.

"They're gone," he announced excitedly to the various people crammed into the overburdened space.

"Who?" one of the boy's relatives asked.

"The bugs! There's none in the corridors!"

What the human said was true. Several of the refugees, Mortalia included, went cautiously out into the passage that led from the habitation blocks up the strut and into the station proper. N'orr had patrolled the route constantly before, but now there was no sign of them.

Excited, nervous chatter filled the block, and several people began to stray to the neighboring zones to see if they, too, had been abandoned.

Mortalia stayed put, the sidearm feeling like a leaden weight in her pocket. Sure enough, someone came for her not long after.

It was one of Kanbos's brutes. He said little but ordered her to follow him. They traveled up to the hub, where Mortalia discovered that the pirates of Port Rathen weren't merely preparing for a mutiny.

The Barony of Letnev had arrived. The hub was ram-packed with people, and every eye was on the central viz projection. It showed ships bearing the Barony's crest – warships – entering the system.

"They're here," Samy said, finding Mortalia in the crowd. "I knew they'd come!"

It was hard not to respond to the human's jubilation with delight of her own, but Mortalia had learned to be guarded when discussing the Barony. Old habits died hard, even with one who seemingly understood exactly who and what she was.

"Then what do we do?" she asked Samy. "Wait? Will they be able to defeat the N'orr?"

Samy laughed and clapped Mortalia on the shoulder.

"You've not been on board Port Rathen for very long, so I'll forgive you for those kinds of assumptions," she said. "But we've done enough waiting."

There was a flash of light, and a cheer went up. Mortalia looked up and realized what had happened. The Letnev fleet had opened fire on the N'orr picket ships, and the brightness of the energy beam fusillade had reached all the way to the station. While the Letnev ships themselves weren't visible yet to the naked eye through the plasticon dome, the wrath of their weapons was.

"We're going to hit these bug bastards where it hurts," shouted a voice. It was Kanbos. He had climbed up next to the viz projector, and now embraced his assembled crews with a broad sweep of his arm. "We've cowered and cringed for long enough. That's not our way! It's time we showed the Sardakk N'orr some proper Port Rathen hospitality!"

There was a ferocious roar, this one loud enough to shake the decking plates underfoot.

"You know your sections, and you know your objectives," Kanbos carried on through the rising wrath of the crews. "Now, go and take them!"

Mortalia looked to Samy, who nodded to her.

"Stick with me, little Winnaran."

Mortalia knew she didn't have much choice.

Samy snapped off a string of instructions as the pirates began to disperse, calling her own force to her. They were as motley a band as any Mortalia had seen running the station, and they grinned like zektra bloodhounds with a scent in their nostrils as Samy addressed them.

"When we go, we go quick and sharp. You know the zones – Strut H, C3 through C11. Speed and surprise are as good a weapon as any beam pistol, so don't hesitate! No hanging back, no helping the wounded until the strut is ours."

None of this was familiar to Mortalia, and her nerves felt like a hard, clenched fist in her stomach. She had faced down gangers and been caught up in crossfire before, she had even once been involved in a heist on a Jol-Nar cred repository, during a desperate period when her benefactors had been unable to reach her. But she had never fought in what was essentially a straight-up military engagement, and she had never risked her life without knowing that her companions were with her.

They loaded and readied their weapons, mostly big, brutal-looking things that made Mortalia doubt the effectiveness of the snub-nose, hard-round pistol she'd taken. She took it out nervously. Samy looked at her.

"Just stick close," she repeated, then added, with a wolfish grin, "The bugs won't know what hit them."

"Haven't they withdrawn anyway?" Mortalia asked, thinking about how the ones patrolling the hab blocks had vanished.

"There are less on board than there were," Samy agreed. "When the Letnev arrived, they drew some back to their ships. But they haven't all gone. They've gathered up most of what's left around the essential systems."

"Do they know we're going to hit them then?" Mortalia asked.

"I guess we'll soon find out. But it's now or never. The Letnev are here, and I think we can both agree, we'd rather them than the N'orr."

That was true, and the arrival of the Barony's forces was a great relief, though she wondered how much the majority of Port Rathen's inhabitants would back that statement.

There was another flash, and she looked up past the dome. Weapons fire between the two fleets was now clearly visible, traceries of red, blue, green, yellow and white brilliance as lance batteries spat and broadsides flared. The N'orr ships around Port Rathen were scrambling to face the onslaught, shimmering as they ignited their shields.

Whether she liked it or not, Mortalia realized she was in the midst of a battle, one that would decide the fate of far more than even Port Rathen.

...

The Second Grand Fleet of the Barony of Letnev had been preparing for this day for months.

The Barony's war fleets, once the most vaunted military arm in the galaxy, had lost their luster. Overreach by a succession of ill-advised barons and a string of shock defeats at the hands of the Sol Federation and the Universities of Jol-Nar had reduced assets to a fraction of the strength they had enjoyed during the First Sol-Letnev War. Yet the final victory against the Ardanil had offered some hope, as had the vital intelligence acquired about the movements of the Sardakk N'orr.

Baronial Command feared they were the target, despite analysis that claimed the offensive was planned to strike at the traditional enemies of the Sardakk, the Jol-Nar.

In response, a preemptive assault had been planned. The First Grand Fleet, traditionally the Barony's finest, had been judged unsuitable following the debacle at the Kenara system. First Admiral Count Zorias had been removed from command – his trial was still ongoing – but intense inter-fleet politicking meant his successor still hadn't been chosen, and space trials were exposing potential weaknesses in decision-making and command-and-control among subordinate captains, all of which had seemingly contributed to the embarrassment against the Hacan.

That was why the Second Grand Fleet had been selected for the strike on Klast. It had been badly damaged after the actions at Texxar and the Viridian Shoals, but with the defeat of the Ardanil, elements of the Third Grand Fleet had been available for drafting, and enough strength had been regained to make offensive operations viable. Admiral Lord Tarzequiel had a reputation as an experienced and competent officer.

It was Tarzequiel and her fleet, therefore, that surged into the Klast system on a battle heading, engines blazing with maximum output. Widowcrusher bomber wings and the fearsome Razor starfighters immediately launched from the holds of the twin carriers, *Countess Malmaizon* and *Might of Prime*, and target locks on the picket drones ranged along the system edge were acquired.

The N'orr responded with the kind of speed and efficiency that left every other military in the galaxy envious. The outlying cruisers closest to the incursion turned and threw themselves into the teeth of the Letnev guns, buying time for the rest of the fleet to shift its axis to face the attack. Sh'ten, Marshal of the Swarm, positioned his flagship, *T'Na Quinarra*, at the head of the formation, flanked by four exotriremes.

The two fleets met head on. The battle of Klast was underway.

Samy's orders were to seize one of the port's defense struts – designated "H" – and recapture the weapons batteries that studded its length. If all went to plan and the other crews secured the shield generators and power banks, Port Rathen would become fully operational again just when the N'orr were busy fighting the Letnev.

Resistance started almost as soon as they reached Strut H. A Hylar with the crew had got the elevator platform working, and it carried them down to the access level, where they found a single N'orr sentry. The insectoid hissed a warning and raised its beam rifle, only to be cut down by a hail of fire.

Mortalia cringed, the noise of the discharges in the confined space hammering at her ears. She hurried after Samy, remembering to keep the muzzle of her pistol lowered and her finger off the trigger.

They stormed the strut's access hatch. She almost stumbled over the body of the N'orr they had put down. Its limbs were still twitching with synaptic impulses, the holes bored in its green carapace by the energy weapons smoking.

Mortalia was close to the back of the assault, and at first could see very little down the strut's main corridor. That changed rapidly as those in front threw themselves against the walls and into doorways to avoid a salvo from the N'orr farther down the gangway.

Samy dragged Mortalia into one of the door arches with her, just as a hail of wicked metal barbs launched by the N'orr weaponry chewed into the deck and walls in front of them. One crewmate, a Saar who had been too slow getting into cover, howled as his leg was brutally lacerated, and he was heaved by his comrades out of the line of fire.

Samy leaned back out into the corridor and returned fire, the energy carbine she was carrying whining and spitting. Mortalia felt frozen and useless, pistol still lowered, senses assailed by the painful stimuli of the barrage contained in the sealed space. She saw the trio of crewmates crammed into the doorway opposite them, two firing while the third reloaded, the metal frame above them shivering as it was struck and dented by N'orr fire.

"Bastard bugs," Samy growled as she ducked back in beside Mortalia and ejected her carbine's spent energy pack, the connector node steaming. Trying to mimic the actions of the others across from them, Mortalia leaned out and aimed her pistol.

She took a precious second or two to pick a target. There were N'orr packing the far end of the corridor, a number in the doorways like their attackers, though others seemed to be trusting in their armor and exoskeletons to take the fire coming at them. Teeth bared in a snarl, Mortalia shot at the closest, the pistol bucking in her grip.

She didn't know if she hit her target. She fired again. For a second, she felt as though she was in the eye of a storm, weapons fire from both sides filling the corridor around her, the air like a living thing, alive with moving and whizzing, zipping, cracking sounds and the passage of metal and raw energy.

She realized that, without meaning to, she had stepped fully out into the middle of the passage.

Samy dragged her back, firing her carbine one-handed from the hip and shoving her into the doorway once more.

"You got a death wish, Winnaran?" she snarled. Mortalia shook her head, unable to find any words.

"Push up," Samy barked at her crew. "Use the doorways! They're slackening!"

It was true. The coughing discharge and the metallic collisions that marked the N'orr weapons had notably decreased. They had also been making that deep susurration Mortalia had heard before at the docking bay, when it had seemed they were about to open up on the refugees, but now the noise of the N'orr battle-buzz had broken down into individual chirring and ticking. Sounds of panic, Mortalia realized.

The pirates advanced down the corridor, their fire intensifying as that of the Norr's' slackened. Mortalia stepped out again and followed, passing more twitching insectoid bodies. Finally, the gunfire ceased altogether, leaving her ears ringing.

"Casualties?" Samy called out.

There was a brace of injuries, but only one fatality.

"Open the doors and get the weapons systems online," Samy urged. She swiped a keypad next to one of the entrances while a Hondril and another human dragged several N'orr carcasses out of the way so they could step through.

Mortalia followed them in, descending a short flight of metal rungs and finding herself inside a weapons cockpit blister, protruding from one side of the station strut.

The cockpit had a circular viewing port, and below it was four great barrels, jutting out into space. They were one of the quad batteries bristling across Strut H's sides, armaments meant to deliver rocket-propelled charges against attacking vessels.

The guns were controlled by several banks of computators arrayed in a semicircle before the port. Several of the pirates immediately rushed to them, hitting activation keys.

"We've got power," one called excitedly as the banks lit up, input boards and viz monitors stuttering to life.

"Harke and his mob must have secured the generator core already. What've we got in our arc?"

It took time for the systems to boot up, but when they did several of the screens showed an array of markers corresponding with the N'orr fleet.

Not wanting to get in the way, Mortalia hung back and looked through the port.

The Letnev and Sardakk fleets appeared to be fully engaged. A blizzard of energy weapons and shield pulses showed where the fight was at its fiercest, two thick knots of warships pounding one another, silhouetting through vessels that still lay between the station and the heart of the battle.

Mortalia realized one salient point – in maneuvering to face the Letnev head on, the N'orr had left themselves with their backs to Port Rathen.

"Firing solutions," Samy called. "Once you're locked, fire at will!"

The pirates knew their business. This was their home, and they were about to defend it. And not only from this battery – Samy's crew had manned half-a-dozen of the weapons blisters on Strut H.

The batteries began to fire, eerily silent in the vacuum beyond the blister – the only hint of kinetic exchange was the shivering of the deck underfoot as the recoil tremored along the strut, and the systems below that fed more ammunition into the quad breeches began to clatter into action.

Mortalia watched the flare of blue fire as the rockets arced away on courses plotted and computed by the weapons operators and their systems, the calculus of annihilation played out over tens of thousands of kilometers.

It seemed wholly unrelated to the heart-pounding, ear-aching fury of face-to-face combat, to the brutal killing and dying Mortalia had just endured. If anything, it was even more terrible. To look upon the beings you were killing, and who were attempting to kill you, was one thing, but to deal death to hundreds, even thousands over such vast distances and extended periods of time felt cold, callous. In a way, it seemed to suit both the N'orr and the Letnev. The former were so bound to the swarm that they would think nothing of killing on command, while the latter were so arrogant and ruthless that ordering the brutal slaying of thousands via lance strikes, battery broadsides and torpedo launches seemed all but second nature.

There was a thump from the doorway leading down into the blister. Mortalia turned, recognizing the sound of N'orr weaponry.

"They're in the corridor!" somebody shouted.

"Why wasn't the door secured?" Samy snapped, abandoning her position at the consoles and storming back to the rungs.

Too late. A N'orr appeared in the entrance to the cockpit, weapon leveled. It coughed and spat its whizzing, wicked steel.

Samy fell.

The Sardakk N'orr followed their brood strategies and attempted to close with the Letnev fleet.

After clashes between the Sardakk N'orr and the Universities of Jol-Nar, military engagements between the Barony and the

Sardakk were among the most infamous of the many clashes that had torn the galaxy apart. Despite the old Lazax efforts to curtail the power of the Letnev, the Barony had built up the grandest fleet of any of the great civilizations, and their reputation as masters of naval warfare was not based only on their arrogant claims. In contrast, the Sardakk N'orr had always been known as the most dangerous when it came to face-to-face combat.

At the height of its power, the Lazax Empire had relied on the N'orr as auxiliaries without compare. The Tekklar N'orr legions had put down rebellions and conquered far-flung worlds for the Lazax, while the famed Tekklar G'hom, said to be the greatest warriors in the galaxy, had acted as the bodyguards of the imperial council and the emperors themselves.

The Letnev were masters of void warfare in all its cold calculus and grand sweep, and the N'orr were masters of world-conquering and close combat, where their strength, toughness, courage and numbers were unmatched. And in their opposite abilities, warfare between them was always desperate and deadly.

The N'orr drove themselves at the Letnev fleet. Sh'ten's chittered and ticked commands were clear – close with the Barony's capital ships, board them, and slaughter their crews. Admiral Lord Tarzequiel, knowing what the N'orr intended, ordered the initial full-speed rush she had instructed into the system to take advantage of the N'orr unpreparedness to cease, and for her fleet to adopt a defensive formation bristling with overlapping arcs of fire.

The Barony drew first blood. A trio of N'orr cruisers led the line of their assault, arrayed ahead of the central phalanx comprised of Sh'ten's capital ships. They knew their duty – to sacrifice themselves by drawing the Barony's fearsome firepower and win time for the exotriremes to close the distance. They did so gladly, dedicating their deaths to the swarm.

But death was not what Tarzequiel intended for them, at least not yet. Ignoring the protests of her subordinates, she ordered her capital ships to focus fire on the exotriremes beyond the cruisers. A concentrated blaze of energy beams overloaded the shields of the N'orr capital ship *D'shun Rey* before gutting it, burning holes the size of small islands in its hull before blowing out its reactor core.

The other exotriremes were punished too, but their shields held and their captains, honor-bound to the swarm and experienced in such bold tactics, never wavered.

Realizing the danger, the Barony was forced to break its tight formation and attempt evasive maneuvers. This normally spelled disaster in such fleet actions, where any inability to support one another would have left the Letnev isolated and overrun ship by ship. But Tarzequiel had a contingency should the N'orr break her lines.

The N'orr fleet possessed a single carrier, but Tarzequiel commanded two, and at her command they unleashed a hail of Ashbringer interdiction fighters. The Letnev starfighter squadrons braved the storm of close-protection fire unleashed by the Sardakk exotriremes, including the powerful systems of the single N'orr destroyer, and threw themselves between their capital ships and the enemy's.

The Ashbringers were renowned as some of the finest starfighters in existence, whether in void combat or engaging atmospherically, but the N'orr were an infamous opponent. Individually their Kess'or *Fury*-class escorts were small and tough, but together they acted with the brood training of the N'orr, creating a cloud of starfighters that moved with deadly grace, surging and sweeping around the exotriremes.

The Ashbringer wings moved to attack positions and met them head on. Each Kess'or *Fury* was armed with a multifiring beam array capable of spitting out a blizzard of firepower, and the hail of energy wreaked carnage on the Letnev. The Barony's fighter pilots showed the steely courage and determination they were famed for, the lead squadrons occupying the shifting swarm of enemy craft while the reserve punched their way through, ignoring the dogfights raging in their wake. Beyond, they braved the defensive batteries of the exotriremes to get close enough to unleash the plasma firebombs each Ashbringer carried, slipping through the shields to deliver their deadly cargo before wheeling up and away. Flames blossomed across the hulls of the N'orr ships, lost to the vacuum.

The casualties among the Second Grand Fleet's starfighter complement were devastating, but they checked the Sardakk N'orr headlong charge long enough for Tarzequiel to reorganize her own capital ships. The Barony maintained a punishing barrage on the N'orr vessels as the two fleets came to close-range blows.

On board *Baronial Glory*, Captain Augustana reported what every Letnev officer feared the most – that at least one N'orr boarding pod had made it through the cruiser's web of defensive fire. Follow-up reports detailed the desperate, useless attempts at holding the boarding swarm at bay, before all transmissions ceased.

The frigate *Monmath* suffered a similar fate, as it was rammed then boarded by the last remaining N'orr cruiser, heavily armored G'hom shrugging off the fire of Barony marines as they stormed the corridors to the bridge. The *Monmath*'s captain, Viscount Ulandro, shattered his poniard uselessly against one G'hom's inches-thick carapace before the hulking insectoid ripped him limb from limb.

But the N'orr could not close with every ship, especially the dreadnoughts and Tarzequiel's flagship. Two of the N'orr capital vessels, *Akla Z'eyh* and *Z'ethran*, were torn apart by point-blank broadsides and lashing energy beams as they tried to deliver their deadly cargo. Another exotrireme, *Mutha'to*, actually engaged the Barony dreadnought *Sire of Magnificence* in a ranged engagement and bested it, targeting the Letnev ship's engines and managing to cross its T to leave it a hulk flaring with venting oxygen and flames. The damaged *Mutha'to* suffered for its victory, however, leaving it listing and wounded, forcing it to disengage.

The two fleets seemed intent on annihilating each other but, like all N'orr, Sh'ten knew his place in the swarm. His orders from the Veiled Brood had not been to fight the Letnev, but to use the Klast system as a staging area for his role in the wider planned Sardakk offensive. The N'orr had other fleets, but that did not mean they could lose this one. Klast itself was of no significance, and the Barony were an enemy for another day.

Sh'ten ordered the Sardakk fleet to withdraw. Instructions that might have met with outrage from the subordinates of other species were obeyed by the Swarm Marshal's dedicated captains. The final N'orr cruiser, which had already lived far longer than any of its crew had anticipated, diverted all power to its engines and set a course for the heart of the Barony fleet.

For the first time since the start of the battle, Admiral Lord Tarzequiel thought she had made a fatal mistake in letting the cruiser live. As it seemed intent on ramming and then boarding her flagship, she loosed a string of panicked orders directing all ships to target-lock the cruiser and obliterate it before it could reach its target.

In the midst of the Barony's Second Grand Fleet, the cruiser was reduced to floating cosmic debris in a matter of minutes.

But it had been enough. Tarzequiel realized too late that it had been a distraction, designed to give the other Sardakk vessels the precious moments they needed to reroute power from weapons to engines and begin to pull away from the engagement zone.

Furious, Tarzequiel initially ordered a pursuit, but when one of the surviving Sardakk ships began to change its heading once more, threatening to turn at bay and board the overeager Barony vessels pursuing it, Tarzequiel decided that she had done enough. The Sardakk N'orr were retreating, pulling away not only from the Barony's formation but also from Port Rathen, which continued to mount a stuttering, long-distance barrage.

The battle of Klast was over.

The hail of barbed metal from the N'orr swarm-trooper's weapon wreaked devastation in the confined space of the weapons cockpit. One shard caved in the back of the head of one of the crewmates at the control station, while another took off the arm of one raising her rifle.

Mortalia was up and rushing toward Samy even as the rest of the pirates in the blister returned fire. The N'orr slumped in the doorway, riddled with wounds.

Several of the crewmates clambered up and began to blast away into the corridor, presumably at more N'orr. Mortalia was oblivious to it all, kneeling beside Samy. She saw immediately where she'd been hit. The barbs had ripped open her stomach and chest. There was blood everywhere.

Samy looked up at Mortalia and tried to speak but choked instead. Then, she slumped back, and her eyes became dull and glassy, like a doll's.

Mortalia stared down at her, feeling helpless, momentarily lost for words. When she found them, it was a bitter string of expletives lost in the hammering report of the weapons fire.

She hadn't known Samy, not really, but she had needed her. She was the one who had brought the Letnev here. She was the one with all the contacts in Port Rathen. Without her, she'd need to try to reach out to the Barony herself, without attracting suspicion. It made things more complicated.

"Keep the quad guns firing," one of the pirates, seeing Samy's death, barked at those crew not holding the corridor. "Keep hitting those ships!"

Mortalia looked up through the porthole, watched as the battle of Klast came to an end, and wondered what in the name of the silver stars she was supposed to do next.

CHAPTER TWELVE
Port Rathen, the Klast System

"That's tragic," Kanbos said.

He was standing, firing out orders and receiving reports from the center of the hub's pit. From what Mortalia had heard, it sounded as though the station had almost been cleared of N'orr.

She had left Strut H when it became apparent the swarmtroopers in the corridor had finally been exterminated. She had made it back to the hub, hoping that Kanbos would remember her, using the excuse of reporting Samy's death to make it into his presence.

"Another few years and she would have been a captain herself," the Rokha said, then seemed to forget his subordinate's passing as he heartily congratulated a scarred Ardanil who had just informed him the power generators had been fully retaken.

"We should contact the Letnev and tell them the N'orr have been driven from the station," Mortalia suggested, knowing she was in no position to make demands. She was in a difficult position – Samy had been the only reason she was able to speak to Kanbos at all, and Mortalia was keenly aware she had no future among the vagabonds and buccaneers of Klast.

What if they decided to keep her as part of their crew? Could she negotiate an exit, preferably with the Barony, that wouldn't arouse suspicion?

"The Letnev have already sent a communication," Kanbos said distractedly. "Their admiral was up there–" He gestured at one of the hub's viz screens. "She almost managed to bring herself to thank us, which is as good as it gets with these blue-bloods."

"I can help you talk with them," Mortalia said, trying not to feel frustrated. She had hoped to be the first one to communicate with the Letnev. Now she was playing catch-up.

Kanbos glanced at her, his green, felid eyes lingering for a moment. Mortalia hadn't met enough Rokha to be able to gauge their reactions easily. It unsettled her, but she pushed on.

"I served the Barony for many years," she lied. "My parents were indentured to one of the nobles on Wren Terra. If you would like, I can assist you as an intermediary."

"Is that why Samy plucked you out of the habs?" Kanbos asked. "She has contacts with them, too. I didn't know the Barony dealt so freely with other species."

"Massage their egos enough and they'll deal with anyone," Mortalia said, trying to sound offhand.

"They'll want to board," Kanbos said. "Stay close. I may have need of you. I'm not going to let them try to stake claim to Klast or treat us the way the Sardakk did. Hopefully they have the good sense not to try to seize the station."

Kanbos was right. Whatever cautious thanks Admiral Lord Tarzequiel had offered in her initial communications, the Barony descended on Port Rathen as though storming an enemy warship. Letnev marines swept up from the docking bays, visors down, kinetic shields triggered and energy weapons thrumming. Their commander demanded that all weaponry on the hub be deactivated – Kanbos refused, and there was a brief, tense stand-off in which Mortalia tried to weigh up approaching the Barony officer and revealing her identity.

A more senior Letnev commander arrived before she could make her move. He introduced himself as Captain ven Kallow of the carrier *Might of Prime* and stated he had been instructed by Admiral Lord Tarzequiel to negotiate the surrender of Port Rathen.

The statement met with jeers and outrage. Kanbos played to his audience, telling ven Kallow that they would not make the mistake of disarming in the face of aggression again.

It soon emerged that what the Letnev really wanted was to refuel and repair their ships at the port. Kanbos agreed to assist, for a price. As the haggling began in earnest, Mortalia dared to break away from the throng of pirates and approach the Letnev marine officer who ven Kallow had superseded. He was standing off to one side and looked at Mortalia with arrogant disdain as she approached, one white-gloved hand resting on the hilt of his holstered pistol.

"I have a request," Mortalia said quietly. The Letnev officer looked at her like she was some sort of slime grub he'd just discovered on the heel of his highly polished boot.

"I am carrying vital information, which I wish to pass on to the Barony," Mortalia hissed, not wanting to pull out her plate in the hub, mindful of how she had been spotted by Samy before. "I need to speak to your admiral."

"Why?" he asked.

Mortalia glanced toward Kanbos and his underlings, but they were locked in an increasingly rancorous clash with ven Kallow. She stepped closer to the idiot marine officer and slipped a hand inside her cape.

The Letnev's look of fear was replaced by guarded curiosity as he saw the small, metallic plate. Mortalia hastily concealed it again as he repeated his question.

"Why do you need to speak to Admiral Lord Tarzequiel?"

"If you recognize what I am you should know I'm not at liberty to say."

"I will forward whatever you need to declare to the admiral personally."

Mortalia let out a hiss of exasperation. She couldn't tell if he was merely an idiot or didn't believe she was who she claimed to be. Whatever the cause, she could think of only one way to leave Port Rathen in the company of the Letnev without attracting the kind of attention she didn't want from Kanbos and his brutes.

She retreated and dared to interpose herself between Kanbos and ven Kallow.

"Perhaps there is a solution to both our problems here, honored commanders," she said, stepping between the two and raising one non-threatening hand as she attempted to bring Winnaran charm to the fore. So often her people were dismissed as administrators, functionaries and flunkies. She could play that role though, when she had to.

"Noble captain, I do not think our desire to retain our independence is unreasonable," she said to ven Kallow. "We have paid in blood for our own liberty. But we are also not naive. You control this system now, but if you wish to make use of Port Rathen's facilities, and do not trust us to aid you, then perhaps we can supply assurances. Tangible ones."

"Go on," ven Kallow said guardedly.

"I propose we permit you to take hostages," Mortalia said, only now looking back at Kanbos as she spoke. She knew she may be going too far, but she was banking on the master of Port Rathen living up to his piratical reputation. Use of hostages was common currency among his kind, and she doubted Kanbos would have any issues sending a few of his less-favored captains to endure the hospitality of the Letnev.

Kanbos's expression was guarded. Understandably, his underlings looked even less enthused.

"Why should we provide hostages for the Letnev when they won't supply any of their own in return?" the bespectacled Hacan demanded.

"My chief purser has a point," Kanbos said. "How many hostages would you supply in exchange?"

"None," ven Kallow said with a sneer. "I wouldn't entrust the lowliest deckhand to you."

Mortalia could have shouted at the captain to stop being so obtuse, but instead managed to intervene before Kanbos took umbrage.

"I'm willing to go, as a gesture of goodwill. Neither of you should be concerned by what the other wants. It's only your pride and your distrust getting in the way of a deal. The Barony has no reason to spread its forces thin trying to occupy Klast, and Port Rathen has no reason not to do business with the fleet and allow it to refill, knowing it will be on its way soon enough. The Letnev have a war to win. Isn't that so, Captain ven Kallow?"

It wasn't the Barony officer who answered her, but rather Kanbos.

"It seems you're pretty eager to go over to the Letnev, Winnaran," he said. "You sound a lot like Samy, when she was convincing me to send the distress packet to the Barony. Just who are you both?"

"Samy is no one now," Mortalia pointed out, with a cold edge. "And I'm not your concern."

While she had been speaking, the Letnev marine officer she had first approached had moved to ven Kallow's side and was now whispering urgently in his ear. The captain frowned, glanced at Mortalia, then gestured curtly toward Kanbos and the rest of the piratical assembly.

"You will provide me with a trio of hostages from those present. Plus the Winnaran. In exchange, we will not make territorial demands of the Klast system, but we do expect to make use of your facilities before our departure."

"You can do that," Kanbos said. "But you'll pay for the fuel and the parts, like anyone else. Don't worry, though, I'll cut you a good price. I know the right sorts of people."

If it was a jest, the Letnev weren't amused. Mortalia didn't care. Her intervention seemed to have taken the sting out of the confrontation, and what mattered most of all was that she was getting off Port Rathen, and hopefully – finally – getting to speak to Admiral Lord Tarzequiel.

The meeting, when it came, was succinct. Tarzequiel seemed to have no love for what Mortalia represented, even if their interests were shared, but she agreed to provide her with a sprinter craft that would take her to a Barony-controlled fueling hub. The place was hardly any closer to the Boreas Gap, but Mortalia was confident she could find further transport from there. Tarzequiel even authorized one of the less-damaged cruisers in the fleet to make a pass by the nameless old junker that had first brought her to Klast, now lying abandoned on the system's edge.

"Why?" Tarzequiel had asked. "Did you leave something on board?"

"In a manner of speaking," Mortalia said.

Wisely, Tarzequiel did not ask her to elaborate.

CHAPTER THIRTEEN

"Here," Marzek said, highlighting the relevant part of the holo display.

Akenzi peered at it and growled.

"You're sure?" he asked the master-at-arms.

"Orbital scans and drone sweeps are all picking up life signatures, and they form a settlement pattern. Hundreds, no, thousands of people."

"But no machinery? No ships?"

"Nothing large-scale, but that doesn't mean their fleet isn't somewhere in-system. We're still searching the moons and there are several asteroid belts."

Akenzi stared at the markings on the holo for a while longer, running through possibilities.

He had anticipated chaos from the moment the Quieron had all but guaranteed him settlement and extraction rights on Gamma Eridius. There had been so much still to organize. Final favors had been called in, more funding secured, shares issued, the fleet assembled, and supplies taken on. Amidst it all several investors had withdrawn at the last minute, some citing market volatility in the wake of the Barony's ill-considered incursion, though Akenzi suspected it was more from Hamlar applying pressure behind closed doors. There had been other problems, too, from a dispute over pay with one of the non-Hacan haulage contractors hired to shift product out of the Gap to the unfortunate discovery that about a third of the victuals taken on for the voyage had been devoured by vekken rodents. An orbital contractor already in place above Gamma Eridius had also provided tectonic scans of the surface that appeared to show little to no traces of osmium deposits, despite the former claims of lying prospectors.

Most of those problems were within Akenzi's ability to solve, and the lack of osmium wasn't a disaster – the tyrentine would be the real earner, and there was plenty of that. Far more serious was the fate that had befallen the first part of the expedition to be dispatched from Hercant.

It had been attacked, all but wiped out by a force bearing no discernible loyalty to any of either the greater or lesser powers. Pirates, and they had shown no mercy.

Akenzi had expected as much. Damage to the advance guard had been factored into the overall operation. There had been reports of piracy in both the Gap and around Gamma Eridius for years, haunting the less well-traveled routes out of the Alpha Wormhole. What he hadn't anticipated was the size and ferocity of the onslaught.

He was in no doubt that Hamlar was to blame. The treacherous Dazeshi was undoubtedly paying the murderous criminals inhabiting the subsector to attack Akenzi's holdings. His contacts on the more illicit side of things had reported shady benefactors paying top aurei for freebooters willing to go out of their way to the Gap. The whole thing was rotten, but nobody had been able to tie anything to Hamlar, and Akenzi knew he wasn't in a position to bring any public accusations, at least not yet. One thing was certain, though – clans Muktat and Dazeshi were at war, even if neither had declared it.

Akenzi had doubled his spending on armed protection, sinking a heavy percentage of his reserves into it. Even more importantly, he'd called Marzek out of retirement. Drusha was an able bodyguard and advisor in military matters, but the old Hacan master-at-arms was the former head of all Clan Muktat's military assets. He had served as a junior officer under Akenzi's grandfather and had risen to the highest rank during the height of Zamaq's power. Now he had agreed to return to serve a third Muktat generation.

"I recommend ground reconnaissance," he told Akenzi as they surveyed the holo together. "They're well concealed in this terrain. There's only so much we can spy from orbit."

"That's a commitment," Akenzi said. "Can't we monitor them as they come and go? If we find their ships, we can strike those and leave them stranded."

"If I had half an ordri's resources at my disposal, yes," Marzek said, the green light of the holo playing across the old Hacan soldier's grizzled muzzle. "But with our current numbers we'll be spread too thin. Once they make a move, we'll be reactive. They'll have the initiative. Better to find out what we're dealing with now."

"Pirate scum," Akenzi said dispassionately. Like all Hacan, he had a vehement hatred of such scoundrels, those devious brutes who harried trade lanes, drove away custom and forced the United Emirates to sink money into military protection rather than focusing on maximizing profits. The fact that Hamlar had stooped to employing such filth was merely more proof of his disreputable character.

"What if we hit them?" Akenzi said as he tried to find a new angle on the problem. "Not reconnaissance. A full-on strike."

"We don't know who they are," Marzek pointed out.

"They're scum in the pay of the Dazeshi."

"Even if that's so, we don't know what we'd be walking into. We're unclear on their numbers, defenses, even if there are more in the area. Gamma Eridius could have a small semi-sentient simian population beyond the psychic frogs, which, by the way, we should avoid aggravating, if we can help it. This could be one of their settlements."

Akenzi's ears flicked with annoyance, and he realized he was baring his fangs as he looked at the holo. He didn't have time for this. The damage suffered by the vanguard of the expedition was bad, but if they also failed to establish themselves here in the face of armed opposition, the whole venture could unravel. He'd be left bankrupted and shamed, eking out a miserable existence as a pauper on some rusting hulk-station in Hercant's orbit.

"Compromise," he said, doing what he did naturally, and negotiating. "Can you mount a limited strike against them?"

Marzek pondered the suggestion, reaching the same conclusion Akenzi had been considering.

"If we do, they'll probably scramble," the veteran Hacan said. "They'll know their position has been discovered, and they'll break for their ships."

"Which will show us where those ships are," Akenzi continued. "And they'll be vulnerable on the move."

"I still don't like that we don't know their identity," Marzek grumbled. "Let me scout it out from the ground first."

"Very well," Akenzi said. "You're willing to go yourself?"

Marzek's mane bristled, and Akenzi realized he had offended him.

"If I'd grown too long-toothed for this, I wouldn't have agreed to leave my wife and grand-cubs and come out to the middle of nowhere with you," he growled. "I'll run it, *and* I'll lead it."

"This is why I asked for you," Akenzi said, clapping a hand on Marzek's shoulder. "You would have been an ordri general by now if you'd joined one of the greater Emirates."

Marzek shrugged off the praise. "Give me one full day-cycle," he said. "And we'll be ready to stake our claim to Gamma Eridius."

Marzek was as good as his word. Akenzi and those investors who had journeyed with him to the subsector gathered on the bridge of the *Rising Sands* as the operation began. The largest monitor's screen had been split with an array of different transmissions, from orbital shots, to aerial footage from drone units, to on-the-ground pickups from head and weapon viz recorders held by the insertion team. The lattermost consisted entirely of Clan Muktat soldiers, many of whom had served under Marzek before.

At Marzek's advice, Akenzi had massed his assets in orbit, ready to move on the pirates as soon as they realized they were under attack. He expected them to flee at the first sign of danger. They were vagabonds who only fought to get paid. They would run, and when they did the orbital and atmospheric strength Akenzi had brought to bear would wipe them out.

"I wish I could be down there," Drusha said.

"You could have gone, if you wanted," Akenzi pointed out. Drusha dismissed the suggestion with a swish of his tail.

"It would be a dereliction of my duty. I am your guardian, little brother. Not a warrior. Not anymore."

Akenzi almost pointed out that he was perfectly safe on board his own ship, but checked himself, not wanting to tempt fate. He glanced sidelong at the investors studying the screen.

Were any of them in league with Hamlar? Spies, or worse, assassins?

He couldn't think like that. Paranoia had been the undoing of plenty of otherwise-successful merchants before him.

Marzek's personal callsign pinged up on the comms array.

"They still haven't moved," the master-at-arms said, voice chopped up by atmospheric distortion.

"Isn't that a good thing?"

"Not necessarily. They must know we've got ships and fliers up above them. But no signs of any unexpected movements or panic."

"Which means it could be a trap," Akenzi surmised.

"Smells like it."

"Then it's well that we're only conducting a limited strike. I will keep our wits about us up here. If their fleet plans on hitting us while our attention is elsewhere, they're in for a surprise. Just go careful."

Marzek acknowledged. Word came soon after that the final sections were in position.

"Just waiting on your word, my magnate," Marzek's voice crackled.

"Go," Akenzi said, his tail swishing with nervous anticipation. "Show this filth the power of Clan Muktat."

Tol couldn't sleep.

She had been dreaming about Malik. He had been gone for decades, but still he returned sometimes to her in her sleep, to remind her of happier times. He had been a human, a doctor like her, and the kindest and most caring person – of any species – she had ever known.

He had died sixty-six years ago, on Loen's World, from a spineplant injury that had proven toxic. It had happened while he had been out foraging for supplies, while Tol had been back with the main body of the enclave, performing another surgery on Ibna. At first the injury had seemed slight. By the time they had realized that wasn't the case, it was too late.

She missed Malik every day. Looking back, she felt certain that his death had been the beginning of the end, not for the enclave, but for her own will to go on.

So many of those they had first embarked with on Mecatol were gone. The blessings of the Hylar – longevity when compared with many other species – had long ago started feeling like a curse to Tol.

She knew better than to waste any of their remaining medication on trying to fight the wakefulness haunting her. Instead, she rose and walked from her home, a stout little dwelling of logs and pine brush thatch on the southwestern slope of the ridge line, down from the towering majesty of Ibna's dwelling within the Eridius Arc and just east of the main tyrentine boreholes that had drilled into the ridge's flank. She was neighbors with the other Nar Hylar, Rondu – they had helped each other build the rudimentary structures when they had first chosen this place for a permanent settlement – a place specifically chosen to be as far from the planet's psychic frog population as possible – along with the assistance of a pair of second-generation humans named Vin and Caldr. Sometimes Rondu would be up still, and they could while away the hours until the new day dawned, talking about half-forgotten lives lived on Nar or debating the ethics of medicine and cybernetics. His light was off though, his window dark.

Not wanting to trouble him, Tol carried on down the forested slope, heading toward the shoreline. She wanted to swim, even if it was dark, to let the tide carry the weight of her existence again for a while. She carried a small, hooded beam lamp with her, using it to find the familiar path through the trees.

Both Tol and Rondu would have liked to live down by the sea, spending their nights fully submerged, but they had agreed with Ibna's assessment that it was too dangerous. Even Zeth, a Jol Hylar, spent his nights slumbering in the tepid water of his containment sphere. It was no way to live really, not for their kind, but Tol supposed it was necessary. It was just one more burden to bear, another ache, adding to the tiredness that had settled like sediment deep in the waters of her soul.

She hadn't gotten far down the slope when something made her pause. There were noises, sounds beyond the sigh and creak of the wind in the trees and the ever-present croaking of the large amphibian creatures that called Gamma Eridius home. A faint thrumming, electronic perhaps, distinct from the generator units that supplied power to the main settlement. As she listened, she heard what seemed like voices as well, though it was hard to tell where they were coming from.

On impulse, she turned off her beam lamp and stood in the dark, gills closed. Was the thrumming growing louder?

She turned in a half circle and caught sight of light. The pale flash of another beam lamp, briefly visible before whoever was carrying it turned away from her, shielding its illumination. It was further south, along the slope.

It seemed she wasn't the only one up and about.

She changed her course, cutting across the slope rather than heading down it, angling toward where she had last seen the light.

It was tough going in the dark. Hylar eyesight wasn't the best, and after almost falling twice and repeatedly banging her knee into logs and trunks, she found herself wryly wishing she'd opted to enhance her eyesight during the last round of cy-implants.

She forged on, doing her best to keep the point where she had last seen the light fixed ahead of her, not wanting to stray. The slope helped to guide her, as she knew she shouldn't find herself heading either up or down, only along.

After a short distance she paused again, listening. No voices, but the thrumming was definitely louder. Perhaps it was coming from the shore after all, echoing back off the waves? Perhaps there was something out there, on the ocean? A trawler of some sort? Had a sea-shuttle touched down from orbit?

And there were the voices again, closer. A hissed exchange, anger warring with a desire to keep as quiet as possible. Moonlight, lancing down between the pines, picked out a hint of movement.

Tol's heart raced, but she was too close to go back. Whoever they were, they'd detect her almost as soon as she started moving again.

She approached them. There were two, hunched and indistinct in the shadows. It seemed they were looking in the opposite direction, but that changed when she inevitably snapped a twig underfoot.

They turned. For a second, both parties remained frozen.

"The empire lives," Tol murmured.

"Forevermore," breathed one of the figures.

Relief flooded Tol. It was the correct response, used when two members of the collective wanted to prove their identity. One of the figures rose and waved for her to approach. She could discern two sets of upper limbs in the moonlight – a Lazax.

She moved to join the pair, finally able to identify them up close. One was the human, Caldr, and the other was Marchu Mal Serrus. Her presence shocked Tol. After Ibna, she was the most senior Lazax with the collective, a former politician on Mecatol Rex and one of the few who had bought into Ibna's warnings that the end of the empire was at hand. She was almost as old as Ibna but bore none of the cybernetic enhancements that were keeping the venerable former ambassador functioning. She was increasingly housebound in the dwelling she maintained close to the Eridius Arc, yet something was seemingly serious enough to have her walking the forest in the dead of night. It didn't bode well.

"What are you doing out here?" Marchu asked.

"I was about to ask you the same thing."

"Caldr came and woke me. He was on watch."

"Quiet," Caldr hissed, waving at them while gazing off into the darkness. He was facing away from the settlement, down toward where the ridgeline began to taper off to the south.

Tol kept her gills shut. She was beginning to wish she had bothered to haul on her enviro-suit before stepping out – she felt dry and clammy. She had been anticipating refreshing herself down at the shingle, but that didn't look like it would be happening anytime soon.

The three of them crouched in the dark, and watched, listened, saw and heard nothing. Tol realized the thrumming noise had stopped.

"What is it?" she eventually dared whisper. "Did something trigger the sentry nodes?"

"One stopped responding, so I went to check on it," Caldr said.

"And?"

"I haven't gotten to it yet. It's out there." He gestured vaguely into the dark. "But I saw movement, and I heard sounds. Like voices or… growls."

"Growls?"

"I don't know," the human hissed, his tone stressed. "I didn't want to trigger a full alarm, so I went and woke Marchu."

That made some sense. Ibna wouldn't take kindly to the

whole collective being roused, not by a second-gen human like Caldr. Marchu was more forgiving.

"And have you seen anything since?"

"I'm not sure," Caldr said, still gazing out into the night.

"We should check the scanners," Marchu murmured. "Find out if they've picked up anything. Drones up in the atmosphere, or even shuttles."

"I thought I heard something earlier," Tol said. "It sounded like… an engine, maybe. A kind of throbbing noise, like an electro-repulser. It was coming from down by the shingle."

"Well, if there's anything in the vicinity the scanners should be able to detect it," Marchu reiterated. "Let's head back."

The Lazax rose and took a few slow, tentative paces. That was when the invaders struck.

It all happened too fast for Tol to follow properly. Dark shapes materialized from the shadows of the undergrowth, and something slammed into her from the side. She barely made a sound as she was driven onto her back amidst the dirt and old pine needles, the impact forcing out any exclamation before she could make it. She half saw Marchu go down too, tackled by a pair of the phantoms.

A hand closed around her throat, big and strong. Her gills flared and scraped, and she screamed. Realizing their mistake, her attacker shifted its grip to clamp down over her mouth.

She tried to fight back. An aged Hylar doctor she might be, but she had been in plenty of scrapes over the decades. She punched against her attacker's flank and kicked up with one knee, aiming for the traditional weak spot on most of the galaxy's mammalians – the crotch.

The blow connected. Her attacker grunted and recoiled, but only for a moment. The fist muzzling her was replaced by a blow to the face. She saw new constellations, and her struggles ceased.

The dizziness passed, but she knew she was outmatched. Still, she fought back, trying to drive herself up off the forest floor, using the slope to her advantage. Her attacker snarled and held her down. It was big and strong and smelled of musky pelt and weapon grease. One of her hands, before it was pinned at the wrist, roved over what felt like some kind of plate armor before grabbing a fistful of fur.

She felt something sharp at her throat, nicking her sagging scales. It was enough to convince her to finally stop.

A light shone in her eyes, blinding her. She heard the sounds of muted struggle from nearby, presumably Caldr and Marchu likewise being restrained. She tried to turn her head away, but was kept in place, a blade to her throat.

Their attackers were conversing with one another in low tones. She didn't understand what they were saying – to her ear, it sounded like a series of bass, predatory growls, presumably the same noises Caldr had caught earlier. And though she didn't recognize exactly what they were saying to one another, she knew what species she was hearing, what race was assaulting them.

Hacan.

The tense silence gripping the bridge of the *Rising Sands* was broken by Marzek's clipped tones coming in over the comms array.

"We're inside their perimeter. The vanguard has made contact. I'm moving up."

Akenzi drew his zenfar tighter, trying to use the silken fabric to disguise how nervous he was. He had come to the Gap to make money, not act like an ordri commander directing operations from his flagship. Yet here he was, the whole venture poised, in the hands of warriors rather than merchants.

His gaze remained fixed on the section of the main bridge monitor that was showing the transmission from Marzek's own head viz recorder. It was set to heat register, painting the woodland ahead in various cold hues, shot through with fiery brilliance whenever the warm bodies of one of the advancing Hacan came into view. That changed as Marzek advanced up what seemed to be a forested slope. There was a blinding, white light from ahead, and the master-at-arms switched the filter to a regular setting. Akenzi saw the white light remain despite the switch and realized that another Hacan was shining a stab beam on the scene now before Marzek.

Prisoners. Akenzi took a step closer to the monitor, trying to discern the trio of figures on their knees in the middle of a tight ring of Muktat soldiers. The viz recorder was on them, though it was hard to get a proper view as Marzek growled at those not guarding the prisoners to spread out farther up the slope.

"Are you seeing this, magnate?" Marzek's voice crackled, addressing Akenzi.

"Yes," he responded. "Just keep steady."

Marzek moved so the view was squarely on the trio. The nearest was a human male, dressed in rustic-looking garments. Beside him was a Hylar female, a Nar going by her colored scales. She wasn't in any kind of enviro-suit, which was surprising.

The last figure was taller than the others, head bowed. She was pallid and bald. Akenzi's ears twitched as he tried to discern his species.

A terrible realization slowly dawned over the Muktat magnate. This particular prisoner had two sets of arms.

Akenzi simply stared, stunned. Then, in a voice that cracked with tension and panic, he spun round and snapped at the bridge crewmember operating the viz monitor.

"Shut it down."

"Magnate?" the Hacan asked, confused.

"I said shut it down! Kill the feed! Cut the transmission! Now!"

The crewmember hurried to obey, and the monitor abruptly blinked off. Akenzi looked back at it and found himself staring at his own reflection in the glassy black mirror, and at the investors gathered behind him. His fur bristled.

They'd seen it. They all had. But it couldn't be. It was unthinkable. Impossible.

"Was that…?" one of the Hacan began to say, faltering in disbelief. "That looked like…"

He trailed off, and it fell to another one to say the very last words Akenzi ever wanted to hear.

"That was a Lazax."

CHAPTER FOURTEEN

Gamma Eridius, the Boreas Gap

Ibna Vel Syd was woken by the news that he had spent so long dreading.

"There are two Hacan outside," Marchu Mal Serrus told him, standing beside his charge cradle. "And more throughout the collective, all armed. Warriors. They want to speak with you."

Ibna closed his eyes again, wondering if he was dreaming. He didn't dream much anymore. For years his sleep had been haunted by nightmares, by phantom memories of the day he had burned the Hall of Cartography on Mecatol Rex, or imaginings of the fiery annihilation of the imperial capital at the hands of the Federation. Now, though, his sleep was deep and black and featureless, difficult to drag himself up from. It was as though each night he sunk into a pit that only grew deeper and deeper. One day he would find he no longer had the strength to rise again.

"Ibna…" Marchu said softly, putting a hand on his shoulder. Ibna's one good eye snapped open again.

"I'm sorry," Marchu said. "There was no way they wouldn't find the settlement if they carried on along the ridge. They threatened to start killing, and it didn't sound like a Hacan bluff."

He raised one hand to the plate of his primary cranial implant, and cycled through his cybernetic visual spectra, finding the one that indicated the locations and vitals of the enclave's children. All were regular, and where they should be. That was something, at least. Any threat to them would be intolerable.

Saying nothing, he pulled himself up, disengaging the charge lines connecting the ports of his cybernetics from the energy hub that stood thrumming beside the cradle. Gritting the stumps of his teeth so as not to groan in front of his old friend, he clutched the side of the bed and hauled himself to his feet, fighting back a rush of dizziness and the dangerous weakness in his one organic leg.

"How?" he rasped, a hint of anger in his tone. "How did they find us?"

"They haven't said. And we don't know who they're working for either."

"Why wasn't the alarm raised?"

"They're professionals."

Ibna grunted at that. He had been a fool to ever think this place could be a safe haven.

Still, he felt the urge to fight back, to resist, rising within him as he came to terms with the situation. They had not come this far only to be cornered and exterminated by felid merchants. He would not permit that sort of end for his people.

He would find a way out for them, as he always did. Through violence or through guile, Gamma Eridius would not become the final resting place of the Lazax Empire.

Marchu offered to help him prepare, but Ibna refused, telling her to go out and keep the Hacan placated. He dressed himself, determined that he at least didn't need help doing that.

His latest implant, synth-tendons in his left arm, were still knitting, and they made him feel even clumsier than usual.

Eventually, though, he was able to pull on his final garment, a heavy overcoat lined with leonid fur. He picked up his moontree staff and stepped out through the roots of the Eridius Arc.

Dawn crept through the forest around him. The air was clear and smelled sweetly of pine trees. Birdsong flitted back and forth. It promised to be a fine spring day.

The two Hacan Marchu had warned him about were standing waiting for him. The nearest was a particularly vicious-looking beast, with a silver mane, a brutally scarred muzzle and a green optic implant not dissimilar from the one Ibna sported. He was dressed in combat gear, a dune spear cradled in his broad arms. He bared old, yellow fangs as Ibna stepped out.

"Greetings," Ibna Vel Syd said. "Welcome to my home."

"You have been target-locked from orbit," the Hacan told him unceremoniously. "We have military assets on the surface as well, surrounding you. Resistance would be futile."

"Do I look like someone who is contemplating resistance?"

"We are not here to negotiate. We are simply making the situation clear."

"Who is 'we'?" Ibna asked. The two Hacan military equipment was nondescript, and he couldn't see any patches or signifiers on them. They were from the same species, but that didn't necessarily mean they were part of the United Emirates. They could be mercenaries.

"You're not in a position to ask questions," the lead Hacan said.

"And yet I just did."

"I have been informed that you are the leader here. You will gather your people and submit any weaponry you possess."

"And if I refuse?"

"I will start killing."

"Why? We are peaceful settlers, nothing more." A familiar

fury built inside him. Sometimes, he envisioned making the whole galaxy suffer for what they had done.

"You are Lazax."

"How perceptive."

The Hacan half turned away and muttered something in his own dialect. Ibna thought he was struggling to overcome anger at his responses, before realizing he was communicating remotely via a savant. Someone, presumably the Hacan's employer, was monitoring their exchange, possibly linked in via the Hacan's optic implant.

The grizzled felid looked back at Ibna and spoke again.

"My strike pack are making this place secure. Any forms of resistance, any noncompliance, will result in the use of force."

"We are at your mercy, noble Hacan," Ibna said, spreading those arms not gripping his staff.

"My magnate is coming here," the Hacan continued. "He wishes to speak with you."

Magnate. It had been a century since Ibna had served the emperor in the capacity of ambassador, but he remembered enough about his life before the empire's collapse to recall that magnate was a rank among the Hacan clans. It seemed as though the interlopers were from the United Emirates after all. "I would be honored to meet him," Ibna went on, continuing to play the diplomat. Privately, he was turning over possibilities, well-worn plans of escape and evasion. He had tried to warn the likes of Marchu and Tol that the increased activity they had noted in orbit over the past months had presaged disaster. He should have acted, rather than allowed himself to slip into the embrace of negligence. He should have shown leadership, as he had done a hundred times before in the century. Ordered the collective abandoned, set out again across the stars, in search of a new home, a new corner of the galaxy not yet ripped apart by warring factions. Somewhere to continue to play the long game and wait out the chaos.

He looked the Hacan warrior in the eye, knowing he was speaking to his master indirectly.

"I look forward to resolving this impasse, face to face."

"We could just kill them," Drusha suggested.

"Is that your solution to everything?" Akenzi snapped.

"Yes."

"Well, perhaps try to think of an alternative for once. I'd rather not start my career as a trader in the Boreas Gap with a massacre."

Drusha glowered at his brother from across the shuttle's transport compartment but had the good sense to hold his tongue. Akenzi knew he shouldn't have snapped at him, but in truth he was still reeling. He hadn't anticipated this. Why would he have? Who in the name of every last grain of the Golden Sands could have predicted that there were still Lazax in the galaxy, much less in the little, remote corner that Akenzi had staked everything on?

Besides the disbelief, Akenzi found it monstrously unfair. It was like some cosmic joke, so crude and shocking that he hadn't quite believed it for hours, until Marzek had delivered multiple viz recordings of the Lazax – not even one, but plural – and their settlement. An entire settlement! With children, even! They weren't alone either. Marzek had reported humans, even a few Hylar, all seemingly acting like the empire hadn't been gone for a century.

And the worst part was that his investors had seen it all. They had watched the capture of the first of those four-armed freaks in real time. He couldn't deny what they had all just seen.

Some had withdrawn their investments, right there and

then. Akenzi was just thankful he'd managed to convince most of them to at least hold off until they knew more. He'd pledged to go to the surface in person.

He knew he could not be hamstrung by shock. Regardless of the misfortune of the hand dealt to him, he could not give in to self-pity. Paralysis would lead to proper, permanent disaster. He had to get the situation under control. And maybe that would mean doing what his brother had suggested and wiping this discovery from existence.

"They must have been running for decades," he said, thinking out loud. "Or even longer. The one that treated with Marzek looked heavily cy-enhanced."

"The galaxy's oldest refugees," Drusha noted.

"I just wish it had been pirates," Akenzi muttered. Drusha let out an amused rumble.

Marzek met them at the makeshift landing zone he had marked out on the edge of the forested ridgeline where the enclave had been discovered. He was in his element, directing the occupation of the settlement and delivering a brusque report to Akenzi as he and Drusha disembarked.

"They're not warriors," he summarized. "Only a few of them are armed. The only risk to security is that we haven't yet been able to make them divulge whether they have ship assets somewhere in-system."

"Well, I doubt they're native to Gamma Eridius," Akenzi said humorlessly. "So, they must have something. Have they told you how long they've been here?"

"Not yet. The settlement itself is crude but seems well-established. They have substantial electrical generation capacity and equipment that's clearly been salvaged from advanced systems. They're also mining the tyrentine. I'd estimate they've been in situ a number of years."

"And nobody found them until today," Akenzi said in wonderment.

"At least no one willing to spread the story," Marzek pointed out. The master-at-arms had a point. What if there were those beyond the Gap who knew of the Lazax presence here? Worse, what if there were more Lazax out there? Of course there were stories, tall tales claiming that some part of the old empire still clung on, beyond the gaze of the great civilizations.

Marzek began to lead them up through the woodland, into a settlement of small log huts with brush roofs. It was neatly arrayed around a series of clearings. There was no sign of anyone besides Marzek's troops.

"I ordered everyone inside, once they'd surrendered their weapons," he explained as they went.

Akenzi wasn't about to question the veteran Hacan on security matters. He followed on, to what he assumed was the heart of the settlement, where he found the leader of the Lazax waiting for him before the bristling roots of a vast tree.

Akenzi had never seen a Lazax in person before. He was tall and gaunt and pale, towering over Akenzi despite the aged stoop to his slender shoulders. His clothing was rough and worn, and he supported himself with an old, slightly crooked staff of polished silvery wood. Most shocking was his level of cybernetic augmentation – it seemed much of his body, including a large section of his cranium and three of his four upper limbs had been replaced.

"Good morning," the Lazax said in a dry, reedy voice before, to Akenzi's surprise, briefly running one finger down his still-fleshy nose, from bridge to tip. It was a common form of Hacan greeting, and Akenzi responded in kind almost without thinking, touching his muzzle, whiskers twitching.

"This was not who I expected to be greeting after arriving

in-system," Akenzi said, having already decided that a neutral disposition would be the best stance to adopt, at least initially. "Exactly whom am I addressing?"

"My name is Ibna Vel Syd," the Lazax said. "I would have prefaced that with all manner of titles once, but they are meaningless now. You may know me simply as Vel Syd."

"I am Magnate Akenzi Muktat, of Clan Muktat, sept of the Emirate of Taneer, of the United Emirates of the Hacan."

"You see, that seemed quite enjoyable. I miss my titles."

"What were they?"

"At one point, Imperial Ambassador. At another, Councilor to his Supreme Majesty and Galaxia Imperator, Salai Sai Corian."

"Grand indeed," Akenzi said, keeping his tone guarded as he tried to gauge exactly who he was speaking to. "You were a senior member of the imperial court, then?"

"You could say that."

"And yet you survived the destruction of Mecatol Rex?"

"I was absent when the bombs dropped. I, and these others with me."

"You must forgive the firmness of my master-at-arms, Marzek," Akenzi said, gesturing at the Hacan warrior. "None of us expected to find… your kind here."

"Nor were you supposed to," Vel Syd said. "Alas, the galaxy has a habit of always catching up with us."

"I did not know there were any Lazax left in the galaxy," Akenzi admitted, deciding not to avoid the obvious any longer. "Have you truly been hiding here since the fall of the empire?"

"No. Our journeys have taken us to many places, some more hospitable than others. Yet we have been upon this particular world for some time. I was almost beginning to hope I had found somewhere to see out my final days." His sharp grimace spoke otherwise.

"Then I fear I must disabuse you of that hope," Akenzi said. "I have been given the right to build a settlement on Gamma Eridius and begin to trade from it. Not only here, but throughout the Boreas Gap. If all goes well, this place will become a hub of commerce."

"You've come for the tyrentine," Vel Syd assumed.

"Yes," Akenzi admitted, deciding to add nothing more.

"And you are trying to decide whether you should wipe us all out," Vel Syd continued for him. He was perceptive, Akenzi thought. But then again, he had claimed to be an imperial ambassador. That, and the mere fact he had survived all this time while seemingly holding together this disparate enclave of exiles, implied he was an individual of uncommon ability. Akenzi knew he would have to continue treading carefully, at least until he had ascertained that he did indeed have complete control over the situation.

"There are some among my venture who would counsel that," he told the Lazax. "Your empire fell with good reason. You are not beloved by any who remain, besides the Winnaran."

"I know how and why the empire fell," Vel Syd said with a flash of bitterness. "I was there when it happened. Quann, the fleet recall votes, the Maandu Edict."

Akenzi did not consider himself a particular student of history, but he knew enough to realize just how senior a member of the imperial administration Vel Syd must once have been.

"There are stories about the Lazax," he said cautiously. "Tales about one who predicted the Federation's attack on Mecatol Rex. He gathered a few likeminded allies and fled before the humans arrived. Are those tales true?"

"What difference would it make if I confirmed or denied that?" Vel Syd pointed out. "What matters is that I am here now, and at your mercy."

"I would rather you weren't," Akenzi said, and decided it was time to commit. "I will be candid. Your existence here is a problem, one of a number I am currently trying to solve. I have two options available. The first is that I leave this place and give instructions to Marzek. He and his warriors go house to house and kill everyone in this settlement. He then evacuates and I level this ridgeline from orbit. This forest will burn. We return and ensure there is no evidence of your existence, right down to casting the ashes of your charred bones into the sea. The second option is that you go from here, and from the Boreas Gap, that you never return, and that you never speak of this encounter to anyone. I will probably still burn the forest once you have left. At the culmination of both solutions, I report back to the Kenara system that I have torched a nest of pirate raiders. I must pick one of those two."

"You would not report what you have found to the United Emirates?"

Akenzi scoffed. "Under no circumstances can your existence here become common knowledge. Maybe I could harvest a little prestige at being the one who uncovered the last of the Lazax. But it would bring all sorts of unwanted attention. Worse, it would cause the great civilizations to take a renewed interest in the Gap. All of that means disaster for me, the end of this venture, financial bankruptcy and disgrace. So, no. You can rest assured I want everyone else to discover that you're here as little as you do."

"What do your shareholders think you should do?"

The question caught Akenzi by surprise, and he had to ask the Lazax to repeat himself.

"You are a burgeoning, entrepreneurial Hacan trader. You clearly have financial backing, as well as the will and drive to make it out here and set up this operation. That means you're working with backers. Shareholders. They will have representatives present here with you, to ensure the venture is progressing as planned and that everything is happening above board. They're probably also aware you've just unearthed the last of the Lazax. So, what do they want you to do?"

"Option one," Akenzi said.

"I suppose the fact they're invested as well means you trust them to keep this a secret."

"They're going to become complicit in whatever I decide," Akenzi said. "They know that if they run and talk, Clan Muktat has the resources to make sure they don't talk for long. But tell me, what would you do? What option would you pick if you were in my position?"

"When I served the emperor, I would have counseled to let you leave," Vel Syd said. "With the threat that you would be hunted and destroyed if you betrayed my mercy."

"And now? Since you don't serve the emperor any longer?"

"Option one. I am not the person I once was. The galaxy has been cruel to me for a very long time, and now I am cruel to it."

"You are advising your own destruction."

"You asked me a question and I answered. I thought you would appreciate that this talk is progressing openly."

"I do," Akenzi allowed, wondering what he was missing. Was this old Lazax really so worn down by the struggles of existence, that he would simply acquiesce to being cut down? Or was there something else at play? Merchant against diplomat, it was a delicate and dangerous game.

"But you have other troubles," the Lazax said. "You admitted as much yourself."

"None that concern you," Akenzi responded.

"There is a reason you're here talking to me," Vel Syd pointed out. "If your allies want to destroy this enclave, and you are leaning toward that option as well, you would already have done it. I would have awoken to a massacre and found myself shot down the moment I stepped beyond these roots. But here you are, talking. Showing restraint, and apparent honesty."

"I like to consider all my options," Akenzi said, knowing he sounded too defensive. "I wish to view a problem like this from every angle, to make sure I do not make a mistake. I cannot afford to, and we Hacan do not like things we cannot afford."

"Then maybe one problem can be used to solve another. That is what you think, isn't it? That is why you are talking to me, and not killing me."

There it was. The Lazax was making his play, bidding to avoid his own destruction. Akenzi almost respected it. Now they both knew where they stood, the proper business could begin.

"What are you proposing?" Akenzi asked, trying to appear thoughtful, considerate. "Walk me through it."

"Unless I am much mistaken, or things are indeed so much different from my days as an ambassador, you seem young for a Hacan magnate," Vel Syd said. He clasped the fingers of both sets of hands as he spoke, the gesture likely intended as giving off an air of thoughtfulness, though subconsciously Akenzi struggled to normalize the motions of a pair of upper arms, even if three of them were cybernetics. "I imagine you come from a clan of some good standing, perhaps a younger son, and you are looking to make a name for yourself. You have poured your talents and energy into this venture, a bold enterprise that promises great reward if it succeeds. But boldness can breed contempt, and it can be mistaken by some for arrogance. You have made enemies, ones who seek to impede you."

"This is all supposition," Akenzi interrupted, showing a flash of fangs, a subtle warning that he did not agree. "Based on the fact I don't have silver in my mane."

"Then let me add firmer facts. We have been here for some years, making this place our home. In that time, I have watched as more travelers have come to this world. Our scanners ping with returns and running lights twinkle in the night sky. From afar we have seen fliers, drones, even ships in orbit. Over the last few months, the activity has become particularly intense. Yet you said earlier that you have only just arrived in-system. You are not responsible for all of what we have been witnessing. There are others here. Other Hacan, or maybe even others from the great civilizations. Rival merchants. Those staking their claim to Gamma Eridius's untapped resources. They are your enemies here, not me or this enclave. And you want to know how we play into all that. You want to know if we can be an asset in your wider struggle, before you destroy us. Hacan are clever and cunning, and you are too much of both to panic and open fire right away."

"Supposition," Akenzi repeated. "With a ring of truth. I can see why you once gave counsel to the emperor."

"I was beginning to fear that age had dulled my mind. Perhaps I have the cognitive implants to thank for my sharpness."

"Say what you claim is true. How could you possibly help me?"

"The details are something we would have to work out. But I'm sure a rogue Lazax collective could be fashioned into some sort of advantage."

"I have no reason to trust you or believe that you have assets that could make a difference."

"We have vessels. Among these, a trio of cruiser ships, concealed on the planet's surface. Let my admission of that serve to help build trust between us, and act as evidence that we have what you call … 'assets.'"

Akenzi looked at the old Lazax, trying to discern his true intentions with every ounce of guile he possessed. He had established Vel Syd wasn't simply going to surrender himself to annihilation, and he had made him place at least some of his cards on the table without giving up too many of his own. But there were risks everywhere. A part of him knew he should just wash his hands of it all, depart immediately and order the settlement wiped out. That would be the simplest solution. Yet it would leave his other problems unsolved.

"I will consider your suggestion," he said, deciding he needed more of that precious resource – time. "And return soon to discuss matters further."

"And I will speak to my people and reassure them that you mean us no harm."

"Then you might be lying to them. I make you no promises."

"I must ask for one then. Swear you will not destroy us before we speak further."

"If you will promise not to attempt to escape, or communicate with anyone beyond this place," Akenzi replied, disliking being beholden to anyone, but willing to compromise.

"Agreed. We are going nowhere. Yet."

"Then I swear by every grain of the Golden Sands of Hercant that we will speak again."

"Very well."

"You trust me to keep that promise?"

"I suppose that depends on what kind of merchant you are. I haven't yet been able to work that out."

Akenzi bared his fangs and saw the Lazax's grip on his staff tighten – he thought he had just made Akenzi angry, but the Hacan was merely showing amusement.

"I like to make profits," he told Vel Syd. "But I also like to make profits that don't involve killing anyone, at least not directly. Until next time, Ibna Vel Syd."

CHAPTER FIFTEEN

Former First Admiral Count Tarquilian Zorias had been sentenced to death.

The ex-first admiral was a shadow of his former self, almost unrecognizable in a drab gray penal jumpsuit and fetters. He had requested to die in his uniform but had been denied. Such a dishonorable end meted out to a fellow aristocrat might have drawn murmurs of discontent from the nobility of Arc Prime in decades past, but no longer – the Barony was in a state of desperate, total war, and the scale of Zorias's failure in such a time of crisis was unforgivable. He had failed to bring the Hacan to heel and had turned them into an enemy with his blundering. The only possible fate left to him was death.

The jury presiding over Zorias's court martial, all of them fellow officers, had been unanimous in its verdict. Zorias was to be executed in the traditional manner. He would be taken to one of the exo-pods in Feruc's shell and then exposed to the thin atmosphere beyond the sealed city, to the bitter chill that held Arc Prime in its perpetual thrall.

The execution was to be transmitted, live and public. A

selection of senior Barony officials witnessed it in person, from the other side of the exo-pod, shielded from Arc Prime's surface by thermal plates and heated plasticon.

Gondar was among them. He was no duke or viscount, so would not normally have been afforded a place among their august kind, but while those not privy to the Barony's inner workings might be confused by the presence of the plainly attired Letnev, all the other senior figures knew him, and knew what he represented. No one would complain about the presence of so senior a member of the Cimm Fenn, the Barony's shadowy intelligence ministry. There were no complaints, and his submission to be present for Zorias's death had been granted without stipulation or delay.

He had not lobbied for this particular sentencing, but he had not needed to. Zorias's handling of the incident in the Kenara system had been the most embarrassing debacle the Barony had suffered since the defeat at Solist. Privately Gondar had been furious, but publicly he had made no comment on his own involvement. His presence with the First Grand Fleet had not been widely acknowledged, and he intended to keep it that way.

The final verdict of the court was repeated before the assembled nobility. Gondar watched Zorias through the clear plasticon. The door between the pod and the outside had not yet been opened, but the disgraced count was already shivering visibly. His face was tight as he fought not to let his fear show. Gondar wondered if such an attempt at courage would impress any of the others watching the execution. It certainly didn't move him.

Zorias had not been afforded the dignity of any final words, so when the verdict of the court was finished being read there was a buzzing sound, and the door to the exo-pod began to lever open.

Zorias didn't utter a sound – Gondar doubted that he could, suspecting the cold and the low amount of oxygen had already stolen the former admiral's breath. He watched with genuine interest as Zorias's violent shivering stopped, and he collapsed onto his knees, head bowed, hands pawing at his chest and throat.

Gondar felt a slight buzz against his wrist and tore his gaze away from Zorias's lingering death to look down at his savant. He was receiving a transmission from Euste Quellar, one of his aides. After a slight pause he accepted the connection request.

"What is it?" he asked curtly.

"Apologies, but Asset 258672 has made contact. You said you wished to be informed as soon as that happened."

"Where from?"

"Out on the fringes. The Klast system. As it so happens, she was picked up by the Second Grand Fleet at Port Rathen, after they routed the Sardakk."

"Picked up? Or did she submit herself?"

"She contacted them. Admiral Lord Tarzequiel agreed to forward a message, and the courier vessel has just reached orbit."

"It hasn't beamed its data packet yet?"

"No, I only know the preliminary information attached to it. But it's downloading as we speak and will be ready for you in a few minutes."

Gondar noticed that several of the noble witnesses to Zorias's execution cast exasperated glances at him. Zorias had collapsed forward, writhing, his face turning purple as he fought to drag in the merest hint of his homeworld's thin polluted atmosphere. His vital signs were the barest blip on the display above.

"Have the packet readied for me," Gondar said. "I'm on my way."

He rose and, with the barest nod to the other witnesses, turned his back on the execution and headed for the exit. He'd seen enough anyway. A few minutes more, and Count Zorias's vitals would cease and the exo-pod would be resealed. A doctor and a pair of assistants would enter the chamber, assess the pale, cold corpse, and pronounce the once-honored nobleman dead. His body would then be incinerated, his named heir and successor would be declared the new Count Zorias, and senior Barony officers would be reminded what fate awaited those who shamed the glorious empire of the Letnev.

Gondar hoped they had all learned their lesson.

CHAPTER SIXTEEN

Druaa, Capital World of the Naalu Collective

The vekken squirmed and bit Z'ffani.

Its large front teeth failed to penetrate the silvery scales of her hand, and she didn't notice anyway. Her mind was elsewhere, submerged in the hissing seas of massed telepathic convergence.

The Crenhees Assembly of Tranquility and Order had gathered, the highest council body on Druaa. One hundred Sen'enn, the masters of the broods, each one honored with a nest-spot within the Assembly Dome. The great building was a marvel of clear crystal that blazed with multi-hued brilliance, the light of Druaa's star refracted down through its geometrically sublime structures to leave the dome's central pit awash with color.

It made the Druaa shine in their nest-seats, causing their scales to glitter like sheaths of diamonds around their coiled, serpentine bodies. One hundred Sen'enn, one hundred Druaa, the leaders of their people, come together to decide not only their fate, but the fate of the galaxy.

The council chamber was silent and still but for the low, rippling hissing and the hypnotic swaying of the Assembly as they communed. None would dishonor this space by seeking to converse with an audible tone. The words they shared – and more – were slipped directly into the minds of each one present, a telepathic congress that Z'ffani had sunk so deeply into, she was hardly aware of her surroundings anymore.

It is clear, Taz'sheen, the Red Scale, thought, the mental words accompanied by an undercurrent of her customary aggression. *We are approaching the decisive point. The galaxy teeters on the edge, ready to fall one way or another. Opportunities abound. The time to stake our claim has come.*

We would risk everything for uncertain odds, Sselth, the First Coil and leader of the council, responded. The flow of the thought-words was cold and firm as they were shared through the linked consciousness. *The great civilizations are not yet spent. Many are desperate, and their militaries are battle-hardened. We may unite them against us.*

No one power can match us now, Taz'sheen assured. *As for the threat of unity, do you think so low of our abilities as negotiators? As deceivers? Have we not deceived the whole galaxy up until now?*

The proud thoughts drew soft hisses of approval from the Assembly. The vekken bit into Z'ffani again, and the slight discomfort finally registered. She raised the large rodent, unlatched her jaw, and swallowed it whole, the powerful muscles of her throat squeezing with peristaltic motion as it forced the doomed creature down her gullet.

Another Sen'enn, Lak'kari, was giving support to Sseth's cautious approach, and the mood of the Assembly seemed to be swinging slowly in the First Coil's favor. That did not suit Z'ffani's intentions. The time for her to intercede had come.

The Druaa didn't merely transmit thought-words, as a lesser telepathic species might. They communed an entire gamut of emotions, a range far beyond the means of interaction used by more primitive beings. When many Druaa gathered together and entered the trance state of a telepathic convergence, their individual consciousnesses were partially subsumed into the whole. Their thoughts intertwined, offering a far deeper level of understanding and easing the Assembly to a more singular decision. It was a superior method of discourse to any in the galaxy, and it had allowed the Druaa to enjoy a level of unity and harmony all other civilizations would have envied, had they even known of the Collective's existence.

If Taz'sheen had her way, they soon would. For centuries the Collective had been building their strength in secret. Even at the height of the old empire's power they had lain undiscovered, surrounded by conquered and colonized people, but shielded from imperial view by their own ability and cunning. They had watched as the Lazax's Imperium had crumbled from within, and as the other supposed great powers had savaged one another in a crude attempt at dominance. All the while, they had laid their own plans.

Now, according to the Red Scale, it was finally time to put those plans into action.

Taz'sheen was the commander of the Collective's military forces, Master of the Twin Moon Legion, and her thoughts matched the bloody hue of her thick, scarred scales, forever underpinned by confidence and aggression. It was an addictive mix, and Z'ffani knew many of the other Sen'enn were swayed by her. Z'ffani herself was sympathetic to the cause of intervention, but she found Taz'sheen's methodologies unrefined.

Uncertainty ran through the convergence, chilling and unwelcome. The Assembly was divided as it rarely had been in the recent past, and the lack of certainty was almost like a physical pain in the hind part of each Druaa's mind.

Z'ffani intended to change that. The plans she had spent years preparing now had to be stated publicly. She marshaled her thoughts, checked her emotions, and passed fully into the current of the Assembly.

My brood kindred, she thought. *Fellow Sen'enn. These are troubled times, and we must be careful we do not misstep. I would not seek a bid for dominance until we have marshaled every advantage we can possibly gain, every edge over each potential opponent we might face. And I believe I have a weapon I can bring before the Assembly, one that will enhance our efforts when the time comes. I have acquired knowledge that might make all the difference.*

How have you come by this knowledge? another of the Sen'enn and a long-standing rival of Z'ffani, D'shasa, demanded, the sharpness of her tone like cold water being poured on her scales. Z'ffani ignored the unpleasant sensation, not modulating the calmness of her own mind to face down the aggression, subconsciously telling the rest of the Assembly that she was in control.

The Yssaril, she responded. *My spy network has reported it to me. The information is fresh and reliable.*

Are the Yssaril ever truly reliable? D'shasa thought.

Who here has not utilized them for the benefit of the Assembly? Z'ffani spoke-thought, allowing a hint of arrogance to color her suggestion. The others knew she was correct – the Naalu Collective had long been linked with the deadly, diminutive species. There had been contact between both cultures for centuries and, unlike all others who had stumbled across their existence, the Collective had chosen not to kill or memory-melt the Yssaril. They had formed a compact, with many Yssaril acting as the eyes and ears of the Collective in the wider galaxy.

Z'ffani's own Yssaril cell had worked hard to infiltrate that part of the Yssaril Guild of Spies hired out by the Cimm Fenn, the secretive intelligence service of the Barony of Letnev. The effort had been targeted and focused, with a single goal in mind, and now, after years of expenditure, it had borne fruit.

The Lazax yet live, Z'ffani declared, relishing the surge of shock that ran through the entire Assembly, the sibilant hissing rising to a pitch. *A small enclave survived their empire's annihilation. But they have been found, and the noose closes around them.*

You only thought to bring this knowledge before us now? D'shasa asked, thoughts laced with reproach.

As I said, the information is as fresh as these vekken, Z'ffani responded, clutching one of the verminous treats caged beside each Druaa's nest-seat and squeezing it until it squealed. *Much still remains uncertain, clouded. But I would not trouble the Assembly if I was not confident.*

Confident, D'shasa repeated. *Have you found the Lazax or not?*

Their likely location is known.

And where is that?

I am sure the Assembly will understand if that information remains known only to a few, for the time being.

The Assembly was divided, Z'ffani could feel it. There was dismay and doubt, but also excitement. This was an opportunity, there to be taken.

Controlling the fate of the last of the Lazax could be a powerful tool during our emergence, another Sen'enn, Z'shen, pointed out. *They could be used as bargaining pieces, or even to claim greater legitimacy for our future role on the galactic stage.*

Even a century after the burning of Mecatol Rex, the shadow of the empire remains long, Z'ffani thought. *By becoming masters of the Lazax, we become masters of the imperial legacy.*

All of this is meaningless if we do not take them, Ssleth pointed out. *If we mount an expedition to wherever they are hiding, it is likely our existence will come to the attention of the other powers. We would be as well following Taz'sheen's proposed course of action and making a wider play, while we still have the element of surprise.*

I am not proposing an expedition, Z'ffani thought, hoping the calm certainty she was building her thoughts around continued to feed into the wider consciousness of the Assembly. *I have sufficient resources at my disposal to mount a covert operation to retrieve the Lazax. I myself intend to travel to their location and ensure that at least some are… persuaded of the positives of returning here to Druaa with me. In that way, we can bring them into our fold with minimal danger or expenditure of resources.*

Z'ffani could sense from the minds of the other Sen'enn that few liked the idea of her making a solo play for the Lazax. No one worried about her chances of survival – few here would mourn her death, and besides, all knew her power, knew the strength of her mind. She was one of the greatest among them, and the thought of performing so dangerous an undertaking alone was of little concern. No, the Assembly feared that if she was successful, they would be in her power. She pushed her suggestion, while the gestalt consciousness was still malleable and open to suggestion.

If we do this, we better position ourselves for the emergence without risking a full commitment. I support the Red Scale's view that it is almost time to strike. But this Assembly has always agreed that we must make every effort to ensure we are in the best possible position when the time comes to make our move. Our kind knows that a single, swift blow is the most likely to succeed. We need to ensure that blow doesn't miss. And if I fail in this undertaking, well… that is little loss to the Assembly, isn't it?

Are you proposing we delay the emergence? Taz'sheen demanded, frustration flaring through the minds of the Druaa as she sought to pin Z'ffani down.

Only for a little while, she clarified. *That is why I think my proposal holds greatest merit – it bridges the divide we can all taste here. But whether my venture meets with success or not, a resolution concerning the Lazax will not take long. After that, we can strike that blow I know you and the Twin Moon Legion ache to unleash, Red Scale.*

There was more hissing, and Z'ffani felt the emotions surging through her own mind, like a discordant crescendo, making her shiver.

K'lani brought it to an end. She was serving as chief Sen'enn, current figurehead of the Assembly, and it was her duty to ensure that the council reached a final accord.

I agree that I see no reason not to permit Z'ffani to attempt this, she thought-spoke. *If she is successful, the stage is set for the emergence. If not… we shall debate our next course of action. How swiftly can the Lazax be brought before the Assembly?*

I intend to leave immediately, Z'ffani responded, doing her best to mask the triumph she felt. *One Druaa month-cycle. If you have not heard from me by then, proceed without me.*

We shall, K'lani assured her. *For the glory of the Assembly. Our time has almost come.*

CHAPTER SEVENTEEN

Orbital Station, Quinz 11

"It's manual work mostly," the Hacan said, looking Vexar and his companions up and down, like a drill master eyeing a particularly scrawny batch of new recruits. "Operation of heavy machinery, long hours."

"But the pay is good," Vexar said, trying to sound hopeful. The big felid made a growling noise that could have been laughter.

"Potentially. Everyone, even laborers, get a share in the venture, so they get a share from the profits, too. It's all in the contract."

He tapped the glassy screen projecting the three-dimensional agreement docket above the desk, causing it to distort briefly.

"So, no profit, no pay?" Lekaan, standing before the Hacan's station next to Vexar, demanded. The felid's ears twitched.

"There'll be profits," he rumbled. "Magnate Akenzi Muktat is running this venture, from top to bottom. The Muktat aren't my clan, but they've been successful recently, and they're getting a lot of backing. This is going to be a highly lucrative undertaking once it gets off the ground."

It wasn't the most ringing endorsement Vexar had ever heard, but luckily for the Hacan hiring foreman, it didn't need to be.

The Resurrectionists just needed a means of getting to Gamma Eridius and without arousing suspicion, and preferably paid for by someone else.

Of course, they couldn't make that obvious, so Vexar and Lekaan were doing their best to appear cautious. There were several separate recruitment agencies operating in systems adjacent to the Boreas Gap, all seemingly run by a Hacan trader called Akenzi, who was looking to, as this recruiter had put it, "open up the Gap." Vexar and the rest of the Resurrectionists had made it to one of the hiring offices in the orbital station above Quinz 11, though they had left *Grand Dominion* concealed with a skeleton crew amongst the asteroid belt trailing the system's edge. Their remaining fuel wouldn't see them all the way through the Gap to Gamma Eridius, and they had agreed that a cutter full of Winnarans heading out to an isolated subsector might arouse suspicion from whichever fueling port they were forced to call upon.

The fact that a Hacan was hiring to take individuals and groups out to Gamma Eridius to work for them was good fortune, but it also made what they were trying to do even more pressing. If Vexar was right, and their goal lay on Gamma Eridius, there was a real danger the likes of Akenzi would stumble across it before them.

"There's a lot of you, isn't there?" the Hacan asked.

"Thirty-four in all," Vexar said, glancing back toward where most of the Resurrectionists were gathered in the office lobby outside, doing their best to look like ordinary down-on-their-luck workers.

"No, I don't just mean them," the Hacan said. "I'm talking about Winnarans in general. I haven't seen any at this station for years, and then two groups turn up barely a cycle apart looking for employment."

"There's another group of Winnarans going to Gamma Eridius?" Vexar asked, genuinely surprised.

"Yes. One of them came here not long ago, asked a lot of similar questions to you. She was alone but said she represented a group of four. All eager to work. Did one of our bulletins appear in a Winnaran enclave somewhere closer to the core?"

"It was a friend who told us about this opportunity," Vexar said, trying not to sound evasive. "Like I said, our crew got laid off at Dagworth. Too much instability given the rumors about the N'orr. We're just trying to find some aurei to get us all back into the inner sectors, where there's more shipping work."

"More shipping, and more fighting," the Hacan observed. "Be careful what you wish for. What have you heard about the N'orr anyway?"

"Same as everyone else. Apparently, they lost a fleet action with the Barony at Klast."

"You can never truly beat the N'orr, there's too many of them," the Hacan said. "Well, I've nothing against Winnarans, so if you're happy to sign, we're happy to have you."

Vexar looked at Lekaan, feigning one last bout of uncertainty, before nodding. He gave his gene signature, authorizing it for their entire group.

"Welcome to the best employers in the galaxy," the Hacan said.

They were given transport to Gamma Eridius three days later. It wasn't much, just a macro freighter with the keel tag B9-09, run by a Hacan captain named Huresh who was currently hauling people rather than goods – Vexar assumed it would be carrying the fruits of their labors back out of the Gap in the coming months.

On the first day-cycle a buzzer in the converted sleeping bays announced that the refectory was open. The Winnarans joined the hundreds of other transportees in the long hall, finding a block of tables near its center. On Vexar's instructions they kept together but were soon garnering attention regardless. The place was boisterous as the laborers met and got to know one another.

It was mostly good natured, though Vexar noted the cold glances a small band of Letnev gave them from across the eatery, and one human got into a spirited argument with Kazi over how many shares they'd been promised in their contract. Most were just curious about the Winnarans and repeated things the Hacan had said – there weren't many this far out, and there were the usual jibes about the old empire and Winnaran loyalties.

The Resurrectionists were experienced in playing the part of the disaffected. They smiled and laughed and feigned outrage over the old suggestions that they were all imperialists and wept for the deaths of those who had once been masters of their parents and grandparents, and the dinner hour largely passed in good spirits.

On the third day-cycle out of Quinz 11, Vexar approached the stranger. She was sitting in the place she had taken every time he had seen her, alone at a table in the refectory's far corner. He took his ration tray and set it down across from her before taking a seat. She looked up, and for a second, he saw annoyance and concern. Then, she smiled.

"I hope I'm not imposing," he said.

"Of course not," she replied. "I was actually thinking of coming over to you. I could use some company. I haven't spoken to anyone for days."

"What about your companions?"

Her expression remained unchanged, though there was a flash of something in her eyes.

"My companions?" she repeated, levelly.

"The three you signed on with. The Hacan who recruited us mentioned there was another Winnaran on the voyage, and that she had signed up herself and three others. Sorry, I just assumed they were Winnaran as well."

"Oh, they pulled. I managed to get the recruiter to redact their sections on the contract. Lucky, or I'd have to be working quadruple hours!"

"For quadruple shares at least." He smiled.

"I'm Mortalia," she said, tipping her head in a belated greeting.

She hadn't given her full name, which was a bit odd, but Vexar understood caution. "My name is Vexar. It's good to meet you." He took a bite of his food. "I don't mean to pry, Mortalia. It's just you're the only other Winnaran on board outside our group, and I felt like I should say hello."

"That's good of you. You all seem very popular with the rest of the passengers."

"Not all of them," Vexar said with a wry smile, nodding toward the Letnev. Mortalia followed the gesture and laughed.

"Well, what's new there?" she said. "The empire might be long gone, but some things never change. The Hylar have the N'orr for enemies, and we're stuck with those pallid bastards."

They shared laughter, and it seemed genuine enough.

"You're welcome to join us any time, not just during mealtimes," Vexar pointed out. "We're all bunked together in Hangar Thirteen."

"Thank you," Mortalia said. "How did you all meet?"

"We were serving as crew on board a merchant cutter from the homeworld," Vexar said. "The homeworld" was how most of their kind referred to the planet of Winnu itself, whether they'd actually been born there or not.

"The trade route got attacked and they decided to cut it. We were laid off. We chose to all stick together – most of us are experienced crewmembers, bridge and upper deck kind of work. One thing led to another, and we ended up out here."

"So why Gamma Eridius?"

"Aurei." Vexar shrugged, trying to sound nonchalant. "What about you? Why did your companions leave you?"

"We were never particularly close. I guess they got cold feet. They reckon there are better routes back to the core."

"Well, heading farther out to get back in doesn't sound like it makes much sense," Vexar admitted. "It can't be easy, though, being one of us and traveling out here alone."

"You get used to it," Mortalia said. "And I know how to handle myself."

"I don't doubt it. Come on over?"

"I'm finished," Mortalia said, tapping her fork against her near-empty tray. "But next time. It'll be good to be with fellow Winnarans again."

Mortalia was as good as her word, sitting amongst them during the next meal. She smiled, and answered the questions posed to her the way she had with Vexar, but other than that didn't engage much with those around her.

"Why did you ask her to join us?" Lekaan asked Vexar afterward, when they were back in their bunks in the converted hold.

"You know we reach out to our own, when we can," Vexar said. "And besides, I haven't asked her to join us, not in the proper sense. She doesn't know anything, besides that we're a group of Winnarans working for the Hacan, much as she is."

"I still expected you to be more careful when we're this close," Lekaan responded. "I don't trust her."

"Why not?"

"She's quiet and watchful. She's hiding something."

"So are we."

"That doesn't make us kindred spirits, even if she's Winnaran. This close, we can't afford any mistakes."

Over the next few day-cycles, Vexar carefully probed Mortalia more about her background, trying to get a read on her views. The Resurrectionists were always recruiting, and it could be that they would soon need every friendly Winnaran they could muster. Still, it always had to be circumspect. Lekaan was right – they were so close to success, after all these years, that it would be tragic to endanger it by trusting the wrong person. Still, Vexar didn't find anything untoward. Mortalia seemed naturally reserved, shy almost. She spoke about how her parents had worked for a merchant guild on Tyrella Maxima, and how her grandparents had been minor administrators for the empire. When Vexar lightly pressed her on the subject of the Lazax, she'd been cautious, as he expected. No Winnaran wanted to out themselves as loyal to the Lazax amongst uncertain company, even other Winnarans. But there had been something there – she had quietly said that, from everything she had heard, her family had been happier and more prosperous living under the imperium.

They closed in on Gamma Eridius, and covert preparations for their arrival intensified. The plan was multifaceted, and delicate. Lekaan and a small section would slip away from the rest of the workforce as early as possible and spread out as they hunted for any hint of what they were searching for. Vexar would do the same amongst those working for the Hacan on the surface. Once contact was made, they would pass word back to the other group and rejoin after Vexar's team had deserted from the labor force.

To survive away from the work sites Lekaan's group would need supplies, a problem solved by the unscrupulous nature of those Magnate Akenzi had hired. The Resurrectionists had pooled the last of their cred resources to bribe one of the quartermasters and had stashed ration packs and survival gear in one of the unused holds, as well as a containment crate that would be among those transported to the surface when they arrived.

It was all going to plan, and in the final days of approach Vexar kept returning to two questions – what would they do if he was wrong, and Gamma Eridius was deserted? Or, even more overwhelming, what would they do if he was right?

Then, during meal break just hours after starting in-system deceleration, Lekaan disappeared.

CHAPTER EIGHTEEN
Macro Freighter B9-09, the Boreas Gap

Lekaan skipped the start of dinner. She waited just round the corner from one of the holds being used as a bunk berth, listening to the chatter of its inhabitants as they headed to the refectory. One was absent, as it almost always was at this time. Mortalia, for all that she now joined her fellow Winnarans in the hall, always either arrived later or left early, and always ate quickly – in fact, Lekaan sometimes doubted she ate much at all. A few days earlier she had noticed her stashing nutrient bars from her tray in her clothing.

Lekaan didn't like her one bit. What Vexar seemed to ascribe to shyness or a reserved nature, she saw as something sinister. There was a furtiveness about the lone Winnaran, and a falseness in her expressions. Her smile never quite reached her eyes.

The Resurrectionists had encountered plenty of dangerous and devious individuals down the years, including fellow Winnaran. It had been a mistake befriending Mortalia, even if she didn't yet know the true reason for their voyage to Gamma Eridius, and Lekaan had told Vexar as much. He had barely listened. His mind seemed wholly occupied by what awaited them, and in a sense Lekaan didn't blame him. It would be easy to overlook a quiet individual like Mortalia.

But Lekaan had no intention of allowing her to slide under the scanner. She wanted to know where she'd taken those ration bars, and why she spent barely half the allotted time in the refectory. Was she hoarding things for her own unscheduled trip to the surface?

She waited until the crowd from the hold Mortalia was bunking in had gone, and then waited some more, until she heard lone footsteps. After making sure they were receding in the opposite direction, she snatched a glance round the corner.

She had been right. Mortalia was heading off, alone, and as Lekaan watched she saw the other Winnaran take a right turn, in the opposite direction from the food hall.

She began to follow.

Her sense of unease grew as she realized Mortalia was headed to the supposedly deserted holds, one of which held the supplies the Resurrectionists had been secretly amassing. Was she stealing from them? Tampering with them? Only Vexar and the quartermaster had the swipe-idents necessary to enter that hold, or so the latter had claimed. What if the corrupt Hacan had sold access to Mortalia?

She followed the Winnaran at a distance, usually keeping one corner behind so she wouldn't be seen if she turned, tracking her by the sounds of her footsteps on the decking plates.

She was relieved when Mortalia reached the hold they had secretly requisitioned and carried on past it without stopping. She didn't go far though. There was another berth beyond it, a storage unit, smaller than the cavernous holds on either side. Mortalia disappeared inside – there was an access hatch but no door, so nothing to lock in her wake. Lekaan pursued silently, her heart beginning to race.

She hesitated before reaching the opening, listening. There were faint noises from within, barely audible over the vibrations of the engines, the hum of air recyc and the creaking hull.

Lekaan dared to lean past the hatchway, trying to get a glimpse of what was happening. The storage space was dimly lit and packed with crates, but she could see Mortalia at the far end, conversing with someone.

She couldn't understand what was being said, but it seemed like an argument. Mortalia gestured sharply, and as she half pointed back toward the hatch, the movement allowed Lekaan to see who she was talking to.

At first, she thought it was a child. The figure was short and slender, only coming up a little past Mortalia's waist. Its body was lightly clad in dark leathers and webbing straps. Its ears were pointed, and its head shaved but for a short topknot. Its eyes were large and pitch-black.

Lekaan saw it and recognized it and, at the same time, realized that if she could see it, it could also see her.

For a short, breathless moment, the pair stared at one another across the length of the storage berth. Mortalia began to fully turn, and as she did so Lekaan managed to throw herself away from the hatch.

She stood with her back to the wall, shaking with a violent rush of adrenaline, wondering if Mortalia had seen her too, wondering also whether she was right about what she had just witnessed – a Winnaran talking to a Yssaril.

The diminutive green species were well known in certain parts of the galaxy. They worked as spies and assassins with few peers. Most infamously, they had been employed by the Barony of Letnev in the early days of the empire's fall, as the Lazax imperium was crumbling, used to hasten that deadly decline. They were dreaded by Winnarans, who had suffered at their hands along with their former masters.

But not, it seemed, by Mortalia.

She heard her call out from inside the berth.

"Lekaan?"

She'd seen her. She had to go.

Lekaan began to run, back along the corridor, toward the refectory. She heard Mortalia calling out again, but Lekaan kept going without looking back.

At one point the Resurrectionists had been stalked by a Yssaril. It had killed one of them, and had alerted its masters – in this case, the Letnev – to their existence, at the time investigating stories of the Lazax's presence in the Jenard asteroid field. They had been hunted right across the sector and had only escaped after one member of the group sacrificed themselves by luring the little green killer into an escape pod on the *Grand Dominion* and launching it.

If even one of them was on board the macro freighter, every member of the Resurrectionists was in grave danger. She had to warn Vexar.

She was almost at the junction that led alternately to the bunk holds and the eating hall. That was when the hatch in front of her levered shut with a thud, seemingly automatically. She hit the release button, then pounded at it frantically when it refused to budge, shouting.

Nothing. She heard footsteps behind her and turned at bay, terrified, wishing she had a pistol, anything at all she could use to defend herself.

Mortalia stood before her, expression dispassionate. The Yssaril were with her, not just the one Lekaan had seen in the storage berth, but two others as well. The trio stood behind Mortalia, and she kept them warded away with a half-raised arm. They looked almost like children, glaring at her maliciously, but Lekaan knew they were anything but.

"Why did you follow me?" Mortalia demanded.

"Curiosity," Lekaan said. Just speaking the word gave her a

newfound strength. She was cornered, and defiance was all she had left. She wouldn't cower before this traitor.

"Does anyone know you're here?"

"They all do. I was sent by Vexar to keep an eye on you."

"I think you're lying. That's a risk I'm willing to take."

"Stay away from them. We've dealt with creatures like those before."

She gestured at one of the Yssaril and it smiled impishly up at her, an unsettling experience.

"You're imperialists, aren't you?" Mortalia asked. "Your partner has been quite guarded about it, but some of your other companions less so."

"We want what's best for all Winnarans," Lekaan said defensively. To her surprise, Mortalia scoffed.

"You think being bound to a crumbling empire, forced to bow and scrape for arrogant fools and being despised by the rest of the galaxy, is what's best for all Winnarans?" she asked.

"I think it's self-evident that what we had is better than what we've got," Lekaan shot back. "And I think I'd rather die than turn to hunting other Winnarans."

"I'm not hunting Winnarans," Mortalia said. "I'm trying to do us all a favor."

There was a sudden shudder, running through the cold duranium at Lekaan's back. Her heart leapt as she thought that the hatch was being reactivated and opened, but then she felt the tremor under her feet as well and saw the lights that ran the length of the corridor dim before regaining full power.

"You're here for them, aren't you?" Lekaan asked, deciding that playing for time was her only hope. "You're looking for the last of the Lazax."

"Much the same as you and your little band," Mortalia said. "They're on Gamma Eridius, aren't they?"

"If I knew, I wouldn't tell you."

"You've come all this way without a more specific location?"

"And you haven't?"

Lekaan wondered how much Mortalia knew and wasn't admitting to, and realized she was probably thinking the same thing about her.

"You shouldn't have followed me," Mortalia said coldly.

The corridor shook again, this time more violently. Mortalia stumbled, and Lekaan seized her chance. She snatched at the treacherous Winnaran, trying to grab her by the throat and pin her close, hoping she could at least convince the Yssaril to unlock the door.

Mortalia punched her. Lekaan thumped back against the hatch, her jaw aching. She realized too late that she was outmatched. The other Winnaran had one hand around her throat and the other pinning her right wrist against the bare metal at her back, her eyes fierce.

"Wrong move," she said.

There was a third tremor, followed by an ear-splitting wail as alarms began to clatter, making them both flinch and causing the Yssaril to hiss.

"Something's... something's wrong," Lekaan managed to pant through the chokehold.

"I know," Mortalia said. "Which is why we've talked enough. I'm sorry."

She let go of Lekaan, turned, and nodded to the Yssaril.

"What's happening?" Vexar shouted to Kazi as an alarm in the refectory began to clatter. Conversations ended and heads turned as the diners looked for the source of the sudden, ear-aching commotion.

Kazi had no idea and admitted as much over the noise. Throughout the hall people discarded their utensils and rose.

A voice cut in over the discord, an automated tone repeated from the speakers that usually heralded the start and end of the meal period.

"All passengers return immediately to your bunk hold. This is not a drill. Repeat, all passengers return immediately to your bunk hold. This is not a drill. Repeat–"

"Let's go," Vexar called to the rest of the Winnarans, most of whom were now looking uncertainly at him. The refectory was already emptying as other passengers hurried for the hatches. A table was overturned, half-finished slop spattering across the floor. Vexar felt a rising sense of panic.

"Keep together," he said to the Resurrectionists as he led them out, looking for Lekaan as they went. It took a few moments to realize there was no sign of her.

"Where's Lekaan?" he called over the continued racket. "Who saw her last? Was she in the hall?"

No one seemed to think she had been. Vexar kept ushering them back toward the hold, and that was when he noticed Mortalia falling in with them.

"Have you seen Lekaan?" he shouted to her as they were carried along. She tapped her ear, indicating she couldn't hear him, but just then the alarms finally cut off.

The rush of bodies heading to the hold faltered as everyone wondered what had happened, and whether whatever emergency had triggered the systems was now over.

It seemed not. A voice crackled over the speakers, not an automated tone, but the panicked growl of a Hacan.

"All hands, brace for impact!"

CHAPTER NINETEEN

The Rising Sands, Magnate Akenzi's Flagship, above Gamma Eridius, the Boreas Gap

Akenzi wished his father had come with him to Gamma Eridius.

He had not felt so isolated in a very long time. For so long now every problem he had faced had been one within his capacity to solve. He was a Hacan trader, born and bred, and it felt as though he'd been wrangling deals, assessing risks and making sure the accounts were in the green since he'd been old enough to grow a mane. He'd already dealt with almost everything he'd encountered in the years of preparation before – the Gamma Eridius expedition meant it was simply happening on a grand scale, and he relished the challenge.

But not anymore. He could never have predicted the venture would collide with the last of the Lazax. That wasn't something any amount of past experience could prepare him for.

"Try to think of it like any other trade bargain," Drusha pointed out when Akenzi, in a moment of weakness, found himself admitting all his troubles to his big brother, back on board the *Rising Sands*.

"That's what it is, when you strip it all down," the former ordri warrior said. "You're negotiating, and you're normally good at that. You've bought yourself a little time. Now do what you need to do."

Akenzi decided his brother was right. He was overawed by circumstances, by the fact that he had unwittingly found the last fragment of the old empire at his mercy. The weight of history and the power of the fates were conspiring to make him think he was helpless, but the opposite was true. He was in control.

While he considered his options in his private cabin, a call came from Marzek over the ship's intercom. The scanners had detected a problem, apparently, and it was recommended he attend the bridge.

Akenzi did so, hardly daring to consider what fresh catastrophe might be waiting for him. The bridge was quiet and empty but for Marzek, Drusha and the actual crew – Akenzi had made sure his business associates were politely confined to their cabins, where they would be unaware of any further developments and, even more importantly, wouldn't be capable of transmitting any messages concerning wayward Lazax to courier ships or system transmission buoys. He was still conducting damage control and was dreading having to meet with them again in an effort to keep them all on one side, but that was a problem for another day-cycle.

"What is it?" he demanded as he swept onto the bridge.

"One of our macro freighters has arrived on the system's edge," Marzek said, the green glow of the holo display underlighting his features and making his scarred muzzle look even craggier and fiercer. "But we're picking up contacts closing in from multiple angles, mostly from the debris fields, here and here."

He indicated a few areas on the display, and Akenzi noticed the barb-like red markers closing in on the representation of the freighter.

"Pirates," he growled.

"Yes. We've got two escorts inbound to link up with the freighter, but they likely won't be enough. I recommend we redeploy our void assets immediately."

That was the last thing Akenzi wanted to hear. If they left Gamma Eridius for the system's edges, it would give the Lazax a free run at escaping, assuming the ships Vel Syd had mentioned were close by.

"What's the freighter carrying?" he asked, reaching up and tapping the air where the holo representation of the spaceship hung. It unfolded with a description of its contents.

"The first wave of workers after the advance parties," Marzek said. "Right on schedule. We thought we'd have the system safely locked down by now."

"And instead, we're debating what to do with rogue Lazax," Akenzi said bitterly, reviewing exactly what the macro freighter – B9-09 – was lugging. "All right. We can't afford to lose that cargo, not if we want to have the slightest hope of starting extraction on time and not running up costs that'll take years to pay off. Issue orders to the rest of the expedition and order a full military redeployment toward that freighter's location. Us as well."

Marzek hesitated.

"There's little reason to endanger yourself, my magnate," he said. "This could well be a trap. It is likely the pirates are operating from those debris fields, and there are probably more of them in there."

"The *Rising Sands* isn't a pleasure craft," Akenzi snapped, in no mood for any more hesitation. "We have shields and guns. This is the second finest vessel belonging to Clan Muktat, and I will not cower before any pirate scum! Send the transmission, and helmsman, plot a course!"

...

The pirates fell upon Macro Freighter B9-09. They had been lurking in the great expanse of void debris that filled one of the system's outer quadrants, close to the most direct route toward the Gap. It was an ideal ambush location, and it would take time for the Hacan to clear it.

There were four vessels involved in the attack. Three were modified civilian ships, all once trade luggers that had been refitted for piratical purposes, with enhanced engine blocks, extra shield layering and cargo holds replaced by weapons batteries. The fourth, the most dangerous, was an old Sol Federation corvette, salvaged from the scrap fields of Bothen and brought back up to full technical capacity. Renamed the *Star Hunter*, it led the attack on B9-09.

The macro freighter's captain, Huresh, had the good sense to trigger his shields as soon as unknown markers appeared on his scanners. He had made runs through contested space before and had been warned by the Muktat to expect trouble as soon as he passed through the Gap. Splitting power between engines and shields, he ordered his big, unlovely transporter to hold course for Gamma Eridius.

The first lance beam from the *Star Hunter* struck the freighter's port side. Energy flared, dispersing in a ferocious flash. B9-09 carried on.

The *Star Hunter* swept toward its rear and crossed behind it, unleashing more lance shots that flashed against the freighter's shields like miniature solar flares. The corvette crossed B9-09's rear and began pounding its starboard side, trying to force it to veer to port and driving it into the guns of the trio of slower-moving ex-luggers.

Huresh held his nerve. In decades gone by, ships such as his would have been easy prey, but every merchant and commerce shipper worth his aurei had invested heavily in shields, engines and armor plating – the galaxy was a deadly place for those carrying cargo and buying gear that would once have been considered military-grade paid dividends.

The luggers finally heaved into range and began adding their firepower to the cruiser's lashing. Now the freighter started to struggle. Unable to maintain shields on both port and starboard, the former dropped, allowing the crude beam turrets the luggers were sporting to begin pounding the hull.

As much as the pirates' natural inclinations were to board and seize the vessel, their orders were to destroy it – they had been promised more aurei than its cargo was worth. All they had to do was wreck it before the Hacan fleet, which had broken from orbit above Gamma Eridius, intercepted them.

Huresh ordered a desperate evasive maneuver – a port oblique, one that lengthened the course to Gamma Eridius, but also caused the luggers to adjust their own heading to keep abreast with their prey, and likewise made the corvette on the other side adopt a wider outward arc, one that brought it closer to the oncoming Muktat ships.

The commander of the corvette, frustrated, tried to get in closer, desperate to rip away the starboard shields. They finally overloaded, and the next lance strike seared a hole in B9-09's aft section, dangerously close to the primary engine block.

Huresh altered course again. The great freighter swung ponderously back to starboard, tacking close to the corvette, which was forced to turn away or risk a disastrous collision with the much larger ship. For a moment the corvette's lance was silent, and by the time it had come back around to bring B9-09 into its arc of fire, the shields were back up.

Huresh ordered his subordinates to cut the engines and divert what power remained to the shields.

All they could do now was try to hold on until the Muktat arrived.

"It must be pirates," Kazi said for the umpteenth time.

"There's no point in speculating until we know more," Vexar pointed out, trying not to lose his temper.

They had been confined to their bunk room. The primary lighting had blinked off as well, reduced to nothing more than the wan emergency strips running underfoot. The hull around them groaned and creaked, interspersed with the odd, powerful tremor. It was claustrophobic, unsettling, and the added stress of not knowing what had happened to Lekaan was almost more than Vexar could take. Only the sight of how badly the other Winnarans were struggling kept him strong. He had to remain focused, for them.

Another impact shook the hold. The rest of its inhabitants didn't seem to be in a much better way. Most of them were on their bunks, clutching the sides, pale or wide-eyed. Some were crying, others muttering to themselves or to each other. Earlier a Saar had thrown up in the corner, and the stench in the sealed space was almost enough to make Vexar want to heave as well.

He focused on controlling his breathing – as Lekaan had once taught him – and thinking rationally. There was nothing they could do to affect whatever was happening to the ship. What mattered right now was keeping everyone else calm.

"Every storm must pass," he told the Winnarans clustered around him, trying to meet each gaze in turn as he repeated one of the old Resurrectionist phrases. "Endure and keep the faith."

"Hit that corvette," Akenzi shouted, gesturing furiously at the pirate vessel whose lance strikes were boring into the macro freighter's flank.

"In range in thirty," Marzek said tersely. "Primed and ready."

Akenzi struggled not to snap uselessly at the master-at-arms. This was his first time in a naval battle, and it felt unbearably frustrating. Though he knew the *Rising Sands* was almost burning out its engines in its efforts to reach B9-09, everything still felt achingly, unbearably slow. It was all he could do not to pace from one control station to the next, demanding continuous updates.

Patience. He could almost hear his father admonishing him. He wouldn't behave like this during the tense moments of a trade deal, so why did he think it was acceptable to act this way during a battle? He forced himself to stay fixed to one point on the bridge deck and wait.

After all, thirty seconds was no time at all.

The *Rising Sands* fired on the *Star Hunter*. The shot was a good one, calculated to perfection by the former's gunnery computators. The white beam hit the pirate corvette's prow, and though its shields earthed the damage, they were almost overloaded by the single hit.

Almost immediately all four pirate ships set new courses, ones that would take them out of the engagement zone. They may well have been able to overwhelm B9-09's shields before the Hacan fleet struck, but to do that they'd be risking their own annihilation, and none of them had come to Gamma Eridius to die.

There was a fifth vessel in the pirate fleet, its flagship, the *Reiver's Son*. It was another former Sol Federation war vessel, a capital ship no less, and the pride of the vagabond fleet's leader, Captain Bazishel. Yet it had not committed to the attack. Bazishel had been advised to do so by the figure currently sharing her bridge as a guest, but she had refused. The *Reiver's Son* was her top card, and she would not lay it out on the deck just yet. There would be a time for that, she assured her benefactor.

So, the four pirate ships turned away before the Hacan onslaught, following the nav-markers they had seeded through the debris field, slipping back into the jagged cloud of drifting rock and flaring gas and vanishing from the Hacan's sensors.

"We should pursue them," Akenzi growled, glaring at the retreating markers on the holo.

"Unwise," Drusha said, and a sweep of Marzek's tail showed his agreement.

"We still don't know how many assets they have in the debris field," the master-at-arms added. "The best strategy would be to sweep it methodically." Akenzi growled again but said nothing more. He was being impulsive, which wasn't like him. What would his father do at a moment like this?

"Order all ships to break off pursuit and rally on the macro freighter," he said eventually. "See it safely through to Gamma Eridius. And tell them to get ferrying their cargo to the surface immediately! Regardless of what we do with the Lazax, we need to try to keep everything else on schedule."

CHAPTER TWENTY

Gamma Eridius, the Boreas Gap

For the first time since the enclave had made the decision to settle on Gamma Eridius, Ibna Vel Syd called for a meeting of the council.

Tol and her fellow Hylar joined the gathering in the circular hut that had been built to accommodate such an event. It had been constructed in one of the small clearings and had rather grandly been described by Marchu Mal Serrus as a center of government and administration.

It had turned out that the enclave hadn't needed such thorough oversight, and Vel Syd, in his mounting lethargy, hadn't seen fit to call a full council meeting since its establishment. The doorways had been boarded up and had to be pried open with crowbars and the inside swept of cobwebs and vermin droppings before the council filed into its musty interior.

All of it happened under the fierce gaze of the Hacan guarding the settlement. Tol had noted that some, including the brutal-looking beast who commanded them, seemed to have departed, but enough had been left to keep guard on the edges of the hut clusters. They had at least been convinced by Vel Syd to remain outside the council building.

Tol knew there was nothing they could do about the unwelcome presence, not until they formulated a coherent response. At the very least, the incursion seemed to have roused Vel Syd.

The council – consisting of a trio from the enclave's notable Hylar population, the eldest human, and the fourteen most senior Lazax – stood in the circle of light shafting down through the spherical hole in the building's thatch roof. There was nothing perfunctory about the meeting. Vel Syd, leaning heavily on his staff, spoke.

"I have conversed with the Hacan," he declared. "Their magnate, Akenzi, is a member of the United Emirates. He is young and perhaps overconfident but seems to have his wits about him. He claims to have come here seeking to mine Gamma Eridius for resources and establish a trade route through the Boreas Gap. He did not expect to encounter us. I believe him, though I do not believe his promise not to destroy us at will."

"That's reassuring," Tol said dryly.

"It is intolerable," one of the other Lazax, Eshkar, exclaimed. She had been a child during the flight from Mecatol Rex, and was now counted amongst the enclave's elders, though she still seemed positively youthful when compared to Marchu or the melding of wizened flesh and gleaming chromatics and synth-plasts that Vel Syd had become.

"We are discovered, and by one of the major powers," Eshkar went on. "Flight is our only hope now."

There were murmurs of agreement, until Vel Syd responded.

"That is true, of course. But it doesn't explain to us just how we might undertake that flight. You need only glance outside to see that they have us cornered."

There was a brief silence, and Tol suspected they were all thinking the same thing – could they fight their way out? The enclave had little in the way of weaponry. Tol had no doubt some among the Lazax and even the humans were still bold enough to want to try, but no one was foolish enough to suggest it.

"Negotiation is our only way out," Vel Syd declared, perhaps louder than was necessary. "The Hacan come here for profit, not mass murder. That is not their way."

"Have you seen the state of the galaxy lately?" Tol said. "I'm sure the Hacan are doing their fair share of killing."

Vel Syd shot her a look, his one organic eye filled with annoyance, and Tol felt a flare of satisfaction. She knew she was wrong to bait the old Lazax, but it came naturally to her now. She had grown bitter.

"The Hacan have problems of their own here," Vel Syd elaborated. "And I hope that we can be of some service in remedying them. In exchange, they will allow us to go untroubled and will say nothing of our presence here."

"You really trust them not to spread word of our existence?" another Lazax, Kyreel, asked. He was second generation, one of the youngest Lazax members of the council.

"No, but word will take time to reach anyone of consequence, provided it isn't sent by the magnate himself. I doubt he will do that. It risks unmaking all his efforts to establish an outpost here."

"But how?" the only human present, an elderly woman named Tyrisha, asked. "You're saying the Hacan will let us go if we help them against these pirates. We have three old star craft and little else. The Hacan must have better ships. What can we do to the pirates that they are not already capable of?"

Ibna Vel Syd told them his plan and, in the aftermath, asked for them to vote on his proposal. Few of those present liked his idea, but no one was able to articulate an alternative. Tol grudgingly agreed with the reality of the situation – the only way out would be if they could make themselves in some way valuable to the Hacan.

The plan was approved, and the council dismissed. All left bar Tol, who asked Ibna to remain with her a moment longer.

"You'll want me with you when the time comes," she surmised, a statement rather than a question.

"There will be bloodshed, violence," Ibna said, his tone guarded. "So I would appreciate the assistance of the best doctor in the enclave. I will make no commandments though. I am too old and tired to order you to do anything."

"We both know that isn't true," Tol said. "But regardless, I have a request."

"Speak it."

"I will come with you on this last effort, for the good of the enclave, and to honor the vows I made over a century ago, to help those in need. Afterward, though, I wish to remain behind."

"You wish to remain on Gamma Eridius?" Ibna asked, his tone sharp.

"Yes. I am done running."

They both knew what that meant. Rondu and Zeth might remain with the enclave, but without their senior doctor, the medical work keeping Ibna fully functional would become more difficult, more fraught. In the past, when Tol had broached the prospect of leaving, Ibna had angrily pointed out that if she did so, she was condemning him to death. Fear of breaking the vows that had held her life together had caused Tol to relent every time. But even her conscience had been eroded. She had promised to protect and preserve life, but she hadn't promised to make anyone immortal.

"You know I will not be able to continue without you–" Ibna began, and Tol felt a surge of revulsion, disgusted at the fact that he was going to once more attempt to shame her into staying, into sacrificing what little of herself remained.

"You will have Rondu and Zeth," she told him. "I am not a Lazax. I am not your subject either. Your empire is dead, Ibna. Fallen and burned up and gone. Ashes scattered across ten thousand worlds. You won't bring it back. The last of your people will wither and die and be consigned to history annals and datacore repositories. That is inevitable, whether you keep running or meet your fate here."

Tol had half expected the harsh words to draw a cold reaction from Ibna, but she wasn't fully prepared for what happened next.

The old Lazax moved toward her with a surety she had rarely seen in recent years. His face was lost in the old room's darkness, but his cybernetic optic gleamed with unblinking, mechanical intensity.

Tol's crest rippled with instinctive fear, and she brought a hand up, as if to ward away a blow she realized would surely not come. Ibna had stopped. His face was still in darkness. Tol stood her ground.

The words, when they came, were not as sharp as she had expected.

"All empires fall," the Lazax murmured quietly. "It is the cycle of things. The natural, inevitable order."

"And it's time to accept that," Tol said, composure recovered, angry at herself for having shown weakness in front of him. It was true that there was a shadow on his soul now, a blight that she feared had been allowed to take hold and fester over the past decades. She would not let him know that sometimes, she feared what he might be becoming.

"Whether you're ready or not, I have," she went on. "I said that I'd make a home here, and I intend to stand by that. I'm not leaving, and you cannot make me."

"Very well," Ibna said, stepping away, back into the light. "I will not give up on my people, on the task I set all those years ago. But nor will I force you to continue on this journey. I accept your decision, Harial Tol."

She pondered his apparent surrender. She knew better than anyone how manipulative he could be, when he needed to be. Was that it, then? She supposed she would find out sooner rather than later.

"We need your help," Ibna declared. "One more time. Will you take Rondu down to the ship?"

"I will," Tol affirmed. "Just tell me when you're ready."

The macro freighter B9-09 began to unload its cargo above Gamma Eridius.

Hacan deckhands saw the bunk holds emptied, and the passengers ferried to the shuttle bays. Vexar did his best to delay the Winnarans' move. He was still searching desperately for Lekaan. She wouldn't have abandoned the cause this close to fruition. She wouldn't have abandoned *him*.

But she was nowhere to be found. None of the non-Winnaran passengers or even the deckhands he'd dared question had seen any sign of her. She had simply disappeared. Vexar was sure something bad had happened to her.

Down in the shuttle bays, as they queued to enter the vibrating old transporters waiting for them at the air lock, Vexar broke ranks to speak to one of the Hacan on duty beside the main hatch.

"We can't go to the surface yet," he told the Hacan. "One of my group is missing."

"What do you mean, 'missing'?" the felid demanded.

"Just that! She disappeared around the time we came under attack. We've searched all the bunk holds, but we need the crew's help to check the storage facilities, the underwalks, the empty bays. She might have become locked in or trapped somewhere."

"That isn't my problem," the Hacan said, baring his fangs, but Vexar refused to be cowed.

"It's about to be," he said. "I want to speak to your superior. Where's the ship's captain?"

"You think he cares about one missing Winnaran?" the Hacan replied aggressively. "Do you know how close we came to annihilation after we decelerated in-system? If it wasn't for the captain, we'd all be drifting space dust right now. You're cargo, nothing more. Now get on that sand-blasted shuttle!"

Vexar was about to snap back when a hand on his shoulder tugged at him, pulling him away. It was Kazi.

"We can't afford this," she said urgently, holding Vexar's angry gaze. "We're too close! Whatever has happened to Lekaan, she'd want us to carry on. That's what we promised to each other, isn't it? That the quest comes ahead of any one individual?"

"You go," Vexar said, yanking out of Kazi's grip. "You know the operation. Take over. I'll stay here and find Lekaan."

"It's too risky," Kazi said, her voice tinged with anger now. "You're going to get the Hacan asking questions. They won't let you stay on board either. You're risking everything!"

Vexar was about to snap back at her when he noticed that another Hacan, an overseer judging by his clothing, had joined the one he had been speaking to. They were now both conversing. Ignoring Kazi's pleas, he swept back over to them.

"What's the issue?" the overseer demanded.

"We've got a member of our group missing," Vexar said. "She disappeared when the freighter came under attack. We've been looking for her ever since, but we can't find her anywhere."

"I can convince the captain to scan the ship," the Hacan said. "He won't want any stowaways. But it will take time, and nobody's going to want to delay the landings while we do that. It'll probably need to be conducted while we head out-system. Time is money."

"I can help you look," Vexar said, knowing he sounded desperate.

"No, you won't. You're under contract, you and all your kind. You're going to the surface, and you're going now, because this shuttle is burning through fuel waiting for you. If you don't, you'll be put in the brig, and then offloaded at the first opportunity. This isn't a pleasure cruiser. This ship is the captain's property, and you're its cargo."

"What will you do with her if you find her?" Vexar asked, knowing everything the overseer had said was true. He had no standing here, no power at all.

"Put her in the brig. Don't worry, Winnaran, we're coming back. Once we're refueled at Amistal, we're voyaging back to Gamma Eridius to take on the first extraction loads. We're as much bound to a contract as you. So, if she's on board, we'll find her, and she'll end up down there like the rest of you in a few months' time."

Vexar couldn't tell if he was merely being placated. He looked at Kazi, and she nodded.

"She'd want us to go, and you know it," the other Winnaran repeated.

Vexar was out of options. He couldn't let the Hacan hold him on the ship, not when all they had worked toward might now be lying just below them.

"Fine," he said, the words tasting bitter. "Let's go."

The labor force was ferried via big, brute haulage transports from B9-09 down to the primary surface camp. It was a place of bare necessities and bustling activity. Rows of prefab structures had been established across a plateau just a little inland from an ocean expanse. There were living blocks and an eatery, storage units, a fuel and motor pool, a comms hub and a medical center. The place swarmed with new arrivals, most of them lugging endless crates and filling flatbed cargo rollers, ferrying gear and supplies up from the disembarkation points. The air was full of the stink of fuel and the vibrating roar of transporters as a constant stream came and went from the plasma-scorched landing fields.

To Vexar's relief, the Resurrectionists were kept together for the time being, assigned to help unpack the rollers at the camp and facilitate the distribution of their contents.

He tried to get a feel for where they'd touched down. Gamma Eridius's soil was dark and tough, its skies leaden, its winds sharp and clear. The planet had a wild air to it. Vexar suspected he would have felt a thrill of adventure as he surveyed the sweep of the green-gray landscape beyond the plateau's edge, but his mind was still occupied with thoughts of Lekaan, and with the momentousness of what they now faced.

Despite the loss, they continued to work toward the plan. The former passengers of B9-09 weren't the camp's only inhabitants – it had been established and occupied by the venture's advanced elements, which included a workforce every bit as diverse as the new arrivals. The Resurrectionists spread among them in the first few days, learning what they could.

It rapidly became apparent that the attack on the macro freighter hadn't been an isolated incident. Rumors were rife. Apparently, the expedition had run into multiple difficulties, all more serious than mere matters of logistics. Pirates were plaguing the system. Those who had been with the advance party told of how entire ships had been lost in a clash that had bordered on becoming a fully fledged naval battle when they had first arrived in-system.

Some claimed the danger of raiders and space-banditry, bad as it was, still wasn't the most pressing concern the Hacan were facing. There had been a huge amount of activity to the northwest, including military fliers. Supposedly the Hacan had discovered one of the pirate bases planetside, though others said there was something else out there, along the wooded ridgeline.

Vexar didn't like to speculate too much on what that something might be. If the Hacan had found the Lazax already, the Resurrectionists might already be too late. What mattered was getting out there and finding out for themselves.

Bit by bit, Vexar disseminated a new plan among his fellow believers. Rather than break in two, they would leave the camp together and strike out for the ridgeline where everyone seemed to think the Hacan had stumbled across something major. If it wasn't related to the Lazax, they would be free to begin searching elsewhere. If it was, well, that was when the real work would begin.

The day before the Resurrectionists were scheduled to make their move, Vexar modified the plan. Mortalia came and spoke with him, while he was busy packing his rucksack in the dorm room they shared in one of the prefabs. Apart from the two of them it was empty, and he realized she had probably been waiting for a moment to catch him alone.

"You're Resurrectionists, right?" she asked him.

He blinked in surprise and cast a hasty glance up and down the rows of bunk beds, fearful of being overheard.

"I'm sorry, I know I shouldn't be talking about it like this," Mortalia went on. "But… that's what you are, right?"

"Who would claim something like that?" Vexar asked cautiously. He hadn't spoken much with Mortalia since they had made planetfall. She had gone back to keeping to herself, and there had been so much going on that in truth, he'd almost forgotten about her.

"I overheard some things," she admitted. "And the way you talk, I mean about… about the empire and stuff. Look, I'm sorry if I've misunderstood but… I think there's a lot of Winnarans who respect what you do or try to do. And I'm one of them."

Vexar looked at her, trying to gauge her sincerity.

"Everyone's talking about what's out there, beyond the camp," she went on. "I thought maybe you were planning on finding out for yourselves. And I thought this might help."

To Vexar's shock, the other Winnaran drew a short, snub-nosed pistol from her waistband.

"Put it back," he said immediately, terrified in case anyone entered and saw what she was holding. Firearms had been strictly prohibited since the start of the voyage, as per the contract. If the Hacan found someone carrying even a single, small piece, all of them could end up imprisoned and then removed on the next transport.

And yet, a weapon was just one of the tools a few of the Resurrectionists felt could prove useful.

"We're seeking… a higher purpose," he told her eventually, still reluctant to fully admit to being a Resurrectionist. Lekaan had always urged caution. "But we welcome Winnarans with similar views. It isn't easy. Most of us have been together for over a decade, traveling all over the galaxy and enduring all the hardship and struggles that entails."

"I'm not a stranger to those things," Mortalia said firmly.

To Vexar's relief, she put the gun away before continuing.

"All my life, I've never really known peace. Never been able to settle. I knew there had to be something more. Like you said, some purpose. So it would be an honor to join others hunting for that purpose. If you'll have me."

"We'll see," Vexar said, knowing he had brought this on himself. He had been the one who had first sat with her in the refectory. But wasn't it right to include her? It had always been the goal of the Resurrectionists to bring Winnarans together, to unite them in the old cause, the cause of empire. They'd sworn to do that one Winnaran at a time, if necessary, from the homeworld to the edges of existence. Late misgivings or not, it was Vexar's duty to induct Mortalia.

"Keep all this to yourself," he told her. "And wait for the word. When the time comes, I'll make sure you're included."

CHAPTER TWENTY-ONE

GAMMA ERIDIUS, THE BOREAS GAP

It happened two Gamma Eridius day-cycles later.

There were rumors of valuable deposits farther east – tyrentine, osmium or something else, nobody seemed to know – and that was where the first extraction site was being established. Workers and machinery were being ferried out. Whatever problems he was facing elsewhere, Magnate Akenzi wasn't hesitating when it came to securing the planet's natural resources.

The Winnarans were picked for the next group to head east and piled on board one of the all-terrain transporters that were moving most of the workers and supplies while proper roads were still being laid. They were bulky, tracked brutes, each one with a pair of Hacan drivers. Neither of the felids were expecting trouble.

On Vexar's orders, Mortalia held them up with her pistol, not long after the transporter left the camp. The two Hacan were ordered off and left standing angry and disconsolate in the wilderness as Kazi took over the wheel and turned the lumbering engine northwest, toward the ridgeline.

From there on, it was a straight run to the forest. They caught sight of the trees not long before they caught the sound of aircraft above them – it seemed the drivers had made it back to the camp and reported the abscondment.

"On foot from here," Vexar told the Resurrectionists as they arrived at the forest. "The transport won't make it through this kind of terrain, and besides, it'll be harder for them to track us."

They split the supplies they'd smuggled between themselves and piled out of the transporter. Nervous, excited energy suffused everyone. A part of Vexar couldn't believe they had made it this far. They couldn't afford to stop though. Ahead, wilderness beckoned, an uncertainty as profound as anything they had faced over the past decade. And yet, they had hope.

They spent the rest of the day picking their way through the forest, following the western slope of the ridge and keeping the ocean they occasionally glimpsed through the trees to their left. There was constant aerial activity, though it seemed the forest was doing a tolerable job of covering them.

"There's a lot further north," Kazi said during a brief pause in which she climbed as high amongst the prickly branches of one of the pine trees as she dared, getting a better view of the aircraft above. "They're constantly circling there, at least three, I think."

"Then that's where we'll head. But they won't be monitoring that stretch of the ridgeline for no reason. Whatever has spooked the Hacan, it's most likely to be there."

They climbed up onto the ridge's spine as they went. It was tiring going, and Vexar permitted a pause around what he judged to be midday. They rested their legs and ate most of the rations they'd managed to bring. Only a few of the Resurrectionists had any experience with wilderness survival, and Vexar doubted they could go more than a few days before things started to become serious. The thought of having to trudge back and surrender themselves to the Hacan, and likely imprisonment, was intolerable.

They set off again, using the aircraft prowling overhead like guiding stars. Kazi fell in alongside Vexar, speaking softly.

"There's something following us."

"What do you mean?" Vexar asked, confused.

"Don't look up," Kazi urged, voice still low. "But I keep catching movement in the canopy. Something's shadowing us. I saw it while I was up there, a glimpse."

"What does it look like?"

"I'm not sure. Small and fast."

"Local wildlife, surely?"

"I thought this place only had large frogs? And why would wildlife be following us?"

"Just keep going, and keep an eye out," Vexar urged, unwilling to entertain Kazi's worries when they had enough concerns to manage already. "If you spot it again let me know, but don't tell the others."

About a quarter of a day-cycle later one of the Winnarans at the front of the group, Zern, tripped.

The other Resurrectionist in the lead hastily called at the rest to stop. Vexar hurried up to join the pair as Zern was dusting pine needles off his jacket.

He saw immediately what had caused the Winnaran's fall. There was something metallic protruding from the undergrowth. It had been hidden by foliage, but Zern had unwittingly exposed it – a cylindrical device, protruding at knee height from where it had been buried in Gamma Eridius's dark soil. Its shell was studded with glassy nodes, and it was contained in a clear, hard plasticon sheath.

"A sentry beacon," Vexar said, recognizing the device. "But it looks inactive."

"There's another one over here," said the other lead Winnaran, Sarina, who had moved off to the left. She brushed aside a large fernlike plant to expose another of the sensors.

"Maybe the Hacan planted them," Zern said.

"But why out here, and why are they inactive?" Vexar pointed out. "There must be something up ahead."

There was a thrumming sound, echoing down through the jagged branches around them. They all looked up, holding their breath as another Hacan aircraft passed low overhead.

Vexar waved the rest of the group up, speaking quietly but firmly.

"I think we're close. Now more than ever, stick together, keep quiet, and move carefully. And watch where you're stepping."

They pressed farther along the ridge, but didn't get far.

"*Ushun reth,*" snapped a voice from somewhere off to the right. It hadn't belonged to any of the Winnarans.

Vexar didn't know what the exclamation meant, but he recognized it as Hacan. He had time to shout at the others to get down before gunfire ripped apart the tranquil woodland.

He dropped to the ground, hearing as he did the battering report of hard-round rifles, and the thudding and cracking noises made by bullets as they ripped into the trees. A shower of pine needles fell all around them as the salvo ceased. They had been warning shots, fired high into the canopy.

"Get up," the voice that had shouted earlier demanded, this time in univoca. "Get up and get your hands up! You're surrounded!"

This couldn't be happening, Vexar thought. Not after making it this far. The urge to brave the gunfire and try to disappear among the trees was almost overwhelming.

"Everyone keep down," he hissed, knowing running could precipitate a massacre.

"Up," the Hacan roared. Vexar could hear twigs snapping and pine needles rustling around them as figures approached.

"Keep down," he reiterated, looking at Kazi, who was lying next to him. She was terrified, her eyes wide, face ghostlike in the shadows of the forest.

He thought about Mortalia, and her gun. What if she tried to fight back? It could see them all gunned down on the spot.

Slowly, he got to his feet, hands raised.

"Don't shoot," he said to the trio of Hacan he found closing on him from the left and right. They weren't overseers or camp workers – these ones were kitted out in dark fatigues and webbing, optic clusters strapped over their manes and eyes, weapons leveled and steady. They moved with the swift, graceful assurance of warriors, doing what they did best.

"And the rest," one barked. "Up!"

"Not until you promise you won't shoot," Vexar said, knowing it meant little.

"You're not in a position to make demands here, Winnaran," the felid growled.

By now they were practically stepping on the Resurrectionists. Several, in a panic, scrambled to their feet, the Hacan rifles swinging to cover them. In moments, all the Winnarans were rising, clustering fearfully around Vexar.

"Keep calm," he told them all, trying to follow his own advice, searching for Mortalia and making eye contact with her. "Don't do anything stupid. It'll be all right."

The other two Hacan kept their weapons raised as the one who had spoken turned away and delivered what sounded like a terse report into a blocky savant strapped to his upper torso.

"We're unarmed," Vexar said, deciding that was the wisest thing to say at least until they started searching them. "We don't mean anybody any harm."

"That's not the report we've received," the Hacan said, glaring at Vexar. "You held up two drivers back at the camp."

Vexar kept silent. The Hacan's savant clicked with a message that seemed to annoy him. He snapped commands to his two underlings.

"Give up your weapons," he demanded of the Winnarans as the other two moved in, beginning to frisk them.

"We only have one," Vexar said, looking at Mortalia and nodding. "Do as they say."

"Any sudden movements, you die," the Hacan shouted. "All of you!"

Vexar saw that there were figures approaching. Two of them were more armed Hacan, but the one between them wasn't. Vexar's heart started to race.

The middle figure was tall and slender, and moved with the difficulty of the senile. Part of his body was clearly cybernetic in nature. The Winnaran stared, trying to make sure he wasn't mistaken. He was terrified he'd made a mistake, that he was wrong about what he saw.

Yet it was true. The middle figure was a Lazax.

Tears in his eyes, Vexar fell to his knees, and the rest of the Resurrectionists did likewise.

He had rehearsed this moment countless times in his head, but years of preparation, of obsession, fled in the passion of the moment.

"My lord," he found himself saying, eyes still cast down in reverence as the Lazax came to a halt. "We have come home."

PART THREE

CHAPTER TWENTY-TWO

Gamma Eridius, the Boreas Gap

Ibna Vel Syd did his best to mask his contempt as he gazed down on the mass of kneeling Winnarans.

"Rise," he said in univoca, gesturing with one of his free limbs, the cybernetics purring.

The Winnarans scrambled to their feet. They were a sorry-looking lot, grubby and dressed in rough, mismatched clothing. They seemed lost for words, staring with almost childlike awe.

"What is your name?" Ibna asked, deciding to keep things simple.

"Vexar Di Valaniari," the Winnaran who appeared to be their leader replied.

That meant nothing to him. He had been taking the air that afternoon, using the opportunity to stretch stiff limbs while pondering whether he had made the right choice or not, rationalizing his choking fury that plagued him like a sickness, all the while under the watchful gaze of several Hacan guards. Every decision he made now felt like it was somehow conjoined with catastrophe. In the past he had been more decisive, which was part of the reason why he'd almost given up on doing anything in recent years. He felt like a shadow of his former self, cy-implants or not. And he despised such weakness.

That was when gunfire had jolted him out of his thoughts, the sound barking through the craggy trees.

It had galvanized him. He had demanded to know what was happening from his guards, but they had seemed unsure, so he had set off himself and told them that if they wanted to keep watch over him, they'd have to keep up. That, or they could shoot him.

The last thing he had expected to discover was a gaggle of several dozen Winnarans, looking like a school expedition that had gotten lost in the woods.

"I am Ibna Vel Syd," he told Vexar, deciding he was too old for further niceties. "Why are you in this forest?"

"We were looking for you, my lord," Vexar said. "That is to say, we were looking for the Lazax! We are Resurrectionists."

And suddenly it all made sense.

Ibna knew of the Resurrectionists. In the past small numbers of Winnarans had happened across the enclave, professing their loyalty to the Lazax and to the old ideals of empire. They were, in Ibna's view, obsessives or zealots who usually struggled to accept the fate that had befallen his survivors. He did not begrudge them their fantasies of an imperial restoration, for he still clung to that ambition himself, though it was befouled and near unrecognizable beneath the grime of a century of loss and failure and flight. But few seemed to have the patience he knew would be required if they were ever to make the galaxy whole again. Most were a liability, offering little in the way of direct assets and risking the enclave's exposure.

He had been forced to quietly terminate those who had found them in the past, knowing that simply sending them away would only attract more attention. He had done so with the assistance of Marchu, Mordai, and a few of the younger, stronger members of the enclave, the ones he knew would follow his instructions no matter what. He had never told the likes of Tol. That would only lead to more trouble.

But he had never encountered a group this large. His first concern was that he would not be able to eliminate them all without the wider enclave becoming aware of his actions.

Yet on the other hand, having such a large influx at such a crucial time might have its benefits. He was supposed to be rebuilding the empire after all, and Winnarans had their uses. Their service was part of the natural order of things.

"How did you find us?" he asked.

"It has been a long road, lord," Vexar admitted unhelpfully. "We have followed whispers and rumors halfway across the galaxy. Many of us have worked toward this moment all our lives."

Ibna was unimpressed by the melodrama.

"If you can find us, then it is possible our enemies can as well," he told the Winnaran, noticing him glance at the Hacan as he spoke. It was, he realized, a somewhat redundant point, though he imagined Vexar might not wish to reveal his sources in the presence of the Hacan.

As though sensing his thoughts, one of the felids growled.

"That's enough chatter," she said. "These Winnarans are under arrest."

"Why?" Ibna demanded.

"They are absconders, from one of the mining camps. They held two Hacan at gunpoint and stole a transport."

"We have come a long way," Vexar admitted. "But we place ourselves under the empire's protection."

Ibna was almost touched but struggled to meet with a mindset that was able to convince itself that the Lazax had any power here. It was borderline delusional. These Winnarans would get themselves killed, and more importantly, they might unintentionally inflict the same upon the enclave. And he must protect the enclave – which was the Lazax future – at all costs.

"You'll be returned to the mining works, immediately," the Hacan told the Winnarans.

"Perhaps they might stay, for a short time," Ibna said to the felid, still of two minds about how he might turn the unexpected arrival to his benefit. He needed more time to assess. "You can keep them under guard, if you wish, but they can be fed and housed. It will not be long before darkness begins to fall anyway, and they are in no state to travel. I will speak to Magnate Akenzi about them."

The Hacan warrior bared her fangs but turned away, speaking into a savant in her own language. Ibna found himself thinking back to the Winnaran assistants he had once had when he was still serving the empire, brave Onni and faithful Erial, both long dead, killed in the line of duty. It had been decades since he had thought about them, and the memory of their loss held an unexpected sting. He almost found himself looking on Vexar with pity.

"They will be separated between different huts," the Hacan finally conceded. "And will submit to a thorough search."

"Of course." Ibna nodded and gestured toward Vexar.

"Your long journey is over," he told the awestruck Winnaran. "Come, walk with me."

Mortalia did her best to hide how badly she was shaking as they reached the settlement among the trees.

Somehow, she hadn't thought this would happen. Despite dedicating most of her life to the search, and despite the mounting evidence that it was bearing fruit, she had managed to convince herself that it would all ultimately be in vain. Of course, the Lazax were no more. Their empire had been torn down. The entire galaxy had conspired, one way or another, to hunt them to extinction.

And yet here they were. Not just the one who had come down to see the Winnarans after the Hacan had fallen upon them, but an entire settlement of them.

She tried and failed not to stare as the party was taken into their midst, but all the other Winnarans were just as wide-eyed, and she supposed it wouldn't mark her out.

The Lazax were even taller and gaunter in person than she imagined. They didn't wear the robes or expensive garments she had seen in the old viz recordings or stills, but rustic attire that matched the roughness of their log and thatch dwellings. It was an entire community as well, old and young and everything in between. The sight of Lazax children watching the new arrivals solemnly from the windows and doorways of their crude dwellings was a particular shock.

And it wasn't only Lazax that seemed to be living in the settlement. There were humans and some Hylar, too. It was as though the galaxy had simply passed this place by and forgotten all about it.

It was all Mortalia could do not to trigger the projector beacon in her pocket right there and then.

At least her efforts had not been in vain. The last months, especially – the brutality of Klast, the struggles of securing a sprinter craft from Letnev territory to Quinz 11, the struggle inveigling herself with these fools. Now, she would make sure it had all been worth it.

They reached a cleared area in front of a vast tree, soaring over them like some great watchtower. The Lazax who had led them to it conversed with several of its kin, as well as a few others – a human and a Nar Hylar – then spoke again with

Vexar. Mortalia wasn't close enough to overhear them, but she didn't want to push her way to the front. Right now, it was imperative that she remained unassuming, part of the group. Everything she had worked toward lay before her. She merely had to wait a few hours more, until darkness fell.

Vexar turned and addressed the group, his expression one of undisguised joy.

"The Lazax have agreed to house us for the time being, and Imperial Councilor Vel Syd has assured me that he will do his best to intercede on our behalf with the Hacan!"

She realized the other Winnarans around her were as exultant as their leader. Some were weeping tears of joy, others embraced. This was the end of the long road they had trod together, the hard, tangible evidence that their faith had not been in vain. Their masters yet lived. Against all odds, the empire was not yet dead.

Mortalia managed to smile and cast her eyes down, hoping it would look as though she was overcome with emotion.

In a sense that much was true, though the emotion was hatred, that slow-burning ember that had kept her going through years of hardship, now roused to a blazing inferno within.

She had sought the Lazax not to worship them, but to kill them, and tonight she would do just that.

The Lazax seemed as good as their word. The Resurrectionists were divided into three groups and moved into rudimentary huts close to the edge of the settlement. Mortalia shared a musty timber room with a dozen other Winnarans, lit by a single, flickering bulb. They were all given blankets and rough bedding, and worked to clear the chimney hole of avian nests so they could start a fire.

Despite the meager accommodation, the Resurrectionists were insufferably happy. Mortalia was thankful that the darkness of the dingy space meant she could remain largely undisturbed off to one side, listening as they spoke of their disbelief that they had found their masters after so long.

Mortalia found it all repulsive. They were hopelessly enamored by some false belief in the glories of days long gone by. She wanted to snap at them to look around themselves, to see the truth. They were packed into a log room that barely had functioning electricity, in a desolate wilderness on the edge of the galaxy! The leader of this enclave seemed to be nothing more than a rotting old coward preserved by cybernetics. His very existence was unnatural, stretched far beyond what was right. It was repulsive, but so was the misplaced loyalty the Resurrectionists were showing.

She looked forward to the horror they were about to experience but focused on playing her part until then. Just a little longer, she told herself, and the galaxy would have its due.

When she judged the time was right, she made her way out of the hut. There were several Hacan standing guard outside. They looked at her warily, cradling their rifles.

"Toilet," she said, pointing at the small latrine hut appended to the structure.

Saying nothing, one of the guards escorted her to it and waited outside. The evening settled among the trees, twilight steadily adopting ever deeper, darker shades as it dressed for the night. She could smell woodsmoke from the fires being lit throughout the settlement and heard the creak of timber and the soft trilling of some local wildlife in the pine branches nearby.

She closed the latrine's door and removed the beacon from her pocket, cupping it in her trembling hands. She closed her eyes, took a breath, tried to push away the tide of emotions, the anger and hate and fear and uncertainty. It was time.

She depressed a series of buttons on the side of the beacon, making sure to do so in the correct order. The kill combination. The device buzzed before becoming an unassuming little projection unit once more. Message sent and received.

Things were in motion now that could not be undone. She hurried back to the main hut and lay down under one of the blankets the Lazax had given her and waited for the screaming to start.

"If I were superstitious, their arrival would feel almost providential," Marchu said as she spooned more fish stew into her mouth. "We need volunteers for the *Syd*. You said they've acted as deckhands before?"

"So their leader claims," Ibna replied. The two Lazax were sharing a dinner within the Eridius Arc, sitting hunched over around a small stove unit while an old liquid-reaction heat generator burbled away next to them, keeping the creeping chill of night out of their old bones.

"If you do want to use them, you'll have to convince the Hacan to let them go," Marchu pointed out.

"I would hope the magnate doesn't particularly care about what happens to thirty-odd Winnaran laborers," Ibna pointed out.

"And do you trust them?" Marchu added. "The Winnarans, I mean."

"I still don't know," Ibna admitted. "There are so many this time it would be difficult to… remove them, the way we have done in the past."

He sensed Marchu glance at him with something approaching reproachment – she had been complicit in dealing with the previous Resurrectionists that had become a liability but had registered her dissatisfaction. Ibna knew his ruthlessness was sometimes almost too much for her. That was not his concern. He merely had the strength to do what had to be done. Protecting the children and their future was paramount.

"The fact they were able to find us at all is disturbing," he went on. "Apparently they followed old stories to a disused refueling waypoint we stopped at during our journey, and they were able to extract and extrapolate logs from there."

As he spoke, he found himself cycling through his cybernetic vision, checking the locator tags implanted into the other Lazax, almost compulsively. He focused on the children, finding all their vitals steady and regular, again feeling grateful to Mordai for suggesting this particular augmentation in the first place. His momentary relief was soon gone, however.

"There is little we can do about traces such as that," Marchu said. "It's why we've kept moving all these years. And why we're going to have to move again."

"You're probably right," Ibna admitted. "But if the Hacan hadn't come here, much of this wouldn't be happening. We must get off-world as soon as possible, but we can only do that if they allow us."

The pair lapsed into silence, Ibna slowly working his way through his own stew. The night outside was quiet – there was a tension to it that Ibna didn't like. He had spoken again with the council that evening, and they had agreed on the final points of the plan. Tol and Rondu had departed for the coast, preparing to make the dive that would bring them to the enclave's main cruiser. Of course, they still had to secure the acquiescence of the Hacan, but all Ibna could do was hope that would be forthcoming. He had tried to leave them with as little choice in the matter as they had left him.

"I don't want to ask for volunteers," he admitted to Marchu as he finished his bowl. The other Lazax looked at him with surprise.

"You barely need to. You know the same ones who have stepped up every time in the past will do so again. We're always ready to do what must be done. Those without the strength have long fallen away."

"No one's strength is infinite," Ibna said, not wishing to cause the conversation to take a morose turn, but unable to stop himself. Marchu looked at him for some time, and he realized she was probably trying to gauge whether or not Ibna was really talking about himself. Did he mean the endurance of the enclave as a whole? Were they really prepared to keep running, waiting, and trusting that the stars would one day complete their cycle, and the galaxy would accept them back again? And how many more dark deeds could the likes of Marchu really stomach, done to keep the enclave safe? She might speak of strength, but Ibna suspected it was waning within her.

"I will command the cruiser," he said. "But I want you to remain here. Take charge in my absence. I want as few members of the enclave up there with me as possible, and that means the rest will be relying on you if the worst should happen."

In years gone by, he knew Marchu would have argued an order like that, but they were long past such things. She had been the de facto chief subordinate of the enclave ever since they had left Mecatol Rex, in a past that, in the flickering lamps that lit the timber bowels of the Eridius Arc, now felt only half-remembered. Without the backing of Marchu, Ibna doubted he could ever have made it away from the imperial capital before annihilation had befallen it, let alone gathered enough individuals to form what had become the enclave. Regardless of the reservations she sometimes showed about the course

Ibna charted, there were none left he trusted more than the former Lazax politician.

"You're sure the Hacan will let us go if we help them?" Marchu asked.

"I'm sure of nothing," Ibna admitted. "But as I said before, if they wished to destroy us, there were easier times to do it. Now that the cruiser is being brought up, they're running out of options. Once the plan has been carried through, the easiest thing would be to let us go."

"Should I prepare *Hurwana* and *Manda* too?" Marchu said. The enclave possessed just enough ships to transport the people of their settlement, but three truly space-worthy vessels of note, but were all concealed on Gamma Eridius's surface. Committing the cruiser named the *Syd* meant they would still have *Hurwana* and *Manda* as a contingency, to get the main body of the enclave away if something went wrong.

"Wait until we're airborne," Ibna cautioned. "Then have Zeth go down and bring them up. Rondu as well. I'll leave him behind, but I'll have to take Tol to help pilot the *Syd*."

"We should've recruited more Hylar before they left Mecatol," Marchu quipped with a wink and then added more seriously, "They have become their own contingent, you know. Now, there are as nearly many of them traveling with us as there are Lazax!"

Ibna found himself laughing softly, the sound coming out as a dry, dull scrape.

"She wants to stay behind," he admitted after he had recovered. "Tol, I mean. She told me after the first council meeting. She's had enough."

Marchu's expression became concerned. "Can we continue without her? Your augmentations..."

"I know," Ibna responded, not wishing to be drawn on the problem at the moment. "Mordai's knowledge will see us through. His passion and abilities are excellent. But I won't keep Tol. She isn't our slave, and I've threatened and cajoled her into staying too many times before. I'm not sure how long she has left. On a practical level, we need to plan for what comes after anyway."

"Then you wouldn't…" Marchu trailed off.

Ibna looked at her, his expression unreadable. "I have thought about it," he said, knowing she wondered whether he would terminate the Hylar doctor, rather than leave her behind and risk spreading knowledge of the enclave's existence. "No one is bigger than the future of the Lazax, not even Doctor Tol. But I believe she would rather die than ever divulge what she has been a part of. Besides, as I said, I'm not sure how much longer she will live."

"I know the feeling," Marchu said with a hint of humor, seemingly relieved that Ibna wasn't planning on ordering the murder of the person who, arguably, had done more for the enclave than any other.

They let the silence slip in once again, lulled by the rhythmic noise of the heat generator. Ibna could feel his thoughts growing heavy as tiredness, forever stalking him these days, crept closer.

A sound intruded on the stillness, breaking the generator's rhythm. A slight scuffling noise, from beyond the roots enclosing them. Ibna frowned and roused himself, realizing that Marchu actually had dozed off during the brief interlude, leaning over slightly in her chair.

The sound came again. Ibna grasped his moonwood staff, the old, polished length a reassurance more than anything. He found his feet and moved toward the entrance to the Eridius Arc, his cybernetics whirring softly, their responsiveness a cruel contrast to those parts of him that were yet flesh and blood.

He walked out between the parting in the roots that served as the door. Beyond was a Hacan guard, who looked at him abruptly, flat ears betraying how he had startled her. She made no aggressive moves though, gazing at him levelly as he, in turn, looked out into the clearing.

It was dark, but for the dim light coming from the neighboring huts. Pinemoths fluttered and darted like phantom wisps through the air. There was a cry from somewhere out beyond the perimeter, some nocturnal beast on the prowl.

Nothing else moved. Ibna sniffed, murmured to himself, and turned slowly to stamp back inside.

CHAPTER TWENTY-THREE

Gamma Eridius, the Boreas Gap

Tol woke the *Syd*.

The cruiser that had carried many of the enclave from Mecatol Rex lay in the depths west of the ridgeline, sunken beneath the hard, gray waves of Gamma Eridius's oceans among their other smaller ships. Such a berth kept its presence off all but the most potent scanners and ensured it would rest undisturbed until the enclave needed it again.

Tol and Rondu went to awaken it from its slumber. Zeth remained on land, a contingency in case some accident robbed the enclave the fellow Hylar.

Night had fallen, and the ocean depths were dark. Tol followed a locator beacon, its receiver fixed over her right eye. She was tired, and the task ahead wasn't one she relished, but it felt good to be beneath the waters once more.

The *Syd* loomed like a vast, slumbering oceanic predator, settled on top of a subaquatic shelf. It had been almost a full year-cycle since they had last checked on the spacecraft. Crustaceans had attached themselves to parts of its hull, watery fronds waving slowly at the pair of Hylar as they located one of the airlocks and input the necessary data to unseal it.

The lock was capable of acting as a drain, and they clutched onto bars on its walls as it sluiced out the brine. Tol felt the unwelcome heaviness return to her limbs. She moved to disengage the interior hatch as Rondu checked a panel next to it, his gills flaring.

"Air recyc is still working," he noted. "That's a good start."

The stale atmosphere on board the sealed craft would have been difficult for anyone else to survive, but it was enough for the Hylar to endure until they got it back to the surface and popped a few of the portholes.

The hatch disengaged with a *thunk,* and Tol ducked in through it slowly, still stretching out her limbs in the wake of the swim. Lighting strips flickered and blinked to life before her, illuminating the corridor leading to the ship's bridge. It was empty, and still, silent but for the slight, dull creaking of the hull around them as it kept the ocean's crushing embrace at bay.

They reached the bridge and slowly began to rouse the ship from its slumber. It took time – two Hylar couldn't compare to a full complement of bridge hands, and more crew would be needed if they were headed back into the void. Rondu checked the integrity systems while Tol nursed power from the core to its outer edges, returning life to that which had lain cold and dead for too long.

The *Syd* responded well. Though old, it was a fine craft. Tol knew that much of it had been Hylar-built. It was sluggish but reactive, and the most important moment of the reawakening – when Tol lit the primary engines and set the vectors to vertical – began without a hitch.

The hull creaked and groaned more loudly as the cruiser began to slowly rise from its watery bed.

"Levels are positive," Tol called to Rondu from across the bridge. "How's the sluicing going?"

"Mostly just the lowermost decks and the bilge to go," he said. Even the *Syd* leaked in places, and over time water had collected in the ship's bowels. Rondu was now draining it out, lightening their load as they continued to slowly ascend.

"Do you think this'll actually work?" Rondu added.

"All the systems have responded well so far," Tol replied, being deliberately obtuse.

"I mean the plan Vel Syd has hatched. It sounds a lot to me like the Hacan want to put us in the firing line while they avoid it themselves."

"The Hacan are merchants and traders," Tol pointed out. "They'll always find someone else to fight their battles for them."

"And Vel Syd's happy with that?"

"The Hacan have us all at gunpoint. Vel Syd's just trying to find a solution to prevent them from wiping us out."

Rondu went quiet, clearly realizing he wasn't going to get any sort of agreement out of Tol in her current mood. Privately, she shared his misgivings, though she also knew there was no point in voicing them – it was too late now to suggest anything else, and besides, she had no practical alternatives.

"I guess it's time we took to the void again," Rondu said. "I never much liked those huts anyway. Maybe we can find a nice water-world somewhere on the edge of existence for the Lazax to settle down on."

Tol resisted the urge to tell Rondu she wouldn't be leaving Gamma Eridius. Besides Ibna himself, she'd informed no one. A part of her was still scared she'd cave at the last moment, that she would end up back on board this ship, bound once more for an uncertain future. It was all she had known for so long.

There would be a time for goodbyes, she hoped. Before then, she had one more job to do.

...

Mortalia waited through the night for the screaming to start, or even just a soft series of taps on the wooden wall that might let her know her companions were setting to work. None came. At some point she dozed off and was woken by the sounds of the Winnarans rousing themselves around her.

Daylight was streaming in through the doorway. She heard another of the Resurrectionists enter the hut, and made sure she kept still and silent, holding her breath while she waited for the horror to break, for the shocking news that the Lazax had been massacred in the dead of night.

Instead, the excited Winnaran reported that Vexar had spoken earlier that morning with the Lazax, and that he wanted them all to gather outside. As the Winnarans started to get up, Mortalia lay for a few moments more, battling with a sudden onset of panic and anger.

Forcing herself to smile and nod at the Winnarans who acknowledged her presence, she rose and hurried out to the latrine. Once inside, she snatched out the beacon again.

Had it malfunctioned? That was surely the only reasonable explanation. She turned the node that varied the strength of its projector, but with an extra twist also allowed her to review past automatic messages. The kill combination was showing as both sent and received.

What had happened? Had the Yssaril, who had followed her faithfully for years, who she had caught glimpses of in the treetops, been overcome, defeated? Or were they refusing to enact the kill command? Had they betrayed her?

What if this was the Barony's doing? It was the Letnev, specifically their covert operations wing, the Cimm Fenn, who had supplied her with her companions from the Guild of Spies, who funded her quest across the galaxy and whose agents had assisted her from the core to the deadzones. What if, at the very end, they had chosen to issue new instructions? What if they wanted the Lazax taken alive?

Mortalia burst into tears. She felt suddenly alone, utterly isolated and overwhelmed.

The anxiety passed quickly, seared away by anger, by frustration that, after so long, she was going to be denied at the last. She couldn't allow that. She had to stay in control.

She had come here with one purpose, and one purpose only, and she would stop at nothing until she had fulfilled it. The final stain of the empire needed to be wiped away. With or without the Yssaril, the Lazax would die.

Vexar watched the Winnarans gather, feeling a surge of pride as he did so, offset by a deep, bitter sorrow.

It all still felt like a dream. To have found the Lazax, to have even been welcomed into their midst, it was everything he had hoped for down the years. But to do it without Lekaan was a cruel blow.

Even in the midst of speaking to Ibna Vel Syd and charting what awaited them next, he was haunted by thoughts of his partner. What had happened to her? Was she still on board the macro freighter? How could she have simply disappeared, especially this close to the end?

There was nothing he could do now, he tried to tell himself. What he was witnessing in this very moment was the realization of everything they had worked toward. She would understand what he had done. Surely, she would even have done the same?

Now was not the time to become undone with emotion. The Resurrectionists still needed his leadership and now, even more importantly, the Lazax had asked great things of him, of them all.

"Good morning," he said once all the Winnarans had gathered outside the huts they had spent the night in. "I hope you all slept well!"

There was some laughter, and smiles. Joy at where their long journey had finally led them still animated the entire group.

"Food is being prepared in the main clearing, but I thought you would want to know this as soon as possible. Earlier I spoke with the Most Eminent Councilor Vel Syd, who once served His Most Imperial Majesty! He has been negotiating with the Hacan and has devised a means for ensuring the safety of this enclave while they depart for territories anew. They wish to take us with them but have asked for our aid in crewing one of their vessels. I informed the eminent councilor that we have experience in such things and would be privileged to help."

An excited murmur ran through the Winnarans, broken only by one voice.

"Why do they want us to crew their ship?"

Vexar realized it had come from Mortalia, standing near the back. Her expression, unlike the Winnarans around her, was cold.

"What do you mean?" Vexar asked, feeling disarmed.

"Why would they need help crewing their ship?" she repeated. "Aren't there enough of them?"

"There are," Vexar said. "But there will be danger involved. That is the point I was going to make next. As we know from the voyage in-system, the Hacan are struggling with pirate raiders. Vel Syd has agreed to help combat them, and in exchange the Hacan will permit us all to depart unhindered."

"So we're going into battle for the Hacan?" Mortalia demanded.

"It isn't expected that the ship we're crewing will be engaged. We should be perfectly safe. Beyond that, I am waiting for further clarity."

He could sense some uncertainty had crept into the group and moved quickly to quash it.

"All of us swore ourselves to the Resurrectionist cause. We promised to give our lives for this. Some of us have already done so. For those of us still here, the time has come to make good on our oaths. We have found the Lazax, and they have need of our aid. Now, more than ever, we must give our all to restore the glory of the empire."

There were mutters of agreement. Vexar felt his own resolve hardening, looking out over the faithful friends and companions he had been through so much with. He carried on.

"It is an honor and a privilege to serve the Lazax. That is what we have all come here to do. The empire awaits!"

The *Syd* broke the surface of Gamma Eridius's chilling swell, great torrents of water cascading from the ship's sleek hull as it halted just above the waves, the wash of its vertical engines churning the sea into a frenzy beneath it.

Tol steered it toward the shore, keeping as low as possible. With a care and precision that came from great experience, she alighted its prow against the narrow shingle and began to lower the primary hatch.

Vel Syd and the rest of the small expedition came down from the ridge. Besides the former ambassador, there was one other senior Lazax, Alarina, who was the most experienced navigator in the enclave, a younger Lazax named Larish who regularly acted as the enclave's lead pilot, and a pair of humans, Keyra and Caldr, both of whom were adept engineers. With Tol and Rondu, the senior bridge command was complete.

After that there was a gaggle of Winnarans, the Resurrectionists who had stumbled into their midst the day before. Tol felt like telling them there was a good chance they'd volunteered for a suicide mission. But she understood the brutal reality of Vel Syd's decision. He wanted to ask as few members of the enclave to risk themselves as possible. These new arrivals were simply less valuable than those who had been together since the beginning.

And if they survived, they would have proven themselves.

"Listen carefully," Tol called as the little crew assembled on the bridge, addressing the wide-eyed Winnarans. "We don't have time to go over things more than once. You've said you're experienced deckhands, so I hope you weren't lying!"

She asked for a show of hands from those who felt most familiar with each station and dispersed the Winnarans among them – engines, shields, navigation, weapons, power. The numbers weren't ideal, but Tol reckoned it could be crewed without too much of a loss of efficiency.

They just had to hope they didn't start taking casualties.

The *Syd* rose as its namesake took the captain's chair, staff still clutched in his one organic hand. The last of the water poured from the old ship, rejoining Gamma Eridius's cruel seas as the vessel climbed farther, arcing up toward the sweeping gray vault of the heavens.

Before it could reach high altitude, one of the Winnarans reported a faulty hatch leading through to the outer hull. Tol ordered them to keep trying to seal it remotely before detailing someone to go and inspect it in person. After the third try the hull finally locked up.

"One of the water drains," Tol surmised, glancing at Vel Syd, who nodded, happy for her to direct the bridge. "Probably rusting, but it's sealed now."

She returned her attention to the engine readouts, watching them for any hint that they were stuttering or might not muster the power necessary to drive them to the stars.

Because there weren't enough crew to watch the ship's internal viz recorders – not continuously, anyway – none of the *Syd's* complement noticed the three small figures who had swum through the bitter waves to scale the vessel's flank while its prow rested against the shingle, or how they had darted in through the hatch they had opened from the outside, slipping into vents and maintenance chutes before the ship was fully sealed.

"I'm going on board," Akenzi said.

Silence followed his words, and he suspected both Drusha and Marzek were trying to articulate an argument against doing just that. They were gazing at the Lazax ship that had risen to join the Muktat vessels in Gamma Eridius's orbit, a sleek, elegant cruiser framed now by the backdrop of the planet's blue-green curve and the light of the system's star breaking over its edge.

"There is no need for you to risk yourself," Marzek said eventually. "You know the dangers they are about to face. And what if they turned against you?"

"We need to make sure they play their part," Akenzi said. "What if they simply flee? The whole plan will come undone."

"Do you think those few on board would abandon the great majority they've left behind?"

"They have two more ships," Akenzi pointed out. "Vel Syd could be using this one as the decoy. By necessity, we have to commit everything we have to this gambit. That leaves the rest on the planet free to make their own escape."

"You think they'd be that duplicitous?" Drusha asked.

"I'm just thinking of ways I could play it, if I was in their position. But it doesn't work if their ship is full of Muktat warriors. So prepare a team, Marzek. A strong one. It's about time I spoke again with Vel Syd."

...

"The Hacan want to board," Alarina said from the comms station.

"Why?" Vel Syd demanded, looking up from the systems report being projected from the arm rest of his command chair.

"They haven't said, it's an automated request."

"Hail them," Vel Syd instructed. "Put it on speakers."

"They've accepted," Alarina said after a moment overseeing the work of the trio of Winnarans assigned to the comms station. "You're going to be audible in three, two, one…"

"You wish to board us, Magnate Akenzi?" Vel Syd called out.

"We do," came the voice of the Hacan over the speakers connected to the bridge's comms node. "I intend to come in person, along with a small armed retinue."

"Might I ask why?"

"To supplement your on board force. From the reports I've received from my surface assets, it seems you're operating a skeleton crew."

"That may be the case, but I didn't think the plan involved us fighting off boarding actions, with or without your help."

"Consider it a little extra insurance. No plan survives contact with the enemy, or so the old Jordian saying goes."

Vel Syd looked across the bridge at Tol, who shrugged her shoulders. It seemed unlikely the Hacan wanted to offer them greater protection, especially if Akenzi was coming in person, but they were past negotiating the finer details. The *Syd* had armed Hacan vessels off its port and starboard.

"We will need to go soon, or the orbital arc is going to bring us into view of the debris field," he pointed out. "If you wish to enjoy our hospitality, magnate, you had best do so swiftly. We will cut engines and come alongside for docking protocols."

• • •

"I still don't like this," Drusha growled.

"Concerned by a hundred-and-fifty-year-old Lazax, big brother?" Akenzi jested as he slotted the weapon into the holster he had strapped to his thigh, letting his zenfar fall over it. He was standing in the prow of the transport berth of one of the *Rising Sands'* shuttles, enduring the brief, tremoring passage between his flagship and the Lazax cruiser.

"You're unnecessarily endangering yourself," Drusha said stoically, unamused. "We don't know what's going to happen to that ship, and there isn't much I can do to save you from a full broadside or an energy beam blast. And do not underestimate their leader. Cybernetics will give him strength and endurance far beyond his years."

"I have full confidence in you, brother," Akenzi said. He knew he was being dismissive, but he didn't have time for Drusha's misgivings. Common sense dictated he remain on board the *Rising Sands* and oversee the coming battle without putting himself in harm's way, but common sense didn't factor in a betrayal by the Lazax. While Vel Syd's cruiser was loose, it was an element he couldn't control, but with a complement of Muktat warriors on board it became a reliable asset. That didn't mean he had to be on board as well, but Akenzi wanted to see the pirate scum destroyed, and the Lazax ship would offer him the best possible view. Now that the time to strike had come, he found himself animated by a kind of aggression he had only rarely experienced before.

"Maybe you should have joined the ordri with me, instead of becoming a trader," Drusha said, and Akenzi was glad to note the humor now undercutting his stern tone.

"I told you, war and trade are as much brothers as you and I," he replied.

"Your courage does the clan honor," Drusha said, the heartfelt comment a surprise to Akenzi. He bowed his head, not entirely sure how to take the high praise, and chose instead to speak to the section of Muktat soldiery packing the rest of the transport compartment behind them.

"Do not antagonize or interfere with anyone once we're on board. But stay sharp. If I give the signal, don't hesitate. Remember that these are only allies of convenience. Never trust a Lazax."

Yet that was exactly what he was doing. There was no time to back out now though.

He recalled for a moment the last time he had faced a trip like this, a shuttle ride to an unknown vessel – the Letnev flagship, back in the Kenara system. He consoled himself with the fact that the odds had been much worse on that occasion, and everything had still gone perfectly. This time he had a force of armed, trained warriors loyal to Clan Muktat at his back.

Akenzi had come to Gamma Eridius to win wealth and glory, and nothing was going to stop him, whether that was other Hacan, pirate filth, or the last of the Lazax.

CHAPTER TWENTY-FOUR

The Syd, Lazax Cruiser, above Gamma Eridius

A single human greeted the Hacan shuttle in the cruiser's docking bay and led them to the bridge. Akenzi kept an eye out for signs of duplicity all the way there but found none.

It seemed the Lazax really had chosen only a skeleton crew, barely enough to man the control stations. Most of them appeared to be Winnarans. Akenzi wondered if they were from his own absconded workforce. Allowing deserters to go unpunished sat ill with him, but the Lazax had been insistent that they join their enclave, and he had judged it a negligible price to pay for the wider plan to proceed.

"Welcome on board the *Syd*, Magnate Akenzi," Ibna Vel Syd called from his command chair, atop a short gantry in the bridge's center. Akenzi took in the sight and felt awed, his fur bristling as he contemplated the old Lazax enthroned. It was as though history itself had been resurrected and now played out before him.

"The ship is named after you?" he asked as he paused with his armed entourage within the main entranceway, wanting to mask his momentary sense of reverence.

"No, after my family," Vel Syd replied. "I make no complaint about your presence here, but I must ask you and your warriors to keep to the edges of the bridge. I'm sure you don't want to interrupt its smooth running."

"Of course not," Akenzi agreed. "Though perhaps you might make a concession for my brother and me? I promise we won't trip anyone up."

"Very well," Vel Syd said, tapping his staff against the deck. Akenzi nodded to Drusha, who gestured curtly to the Muktat soldiers. They spread out around the edges of the bridge, while Akenzi and Drusha walked to its center, mounting the gantry platform to stand alongside Vel Syd's chair.

"I must admit, I didn't imagine I would find myself alongside a Lazax on his command deck when I first set out for the Boreas Gap," Akenzi declared.

"Reality rarely matches our hopes or expectations," Vel Syd stated with a dourness that Akenzi was getting used to. "We have our course ready, if your own fleet is prepared?"

"It is," Akenzi replied.

"Come to a new heading, thirty-eight by five-six," Vel Syd said to his mismatched crew, stirring them into a flurry of activity. He triggered a holo from his command chair, indicating a Hacan ship that was highlighted amber on the display.

"And get me firing coordinates for this vessel. Macro Freighter B9-09."

"We're to fire on that Hacan ship?" one of the Winnarans spoke up in the moment's silence that followed.

"We are," Vel Syd affirmed, glancing briefly at Akenzi. "Do not worry. The Hacan are aware. The freighter's cargo has already been unloaded, and it has been fully evacuated."

"And I am paying its captain more than enough for a replacement," Akenzi added.

The other deckhands got back to work, but the one who had spoken up appeared distressed.

"That was the ship we came in on, sire," he said to Vel Syd. "One of my… companions was left behind on it. She went missing just when we broke in-system."

"If she was found, she'll have been part of the evacuated crew, I'm sure," Vel Syd declared. "Was there a reason she went missing?"

"I don't know, sire. It's a mystery I was still intending to solve."

"And I'm sure you will, when we make contact with B9-09's crew planetside, after this is all over," the Lazax declared brusquely. "Now, do I have my firing solution yet?"

Akenzi briefly thought the Winnaran was going to do the unthinkable and argue with his master, but after another moment's hesitation he turned obediently back to his station.

"Target locked," a Nar Hylar called from the gunnery station. "Prow cannon primed."

"Open fire," Vel Syd ordered.

The *Black Scale* lay still and silent, floating like a small shard of space debris on the edge of the sector it had just entered.

Z'ffani was as cold as the systems of her ship, coiled within the single nest-berth that acted as its cockpit. Like all Druaa she was capable of a form of extended hibernation, one that could be entered into during interstellar travel. Most preferred to do so as part of a wider brood nest, but Z'ffani was not distressed at her isolation. She preferred her own company, not having to worry about the voices and emotions of others filling her head unbidden. Out here, the sole crew member of the small, barb-like *Fractal* 6-class voidcraft, her thoughts were her own, and her emotions were clear and settled.

She had made good time to the Boreas Gap, then on to Gamma Eridius, guided by the traces of the beacon echoes her spies had left in their wake, at fuel hubs and remote space stations. There were no firm messages – such a thing was too difficult to do regularly, even for the Guild of Spies – but she trusted her Yssaril.

They had reported faithfully to her for years now, hunters working alongside an unwitting beater, a naive, hate-filled Winnaran called Mortalia. The Barony of Letnev had recruited her while she was still young, adding her to the network of informants, spies and assassins they employed across the galaxy. Mortalia had been granted her wish, to hunt for the Lazax. Officially the Letnev had pronounced the end of the imperial line decades earlier, even though the original aggressors had been the Federation of Sol, but what the Barony declared and what it really believed were often two very different things. Having a small number of agents following up old rumors did no harm, though Z'ffani doubted Mortalia's handler would have really thought she would actually find the empire's last vestiges.

Then again, they probably also didn't realize that the Yssaril they'd deployed alongside the embittered Winnaran were double agents, whose true loyalties lay with Z'ffani. Contrary to the Letnev's orders, their instructions were not to kill any Lazax they came across, but to tell Z'ffani of their existence.

Now their efforts had finally borne fruit. She would claim the Lazax and use them to ensure the Druaa were in the best possible position as they struck out into the galaxy. In doing so, she would also be able to secure her own place high within the Assembly, above lesser, petty Sen'enn like D'shasa and Z'shen.

But first, she needed to regain her strength. She had only herself to rely on, and while that was as she wished it, it meant there would be no room for the sluggishness that so often followed hibernation.

She unsealed one of the vacuum pods within the *Black Scale* and triggered its metabolic reaction process, causing its contents to thaw out. The vekken within woke from its own hibernation, starting to wriggle and chitter. Z'ffani gripped it and gulped it down. Even in the depths of space, Druaa despised cold, dead food.

As she felt it squirming while it digested, she reviewed the last transmission she had received. It had pinged up on the curved shell that acted as the cockpit's hatch and viewing port. The sender apparently came from one of the old, long-disused message nodes strung out through the system, the ones planted there by the Lazax when they had still ruled Gamma Eridius. The ingenuity of the Yssaril never ceased to impress her.

The transmission consisted of a set of coordinates, ones that Z'ffani had already triangulated to Gamma Eridius's surface. She would already have set the *Black Scale* on course for the planet's orbit, but for the second part of the message, which consisted of a simple red diamond shape, one that held a basic universal meaning.

Wait.

Bazishel sent word to Hamlar while he was sleeping.

It was the beginning of the night-cycle, and the pirate captain usually knew better than to disturb him, so it was immediately apparent that something untoward was happening. The Hacan magnate rose from the private berth he'd commandeered on board the *Reiver's Son* and made his way to the bridge, accompanied as ever by his bodyguards, Naru and Selyne.

"What is it?" he demanded as Bazishel greeted him with an irreverent swish of her tail.

"Something's happening around Gamma Eridius," she said. Bazishel was a Hacan too, though Hamlar barely deigned to accept they were from the same species. She belonged to none of the emirates but had been born into a rogue pirate clan. She was, as far as Hamlar was concerned, just part of a long list of undesirable allies he had recently become acquainted with.

"There's movement in the planet's orbit, and energy returns. Big spikes. Shields, and almost definitely weapons fire."

Bazishel ran a hand through the square, boxy shape of the bridge's stuttering holo display, the passage highlighting what she was talking about.

"That's the macro freighter you failed to take when it broke in-system," Hamlar said, identifying one of the markings on the display. As he watched it turned from amber to red.

Bazishel bared her fangs at the slight she perceived in Hamlar's words, but after a tense moment, confirmed he was correct.

"It's dead in its high orbital anchorage," she said. "Out here in the debris field we're too far away for even long-ranged viz scans, but from the patterns of the energy readouts, it looks like something gutted it. It's burning."

Hamlar's tail swayed in consternation as he tried to gauge what was happening on the distant planet. He had come to the Gap in person to oversee operations – these matters were too important to be left to others. In the weeks since his arrival, though, he had grown frustrated with Bazishel's reluctance to launch an all-out attack on the Muktat assets around Gamma Eridius. The pirate captain had insisted on skulking with her five vessels in the asteroid field along the system edge, concealing her numbers and precise location and venturing forth to attack the Muktat ships as it arrived in-system. That strategy was not without merit, especially after the advanced elements of the Muktat venture had been ravaged during the first ambush, but the last attack on the macro freighter had been a debacle. Akenzi had turned at bay, and all Hamlar's threats and instructions hadn't been enough to stop Bazishel from disengaging and scurrying back to the safety of the space debris.

This was the price he paid for hiring such criminal filth. His chief military advisor had recommended he deploy the Dazeshi's own fleet assets to the Gap, but he had ruled out such an extreme course of action. Since the humiliation he had suffered because of Akenzi – forced via private channels by the Quieron's underlings to relinquish his complaint against a Muktat venture into the Gap – there was little he would not consider when it came to taking vengeance against the arrogant, upstart young magnate. But starting a full-blown clan war was not an option. There had to be deniability, even if he himself had ventured to the Gap to oversee privateer operations in person.

He had wanted to watch as Akenzi's venture fell apart, and even be present to see the magnate killed or captured. If Akenzi was taken, they could extract a ransom that would not only destroy the Gamma Eridius venture but bankrupt the entirety of Clan Muktat.

All that Hamlar had been looking forward to, and yet suddenly, there was uncertainty. What was happening on Gamma Eridius? Why was a macro freighter burning?

"Do you have any other assets in-system?" he demanded of Bazishel. "Anything that could have hit that?"

"No," she said defensively. "Whoever's attacking them, it isn't anything to do with me."

Hamlar let out a low, uncertain growl.

"We need to get closer," he said.

"I'm not leaving the debris field," Bazishel said stubbornly. "It could easily be a trap."

"Send one ship," Hamlar instructed. "Or have you forgotten who's paying you, again?"

Bazishel prevaricated, and Hamlar was about to repeat his order when the renegade Hacan highlighted a different part of the holo.

"We might not have to. Look."

Hamlar noted that a new marker had appeared on the display and was seemingly exiting Gamma Eridius's high orbit. As he watched, the holo plotted an estimated course, one that carried the mysterious new craft past the debris field.

"More energy returns," Bazishel added. "They're exchanging fire. And the Muktat are pursuing."

"That doesn't make any sense," Hamlar said, but he could see that what Bazishel was claiming was true. Traceries showed beam weaponry being directed at the lone vessel by the Muktat war ships, which were turning and aligning on courses that would take them after it.

"Identify that ship," Hamlar snapped.

"Already running scans," Bazishel responded tersely.

It took a painfully long time. Hamlar tried not to fret, watching as the ship extended its lead over Akenzi's pursuing vessels. Whatever it was, it was fast.

"Well?" he eventually demanded of Bazishel, who had stalked over to the bridge station busy trying to tag the ship. Hamlar noticed her ears twitch, her golden gaze locked to one of the computator screens in apparent consternation.

"It's coming up with specifications that match a modified civilian cruiser," she said.

"But who does it belong to?" Hamlar demanded. "Is it Federation? Barony?"

The only explanation he could come up with, besides a lone raider making an opportunistic run on Hacan assets, was a scout vessel belonging to one of the great civilizations that had been caught prowling about Gamma Eridius's orbit.

"That's the problem," Bazishel said. "The only match we're getting is in the archival files. It's a private vessel, supposedly belonging to a Lazax. An imperial politico called Marchu Mal Serrus. She must've been dead for years."

"Lazax," Hamlar repeated disbelievingly. "It must've been captured at some point by pirates."

"I know every raider who operates in this subsector, and none of them have an old Lazax ship on their books," Bazishel said. "That isn't something you just come across or steal for that matter. Old imperial tech can set you up for life, and a whole ship in working order…"

Hamlar had no doubt she was telling the truth. But a Lazax ship, out here in the Boreas Gap – it was inconceivable.

And if it wasn't stolen, that left only one other obvious alternative.

"What if it really is the Lazax?" Bazishel asked, voicing words Hamlar wasn't even ready to entertain.

"Impossible," he said. "The empire has been gone for a hundred years."

"The empire, yes," Bazishel said. "But even if the Imperium was destroyed decades ago, that doesn't mean all the Lazax were as well."

Hamlar stood, considering the possibilities, trying to rationalize them, and as he did so, he watched the marker representing the strange vessel creep closer. Akenzi's Muktat vessels were still giving chase, but the gap was widening.

"If there was an old imperial enclave on Gamma Eridius, and that fool discovered them…" he mused, still not wanting to acknowledge so unthinkable a possibility.

"If your rival captures the last Lazax in the galaxy, he might be able to leverage them," Bazishel said. "Other powers would be beholden to him, and not just the United Emirates."

"Get that ship up on the viz, maximum magnification," Hamlar ordered. One of the bridge monitors flickered and came to life, the image blinking as it rapidly enhanced.

Hamlar found himself looking at a sleek cruiser, its engines blazing as it powered away from Gamma Eridius. It matched the description from the stellar archives of the *Reiver's Son.* It was as though the old empire had risen from the grave, right before his very eyes.

"They're trying to escape out-system," Bazishel noted. "Making for this acceleration point, here."

She highlighted a new part of the holo chart, not far past the debris field.

"And that puts them within striking distance of us," Hamlar said. "But it could be a trap."

"What're you suggesting then?" Bazishel asked, her previous caution seemingly evaporating before the temptation on offer. "That we sit here and do nothing, and watch the biggest payday of our lives power past and accelerate out of the system? And what if your rival catches up with them before they can make it up to speed?"

That was unthinkable. Knowing the sort of luck that seemed to attend Magnate Akenzi, it would be typical that he'd somehow manage to capture the last of the Lazax.

"Prepare a new heading," Hamlar ordered, making his mind up. "For all your ships, including this one! We're not holding anything back this time. Put us on course to intercept that vessel. And get a boarding party ready, too."

CHAPTER TWENTY-FIVE

THE REIVER'S SON, PIRATE FLAGSHIP, ON THE EDGE OF THE GAMMA ERIDIUS SYSTEM

As they had done on two previous occasions, Bazishel's fleet of buccaneers surged from the debris field and fell upon their prey.

Star Hunter again led the way, but this time *Reiver's Son* was with them.

"Cut them off," Hamlar instructed, but Bazishel was already snapping orders to that effect to her comms station. *Star Hunter* roved ahead, getting between the Lazax vessel and the system's nearest straight acceleration point toward the Gap. A thin red line appeared on the viz, showing the first lance strike lashing at the mysterious ship.

"They're trying to come to a new heading," Bazishel said, the green of the holo reflecting back in her felid eyes. "Too slow, though. We'll soon have them!"

Hamlar saw she was correct. The Lazax cruiser was attempting to flee before both the Hacan and the pirates, but the *Star Hunter* had it for speed. He saw the markers on the holo once more conjoined for a split second by a red beam. A cheer went up from the bridge crew.

"What happened?" Hamlar demanded, concerned that, in their eagerness, the pirates might have destroyed the prize.

"We've clipped their wings," Bazishel growled, fangs bared triumphantly. "An engine hit. They're already losing power. We've got them."

Hamlar's gaze darted to the markers representing the oncoming Muktat ships. They were closing fast. It was going to be tight.

"Have the rest of your ships engage the Muktat, hold them up while I take a boarding party and bring the Lazax to the acceleration point," Hamlar told Bazishel. He briefly thought she was going to argue, but instead swept her hand in a gesture of affirmation.

"Boarding pods are primed," she said. "Are you sure you want to go in person?"

Hamlar considered the possibility it could be a trap, but he also didn't trust Bazishel not to claim any Lazax for herself.

"My clan warriors will assist yours," he said.

"Very well. I'll cover your withdrawal once you have control of their ship."

Hamlar snapped at his twin bodyguards, Naru and Selyne, who swept from the bridge. As soon as he was gone, Bazishel turned to one of her subordinates.

"Take a second pod," she said. "And kill that fool as soon as the ship is secure. We're not splitting this prize with anyone."

"Enemy ship closing to boarding range," one of the Winnarans working feverishly at the bridge station called, glancing back at Vel Syd. He in turn looked up at Akenzi.

"Are your warriors ready?" he asked the Hacan. Akenzi had already ordered most of his boarding force to deploy to the starboard midsections of the cruiser, facing toward the oncoming pirate fleet.

"They are," Akenzi replied. "You can trust Clan Muktat. We aren't all just traders, are we, brother?"

His one-armed sibling and bodyguard didn't reply verbally but bared his fangs. The wicked display combined with his broad frame and scarred features seemed like answer enough.

Ibna leaned forward in his command chair, two hands grasping his staff, resting against it. It was made from moontree wood, the same substance his ambassador's staff had once been fashioned from, though without the circuitry inlaid into it that could interface with Lazax technology. This was a simple crook, worn and tough. Sometimes it reminded him of how he, too, was not what he once was, how he'd been whittled down and hardened. Right now, though, he didn't feel the same weight that was usually bearing him down. There was a thrill to what was happening, desperate and dangerous though it was. It reminded him of his younger days, representing the empire during the most perilous of assignments. Despite the fact that they were essentially acting as bait for the Hacan, the immediacy of it all helped drive out the old, familiar doubts and fears.

"I thought you said you didn't think we would be boarded," Ibna said to Akenzi, the reproachment twinned with something akin to dark amusement.

"My warriors will ensure not one pirate steps foot on this bridge," Akenzi replied with all the self-confidence Ibna had come to expect of him. "We only have to hold them off long enough for my fleet to engage them. Then we'll have the battle they've been so desperately avoiding."

"While we're sitting in the middle of it all."

"Lazax ships have good shields. We'll be fine. Or do you think I'd be on board if there was the slightest danger?"

Ibna suspected Akenzi's presence was more to do with a desire to ensure he followed the plan and an inability to delegate when it came to decisive moments, but he kept such thoughts to himself. It had put the Hacan into his power, to a small degree, and he welcomed that.

"They're firing their boarding pods," another Winnaran reported.

"Brace for impact," Tol added from her station.

Ibna remained seated, leaning forward. He wanted to feel it. He noticed Akenzi take a grip of his chair's back, using it as a brace. He decided not to chastise the Hacan. As much as it seemed they still didn't fully trust one another, they were in this together now, facing death side by side.

There was a series of crashing impacts, three in quick succession, setting the whole bridge shaking. Ibna found himself almost thrown from his chair, but steadied by his planted staff, the vibrations running through him. The retinal display over his enhanced vision blinked a warning, but he deleted it with a thought.

"Damage report," he demanded, looking to the crew stations as the worst of the tremors subsided, the hull around them groaning.

"All impacts on our starboard side, along the midsection," one Winnaran said, bent over her console as her eyes scanned the displays. "Three hits. They're boring through the outer hull."

Ibna realized that if they survived this, the *Syd* was going to need a lot of repairs.

Akenzi's brother snapped something into his savant, presumably orders to the clan warriors to prepare to repel boarders.

"We're in your hands, magnate," Ibna told Akenzi. "Let's see how the Hacan fight."

Bazishel's crews were proficient in the boarding and seizing of vessels, and the warriors of Clan Dazeshi were no less skilled in their profession. All three boarding pods drilled through to the outer corridors of the *Syd's* starboard side. The outer plates, beneath the terridium-tipped drill bits, were layered with shaped explosive charges, and they detonated once past the bulkhead, blasting a wicked storm of shrapnel at whatever might be waiting for the boarders on the other side.

If the Muktat soldiers had been on the other side of the pods, they would have been shredded, but they were just as good as their opponents. They had abandoned the sections of corridor where the pods had burrowed in and waited for the telltale *whump* of the charges detonating. Then, they pushed back in, swiftly levering up the decking plates that provided access to the underbelly of the corridors to use as makeshift barricades.

The prow hatches of the pods blew open, accompanied by a flurry of scatter-burst charges that filled the corridor with disorienting light and noise. The boarders stormed out in their wake, opening fire indiscriminately.

A hail of solid rounds and energy bursts filled the corridors, scarring and gouging the *Syd*. Pirates dropped, hit from left and right, blood spattering the walls and decking plates.

Speed and aggression were the only hope for the attackers. The Muktat were outnumbered, and though they were able to pour fire into the confined space before them, the hail of return shots rapidly started causing casualties among them as well.

Hamlar knew almost as soon as the thunder of the gunfight filled the corridor before him that something had gone wrong. Unlike their pirate allies, his Dazeshi had blast shields, and were able to form a defensive phalanx as they pushed out from their own pod. Hamlar, remaining for the time being in its red-lit confines, heard the reports from those in the vanguard over the boarding party's shared savant channels.

It wasn't Lazax waiting for them. It was Akenzi's runts. Muktat.

That could only mean it was a trap.

"Push out, kill them," Hamlar snapped into his own savant, ears twitching and aching from the fury of the confined firefight. There was no going back now.

He only hoped Akenzi was somewhere on board. He was done showing restraint and working in the shadows to undermine the arrogant upstart. Now, he just wanted to kill him.

"Three different points of penetration," Drusha noted. "And that one is Hacan-only."

He pointed toward one of the displays on the bridge's internal control consoles, showing the action playing out on the ship's starboard side. Akenzi had already noted the same – while two of the boarding parties were mismatched rabbles, one was comprised only of Hacan.

"They have to be Dazeshi," he growled, fury coloring his words. "I knew it! I knew those bastards were behind this!"

"Will your warriors hold them?" Vel Syd asked from his chair.

"Of course," Akenzi snapped at him, but a glance at Drusha told him it was less certain than pride would allow him to admit.

"If they don't, I'll be the first to meet them," Akenzi added darkly.

"Your ships are approaching engagement range," Vel Syd noted, drawing Akenzi's focus away from what was happening within the ship and toward the holo display showing the spread of the surrounding fleets. The pirate ships had swept down on the lone Lazax cruiser and had now surrounded it, but the wedge of Muktat zebeks hastening toward them from Gamma Eridius were almost in range of the corsairs.

"We are fortunate they decided against simply destroying us," Vel Syd carried on.

"Their curiosity got the better of them, as we knew it would," Akenzi said. "Hold for a little longer and my ships will rip these wretches apart."

"I am sending part of the crew to ensure the engines are still fully functioning," Vel Syd declared. The cruiser had taken a hit to its secondary power drives, albeit the Lazax had assured him it had only been a glancing blow. Still, they had deliberately bled power, intending to let the pirates believe they'd scored a damaging strike. It was all part of the choreography that, along with the destruction of B9-09, was supposed to convince the pirates that the Lazax had surprised the Muktat as part of a desperate escape. The damage to the engines should have been negligible, but Akenzi supposed Vel Syd's request was reasonable.

"Do you need warriors to accompany you?" he asked the Lazax.

"No," Vel Syd said. "The aft section between us and the engines is not part of the current engagement zone."

He issued a series of instructions to his small crew, and several Winnarans along with a Hylar were detached from their stations and hurried from the bridge.

"That might be a problem," Drusha noted, drawing Akenzi's attention back to the viz screens. He saw what his brother meant.

The Dazeshi were breaking through.

The *Black Scale* triggered its cloak and slipped between the warring ships toward its prey.

Such advanced technology on so small a craft was rare outside of the Universities of Jol-Nar, and even more so now, with the Hylar solely focused on their war effort. But the Druaa had long experience with tools that aided their subterfuge, and Z'ffani had paid the price necessary to secure a craft with the capabilities of the *Black Scale*. It meant that she was able to approach the Lazax cruiser unnoticed though, in truth, even without the cloaking device, it was doubtful anyone would have noticed the one-person craft on their scanners for very long. The Hacan and pirate fleets had opened fire on one another as the distance between them shortened, and though they were both still at extreme range, they were intent on pounding one another into submission on either side of the cruiser that was apparently their prey.

Z'ffani artfully wove the *Black Scale* between the energy beams and the predicted pathways of hard-round shots, until she was able to roll in under the cruiser's midsection. She then triggered the *Black Scale*'s magnetic actuator, causing it to clamp to the underside of the Lazax vessel. After the connection had been made, a dematerializer ring began to sear a perfect hole in the ship's hull.

While she waited for the point of ingress to finish being bored, Z'ffani reviewed the results of her final, close-range scan of the vessel. There were over a hundred life forms present, and it was clear the pirates had already boarded the ship. Still, Z'ffani believed she would be equal to the numbers she was about to face, especially since she could already feel the small, razor-keen minds of the Yssaril on board. It would be good to be able to use them as a direct asset, rather than a distant, long-term strategic piece.

Besides, no one on board would ever have encountered a Druaa before, much less tried to fight against one.

The dematerializer finished its work with a thump and a hiss of hyper-cooling metal. Z'ffani grasped the roof of her cockpit and began to uncoil, hauling herself up through the tunnel bored into the cruiser's hull and into the underbelly beneath its lowermost decks.

CHAPTER TWENTY-SIX

THE SYD, LAZAX CRUISER, ON THE EDGE OF THE GAMMA ERIDIUS SYSTEM

"How's the coupling?" Vexar called out. "Is it still fully connected?"

Mortalia was tempted to tell him it was while simultaneously breaking the engine's hardwire connector, but knew there was too great a danger of such duplicity being discovered.

"It's good," she confirmed, giving the heavy cable one more tug to confirm it was properly seated in the power port.

"Readouts are showing we're back to full capacity," the Nar Hylar, Rondu, called from the computator platform overseeing the primary engine block. "Looks like we're good to go."

Mortalia, Vexar and another Winnaran, Marwell, had been plucked from the bridge crew to accompany Rondu to check on the aft engines. Mortalia had been concerned it would bring them close to the ongoing boarding action, but the only evidence of it this far back was the faint reverberations of gunfire echoing down the corridors, mostly subsumed by the thrum of the power stacks that dominated this particular deck. They had taken a hit earlier from a glancing lance strike but seemed to have suffered no lasting damage. The cruiser was still capable of full maneuver.

"We should get back," Rondu declared, climbing down the short ladder from the computator platform to the engine block's main deck. "They probably need every hand on the bridge, especially if it looks like the boarders are going to break through."

"Do you really think we'll be able to make the difference if they do?" Marwell asked. He was one of the older Resurrectionists and seemed to possess a morbid streak that Mortalia almost respected.

"We'll fight to the last and make them pay for every corridor they try to take," Vexar said with the opposite fervor that privately sickened Mortalia. "This is an imperial ship, and it will stay that way!"

Rondu led them out of the aft section, heading back in the direction of the bridge. The hatch to the engine block refused to close on the first attempt, and Vexar volunteered to hang back and ensure it was properly sealed.

As Mortalia carried on after Rondu and Marwell, she felt a chill run down her spine. Malfunctioning hatches – caused by covert magnetic scramblers – were a common trick used by her former companions to separate and corral their prey.

She had no idea if any of the Yssaril had made it on board before the cruiser had departed Gamma Eridius. She had tried to use her beacon again, but it was now dead, unresponsive, as though it had somehow been deactivated remotely. She was frantic with fear and anger at being abandoned by her supposed allies but had determined to make the most of the situation. Surely, in the midst of a desperate naval battle, she could engineer the destruction of at least those few Lazax on board, then bluff her way back to Gamma Eridius?

But if the Yssaril were on board too, maybe there was still

some hope that they were obeying the orders she had given them after all?

They'd barely made it up to the next deck when her suspicions were confirmed. Marwell had taken the lead and died without a sound as he hurried past a comms alcove, the space intended to provide a means of communicating with the bridge for crewmembers working in the ship's aft. A shape darted from the alcove. There was a flash of steel, a surge of blood, and Marwell dropped to his knees clutching his throat.

Rondu shouted something, words lost in the sounds of the nearby engines and the battering report of gunfire coming from the embattled sections up ahead. He reached for the pistol he had strapped to his hip, but the old Hylar was too slow. The Yssaril – alone, it seemed – was on him in a blur, leaping and hitting him in the chest with the full weight and momentum of its small body.

The pair went down together, the beam pistol clattering across the mesh decking. Mortalia stood, frozen, watching the Yssaril's knife dispatch the Hylar with the same quick efficiency as the Winnaran. Blood burst from Rondu's lips and then his gills, and he shook violently. Mortalia was reminded of a fish thrown onto the shore, spasming in its final death throes.

The Yssaril remained perched on the Hylar's chest until he went still. Then he rose, and fixed Mortalia with his large, black eyes.

"Where have you been?" Mortalia demanded of the Yssaril, feeling her anger spike at such a sudden, deadly reappearance. "Why haven't you responded to my instructions?"

The killer said nothing. Instead, he took a step toward her, his eyes not leaving hers, the blood on his knife still drizzling down onto the floor and running between the mesh.

"What're you doing?" Mortalia snapped, sudden dread gripping her. The Yssaril was showing none of the deference she had grown accustomed to. She had a horrible sense that it was about to pounce on her the way it had done with the Hylar.

"Wait," she began to cry out, raising an arm, but like all those before her, she was too slow. The Yssaril lunged, and when she tried to back hastily away, he kicked at her ankle, expertly hooking it and tripping her.

She went down on her back, grunting with the impact, trying to kick and swat the vicious killer away, but he was on her, a knee in her sternum, a hand pinning her wrist, the knife at her throat.

There was a crack, and the burning ozone stink of an energy discharge. The Yssaril poised, knife raised above Mortalia, Rondu's blood dripping down onto her pale, wide-eyed face. Her eyes traveled from the red razor-steel to the Yssaril's chest – there was a smoking contusion in the bared green skin. A cauterized beam wound.

The Yssaril let out a high-pitched keening sound, then slipped off Mortalia, rolling onto the deck. He writhed for a moment, clutching the injury, then went still.

Mortalia scrambled to her feet and pressed her back against the wall, looking from her dead former companion to the individual who had just shot him with Rondu's pistol – Vexar.

The Resurrectionist's aim was trembling slightly, but it had been firm enough to make the shot that had saved Mortalia's life.

"Thank you," she said amidst a surge of genuine, limb-liquifying relief. Rather than lower the sidearm, Vexar switched his aim from the Yssaril's corpse to cover Mortalia.

"I heard you speaking to it," he said, his tone cold, accusatory. "I heard you giving it orders, like you were its master."

"Did it look like I was its master just then?" Mortalia exclaimed. "Another second and it would have opened my throat like it did with the others!"

"What did you do with Lekaan?"

The question caught Mortalia by surprise, even though she supposed it shouldn't have.

"Who?"

"Stop lying! On board the macro freighter, Lekaan went missing, and you turned up just when the pirates were attacking! Are you telling me that's just a coincidence?"

"What does that have to do with anything? I didn't know Lekaan and I definitely don't know what happened to her!"

"I don't trust you," Vexar declared. "I did, but maybe I shouldn't have. You can explain yourself once we get to the bridge. Come on, move."

Mortalia thought about going for the snub-nose she still had tucked into her waist belt. Vexar had either forgotten it or was stupid enough to not demand she surrender it. She wondered if he'd shoot if she went for it, or if she could face him down and win. Just from the way he held the beam pistol, he didn't seem familiar or comfortable with firearms.

"Come on, move," Vexar shouted, and waved the weapon. Mortalia decided there was as much a chance he'd shoot her accidentally as he would on purpose. It was ironic – considering the number of battle-hardened brutes who had tried over the years – that he had been the one to kill one of the Yssaril.

The fact that he had decided to take her prisoner wasn't even her biggest problem, she decided. The worst thing was that her Yssaril had just tried to murder her. There was no longer any doubt they had betrayed her, although she didn't know why. And with two more likely still loose on the ship, a packed bridge was quite possibly the safest place to be, at least until the real carnage began.

"You're making a mistake," she told Vexar as she raised her

hands and moved along the corridor, stepping over the bodies in her way.

"You can tell that to the Lazax," Vexar replied.

Z'ffani passed beneath the decks of the Lazax cruiser.

The confined nature of the crawl spaces, service hatches and access tubes posed no difficulty to her. Her sinuous, serpentine body was capable of slipping through gaps few other creatures of similar size would have contemplated attempting. It allowed her to pass beneath the feet of her prey unnoticed. The whole time, she cast the barbed net of her mind wide, her complex Druaa consciousness, multifaceted like the glorious rays of light refracting through the Dome of Shan on Druaa, touching upon the thoughts of those struggling throughout the ship.

It was a place of wrath and bloodlust, pain and fear and death. A place of war. She followed the tremors that were vibrating the decking, slipping her glittering, grease-streaked coils through the ship's guts toward where the most furious fighting was taking place. Attackers were attempting to board the vessel and fight their way up to its bridge, while others sought to stop them at any cost. Some bore particular antipathy for one another – both of those most ferociously opposed groups were Hacan, she realized. Rivals, clan enemies. Those were always the most bitter of struggles. Were it not for the harmony of the Naalu Collective and the melding of consciousness, Z'ffani suspected her own people would be prone to the same foolish, self-destructive tendencies.

Thankfully, the Druaa were a higher life form, and the strength of Z'ffani's powers unique to her species. The Hacan's deficiencies suited her fine, however. It would make her job much easier. She had been right to do as the Yssaril advised and wait.

The important thing was that the Lazax were present. She could feel several, located on the bridge. Their minds were not as she had anticipated, though she avoided probing them yet – she did not wish to reveal her presence too soon, even if she was certain they wouldn't be ready for her when she did.

There was work to be done. And it started with killing everything on the ship that wasn't a Lazax.

"They're hitting us hard," Naru growled as she crouched in front of Hamlar in the entrance to the boarding pod.

The Dazeshi had made some headway against the Muktat defenses, but not much. The corridor immediately outside the pod had been cleared, but beyond that the Muktat were standing firm, interlocking patterns of fire meaning that, even with their blast shields, the Dazeshi weren't able to advance any further into the blizzard of metal and energy beams.

"What about the other two assaults?" Hamlar demanded, meaning the two pirate boarding actions that should have been happening on either side. "If we can link up with them, the Muktat will collapse."

"They're not answering over comms," Selyne said. "Either they're deliberately blocking us, or they're all dead."

Hamlar wasn't sure which possibility was worse. He bared his fangs, beyond frustrated.

"We need to break this deadlock," he said. "This has already taken too long. The Muktat fleet will be engaging Bazishel. We must capture the bridge and the engines, take control and head for the acceleration point."

"Perhaps we should think about evacuating instead," Naru pointed out. "There are escape pods nearby. We could return to the *Reiver's Son*. There probably aren't any Lazax on board here with us anyway."

Hamlar had to concede she was probably correct. This was almost certainly a trap, and Hamlar had allowed himself to walk right into it. He had let his hatred of the Muktat get the better of him. Now he was cornered. If he was captured alive by the likes of Akenzi – it didn't bear thinking about.

"How far are the escape pods?" he began to ask, but a voice on Selyne's savant made him pause. She demanded the sender repeat his message, then looked at Hamlar.

"We've broken through," she said, sounding almost disbelieving. "The left-hand corridor, up toward the starboard docking berths. The Muktat there are all dead."

"How?" Hamlar asked, wondering if this was some new trickery from the devious rival clan.

"It's… unclear. Taresh is leading that section of the boarding team. He says it seems as though they turned on one another."

That was difficult to believe. For all the contempt Hamlar held for the Muktat, they were a loyal clan. He had spent months trying to find spies, traitors and informants within their ranks, and had failed to recruit any. The idea that one would turn on the others in the midst of a boarding action, one in which they were winning…

"I'm going forward," Hamlar said, rising with a swish of his tail and drawing the weapon at his hip. "I want to see what's happening."

"We wouldn't advise that, magnate," Naru said, exchanging a pointed glance with Selyne. "The situation is still unclear and contested. As you said yourself, this could be another trap."

"I've hung back here for long enough," Hamlar snapped. "I'm going to find out what in the name of the Golden Sands this all means. You can do your job and protect me, or you can stay here. Either way, I'm going."

...

The report from Taresh seemed to be correct. Hamlar passed along the corridor toward where the Dazeshi boarders had made their breakthrough. The space was scarred by the ferocity of the tightly confined battle, the walls, ceiling and decking blackened by energy burns and pockmarked where hard rounds had chewed chunks out of the ship's interior. Bodies still littered the walkways as well, both Dazeshi and Muktat, their blood puddling on the decking plates.

Such a brutal end to so many Hacan lives almost gave Hamlar pause, but he carried on, thankful he had worn more practical combat gear instead of his usual zenfar robes, so he did not run the risk of them trailing in the blood.

This was negotiation at its most aggressive, and Hamlar would not lose to upstart sled-draggers like Clan Muktat.

He met Taresh at the last barricades the defenders had been holding. They were ingeniously formed from decking plates that had been levered up so they stood vertically. Their fronts were a twisted, fused mass of metal, battered almost beyond recognition by the intensity of the firefight, but behind them were heaped half a dozen Muktat corpses. Taresh and two more of his boarding team were standing over them, their flat ears pointing toward their uneasiness despite their apparent victory.

"We noticed they had stopped firing," Taresh said by way of explanation. "We thought at first it was a trick, so we waited, but nothing happened even after we started to advance. We found this barricade like this. No survivors. I don't think any even managed to retreat."

"If you didn't kill them, what did?" Hamlar asked.

"It looks like they shot each other," Taresh said, stooping to indicate various wounds.

"Point-blank hits, so close they ignited their fur. This one looks like he clawed this one to death while he was being shot. It's like they went completely feral."

"Why?" Hamlar wondered aloud. "It doesn't make any sense."

"I don't know, my magnate," Taresh admitted. "We weren't going to break through here, but now the rest of my strike team have spread out beyond this corridor, and we're meeting no resistance. It looks like we've got a clear run up to the bridge."

A sense of unease crept over Hamlar, piercing the raw aggression that had animated his thoughts since the boarding began. Something was wrong here, and yet he couldn't fathom what. But they couldn't afford to stop now. Trap or not, they would only discover what awaited them by pressing on.

He was about to order Taresh to storm the bridge when one of the other Dazeshi boarding members cried out and clutched his head. His other companion, and Taresh, all looked suddenly uncomfortable, as though suffering from some sort of acute pain.

"What is it?" Hamlar demanded, feeling nothing himself.

"It's in my head," the first Hacan snarled through clenched fangs. "It's on board and it's in my head … I can't …"

Hamlar took a step back from the struggling warrior, alarmed, yet still wasn't ready for the moment when the pained Dazeshi suddenly ceased gripping his skull like it was about to burst open and instead snatched up his energy carbine.

Naru and Selyne were, thankfully, faster than the traitor. One shoved Hamlar to the side as the other lashed out with her claws, choosing her natural weapons as quicker options compared to the weapon cinched to her chest.

She raked open the Hacan's throat just as he discharged his carbine, the crack of the shot painfully loud to Hamlar in the confined space. He stumbled, Naru almost knocking him over, but the burst of energy missed them both, searing black, fused markings into the plasticon at their backs. The Hacan's mane turned dark red with blood, and he slumped against Selyne as she tackled him to the ground.

"What are you doing?" Hamlar shouted uselessly at the second Dazeshi warrior as, trembling, he, too, slowly raised his carbine.

"Can't you hear it?" the Hacan pleaded. "Can't you hear the hissing? I-It's underneath us. It wants you to die!"

And suddenly, Hamlar understood what the panicked warrior meant. There was a susurration on the edge of his consciousness, in the strange, gray area that seemed to lie between mental thought and physical sensation. It began to rise rapidly in pitch, filling his hearing, then his whole mind, making him forget himself, forget everything besides the hypnotic rise and fall, like wind breathing through rustling leaves, or a gentle tide whispering up a stony shore.

The discharge of the carbine brought him back, if only momentarily. He briefly thought he had been shot, then realized it was the second of his warriors who was down, hit at point blank by Naru's carbine.

"We need to go," she urged. "There's… there's something here. We can't protect you from it. From ourselves. Not for long."

"Yes," Hamlar agreed. He could still feel the hissing, more pure sensation than just a sound. It made his fur bristle and caused him to instinctively snarl. It was inside him, inside his skull. He could understand why the others had clutched at their heads.

"What is it?" Hamlar asked as they began to run along the corridor, feet making the decking plates ring. It was a stupid question, he knew. None of them had any idea what this was. Some deadly tool unearthed by the Muktat? But then even a cunning runt like Akenzi surely wouldn't have used it on his own bonded clan warriors first? Perhaps it was the Lazax? Some terrible old weapon belonging to the empire, either accidentally unleashed by the Muktat on friend and foe alike or deployed by the Lazax themselves. Maybe they were on board after all?

Hamlar could find no answers before there was a clang as Taresh fell to his knees, crying out in pain or frustration, or both. Hamlar half turned and found himself gazing into his warrior's eyes.

"I am sorry, my magnate," Taresh growled through clenched fangs, then raised his beam pistol and turned it on himself.

Hamlar stared in horror, but Naru snagged his mane and began dragging him along again.

"Keep moving," she urged, voice barely audible above the hissing. It grew stronger again, drowning out everything else in Hamlar's mind.

That was when the creature struck.

It dropped down from an air recyc vent, squarely onto Selyne's shoulders.

It was small, green, and wielding a telescopic spear that it extended with a deft twist of its wrist, plunging the weapon down through Selyne's shoulder and into her torso before the Dazeshi bodyguard could react.

Though she had suffered what could only be a mortal wound, Selyne still lashed out with the ferocity of a born warrior. She twisted and flung her assailant against the corridor wall, the movement becoming a stumble as her strength deserted her and she fell with her killer.

This enemy, at least, Hamlar recognized. Yssaril. Spies, assassins, mercenaries with the ability to turn practically invisible. They had most famously been used by the Barony of Letnev against the last fragments of the Lazax Empire, but they were mercenaries by nature and had regularly been hired by one or another of the great civilizations.

Whether they had been brought by Akenzi, the Lazax, Bazishel or whatever mysterious thing was causing the hissing, Hamlar had no idea. All he was certain of was that he had made a terrible mistake choosing to board this ship.

He attempted to run back the way he had come. Instead, he tripped on Taresh's corpse and went sprawling, striking his head off a bulkhead. He was vaguely aware of Naru screaming and opening fire on the being that had killed her sister, the energy shots whipping over him. It was fast though, incredibly so. Despite having been thrown against the wall by Selyne, it leapt lithely up and away from the arc of fire unleashed by Naru, her beam pistol searing holes into the corridor all around it but not touching it.

The thing's spear was still wedged in Selyne who, incredibly, was not only still alive but was trying to rise once more, her bared fangs red with blood. She snatched for the Yssaril and managed to snag its ankle with her claws, momentarily impeding it. Naru's weapon was whining though, drained of charge. Shrieking with frustration, rather than reload, the Hacan threw the empty weapon at the Yssaril and lunged at it, her claws out.

It had drawn a short knife, which it used to stab Selyne's wrist, expertly severing tendons and causing the bloodied Hacan to immediately relinquish her grip. It just had time to throw itself back to avoid an eviscerating swipe of Naru's claws, but before she could recover from her furious lunge it had kicked back off the wall behind it and powered in through the charging Hacan's guard.

The Yssaril stabbed Naru with its short knife more times than Hamlar could count, a blur of thumping blows delivered under her arm, where the body armor she was wearing ended at the joint. With a throat-shaking roar, Naru threw the Yssaril back and swiped again.

This time the assassin had no more room to maneuver. The Hacan's claws savaged its chest, ripping green flesh and sending dark blood surging. The Yssaril shrieked, but the wound only seemed to drive it into a frenzy of its own. It leapt on Naru again and rammed its short knife into her eye socket with a hideous crunch.

Naru made a keening sound deep in her throat and stumbled, but she didn't go down. Selyne had somehow regained her feet behind the Yssaril as it twisted and tried to grind its knife deeper in her sister's skull.

With the spear's haft still protruding from her shoulder, Selyne snatched the Yssaril from behind and pinned it with her claws. Gagging on her own blood, she plunged her fangs into the assassin's neck, savaging it as it shrieked again.

With the knife still protruding from one eye, Naru did the same from the front, digging her fangs into the other side of its neck. Its wailing became ugly gargling noises as the dying sisters ripped out their killer's throat.

Slowly, the gory, entwined trio slid to the floor. The Yssaril was dead, its body drenched in dark blood. Naru slumped over it, twitching, both lying against Selyne now, who was sitting with her back against the wall. She made eye contact with Hamlar, her crimson muzzle opening as if to say something, but the last of the ferocious, murderous strength that had driven her was gone. She went still and silent.

Hamlar remained where he had fallen for what felt like an age, staring. It was the most violent thing he had ever seen.

Eventually, something roused him from his shocked stupor, a sound, a sensation.

The hissing had returned.

"No," he whined, pawing at his head and scrambling to his feet. He stumbled through the blood of those who had died saving him, running.

CHAPTER TWENTY-SEVEN

"What are you doing?"

The words stung Vexar – they were an accusation, delivered by those he held most dear. Vel Syd had risen from his chair on the command gantry and every eye on the bridge was turned toward him. Vexar had entered with Mortalia ahead of him, the beam pistol still aimed at her.

His heart was racing. He began to speak, stumbling over the words in his haste to explain himself, in his desperation to make it clear that she, and not he, was the traitor here.

"We were attacked. The others are all dead. I… I think Mortalia was part of it."

"What do you mean?" the Hylar named Tol demanded, stepping away from her station. "Are you saying Rondu's dead?"

"Yes," Vexar said, his throat dry. "Something attacked them."

As he spoke, he noticed that the nearest Hacan warriors around the edge of the bridge had raised and primed their weapons. They were pointing them at him, not Mortalia. He knew he should lower his beam pistol, but his arm seemed stiff, stuck, still trembling as he kept the pistol pointed at Mortalia.

"It's her," he almost shouted, knowing he sounded dangerously incoherent, but struggling to frame his thoughts. "She isn't one of us! A Resurrectionist, I mean! She… she joined us at Quinz 11. Claimed she was just going to Gamma Eridius to earn aurei. But she spoke to it! She told it to obey her!"

"Vexar," Vel Syd said sharply, cracking his staff onto the deck to get his attention. His cybernetic eye glowed dangerously. "Lower the pistol."

"I can't," Vexar said breathlessly. "S-She might try something."

"He's deranged," Mortalia said, looking at the rest of the bridge pleadingly. "It's true, something attacked us. I don't know what it was. Some small, green creature. It murdered Marwell and Rondu with a knife. It was about to murder me as well!"

She pointed at the blood on her face, still fresh. The blood from the creature's knife, Vexar knew, but he stumbled over his words again as Mortalia carried on.

"Vexar shot it, but then he had some sort of breakdown. He started making these accusations, and he turned the weapon on me! I haven't done anything! I don't know what he's talking about!"

"What happened to Lekaan?" Vexar shouted, a surge of frustration finally giving him a degree of focus, of clarity. "What did you do to her?"

"I don't know what he's talking about," Mortalia replied, speaking up at Vel Syd, her tone desperate. "Please, don't let him shoot me."

"Vexar," said a familiar voice. He blinked and realized Kazi had left her station and approached him. Gently, she put her hand on his raised arm.

"You know I don't trust her either," she said to him, softly, turning his face with her other hand so they were eye to eye. "But you need to lower the pistol. We'll work this out."

The Hacan soldiers had moved closer, the whine of their leveled energy weapons loud in Vexar's ears. He swallowed hard, trembling, and finally found he was able to slowly lower his arm.

Kazi took the pistol off him and stepped back.

"Thank you," Mortalia said, dropping her own arms.

There was a pounding at the main bridge hatch. Half of the crew leapt with fright, and the Hacan turned their weapons on the entrance.

"Have they broken through?" Akenzi snapped at Drusha.

"I don't know," he growled, moving to check a bank of viz monitors. He stared for a moment, then gestured wordlessly for Akenzi to join him.

The magnate hurried down from the command gantry and stood alongside his brother. He found himself looking at the last thing he had expected to see.

According to the viz recorder monitoring the corridor immediately outside the bridge's primary hatch, Magnate Hamlar Dazeshi was attempting to gain access. He was seemingly alone and spattered with blood. Akenzi had to do a double take, wondering if he was imagining things.

"He's here," he said. "That Tuuran whelp is actually here."

"What is it?" Vel Syd called. Akenzi was too shocked to consider the ramifications of telling the Lazax his most relentless opponent was currently right outside.

"It's Hamlar," he replied. "The magnate of the Dazeshi clan. He's my greatest rival."

"He's a Tuuran-rutting bastard," Drusha added in Hacan, but Akenzi ignored him.

"He's been trying to undermine my venture to the Gap from the beginning. I suspected he was behind the pirate attacks. I assumed the Hacan boarding us were his warriors, but I didn't think he'd be in the Boreas Gap, let alone leading them."

"Are his warriors with him? You said they've broken through?"

"It looks like it's just him," Akenzi said, staring at the viz screen like it was some digital anomaly. Hamlar had been beating against the hatch but was now alternating between glancing up at the viz recorder monitoring him, and looking back over his shoulder, down the corridor.

"He looks like he's trying to get away from something," Drusha said.

"Perhaps he's running from whatever it was that attacked the engine party," Akenzi replied, trying to rationalize what he was seeing. "If there's a third faction on board that's been attacking both the pirates and ourselves, it might explain how our defenses have been breached?"

"Or it could be a trick," Vel Syd pointed out.

Hamlar beat against the hatch again, calling out, though his words were too muffled to understand. Akenzi looked between the display and the entrance.

It appeared for all the world as though the Hacan who wanted him reduced to ruin, or worse, was currently, desperately trying to surrender to him. And as much as the thought of having Magnate Hamlar in his power appealed, something was clearly very wrong.

"What do we do?" Drusha asked softly, again speaking in the Muktat dialect. He was looking at the Lazax and the Winnaran, but they seemed as confused and uncertain as the Hacan.

"Open the hatch," Akenzi said. "Take him."

"If I open it, and he has forces ready to storm the bridge in the adjoining corridor, there'll be little we can do to stop them," Vel Syd said. "Most of the viz recorders in the rest of the ship are down. We're blind to what is happening elsewhere, as the death of Rondu proves. But we are secure here as long as the hatch remains sealed. There is little reason to open it."

"Just do it," Akenzi snapped, turning sharply toward Vel Syd. "If we take that Dazeshi fool, this all ends. The pirates will have lost their paymaster, so they won't have a reason to risk themselves against us. I can return to the tri-system and present Hamlar before the Hacan Council. I can have him tried for piracy and propagating a clan war. The Dazeshi will be broken, and Clan Muktat will be secure for a generation."

"None of which explains why I should risk my ship and my crew," Vel Syd said coldly.

"There's no one out there," Akenzi all but shouted. Vel Syd remained unmoved, so he gestured at Drusha instead.

"Open the hatch."

Several Winnarans rose from their stations, but the Muktat soldiers had their weapons leveled again in an instant, covering the whole bridge.

"Let us not be foolish," Vel Syd called sharply, again using his staff for emphasis. "You've made your point, magnate. Let the consequences be on your head."

The Lazax gestured at one of his simpering crewmembers, and the Winnaran unlocked the hatch remotely.

The heavy blast door levered open. Drusha moved toward it and lunged through. Hamlar emerged onto the bridge with Akenzi's brother gripping him by the mane, blood-spattered and flat-eared.

"We have to get away," the Dazeshi magnate stammered before Akenzi could even begin addressing him. "We have to get off this ship, before it kills us all!"

"What are you talking about?" Akenzi snapped. This wasn't the triumphant encounter he had envisaged – Hamlar seemed too shocked and afraid to even display surprise at Akenzi's presence on the Lazax ship.

"Can't you hear it?" he asked, then stopped, apparently searching for a sound inaudible to anybody else on the bridge. "The hissing."

"Cease this foolishness," Akenzi snarled at him, gesticulating angrily at the comms station. "You will call off your pirate pets immediately. Do that and I might just advocate a degree of clemency when we make it back to Kenara!"

Hamlar charged at him, ripping out of Drusha's grip so forcefully that Akenzi's older brother was left with a fistful of the Dazeshi's mane.

Akenzi yelped as Hamlar, stumbling past the nearest console blocks, grabbed the front of his armored vest, and every weapon on the bridge was leveled in their direction. For a second, he imagined Hamlar's fangs at his throat, but instead the rival magnate just gripped him muzzle to muzzle, their gaze locking. His eyes were wild, feral.

"There's something on this ship, and it's killing everyone. If you are not its master, it will kill you next. Do you understand?"

Akenzi yanked himself from Hamlar's feverish grasp, and then Drusha was on him, slamming the Dazeshi against the nearby consoles and restraining him.

"You saw them, didn't you?" the Winnaran who had come onto the bridge earlier waving a beam pistol shouted at Hamlar.

"Yssaril," Hamlar growled, making no effort to fight back against Drusha. "One slaughtered my guards. But that isn't what I'm talking about! Something is on board that is breaking the minds of your warriors and mine, Akenzi. It drives itself into your mind! It will make you do terrible things!"

"There are Yssaril on board?" Vel Syd demanded, looking back at the Winnaran. "Is that what attacked you?"

"I don't know what Yssaril are," the Winnaran admitted, pointing a furious finger at the one he had brought in as a prisoner. "But she was commanding them!"

Akenzi was still trying to make sense of the situation when he heard the hissing. He was barely conscious of it at first. It lightly caressed the back of his mind, growing slowly, pushing away other thoughts until, belatedly, he realized it rang in his ears, inside his very head, a slow, steady rattling that made his fur stand on end.

He looked at Hamlar with a plunging sense of horror.

"You hear it, don't you?" the Dazeshi exclaimed.

One of the Muktat warriors on the edge of the bridge cried out.

"Stop him," Hamlar shouted. Akenzi opened his mouth to speak, but too late.

The Hacan soldier opened fire.

CHAPTER TWENTY-EIGHT

The bridge descended into chaos.

The Muktat warrior fired indiscriminately into the center of the space, a hail of plasma bolts cutting down two Winnarans at their stations and hitting another Muktat on the far side.

Akenzi threw himself to the deck as a second burst cracked overhead, searing into the command gantry.

There was more gunfire, this time from another of the Muktat, standing close to the first shooter. Reacting faster than those around him, he turned his carbine on the traitor and brought him down with a flurry of close-range hits, punching crimson bolts through his armor.

Briefly, Akenzi thought the danger had passed, but then the warrior who had brought down his kin clutched his head and stumbled. A few moments later and he was the one firing wildly, screaming with pain even as he did so.

The computator station above Akenzi sparked and blew as plasma bolts pounded it. Drusha hauled Hamlar to the deck just across from him as the same flurry whipped at the station they were now sheltering behind.

Akenzi clenched his fangs, heart hammering. One thought pierced the fog of adrenaline and panic – for all his wits and cunning, surrounded by death and gunfire, he had no idea what to do.

Mortalia went for her pistol.

She yanked the snub-nose out and flung herself past the nearest control station even as bolts blew through it and sent smoke and sparks broiling through the air.

She didn't understand what was happening, but she knew one thing – this was going to be her last chance.

Oblivious to the carnage around her, she ran to the base of the command gantry and raised her pistol at the Lazax seated above her. He hadn't moved, seemingly frozen amidst the chaos.

"This is for my parents," Mortalia screamed. "And for all Winnarans!"

She fired. The Lazax was hit, punched back into his chair.

With a clatter, his staff fell to the deck.

"No!" Vexar screamed.

He threw aside Kazi and flung himself on Mortalia, slamming her head against the struts of the command deck as they went down together.

Blind rage filled him. He was unaware of the shouting, screaming and gunfire all around. Unaware of anything other than the traitor under him, her pistol falling from her grip, her hands grappling with him as she tried to force him off.

He hit her, once, twice, three times. Blood ran down her pale features.

"Traitor," he howled, spittle flying. "What have you done?"

Hands grabbed at him, dragging him up and off. He fought back, desperate to punish this devious murderer, this assassin who had deluded him and tricked him and sought to kill all that he loved.

Someone hit him, so hard that he stumbled. The sudden pain pierced the frenzied fog that had swamped his mind.

"She's down," Kazi said, yanking him round to face him. "Now for the love of the empire, find some cover!"

Tol heaved herself up onto the command gantry, her aches and pains momentarily forgotten. Disdaining the energy shots that were scything through the air around her or burning into the metal, she knelt where Ibna had collapsed off the chair and onto the deck, her eyes scanning for where he had been hit.

"Tol," Ibna rasped, his one organic eye flickering as he looked up at her, seeking focus.

"Gunshot wound to your left side," she said, noting the dark patch around the hole in his rough old robes. "Hold still."

"You should get down," Ibna wheezed. "There's shooting…"

Tol ignored him as she worked, pulling aside the cloth and tugging at the undershirt beneath. Her mind ran through the long list of surgeries she had performed on Ibna, trying to assess the likely impact against where he had been shot.

"Get the rest out," the Lazax was saying, one cybernetic arm clutching at her, the grip unyielding and painful. "The children… the future… Tell Marchu. Don't let them die on Gamma Eridius."

"Let go," Tol ordered firmly. "And stop being so melodramatic. You've taken a hit to your synth skin. The bonding's broken so it'll hurt, and the fact there's a hard round still embedded won't help. But you've not had any of your original organs penetrated."

Ibna grunted, looking down at the injury, the meeting of wizened flesh, artificial skin and chromatic metal laid bare. He let go of Tol's arm.

"I wouldn't recommend trying to get up just yet though," she added as more shots punched into the back of the chair above them.

"Stop," Akenzi yelled, but nobody was listening.

It seemed as though at least half of the Clan Muktat soldiers on the bridge were shooting at the crew, or at each other. Everyone else had gone to ground, but the fact that Akenzi's supposed guards had been arrayed all around the space meant they were currently in the middle of a wicked crossfire.

"It's underneath us," Hamlar shouted, trying and failing to rip his way free from Drusha. "They said it was in the vents beneath the decks! You need to flush the systems! That's why I came here! It's the only chance we have!"

"What is it?" Akenzi shouted back, cringing as a bolt blew out the computator above him, sparks singing his mane. "What did you bring on board?"

"We didn't bring anything! I don't know what it is, but it gets in your head! I know you can hear it now!"

Loath as he was to ever admit Hamlar was right, Akenzi could indeed hear it. More than that, he could feel it. Like something in his head, coils of glittering scales, slowly tightening around his mind, their hiss and rattle scraping his brain free of any other thoughts.

"It's targeting the ones with weapons first," Drusha called out from next to Hamlar, no longer trying to restrain him.

"What?"

"If it's controlling some of us, it's going after the best-armed first. Making them kill each other."

Akenzi realized his brother was right. He was suddenly thankful he was only packing a beam pistol.

"I don't think it has the ability to get into everyone's head at once," Hamlar said as wayward shots seared holes in the decking plates between the two magnates. "It will pick us off a few at a time!"

"How do you know it's under us?" Akenzi demanded.

"Can't you feel it? When it connects with you, you can sense it, or some of what it's feeling. Scales. Dark, narrow spaces. I think it must be nearby. Under us."

Akenzi had no doubt anymore that Hamlar was telling the truth. Something, somehow, had used the chaos and confusion of the boarding action to strike. Whether it had been lurking on the Lazax ship since Gamma Eridius, or had gotten on board since then, didn't matter. It had to be stopped before it turned them all against each other.

"Vel Syd," he shouted, looking up at the command gantry. The chair was empty, smoldering with blast holes. "Vel Syd, can you hear me?"

"I can hear you," called the Lazax's voice, to Akenzi's relief. He wasn't sure if he'd been hit during the carnage, but at the very least he was still conscious.

"We need to purge the systems! Something on board is causing all this, and it's probably nearby! Under us! We need to find it and kill it, before it takes us all!"

"A final system purge needs authorization from you," Tol said as she crouched, hunched over, next to Ibna. "From the chair."

"Do you know what's causing this?" Ibna asked.

"No," Tol admitted. She had been trying to make sense of what was happening ever since Vexar had reappeared with one of his own Resurrectionists held at gunpoint, but so far, the puzzle was missing vital pieces. She could feel what the Hacan magnate had been raving about – a pain in her head, a slow, hypnotic rattling. It was barely strong enough to make its way past her subconscious, but she had no doubt it was the same force that appeared to have driven some of Akenzi's warriors wild.

"We know there are Yssaril on board," she continued. "We know how deadly they are. Perhaps this is one of their weapons."

"Do you feel what they're talking about?" Ibna asked.

"You don't?" Tol responded. "A … a kind of hissing. It's … unsettling."

"Nothing," Ibna confirmed with a shake of his head.

"Interesting," Tol mused, the cold, detached, clinical part of her brain compartmentalizing that for later review.

A plasma bolt cracked into the base of the chair beside her, searing and melting the metal, and another slashed so close by she felt the deadly heat of its passing.

"No reason not to flush the systems," she said with a grimace. "Let's just hope the Hacan are right."

Ibna nodded. Then, expression set, he reached up with his one remaining organic arm and pressed his hand against the side of the command chair. It spent precious seconds checking for Lazax gene idents, then unlocked.

He did his best to input the necessary orders without pulling himself up into the shot-scarred chair itself. It was awkward, and the pain of his injury was obvious on the remaining flesh of his face. Finally, though, arm trembling, he stabbed the accept marker.

An automated voice spoke out over the comms bank, announcing a manually triggered system purge would be commencing in thirty seconds. Tol tugged Ibna back down to the meager cover of the gantry deck as the fire around them intensified.

...

Akenzi counted down the seconds. After thirty it seemed nothing was happening, then, with a sense of breathless relief, he felt the whole bridge begin to tremor.

There was an electronic whine, its pitch competing with both the gunfire and the hissing inside Akenzi's head. After reaching a painful intensity it cut off and was replaced with a solid *whump* that caused the shaking to redouble.

The *Syd* flushed its underbelly. The dense cables and knots of wiring snaking beneath the bridge experienced a surge, and the pipes and valves briefly became superheated as the power was rerouted from shields and engines to the ship's hardware core. It was designed to burn blockages and restore idling or flagging systems to full capacity ahead of a redirection of power, often from prow to aft engines or as part of a sharp navigational change. The vessel was reinvigorating itself, and in doing so Akenzi could only hope it purged whatever horror lurked in its depths.

His thoughts were answered almost immediately. The hissing was replaced by a shriek that seemed to issue not from the decking plates beneath them, but within the confines of his own skull.

He cried out, clutching his head, the pain momentarily overwhelming. Then it was gone, the scream echoing away into his subconscious, melding with the memory of his own cry until they were indistinguishable.

The first thing he noticed in the aftermath was the quiet. Not only had the deck stopped shaking and thrumming, but there was no more gunfire. All that was left was the occasional fizz and spark of the damaged console stations and the moaning and whimpering of the injured. After the carnage that had reigned moments before, such near-silence was shocking.

"System purge, complete," droned the bridge's automated voice.

Akenzi looked toward Hamlar and Drusha. The Dazeshi magnate was as stunned and looked as uncertain as Akenzi felt, but Drusha was already on the move. He had risen from his battered cover and headed over to one of the other bridge stations, stepping round the Winnaran cowering there.

No shots snapped at him. Akenzi dared to glance over the wreckage he was crouched behind and found most of his nearest warriors – those who were still alive – staring about themselves in apparent confusion.

"It must have worked," he said, seeking any hint of the accursed, dreadful hissing. There was none.

"Did you hear it die?" Hamlar breathed. "It screamed. It screamed inside my mind."

"It's not dead," Drusha said bluntly. It was only then that Akenzi understood what his brother was doing. The station he had gone to was the one holding the viz monitors.

Akenzi got up and hurried to his side. Most of the screens had been shot out, but a few still functioned, and Drusha had cycled through them, hunting for ones not destroyed during the boarding action. Akenzi looked for what he had spotted but could see nothing besides stills of the ship's corridors, empty apart from the dead.

"Did you see it?" he asked urgently.

Drusha said nothing but manipulated the station's input board. One of the images froze then rewound a few seconds.

Akenzi witnessed a sight that chilled him to the bone.

Something burst up through a maintenance porthole in the deck. It was long and sinuous, though its upper body resembled something akin to a human or Letnev woman, albeit one covered with serpent-like scales. Part of those scales seemed broken and blistered, and the thing writhed with apparent pain as it hauled itself up onto the deck, steam rising from the hole behind it.

It moved with darting quickness, sweeping down the corridor with a thrust of its tail. In a few moments it was out of sight.

"Have you ever seen anything like that?" Akenzi asked Drusha.

"No," the former ordri warrior admitted. "I just hope that's the only one on board."

The raw adrenaline powering Akenzi was now fully gone, drained by the realization that there was something utterly unknown to any of them on board. The galaxy was a place full of mysteries, and Akenzi considered this the worst possible time to be reminded of that truth.

CHAPTER TWENTY-NINE

THE SYD, LAZAX CRUISER, ON THE EDGE OF THE GAMMA ERIDIUS SYSTEM

It had been decades since Z'ffani had last experienced such pain.

By the time she had realized what her prey were doing, it had almost been too late. She had been burned by electrical discharge and by the heat of surging power capacitors. The pain had fueled her, and she had been able to pry her way up onto the main deck.

They had flushed her out. They were clever. But all they had really done was make her angry.

The lone Druaa slithered along one of the scarred corridors close to where the boarding action had taken place, slipping around the bodies and through their blood, leaving a crimson wake behind. The cold liquid helped soothe the pain of her burns. She kept moving until she reached an area where the viz recorders she had noted on the ceilings had been shot out or were inactive. She was safe from the prying eyes of those on the bridge, for the time being.

It had been progressing well, until she had overplayed her hand. She had worked her way through the ship's bowels, mind-breaking and killing as she went, but the bridge had proven to be too much. There were too many of them, and now she had no doubt they were aware of her presence.

She would need to get closer to them again if she wanted to resume the slaughter. Though her telepathic control was impressive even for her kind, like all Druaa the range of her abilities was not limitless. Nor were they without cost. She was drained, exhausted by the mental effort of bending and snapping so many wills, of driving so many to kill those they had once counted as friends and comrades.

Perhaps such a brutal solution was not the ideal one. She had not come this far to discard subtlety for blunt force. The Naalu Collective were natural manipulators, and she was, arguably, the most powerful of all. She could do more than puppet a few warrior brutes from the lesser civilizations.

She found a cabin berth off one of the battle-scarred corridors and coiled up in it, rattling softly as she tended to her wounds with her forked tongue. Then, she closed her eyes, settled herself and forgot her pain and exhaustion. She reached out once again with her mind.

They would give her what she wanted, whether she was in their heads or not.

"I have never seen its like before," Vel Syd admitted.

The former ambassador and his fellow Lazax, Alarina, along with Tol and Vexar, had joined Akenzi and his bodyguard as well as the other Hacan magnate at the viz monitors. They had rewatched the nightmarish emergence of the serpentine creature half a dozen times. None could put a name to it.

Tol knew of several lesser species the galaxy over that shared characteristics with the reptilian snake-species that existed on many habitable worlds. She had never heard of any with the ability to possess the mind. Telepathic species were extremely rare and, to the best of her knowledge, confined to two known groupings, neither of which traveled in any numbers beyond their home systems, or shared characteristics with giant serpents.

"Perhaps she knows," Vexar said coldly, and gestured at the captured Winnaran.

Mortalia was being held nearby by two of Akenzi's Hacan warriors. Her scalp and nose were bloody, and she simply glared as Tol looked over at her.

Without Vexar's intervention, she might well have succeeded in assassinating Vel Syd. The old Lazax was still suffering from his wound, but Tol had patched it with an antiseptic tyrentine synth bond, and without internal bleeding or rupture she was confident it could wait for further treatment. It seemed Vexar had been right about her treachery, although why a supposed Resurrectionist would want to murder a Lazax, Tol had yet to work out. Right now, there were more pressing matters.

"Do you know what this is?" she asked the baleful Winnaran, stepping aside and gesturing at the monitor. Mortalia just shook her head.

"Bring her here," Vel Syd commanded. There was a coldness to his voice that gave Tol pause.

The Hacan grasped the Winnaran's arms and marched her to the display. All eyes turned to Vel Syd.

Tol wasn't sure which part of his expression was more terrifying – his natural organics or the metal of his cybernetics. The Lazax took a step toward Mortalia, his enhancements purring, and suddenly he loomed over her. For a moment, the defiance flushed from the rogue Winnaran's face.

"Did you bring this creature on board?" Vel Syd asked softly, almost deadly. "Are you working with it?"

"No," Mortalia said, suddenly unable to meet the glare of the Lazax's optic implant.

"You've never seen it before? You've no idea what it is?"

"I have as much an idea as you seem to."

"But you know what the Yssaril are," Vel Syd pressed. "You're working with them. Why?"

Mortalia said nothing.

"We need to know how they're connected," Tol spoke up. "And you know more than any of us."

Mortalia seemed to rediscover a fraction of her defiance. She glared at Tol, then abruptly asked to be allowed to remove something from a pocket. There were cautious glances, and Vexar tensed up, but Vel Syd nodded, and Akenzi told one of the guards to release her arm. Slowly, the Winnaran withdrew something before tossing it onto the input board in front of the monitors.

It was a small metal plate. Tol leaned over to inspect it and recognized the crest immediately. It belonged to the Barony of Letnev. More specifically, the Baronial coat of arms bore the subdivisions denoting the Cimm Fenn, the dreaded security agency.

"You're working for the Barony?" Akenzi asked.

"Yes," Mortalia said. "Almost all my life."

"But why?" Vexar exclaimed angrily, and Tol tensed up as he took a step toward the prisoner, before Drusha interposed himself between the pair.

"Why would you work for those who hate us, who hate everything we stand for?" Vexar carried on regardless, face flushed with rage.

"The Letnev don't hate us," Mortalia snapped back, her anger ablaze once more. "They just hate fools like you and your little cult. Misguided idiots who think that somehow things were better when one civilization ruled all the rest, including us. The Lazax were corrupt, power-hungry tyrants, and when the rest of the galaxy had endured enough of their misrule, they made sure we suffered the consequences. How many Winnarans sacrificed their lives trying to preserve their four-armed masters? How many were purged because of their association with an empire that only ever viewed them as useful servants? And you would glorify that? Try to recreate it?"

"My people made many mistakes," Vel Syd said sharply, cutting in before Vexar could respond with a tirade of his own. "I know better than most the sacrifices of the Winnarans. But now is not the time to debate your people's place within the empire. As Doctor Tol said, there is a threat on board this ship, and it seems intent on killing us all, regardless of where our loyalties lie. So, if you wish to live, Mortalia, and maybe yet take your revenge, you should tell us what you know, if not of this creature then of the Yssaril, and why you brought them here."

"The Cimm Fenn assigned them to me," Mortalia said, glaring up at Vel Syd. "There are three of them. Or there were three. He shot one–"

She gestured at Vexar.

Hamlar spoke up. "My bodyguards died killing another. Damn those camouflaged…"

"So, unless it was caught in the system purge, the third is still loose," Vel Syd mused. "But you said they weren't obeying you any longer? That one tried to kill you? Or was that a lie?"

"My instructions from the Cimm Fenn were simple," Mortalia said. "If I ever managed to locate any surviving Lazax, I was to issue a kill order to the Yssaril. They would… take care of the rest. When I joined the Resurrectionists and we discovered the settlement on Gamma Eridius, I sent out that instruction. But the Yssaril did nothing. I have had no contact with them since then, except earlier, when one ignored my orders and tried to cut my throat. So either they have betrayed the Barony, or the Barony has betrayed me. Perhaps their true instructions from the Cimm Fenn were simply to locate the Lazax and then kill me. Why, I don't know."

"We do not know if this creature is in league with the Yssaril, or if it is mere coincidence," Tol pointed out, seeing an expression of murderous rage pass over Vel Syd's face at the mention of killing their enclave. "At least with the Yssaril there is a way to fight them. But this other interloper possesses potent telepathic abilities, and there seems to be no way to–"

A pain in her head interrupted her. She flinched, clutching at her temple. Those around did likewise, all but Vel Syd, who looked nonplussed.

"What is it?" he demanded.

The hissing had returned. This time, though, there was more. Tol steadied herself against the side of the viz monitors as she heard a voice, feminine, soft and lilting with a rise-and-fall cadence that matched the pace of the swaying susurrations.

Greetings, servants of the great civilizations. Are you impressed by my power? By how tightly I can grip your little minds? You are likely trying to discern a way that I might be stopped, but there is only one way to guarantee you will leave this ship alive. I have not come to kill, but to preserve. Bring me the Lazax. By their own will or by yours, have them leave the bridge. I will depart with them, and no more harm will befall you.

The voice became silent, and the hissing slowly receded. With it went the pain. Tol straightened and saw the same dismay in the eyes of those around her. All but Vel Syd.

"Did everyone else hear that?" she asked. There were nods, but when she looked pointedly at the Lazax he shook his head.

"Who else on this bridge did not hear that voice?" Tol called more loudly, addressing the rest of the crew. Only two other Lazax raised their hands – the pilot Larish and Alarina, the navigator.

"Why couldn't we hear it?" Vel Syd asked Tol. "I have heard no hissing either. I am not connected to whatever this creature may be."

Instead of replying immediately, Tol hurried over to the station Larish was manning and spent a few moments inspecting his head.

"I have a theory," Tol declared as she returned to the huddle of Vel Syd, Mortalia, Vexar and the Hacan. "But it's only that, a theory. I might ask you to stake your life on it though."

"What does it want with the Lazax?" Vexar wondered aloud.

"Likely what everyone else wants with us," Vel Syd said dispassionately. "To kill us or control us. We are the most valuable pawns in the galaxy."

"We cannot possibly allow it to take them," Vexar exclaimed.

"Three sacrificed for the many," Hamlar said, looking at Vel Syd and the other Lazax on the bridge with a grimace.

"We have done nothing but aid you and you would still sacrifice us? The universe refuses to surprise me," Vel Syd snarled.

"But what guarantees do we have that it can be trusted to leave once it has them?" Akenzi pointed out. "It is a bad trade."

"We certainly injured it," Drusha added. "It was attacking without restraint, now suddenly it wishes to negotiate? We have it out in the open and possibly weakened."

"Yet it still has the power to enter our minds," Hamlar said. "As long as that is the case, it has an advantage over us!"

"And there's still a Yssaril somewhere on board," Mortalia said.

"We have to locate and confront this thing," Vel Syd stated, his tone commanding the attention of the others. "And it has just given us a way of doing that. If it is the Lazax it wants, it is the Lazax it will get. I will go and seek it out. But first, Tol, you must tell us your theory."

"You cannot," Vexar began to say, but Tol spoke over his protests.

"There is one connection shared by you, Larish, and Alarina that is enjoyed by no one else on this bridge. I think it might be the key to overcoming this creature. But it might also mean sacrificing one of you."

"I have faced down danger many times before," Vel Syd said. "I have no intention of stopping now. Tell me your plan."

CHAPTER THIRTY

The Syd, Lazax cruiser, on the edge of the Gamma Eridius system

Z'ffani felt her prey leave the bridge.

She had been too distant to properly discern between them, too weak to drive her mind into theirs and enslave them to her will. Slipping words into their consciousness was the best she could do for now, but it seemed as though it had been enough.

It did not surprise her. The horror of first contact with a Druaa who was going out of her way to kill and terrorize was something she was sure none of them had ever experienced before. But terror was nothing more than a tool, one more means of manipulation. She had others, and she intended to employ them.

She uncoiled from the berth she had made her temporary nest, her eyes shut, questing out with her mind once more. There were four beings she could now sense. She could not read their thoughts, but she could feel an imprint of their emotions – one was a Winnaran, one a human, and three Lazax. They were curiously dull, but that did not matter. Beyond the bridge and its thick hatches and bulkheads, and now isolated from the rest of the ship's crew, their minds were more open to her, more amenable.

The presence of the human and the Winnaran were a surprise. She had demanded only the Lazax, so why send out two more?

Z'ffani swayed as her physical form subconsciously mirrored her telepathic efforts. Her thoughts wrapped around their minds like the coils of her own body, squeezing, taking control. They were amenable, yes. They would obey.

She forced a thought into their heads, a simple imperative, though it was about all she could manage for the moment.

Walk.

As she had hoped, she felt them begin to move. Maintaining her tight mental grip on them, she fully uncoiled her own body and left the berth, the pain of her injuries now forgotten, subsumed by the telepathic congress that dominated both her mind and theirs.

From a distance, she led them down to the cruiser's midship lower hold, where the *Black Scale* had bored its way into the vessel's underside. It was a storage space, dark and damp-smelling, filled with crates and tarpaulin-covered equipment, including what appeared to be several antigravetic, atmospheric speeders. A porthole in the deck had allowed Z'ffani to access it via the maintenance crawlspace the *Black Scale* had breached.

She felt another mind within the hold with her but dismissed it. She had already instructed it in its new duties, now that the main task it had come here for was almost complete.

Her prey arrived. Their constrained, puppeted thoughts entered the hold, their proximity allowing Z'ffani to further tighten her grip on them.

She shadowed them briefly, remaining out of sight, coiling through the darkness that clung to the hold's edges while she watched them. It was as she had thought, a human, a Winnaran, and three Lazax. She would only take the latter. The *Black Scale's* cryo-coffins would not have room for anymore.

Another imperative, driven into the meat of their cortexes.

Stop.

The five obeyed, though three seemed to stumble and falter. Z'ffani wondered if she was gripping them too tightly.

She approached them. One of the Lazax immediately caught her attention – he was aged, and heavily enhanced with cybernetics.

She hadn't expected to find an actual surviving member of the empire, only the descendants. This made the prize even more valuable.

Z'ffani was about to instruct the Lazax to kill the human and the Winnaran, satisfied that she would have no further need of any puppets, when she noticed something that did not belong. Movement. Motion from the second Lazax, the younger of the trio, that she had not instructed. The Lazax was reaching into the robes he wore, pulling out something. A beam pistol.

The Druaa experienced a moment's pure panic. She tried to tighten her grip on the Lazax's thoughts but realized she could not. The dullness she had noted before had returned. It was as though she was trying to grip a shard of ice as it melted in her hands and slid through her fingers.

In desperation, she lunged forward while lancing a command into the minds of the others.

Stop him.

The imperative had the desired effect. The human and the Winnaran were the closest to the younger Lazax, and they turned without any hint of resistance. Together, they tackled him. The other Lazax obeyed, but without the same responsiveness as the human and Winnaran.

The weapon went off. Z'ffani flinched, but the crimson energy beam went wide, and the trio fell to the deck, struggling. The last Lazax, the one with the staff, finally stepped in to help restrain his younger companion as well.

Hold him, Z'ffani demanded of her puppets before leaning over the prisoner.

She had never known a sentient species capable of resisting her abilities, not to this extent. A fully mature and experienced Druaa was one thing, but Z'ffani was a master of mind manipulation. Such defiance was shocking to her. She had to find out how this younger Lazax had managed it, to ensure there wasn't some potential weakness that others might exploit when the Naalu Collective finally made its play.

She hissed with displeasure as she leaned close, waving aside the Lazax with the staff. She noted the one who had been pinned had a cranial scar. Some work had been conducted upon his skull. Subtle cybernetic implantation? Could that be the connection? Maybe the prisoner's mind was not the electrical wetwork of neurons and fatty nodes that Z'ffani could easily manipulate. Perhaps part of it was hardwired, and Druaa telemancy had no hold over the mechanical.

It was something she would have to take back with her to the Naalu Collective, a warning about the dangers of the cybernetic. But even as she considered the value of such information, she experienced a revelation.

Whatever technology the pinned Lazax might possess implanted into his skull, it was minor compared to the cranial modifications of the elder.

She turned, whiplash-fast, but still too slow. The staff-wielding Lazax had moved behind her while she'd been coiled over the prisoner.

The Druaa felt a burst tof pain across her skull as something cracked into it.

She fell.

Vexar and Caldr cried out and let go of Larish, clutching their heads, as though Ibna had struck them and not the serpent. Alarina brought out her own weapon and trained it on the human and Winnaran, just in case the snake-like creature's influence lasted longer than they would expect.

Ibna ignored them and hit the creature a second time with his staff as it tried to rise. It slumped against the deck, stunned.

Ibna knew he had to act fast, though that was a struggle at his age. He stepped heavily over to the pistol Larish had dropped when he had been snatched.

Vexar and Caldr, knowing they had no defense against the creature's form of control, had deliberately left the bridge unarmed, so they couldn't be controlled into using weapons against Larish, Alarina, or himself. They had banked on the creature not immediately understanding that its form of control did not seem to extend to those with cybernetics or cranial chips. Like most of the younger Lazax in the enclave, Larish bore a monitoring implant in his skull, intended to allow Ibna to keep an eye on the enclave's future. Tol had gambled that it would function in much the same way as Ibna's more extensive surgery, breaking up the synaptic impulses this creature appeared to be able to mentally latch on to.

Groaning with effort, Ibna managed to reach down and snatch Larish's fallen pistol in one of his mechanical hands. The creature was stirring, its eyes fluttering. He stood over it.

He knew that the person he had once been would have hesitated at this point.

But that had been a long time ago.

Nothing mattered more than the existence of his people. Not even this *thing*.

He shot the creature through the head.

"Is it done?" Akenzi asked as the four who had left the bridge stepped back into the control center. He resisted the urge to order his surviving Muktat warriors to cover them with their firearms, hoping there was really no chance they weren't all under some diabolic control.

"It's done," Vel Syd replied. He leaned heavily on his staff. "You should send a few of your warriors down to retrieve the body. I imagine it will be of some interest."

"You still don't know what it was?"

"No, but Doctor Tol's hypothesis was correct. It was unable to exert mind control over those of us who have undergone cranial implantation."

"And what if it wasn't alone?"

"Then I suspect we would be dead by now. The last Yssaril must have perished with the system purge, or else it would surely have gone to that creature's aid."

The bridge shuddered, and Akenzi glanced with concern toward the shield display. Another errant strike, misplaced by the ships locked in combat around the cruiser.

The pirates and the Muktat fleet were hammering at one another. Akenzi dreaded the thought of the damage being done to his vessels, the loss of precious ships, but at that moment it couldn't be helped. It would mean nothing if they lured the reavers into an open battle, only to then lose it.

He had already tried to use the bridge's communications systems to warn the pirates he had captured their paymaster, and advise them to surrender or withdraw, but they didn't seem to care, and Hamlar had admitted they might have simply betrayed him.

With the brief, unifying panic caused by the serpentine creature's incursion over, Akenzi's disgust for the rival magnate had returned, while it seemed Hamlar had regained some of his arrogant pride. Akenzi had already ordered the Dazeshi seized and kept at gunpoint, a fact that Vel Syd did not seem intent on reversing now that he had returned to his bridge.

"We need to at least chart a course out of here," Akenzi said, looking at the markers representing the hail of ship-to-ship, defense battery and starfighter fire transfixing the space around the cruiser. "We're right in the middle of it!"

"By design," Vel Syd pointed out, unhelpfully. "You have your battle, magnate. We have done our part."

"Vel Syd," called out the other elderly Lazax, who had maintained her post at the navigation station. "There is motion on the scope, along the system edge. Possible contacts. Something's coming through the Gap."

Vel Syd made his way over to the nav post, Akenzi joining him, uninvited. He was trying to gauge what the cruiser's sensor array was picking up.

It quickly became apparent that it wasn't good news.

"Those are Barony markers," Vel Syd said darkly. "War ships."

"It can't be," Akenzi said hoarsely, gripping the side of the main sensor display and leaning over it, his eyes scanning it. "Surely they can't have spared forces from the front?"

Akenzi heard a sound, so unexpected he didn't recognize it at first – laughter. He turned sharply and saw that it was coming from the Winnaran who had been seized by her compatriots, Mortalia.

"What did you do?" Vel Syd demanded, showing sudden alacrity as he stormed over to her. The cold laughter died, replaced by a look of fierce, bitter triumph.

"Did you really think I would come all this way without telling the Barony where I was going?" she demanded.

"They're here for you," Akenzi said accusatorially, gesturing at Vel Syd and the other Lazax. "You've led them here!"

"Then I suggest you get off this ship as swiftly as possible," Vel Syd replied. Akenzi turned back to the nav station.

"Highlight my flagship and hail it on comms," he said, though the Lazax in charge was looking at Vel Syd rather than him.

"The pirates are disengaging," she said. "Scattering. If we don't want to be sensor-locked by the Barony, I suggest we do the same."

"What will you do about the enclave on Gamma Eridius?" Akenzi asked. "If the Barony is hunting you, and they discover Lazax living in what's supposed to be my trade outpost…"

He barely dared consider what might follow. Loss and disgrace was one thing, but given the history he already had with the Letnev, he doubted any of them would get out of the system alive.

"My people have put our lives in harm's way to assist you, Magnate Akenzi," Vel Syd said. Akenzi immediately disliked the Lazax's tone, feeling somewhat threatened. "Several of us lie dead, and the survival of the rest is far from certain. I must ask you to do something in return, something that I hope will improve both our chances, and yours. Then I expect you to erase the existence of the Lazax from your memory."

"Speak it," Akenzi said, knowing there was no time for grandstanding, again eyeing the sensor display showing the locations of the Muktat ships, the fleeing pirates, and the Letnev still arriving in-system. There were over a dozen capital ship icons showing now among their fleet.

"I must ask you to return to your flagship and plot a course directly toward the Barony's fleet, immediately."

CHAPTER THIRTY-ONE

THE WRATH OF SSAMRAC, FLAGSHIP OF THE BARONY OF LETNEV'S 4TH GRAND FLEET, ON THE EDGE OF THE GAMMA ERIDIUS SYSTEM

"What do you mean, Hacan war ships?' Commodore ven Veen barked, rising from behind his command console.

Gondar managed to hold back the urge to snap at the fleet's nominal commander to sit down and be silent, as the petty officer manning the bridge's sensor array hastily repeated her findings.

In fairness to ven Veen, it was not what Gondar had expected to find either. There had been rumors of greater activity in the Gap, and increased Hacan involvement, but this looked like a strong section of a clan fleet.

And they weren't alone. The holo chart was showing traces of other ships scattered throughout the system, most of them too far out to pick up anything more than their vague presence and heading. The in-system sensors and equipment of the Letnev war ships were still coming online after the deceleration through the Gap, and it would take time to make proper triangulations.

"Traces of recent weapons fire and energy shield impacts," the petty officer added to her report.

"It seems we have stumbled across a naval engagement," Gondar said.

"Whoever is fighting who, they are no match for this fleet," ven Veen declared, clearly trying to hide how flustered he was with braggadocio. Gondar had assured him there would be no force to challenge them on Gamma Eridius besides the filth they were hunting – a part of him had always been suspicious that there were Lazax still alive in the galaxy, and now the nurturing of Asset 258672 had paid off. Or it would have, if her information was found to be accurate. In her last report she had told of her intention to follow traces of the Lazax to Gamma Eridius, and the evidence had been firm enough for the Cimm Fenn to act.

But the Hacan had upset matters. The Barony fleet was five times larger, capable of annihilating them, but that was not the reason they had traveled all this way from Arc Prime. After what had happened with Admiral Zorias, van Veen was clearly nervous. The Baron had made it clear he didn't want another incident with the United Emirates.

"They're approaching us," the scan officer said. "And hailing us."

"Are their weapons muzzled?" Gondar asked.

"Yes, but shields up."

"Put their transmission through. Visuals."

The main holo display in front of the command console beamed up, and Gondar and ven Veen found themselves gazing at a Hacan, garbed in traditional blue and silver robes.

Gondar recognized him.

"Magnate Akenzi," he said before ven Veen could speak, not intending to let the navy idiot cause a debacle the way Zorias had. "We meet again."

"Gondar," Akenzi said, recognizing him, though it was hard to gauge whether he was surprised. "There is a face I did not expect to see again. I can't deny I'm glad, though. Those pirate vagabonds almost had the better of us."

"Pirates?" Gondar said, glancing briefly at the other ships on the display, spreading out through the system and away from the Letnev fleet.

"The whole Gap is lousy with them, I'm afraid," Akenzi said. "At this very moment an abandoned reaver nest on Gamma Eridius is being torched by my forces. That was what caused their fleet lurking here on the system edges to attack. If you wish to help me hunt these animals, I will accept your aid. I'm sure the United Emirates would be pleased to hear of cordial relations given the recent… misunderstandings between our two peoples."

Gondar briefly considered telling Akenzi the purpose of his visit. If the Hacan were setting up a trade outpost, they might have already discovered the Lazax. Gondar was sure a cunning magnate like Akenzi could be convinced to hand them over. But if Gondar admitted his intentions, he would risk his assets, even open the Barony to further ridicule if the intelligence was inaccurate.

"We are not here to hunt pirates, and we were unaware the United Emirates had a stake in the Gap," he said instead. "Regardless, your right does not supersede ours. We have come to claim this system in the name of the Barony."

"That is unfortunate," Akenzi said, interlocking his hands before him. "We seem to be at something of an impasse then, as I have claimed this system for the United Emirates."

"There is no impasse," Gondar said. "You are outgunned, Hacan. You will withdraw all assets and depart immediately."

"Or what?"

"We will destroy you."

"Do you have authorization to do that? To fire on ships

belonging to a clan of the United Emirates? Did the Barony even expect to find us here when you set out?"

Gondar began to speak, but Akenzi carried on.

"Do not worry, my pallid friend! I know you are a being who appreciates the importance of negotiation. So let us talk. I have no doubt I could be induced to relinquish my claim and evacuate the system, for a price. It will take time though. A great deal of aurei has already been spent, and the mining operations are already underway!"

Gondar could not have cared less about Hacan profit margins or mining operations. He looked again at the uncertain markers representing the other ships in the system, seemingly fleeing after a space engagement. He remembered the shame of the tri-system incursion, how this Hacan magnate had shamed him, had shamed the entirety of 2nd Fleet. Akenzi had been devious, treacherous. He had been stalling for time.

"There will be no negotiations, not this time," Gondar said. "We are making a direct course for Gamma Eridius."

"Then we shall escort you," Akenzi replied.

"We hardly have need of an escort," Gondar said tersely.

"Then allow me to be honest," Akenzi responded. "If you had not arrived when you did, I doubt there would be a great deal of my expedition remaining. The reavers may have scattered for now, but they will undoubtedly regroup. If you wish me to actually make it safely to Gamma Eridius to remove my assets ahead of your occupation, I fear I am the one who must request an escort."

"The Hacan ships are coming about," ven Veen muttered. Gondar glanced toward the navigational terminus, seeing the markers representing Akenzi's battered little fleet beginning to swing around, baring their aft sections as they formed up in front of the Baronial ships, on a heading for Gamma Eridius. In such a position a single salvo from the Barony would annihilate them. But that, in a sense, was their best defense.

Gondar had great influence among the nobility of Arc Prime. There were none among the Barony's spymasters and enforcers who wove a more tangled web. But part of Gondar's success rested on knowing his own limits, and he doubted even he could explain why the 4th Grand Fleet had obliterated a small force of Hacan ships that were requesting their assistance after surrendering the system to them.

"Cut transmission," Gondar ordered.

"Let me know the moment there's an energy spike," Akenzi said, hardly daring to breathe as he watched the Letnev fleet begin to form up to their rear. Turning a back on an enemy was beyond foolish, but then everything he had been doing since leaving Vel Syd's cruiser had been an attempt to convince the Letnev that they weren't actually the enemy.

"Maintain this course and pace," he ordered his helmsman. "Don't let them bully us into going faster. Frustrate them if need be. We need to keep their eyes on us."

It was desperate, but it seemed to be working. Akenzi had been privately horrified when he realized the very same Letnev they had held hostage was with the invading fleet. Surely he would spot that Akenzi was once more employing delaying tactics?

Hamlar's pirate scum had unwittingly added verisimilitude to the deception. It was clear that a genuine battle had been raging prior to the Barony's arrival, and that the disparate pirate ships were now scattering across the system. The Letnev fleet really had saved Akenzi's ships, and now in their own way the pirates were doing the same. It would be a brilliant coup, if it worked. All they could do was maintain the distraction, and hope that the Lazax's swift cruiser was making good time. Certainly, it had already passed out of range of the Hacan ships – the furthermost scan put it close to Gamma Eridius's orbit.

"What if they don't evacuate the rest of the enclave in time?" Drusha wondered.

"Then we'll be running with them," Akenzi replied humorlessly. "Is Hamlar secure?"

"He's in the main brig, under guard," Drusha reassured his brother.

"Keep it that way," Akenzi said. "He's the only hope we have left."

Everything since arriving at Gamma Eridius had been a disaster, yet somehow, there was still a chance Clan Muktat would make it out with its wealth and reputation intact. Akenzi had known as soon as he realized the Barony had deployed a major incursion fleet that they were, at best, intending to claim Gamma Eridius for their own and, at worst, were specifically hunting the Lazax. Either way, he was in no position to stop them claiming the planet and, in doing so, ruining every effort he had made to establish a trade outpost.

The venture was over, and he accepted that. But all was not lost. He was waiting until they got clear of the system before putting a simple proposition before Hamlar. In exchange for not informing the Hacan Council that Clan Dazeshi had been directly involved in pirate attacks and fomenting a clan war, Hamlar would make a series of vast payments to the Muktat coffers and, even more importantly, sell shares in his own most lucrative enterprises directly to Akenzi and the other stakeholders in the Gamma Eridius expedition.

Akenzi knew that if he handled it right, he might make more aurei out of this situation – and with a fraction of the work – than he would have from claiming Gamma Eridius.

"Hold the course," he repeated. "And pray to every sand spirit you know that they follow."

"*Hurwana* and *Manda* are in position," Alarina said. Vel Syd hobbled over to assess the two ships on the main console. His command chair had been so riddled during the firefight on the bridge that most of its inbuilt systems were no longer functioning. He'd taken to the main deck instead, leaning heavily on his staff as he moved from station to station.

"They have the heading?" he asked Alarina urgently.

"Yes. Course-locked for the system edge, and the acceleration coordinates have just finished transmitting."

"Then launch the shuttle and let us be gone," he said. "The Hacan will be able to delay the Barony for only so long."

He watched the single transporter arc away from the cruiser, back down toward the blue curve of Gamma Eridius, aiming for the sea that lashed the shoreline beside the burning enclave. In the small craft's wake, he felt the rising throb of the engines shivering through the deck underfoot and was again thankful for the speed of the cruiser named in his honor. Thankful, too, that Marchu had followed through with the precautions they had discussed prior to setting out. If the other two ships belonging to the enclave hadn't already been awoken, there was no chance they would have been able to slip away ahead of the oncoming Letnev fleet.

As per Akenzi's advice, they had set fire to the settlement before leaving, making it appear like a pirate holdout that the Hacan were in the process of destroying. Hopefully in doing so, any trace of the Lazax would also burn.

Vel Syd spent a moment pondering the irony of that, gazing at the representation of Gamma Eridius on the console. He had always known that this place was not the Lazax's new home, that it would not be the cradle of his civilization's rebirth. Those who had first brought down the empire would never stop hunting them. There could be no rest, and no peace.

The whole universe was their enemy.

At least the lethargy and anxiety were gone. The tiredness he felt had only grown with inaction, but now it had been banished by the certainty of the task before him. He knew where they were bound. The road was long, achingly so, but it was straight and firm. He had resolved that he would follow it, with the last embers of the empire, out beyond the furthest reaches of the galaxy, into the darkness between dying stars, to a destiny that would once have been unthinkable. He would continue, on and on, exhausted but unbroken, safeguarding the future of his species, and not stopping until the countless fallen had been avenged, and a Lazax once more sat upon the throne of Mecatol Rex.

Mortalia half expected Vexar to kill her.

The Resurrectionist Winnaran and one of his companions had been ordered by the Lazax to take her to the cruiser's brig. They remained silent as they did so, though she could still sense Vexar's smoldering hatred, the zeal of a fanatic confronted by a militant nonbeliever.

He finally broke his silence as he ushered her into the brig itself.

"Your masters are too slow, traitor. We are about to begin the acceleration out-system."

"Why not just kill me?" Mortalia demanded.

"Because the great Ambassador Vel Syd, in his wisdom, has demanded you be kept alive. Think of how merciful he is, and just how unworthy you are of it."

"Spare me," Mortalia hissed.

"Sadly, that is exactly what I have been ordered to do."

He made to leave, his companion watching him closely, as though afraid he might still lunge at her – Mortalia's head yet throbbed from the beating he had given her on the bridge.

"One more thing," he said.

"What?"

"What did you do with Lekaan?"

Mortalia simply glared at him. Her wrists had been bound with a magnetic cuff, but part of her still wished Vexar would lash out, so that she could strike back. The hatred between them was almost electric.

"You'll tell me one day," Vexar said darkly, when it became clear Mortalia wasn't going to answer. Then, the door sealed with a compressed thump, and she was alone.

She spent some time pacing the spartan prison cell, gripped and pulled one way and then the other by the tides of anger and remorse. She had failed. And yet, she still lived. It wasn't over yet.

She eventually settled, sitting on the side of the brig's fold-down bed and focusing on the water station opposite, listening to the rhythm of the engines, rising to a deep, sonorous vibration as the cruiser prepared to accelerate. And as she sat, seeking to clear her mind and rediscover her deadly focus, she caught something amidst the engine throb. The faintest knocking, coming from the brig's air recyc unit overhead.

Tap-tap… tap-tap-tap.

Mortalia smiled.

EPILOGUE

The sky was full of warships.

Tol stood on one of the rocks jutting out into the cold gray of the ocean, bathed in its spray, looking up. They were low, bulbous troop carriers and arrowhead-like frigates and escort vessels, grazing the under edge of orbit. Dark swarms of atmospheric craft swept around them, at this distance looking like tiny insects surrounding their hives.

The Barony of Letnev had claimed Gamma Eridius.

In doing so, they had searched the ridgeline from end to end, three separate, exhaustive sweeps. They had picked over the charred remains of what had once been the enclave.

They had failed to detect Tol. She had swum too deep for that, only reemerging when her savant told her their scanners had moved on.

The shuttle that had brought her back to the surface was too deep as well, sunk to the bottom of the ocean. Even she wouldn't be able to retrieve it now. That did not trouble her.

"You know Gamma Eridius will change?" Ibna had asked her, as she had prepared to leave the cruiser before it escaped the system. "You know that even if the Letnev don't find any trace of you, they will begin to strip it bare, and then the other civilizations will remember how valuable the planet is. War will follow, and it will happen even faster if word spreads that it once concealed the last of the Lazax."

"I know," Tol said. "But by then I'll be gone."

Ibna had not questioned how she intended to get off-world. He was too wise for that.

Tol thought about Ibna, about the folly he was engaged in, the century-spanning tragedy that she had made possible. She thought about the way he watched over all of them with his implants, monitoring heartbeats and breaths as if he was some sort of omnipotent entity. She thought about how she had once tried so hard to make a difference, not just with the Lazax, but across the galaxy. Decades of striving, of loss and sacrifice and a few precious successes.

"Are you going to kill me?" she had asked Ibna as they neared Gamma Eridius's orbit. The fact that he had shown no surprise at the question confirmed more of Tol's thoughts – he had changed, and was changing still, not for the better. There was a darkness upon him, that deep sediment slowly but surely weighing him down toward cold, unfathomed depths. She suspected there was little now that Ibna would not do to preserve himself, and the enclave, even more so after coming so close to disaster.

"You think I would kill you in cold blood, after all you have done for us?" he had asked. "After all you have done for *me*?"

"I think you would consider it."

"Then you would be correct."

There was no humor in his tone, no warmth in the gaze of his sole organic eye. His voice was like a blade, his cybernetic optic like the targeter of a weapons system. Tol had shivered.

"But I trust you," he had continued. "More than almost anyone in this enclave. I know you, Harial Tol. And I would reward your good service down the years by sparing your life, and letting you leave."

Tol had almost laughed bitterly. How like a Lazax to describe the dedication of the greater part of her existence as "good service down the years."

"Where to?" she had asked. "Where are you taking them?"

"To the place I always intended to go, if the mass-drive hadn't given out, if the universe hadn't set infuriating obstacles in my path," Ibna declared. "Hazz."

The name meant little to Tol. She knew it vaguely, as a small star on the edge of existence. A fitting place, she thought, for the last of the Lazax.

"You go into the dark, Ibna Vel Syd," she had warned him.

"We entered it a long time ago," Ibna had replied, turning away. "Swim for the light, Tol, while you still can."

Now she stood on the shore and watched the warships high above, hunting those who had already fled.

Her mind turned to Malik, and the span of happy years at the heart of it all. She thought about home, far-off Nar, and wondered whether its waters were still warm and its sands white. She hoped so.

The waters here were not warm, and the shores were craggy, dark shingle. They were, in their own way, beautiful.

Tol shook the stiffness from her limbs and dove down into the crashing waves. The water embraced her like an old friend, and immediately she felt young again, that terrible weight that seemed to be forever bearing her down banished in an instant.

She forged deeply through the whirling currents, dancing with them, alternately fighting and following them, like a young Nal child at play. When she eventually tired, she would rise again and return to the shore for a while. But she knew that, one day soon, she would not come back up. That thought was a comfort.

Ibna Vel Syd, the Lazax, and an empire burned beyond recognition – none of it was her burden any longer.

She had enough time to enjoy the waters of this world and sink to its depths and let herself be forgotten, while the rest of the galaxy carried on to wherever the long road was taking it.

ACKNOWLEDGMENTS

My thanks to the Aconyte publishing team, from my talented and ever-patient editor, Gwen, to the copyeditors, proofreaders, printing, distribution, and marketing, as well as to Tobias Roetsch, the talented artist who somehow topped the work he did for *Empire Falling* with this book's cover.

ABOUT THE AUTHOR

ROBBIE MacNIVEN hails from the highlands of Scotland. A lifelong fan of sci-fi and fantasy, he has had over a dozen novels published in settings ranging from Marvel's *X-Men* to *Warhammer 40,000*. Having completed a doctorate in Military History from the University of Edinburgh in 2020, he also possesses a keen interest in the past. His hobbies include historical re-enacting and making eight-hour round trips every second weekend to watch Rangers FC.

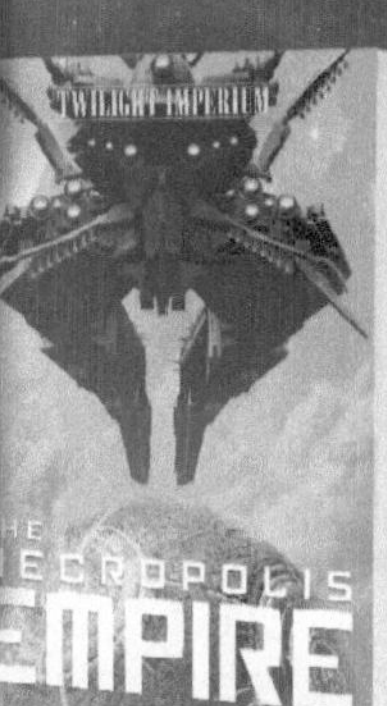

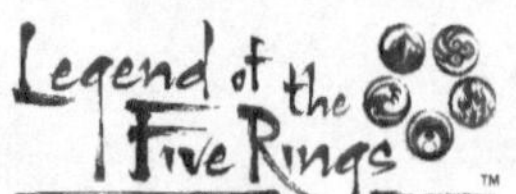

TWILIGHT IMPERIU

WORLD EXPANDING FICTION

ACONYTEBOOKS.COM

@ACONYTEBOOKS

9 781839 083037